BREEZES AND BODIES

WOLF SHIFER KINGS

BOOK FIVE

BELLA MOONDRAGON

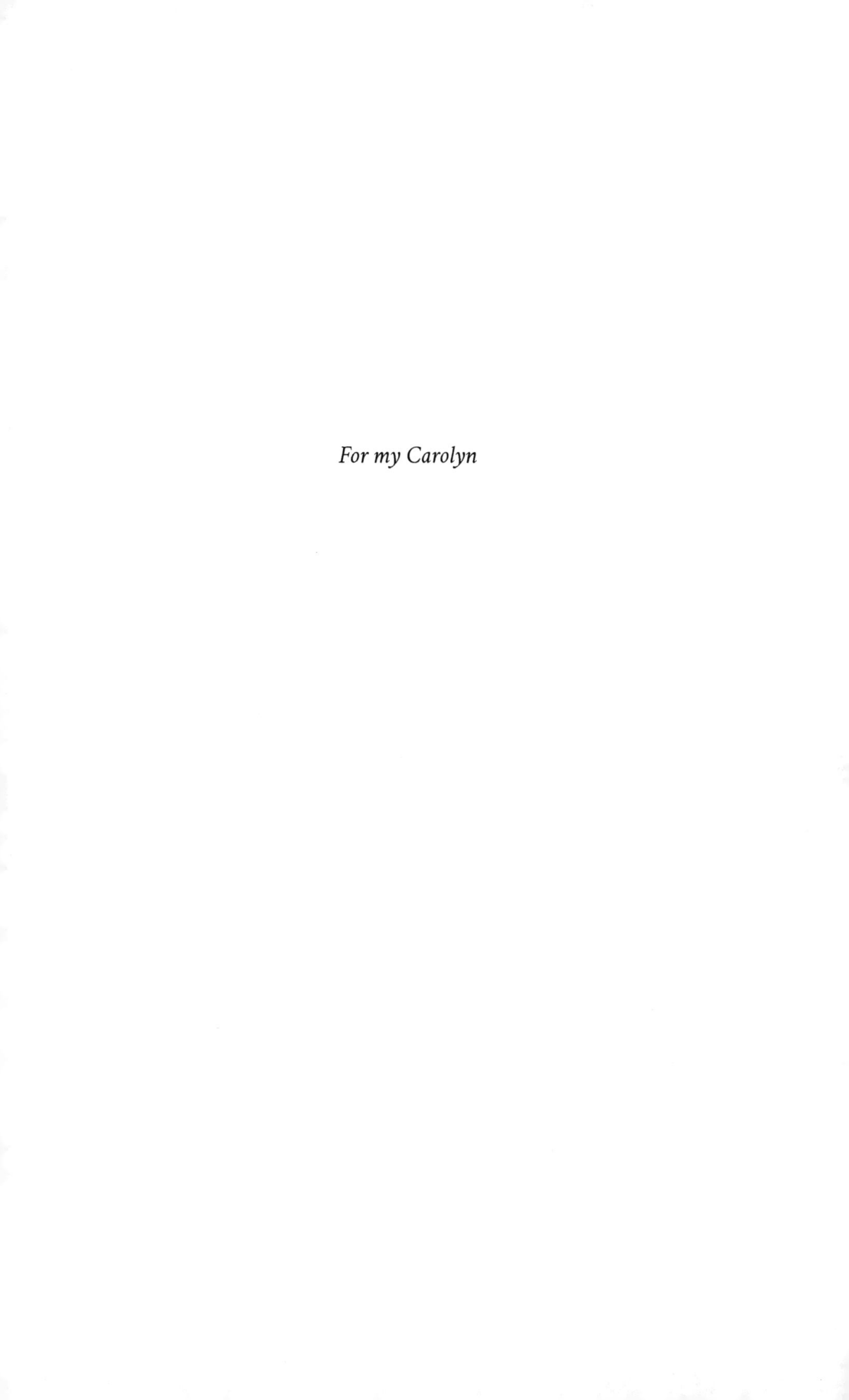

For my Carolyn

CONTENTS

WAKE UP

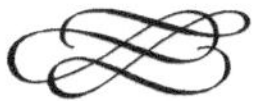

Ingrid

A WARM BREEZE SKIMS MY BODY FROM TOE TO TIP AND SENDS something rustling around my head.

Not something. Tall grass, almost taller than I am when standing. It's the tall grass I spent the Haze in.

With my mate!

I squeeze my eyes shut, not ready to see him yet. His arm must be the warm band across my stomach, the only thing blocking me from the morning breeze. Well, warmish. Last night, I thought he was hot as a fire, but something about sleeping outside must have cooled his skin. That's hardly a deal breaker, after everything my siblings have been through.

There were so many people at the party last night. Delegations from all over came to gawk at the reunited—sorry, celebrate the name blessing of the twin princes. Kingdoms I've only ever read the names of managed to send a representative or two.

Or maybe the man draped across me isn't one of the boring nobles I spent the whole night avoiding at all. Maybe the Goddess knows I'm not built for a life of state dinners and stiff diplomatic greetings. One final scandal to end the line of Solberg siblings, and one I wouldn't mind a shred.

I saw almost nothing of him last night. Until now, I sort of thought everyone was lying when they talked about how little you can perceive during the Haze, but I don't know anything about him other than his coat. Deep brown or black, impossible to say. That, I suppose, and his smell. Candace could tell me his pack from that alone, but she's got the sort of nose people write songs about.

For now, I let my mind wander. I picture a tall, dark, handsome prince from a far-off land, mentally push him aside, consider a sooty soldier or day laborer. Someone who has stories, who's lived a life. Who does something real with their hands rather than sitting around thinking pompous thoughts all day?

An artist, maybe. I never really wrapped my mind around sculpture, but there is something visceral about it that seems to match the intensity with which my mate handled me last night. Like he's used to grabbing the world and making it what he wants.

I run my thumb over the tender spot high on my left breast. The ridges of the final mark are still developing, but I can try to read them with my fingers.

No. I overheard Finn and Xandra talking about a compromise between traditions—there aren't tents, like there would be in Dun's Crossing or many other kingdoms, but there are clothes on the path back to the palace. I wriggle out from under my mate's arm, trying not to wake him without opening my eyes. I'll grab us clothes so we don't have to immediately run away if he's the embarrassed type.

The sculptor in my mind is the opposite, but the Goddess can only do so much for me.

I push through the evidence of our night together–hair, fur, and dried sweat on the ground. The grass finds tiny slivers and slashes it left in me last night, but I care as much now as I did then. I've found my mate. He could be anything, anyone, and he might make me perfectly happy. I didn't realize how much of an improvement that could be over "pretty damn" happy until last night.

I hum the melody I've been composing for a few weeks, my fingers itching for my lute. After last night, I know exactly what the ending needs. I was trying to keep the whole piece too light; that was why it felt unfinished. It needs a bombastic conclusion, a climax of sound that will leave listeners feeling emotions they weren't sure they could feel. That will be perfect.

Avoiding pockets of other murmurs, following trails already trampled in the high grass, I find my way to a table piled with robes. I didn't even look at him enough to know what size he might wear. He seemed much larger than me last night...

I grab two simple undyed robes of the exact same size and hurry back the way I came. If he really is my other half, he'll find this hilarious. I'd like to start our life together laughing. I've never really gone in for superstition, but that seems like a good sign.

Finding my way back is as easy as walking a straight hallway. His smell is impossible to miss, impossible to wander away from. I feel more like a fish on a line than someone navigating pathless grass.

When I reach him, he's still asleep. The morning sun makes his skin glow, though the grass casts strange shadows, turning it more gray than the soft brown I think it truly is. His arm is flung over his face, and he lays half on his side, but hair the same brown-black as his coat flows past it. Short hair—that rules out a number of kingdoms, including Moonlight Beach.

I clear my throat. "Good morning."

Nothing. A heavy sleeper. Certainly not the worst problem, but irritating right now.

I kneel next to him and set the robes aside. "Um, hello?"

Still nothing. I'm finally ready to look at him. Can't he wake up and look at me?

"Hello?" I grab his arm and shake it a little. "Goddess above, you sleep like the dead."

I shake his arm harder, and it finally moves off his face.

If I could take a breath, I'd scream, but my lungs are brutally empty. I open and close my mouth uselessly. Am I trying to say something? What is there to say?

My mate, the man who is supposed to be my other half, who I spent one wonderful night with and have never really looked at, isn't just sleeping like the dead.

He is dead.

My hands shake as I drop his arm, but it doesn't fall back over his face. I wish it did. His eyelids are swollen and nearly crimson, like they're about to burst with blood. Purple veins crawl out from them, almost down to his mouth. His lips are what make me realize the cast to his skin isn't just shadow. Lips I remember being rosy last night are now somewhere between gray and blue, with a single spot of dark gore at the center.

Did I kill him?

No. There is no way. Or, if something I did is the cause, it was going to happen soon anyway. Last night was primal, unrestrained, but it wasn't dangerous.

Something else must have happened. Someone else. I don't recognize these symptoms, but I've seen veins like this before. The wolfsbane scar Estrella will carry for the rest of her days doesn't look completely dissimilar.

But why now? Why wait until I was asleep in his arms?

Why leave me alive?

I shiver and pull one of the robes on, even though I know I'm not reacting to the cold. Someone was here. They did this.

Or this place or something inside him. It just can't be me.

I gather my knees to my chest and hug them. My bite aches more than a bruise should. It's the deep throb of real pain I should've noticed before waltzing off to grab a silly joke he'll never laugh at. I search for his mark, even though I know it's on the side of his neck, still cradled between his shoulder and the side of his head. Not seeing it is almost like relief.

At the very least, it's enough to let me take what feels like my first breath since I moved his arm. I need to do something other than just stare at him. Eventually, someone will come looking for us. The longer I wait, the worse...something will probably be. I gnaw on my thumbnail.

Who is he? Parts of his face look familiar, but it's almost impossible to tell with all the swelling and discoloration on his face. It doesn't help that everyone was perfectly polished last night, and the man in front of me now is a rumpled ruin. Numbly, I reach out and stroke dark hair out of his face, as if that will make a difference.

Some kind of product sticks to my fingers. The sort of thing that would help hair stay up and together.

And I know who he is.

Prince Amval Som. The stuffed shirt, who had no sense of humor and still made sure to tell me he didn't think I was funny. Joli's oldest brother.

Oh, Goddess.

Candace. I can ask Candace for help. She'll know what to do.

But she'll have to tell someone else to be able to do it. King Andri still insists Hollis commands the army, and Candace doesn't want it enough to fight him for it, so he's the only one who can order their guards around. And as much as I love her, she doesn't have the stomach for this. I don't even know what I'd ask her to do without help.

I yank my hand back, squeeze my eyes shut, and mind-link Finn. *"I'm in trouble."*

He takes a few minutes to reply. Apparently, raising twins hasn't made waking up in the morning any easier. But he's the only person I can trust with this who's tough enough to take it, the only one who's here and has the power to handle it. Who I think will handle it the way I want.

"Trouble?" he asks sleepily.

Everything I know spills out in awkward phrases. The Haze, the robes, the man who's dead. My mate. I still haven't stopped staring at him. The body that was once him.

"Shit," Finn says when I'm done.

"I don't want anyone to know, I whisper. That I was... that he and I...."

I can't say it. No one ever gets a second mate.

"I'll organize a discovery as soon as you're gone," Finn says immediately. *"Vedran can help you hide the mark while it develops."*

I can hear Xandra in his voice, and I want to be glad he found her, but that just makes it impossible to breathe again. Something vital has been sucked out of the air. It doesn't matter how much of it I suck in. My lungs are starving.

His scent, I realize. It's fading.

I break the link with Finn before he hears the choked noise that drags out of me. My mate is disappearing in front of my very eyes. I need a minute before I can skulk off and pretend this never happened.

"Prince Amval?" someone calls.

I flatten myself to the ground and then rear back up when that brings me too close to his destroyed face. Goddess, what I wouldn't give for one memory of it, not in the ballroom and not like this.

"Amval?" they yell again. A woman, I think, but too young for his mother and too old for Joli.

It doesn't matter. Anyone looking for him is a problem. I need to get up and leave. This isn't the discovery Finn is probably currently planning, but it'll do.

I will my legs to stand. My bite screams at the idea of leaving the only place I had him.

The grass parts, and I turn.

Another of the Som sisters. Something with a K. She looks from me to Amval, horror growing in her amber eyes.

"Amval!" she shrieks.

SWARM

Ingrid

When Kieran and Raven claimed the kingdom, I watched the news spread through the castle windows. It started slowly—just a few dark specks of people in the roads. But those specks swirled, collected more to their cause. Like a cloud of gnats in the forest, swelling and pouring through the streets until I couldn't even see the stone underneath them anymore. That was when the cheering reached us.

Kieran's name, chanted over and over again. Louder and louder.

That was also when I stopped watching. I was glad they weren't swarming to take revenge on the man who killed their king, but that kind of power is always terrifying. It makes you feel small.

Small might be the only way to describe how I feel right now.

The princess's scream punctured the warm quiet of the morning. After the first flock of birds took flight, there was a moment of silence where I thought I might escape without the whole world knowing what happened.

Then, the grass parted, and the first pair of blushing new mates joined us.

There are at least a dozen now. Some are holding hands and clinging to each other. Some stand apart, clearly caught in the Haze last night but alone this morning. I must have stood up at some point because I'm just one of a crowd of identical robes.

"Just send someone," I tell Finn through the mind-link. *"Quiet discovery is out of the question."*

I'm sure he replies. I'm sure he says yes. I don't listen.

The princess—Kaloni, I've learned from the murmuring crowd—clings to Amval's body, openly weeping. I can just barely see her through the field of shoulders, her dark hair falling over both their faces.

My bite aches hollowly. She's the one who deserves to be at the center of this moment. I'd rather be back here, one of the many. Even if that is the man who could have been my mate. The Goddess may have picked him out for me, but I didn't know him.

Hell, I didn't even like him last night. Before the Haze, at least. My fingers burn where I touched him after I realized. Like I stole those moments from Kaloni, or Joli, or anyone else who actually knew and cared about him.

He's a stranger to me.

A fated stranger who died in my arms.

"Is Lightning Cape at war?" someone mutters next to me.

"I didn't think so," someone else replies, "but I heard some remnants escaped Tansy Beach before they reunited."

"Do you think that was the girl he was found with?"

"Maybe."

I stare at the trampled grass. How long will it take the grass to recover? How long will everyone walking past here have to remember what happened?

How long will it take me?

A man in a loosely tied robe pushes through the crowd. "Excuse me. I don't have any of my tools, but I am a healer."

"He isn't—" Kaloni breaks into another sob.

The man kneels beside her. "I understand, but I may be able to tell you more about what happened."

She peels her fingers back from Amval's arm. The bone-white pressure lines fill sluggishly with blood again. Some late arrival yelps in surprise or disgust as his face lolls toward the watching crowd. My stomach churns.

As the healer studies the body, I think about leaving. Just taking a few steps back, slipping away, leaving an empty spot in the cluster no one will think twice about. I've done it a thousand times. In this chaos, it won't even be hard.

My feet don't move.

I beg them to. Nothing good can come from watching Kaloni's matching eyes water, studying the way she gnaws on her matching lips. It only lets me wonder if he did that, or if he noticed that she did. The way she's clinging to him implies they were close. How close? Was he close to all of his siblings?

These are all the kinds of questions one usually asks about someone they're getting to know. But there's nothing to know here. That door is closed, and the only open window leads me far away from here.

Another woman shows up—a familiar one. Lieutenant Hana, now one of Finn and Xandra's chief advisors.

"The Luna and Alpha send their regrets," she says. "May I see?"

Kaloni gestures vaguely. The man already kneeling beside Amval looks affronted.

"I am already at work here, madame."

"Lieutenant." She squats beside him, ignoring everything else he said. "I assume you've checked for rashes?"

The way he turns red tells everyone around that he absolutely hasn't yet. Murmurs, followed by a few quickly covered laughs, dot the gathered crowd. Kaloni looks accusingly in the direction of the laughers.

I clutch my robe and pray she doesn't realize how small the one I brought for him is. He wouldn't have found it funny, I know now. Or I suspect. His parting jab implied he has a sense of humor, somewhere. Just maybe a bad one.

My mark throbs. What am I doing? Taking jabs at a dead man's sense of humor?

Take a step back, I tell myself. *Just one.*

A third woman enters the ring at the center of the crowd, claiming to run an apothecary. She, of course, has her own opinions about what might've happened, and she's happy to announce them without even getting within a few feet of Amval.

"A curse," she declares. "The new Luna and Alpha didn't have this land blessed properly before they began construction, so it is cursed."

Hana scoffs. "I was at the blessing."

I don't hear what the third woman says. It doesn't particularly matter. Hana has to be who Finn sent; she'll keep the situation under control, make sure no crackpots like the curse lady get control of what's going on here. I can leave. I should leave. This is in the hands of people far more equipped to deal with it now.

But I can see the sunlight in his hair. Just that, now, with how the crowd is shifting. It's the only part of him undamaged by whatever happened, and Goddess above, it's beautiful. I know why I couldn't tell whether his fur was brown or black—it seems like every other strand changes color, like the striations in rich, dark wood. It's warm like wood, too, all the brown and black tinted just slightly red. I know, even from here, that it's been soaking up the morning's heat. When I touched it, I could barely feel my hands, but stroking through it would be like petting a cat that was dozing in the sun. Nothing more peaceful or homey.

I shut my eyes and take a deep breath. Foolish. His scent is nearly gone, between the endless drag of time and how many other people are here. Evidence of our one night together, trampled. My lungs seize and choke on nothingness.

I've never even had a fucking cat; I just pet the ones in the stable sometimes.

Someone pats me on the back. Words of support whisper through the air—empty ones, like *Isn't it awful?* Or *I can't look either.* A scream builds in my throat. I don't belong here. I've got no real right to that body on the ground. But if I don't, none of these complete strangers with their platitudes and their hungry eyes certainly don't. At least I touched him once. At least I might've cared about him. At least he was my only chance at true love.

"If it were an insect sting," Hana says with aggravated patience, "don't you think we would have found a stinger?"

Somebody splutters a reply. I manage to take a step back.

It's like growing wings. I turn on my heel, ready to run.

And I see Joli. She looks younger than she ever has, the four years between us stark in the roundness of her shocked face. She deserves more than to be just one of the swarm.

My feet carry me over to her. She looks up at me, expression unchanging.

"I'm sorry," I say.

"For what?"

For being here. For not leaving when I had the chance. For ever coming out last night.

"For him."

"So it's true." Her words are as dull and hollow as the ache of my mark. "Kaloni said, but…."

I put a hand on her shoulder. Mother taught me all the right things to say at times like this, even the ones in her home kingdom when she was sure Father wouldn't overhear, but they feel worthless now. I was Joli's age when Father died, but I've never lost someone I really loved.

Only people I could have.

Joli doesn't brush me off. She just stares blankly through the crowd. I wonder if she can see his hair, if she's thinking about how much it looks like her own. I am.

"It shouldn't be like this," she says.

"It's bullshit."

She shakes her head. "No—well, yes, but—Amval, he shouldn't be a curiosity like this. In Lightning Cape, you don't poke at bodies. You keep them somewhere cool and dark until the spirit is released into the sky at their funeral." Her eyes water. "He deserves his privacy."

For the first time, I think I understand a little of what Candace sees when she looks at me. Responsibility hits like a lightning bolt. I can't fix anything that happened, can't scrub this mark off my skin or return to the moment before I saw his swollen face. But I can fix this for Joli—for all the Soms. And then I'll leave them alone.

I take her hand, lift my chin, and shout, "Hey!"

Every head turns toward me.

"This man was the Crown Prince of Lightning Cape." I march forward, pulling Joli with me. "We may not be on their land, but their laws dictate that he needs to be protected, not inspected."

Shock is a powerful weapon, I've learned. The crowd parts. Joli stumbles the first few steps, but quickly, she falls into rhythm. Tears streak down her face, but she holds her head almost as high.

"I volunteer as intermediary between Moonlight Beach and Lightning Cape," I declare. "Everyone else, go about your mornings. Somewhere else. Information on his service, if it is public, will be made available." I glare at the people around me. "Later."

Shock carries them into wandering away, heads bent together as they talk. Joli and I reach where Kaloni and half a dozen healers, apothecaries, and other attention-grabbers sit with Amval's body.

"The order to disperse includes you all," I say.

Hana nods at me and begins hauling the first man to his feet. Clearly, he is going to be the hardest to dislodge. Between her soldier's bearing and my refusal to budge, the pokers and prodders all leave.

Mostly. I can see Hana a few feet away in the grass. I'm going to need her for what comes next, and she knows it.

Joli throws herself onto the ground, grabbing at Amval and Kaloni as her tears flow freely. I crouch beside them, far enough away that I can't touch him even by accident.

"People arrived so quickly," Kaloni says thickly. "It was all too overwhelming to speak up."

I don't look at him. I can't. "Joli said something about the cool and dark?"

"Yes." Kaloni offers me a wobbling smile. "We have caves in our shoreline which keep our dead safe while still allowing them to taste the wind."

I haven't even had time for a tour of Moonlight Tower yet, but I saw a pile of spades speared into a massive mound of dirt behind the stable when we arrived. They've been digging. "Would underground work? No wind, but he'll be safe."

"That is all we can truly ask." Kaloni seizes my hand. "Thank you."

"Anything for"—him—"an ally."

WHO DID IT?

Ingrid

Hana deposits Amval's body in the large, empty hollow below Moonlight Tower. Right now, there's no way of knowing whether it's going to be a dungeon, cellar, or both. The crowd of Soms—two parents, seven remaining siblings—look around at it with tired eyes. Maybe they're thinking the same thing. Maybe they're just comparing it to the seaside caves at home.

If I could see them, would I understand more about Amval?

Of course not. No one would learn a thing about me walking through the Solberg family crypt. There are no answers in this death.

King Iraj clings to his wife, Queen Zephira's, hand as she murmurs a prayer over the body. All nine of them stand quietly over their tenth. No answers there either.

But answers have to be somewhere. Things like this don't just happen.

I sidle over to Hana. "Will there be an investigation?"

The corners of her mouth tug down. "Yes."

She looks at Amval, not at me, and I realize what has to happen. Because I didn't escape in time. Because Kaloni found me with him.

There will be an investigation, and I am the very first suspect.

"CAN WE GET YOU ANYTHING ELSE?" XANDRA ASKS, LOOKING BETWEEN me and Beta Sahin, the slab of staunch Lightning Cape muscle standing in the corner of the windowless sitting room Hana escorted me into.

She's doing her best under the circumstances. At her insistence, I have a full plate of breakfast I haven't been able to touch yet and one of my own dresses to wear. The king's Beta vetoed a bath, which means the remainder of Amval's smell still clings to my skin. The charcoal feels more like an omen now—not ready to burn again, already burnt out.

I shake my head. What I want is a bed to sleep away the day. Maybe a few days. I don't have the answers they're looking for, and that doesn't change anything.

"Then we should get started." She sits in the armchair across from me and crosses her legs, displaying the masculine pants under a skirt that barely hits her knee at the front. It was my idea, but she wears it better than I dreamed. She looked good in the dresses in Tarrin, but she never looked comfortable. "You were found with Prince Amval's body."

"I know," I reply. "I was there."

She offers me a tired smile. Every expression is tired now. Apparently, the twins are much less cherubic when not dressed to the nines and half asleep. "How did you come to be there?"

"Bad luck?"

Sahin tightens his grip on the sword at his belt.

"I'd like to know how you do under interrogation after a couple of hours of sleep and discovering the potential love of your life is dead in your arms," I spit.

His eyebrows shoot up.

"This is not an official interrogation," Xandra says, sharp and fast.

Technically, nobody knew we were mates. Nobody other than Finn, and judging by her attempt to cover my slip, Xandra.

Now, all of Lightning Cape will know.

"Is it correct to say you were caught in the Haze and drawn to Prince Amval?" Xandra asks gently.

I huddle back onto the couch, away from my breakfast, and nod. Interview, interrogation, it doesn't matter. It's only a matter of time before my mouth runs away with me.

"Did you mate?"

Memories cascade through my mind. They felt like the beginning of something. A chance to be happier than I've ever dreamed.

Foolish. I am more than happy enough.

Xandra nods. My silence is enough of an answer. "Did he seem injured or ill?"

Leather creaks as Sahin tightens his grasp again. Xandra sighs.

"I am sorry. We don't have an official policy for this yet, so they are allowed far more latitude over the investigation than I would like for them to have," she tells me through the mind-link.

Out loud, she says. "Did he seem injured?"

"He seemed whole and uninjured." I spear the Beta with my gaze. "Trust me. I made a very thorough inspection."

He grimaces at me, but his orange-brown eyes slide away from mine. I smile grimly. He should feel at least as shitty as I do.

Or should he? For all I know, the king's Beta wasn't the distant sword Father's was to me when it came to Amval. He could be grieving something like a nephew, maybe even something like a son. All I know is that King Iraj said he would supervise, and Sahin appeared instead.

I pick at my thumbnail. It's slightly less obvious than chewing. If I had my lute—

I'd look like the guiltiest person alive, plucking chipper tunes as my sister-in-law asks me about my dead mate.

Xandra clears her throat, jarring me from my thoughts. "What about sickness? Did Prince Amval seem ill?"

"I don't think it would've shown during the Haze if he were." Last night, I felt unkillable, all instinct and adrenaline.

Xandra nods. Even Sahin has the decency to look like he believes those words coming out of my mouth. He must have a mate.

"Did you see anyone strange?" Xandra asks.

I hear Anwen's voice in the back of my head, telling me to lie. I know I didn't kill him. Everything would be much easier if I sent Xandra and all of Lightning Cape off on some wild goose chase for a mysterious figure in the night, a murderer for them to pin all their hopes on.

But then I'd never know the truth.

"I didn't see much," I say. "Certainly nothing obvious."

Xandra is too good at politics to actually frown, but her brow puckers for a heartbeat. She was hoping for a different answer. Maybe she was hoping I'd lie, too. "All right. I have to ask about the morning now."

Sahin leans slightly forward, and I realize he thinks I did it—whatever *it* is. Since he has a mate, he knows it would be nearly impossible to do during the Haze itself, so he figures it happened in the morning. He thinks there are going to be holes in my story, that I'm going to slip up.

Shit, I'm almost glad he's here. If this whole not-interrogation is Xandra gently asking me questions….

This way, I have an enemy. Someone to prove myself against. And that beats thinking about my burning, dry eyes or the hollow ache in my chest any day.

"As best I can tell, I woke up after it was done." I unfold myself and sit forward, making my testimony right to Sahin. "He was…already cooling."

Xandra closes her eyes, almost wincing. Sahin looks away from me. He doesn't want to hear this in this kind of detail—but if he wants to suspect me, he can endure whatever I damn well please.

"But not longer after. His scent was still thick in the air, and it dissipated as the morning continued." Details slot into place in my memory, details I barely noticed that become clues in retrospect. "The grass was trampled in two directions away from where we were, the way I came from and the way he did." I blink slowly as realization dawns. On human feet, alone as I got robes, I didn't trample more than a blade. "A person could've reached us without leaving a trail. Or a wolf could've followed one of our paths.

Sahin coughs, but I can hear the incredulous snort anyway. He thinks it's convenient that now there's a way for someone else to get to where we were. Xandra pats my knee, encouraging me to continue, but I don't need it. Those paths seemed damning until a minute ago.

"His face was covered, but he had an arm over my waist," I say. "That's a strange way to fall asleep—unless someone positioned him like that to make sure I would discover he was dead in the most dramatic way possible."

"Lightning Cape can draw its own conclusions," Sahin rumbles, the first words I've heard him say in a while. There's a jagged edge to them, like he's just waiting to be able to kill me.

He'll have to wait. I'm onto something, and I know it.

"I'm a heavy sleeper. Everyone knows that." I stand slowly, staring at Sahin.

Xandra's comforting hand on my knee has become a restraining one, suggesting firmly that I sit back down. I compromise on staying where I am instead of storming across the half-decorated room. By the tightness in her face, it's not the compromise she would've chosen.

"Lightning Cape knew nothing of you until we found you beside our fallen prince," Sahin replies.

"Unlucky, then, that he happened to die beside someone so unlikely to wake up while he did." I study the towering Beta. He has maybe six inches on me, but he's less broad than Father or Kieran. The emphasis on riding and magic makes all the strongest in Lightning Cape slightly leaner than those in other places. He is armed, certainly extremely magical, and furious, judging by the clench of his jaw. But is that defensive anger? "Where were you this morning? Who else is being unofficially interrogated? I spent last night with Prince Amval, it's true, but I missed an awful lot of last night."

Xandra squeezes my leg, begging me to stop. I know my mouth is way out ahead of my thoughts, about to get me into trouble again. But I can picture Sahin creeping through the night, looming over the pair of us, ripping away everything the Goddess just promised us.

He opens his mouth to reply, his eyes narrowed.

Someone knocks on the door. We all turn as Hana steps in.

"Apologies, Luna Xandra." She bows. "I've been talking with the other...healers who saw Prince Amval's body before it was sequestered, and we believe we've come to a conclusion about what might have happened."

Xandra stands, blocking me from Sahin. He has the good sense to turn toward Hana, even if his eyes gleam like he thinks I'm about to be caught.

"Tazi, from Lightning Cape, actually made the connection." Hana inclines her head toward Sahin, making me dislike her for just a second. I thought she was above politics. "We think it was the Carmine Pox."

Sahin's face drops. His warm skin turns an unpleasantly familiar gray.

"Goddess above," Xandra mutters, going pale. "The twins?"

"Safe." Hana glances at me. "They'll be kept far away from any infection."

Infection. He was sick. There's no conspiracy, no second set of tracks to be looking for. Just the worst luck imaginable.

"Wait, infection?" I ask.

"The Carmine Pox takes two forms," Sahin says somberly. "One is passed through the air and is highly contagious. Some decades ago, it nearly destroyed Lightning Cape, Tansy Beach, and Whaleberry Harbor."

"And the other form," Hana says, "is carried in the blood of the few who survive."

"Alpha King Notu, Prince Amval's grandfather, carried it." Sahin lowers his head. "His abrupt death in the night made Alpha Gavin's overrunning of our kingdom all the easier."

Everyone in the room looks shaken by the revelation—everyone but Xandra, who seems slightly comforted by the reminder that what happened to my mate might have been a quirk of his family, nothing that could affect her twins.

Just a quirk. Just luck.

Just on the night we first met.

"I am so sorry to have put you through this," Xandra says suddenly.

I look around for who she's talking to and discover she's staring at me.

"As am I." Sahin bows shallowly. "The Carmine Pox kills without warning and without impetus. Please, accept my apologies on behalf of all of Lightning Cape—and my condolences for your loss."

I open my mouth and close it again. My head hurts from how fast everything changed. Sahin can't have switched so quickly—a moment ago, he looked like he wanted to run me through.

But there aren't any answers in their faces, either.

THE PAST RETURNS

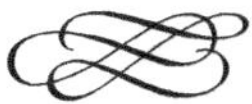

Ingrid

In the end, Raven comes to find me.

The Carmine Pox seem to be magic words. Xandra disappears with Hana, presumably to check on the twins and make sure the inherited form hasn't somehow turned into something worse. Sahin offers me a final, apologetic nod before stumping out. And then I just sit there.

Where else should I go? I doubt there's anywhere in this castle that isn't talking about Amval or me, and if somebody asks me about it....

I've just been cleared of murder. I don't particularly want to put myself up for suspicion again by committing one in broad daylight.

So I'm still sitting on that same damn couch when Raven knocks softly then pushes the door open. Vespera dozes on her hip, her tiny, peaceful face the exact opposite of Raven's worried one.

"Everyone has been looking for you," she says.

"I was never lost," I reply.

She steps in, shuts the door, and sits on the couch beside me. A few inches away. She always sits like that with us until we pull her closer, like there's still a tiny part of her waiting for us to call Mother for crossing the invisible lines that dictated our childhood. I've spent years pulling her across them now.

Not today. My hands lay still in my lap.

"I am so sorry," Raven says.

Those words have lost all meaning much faster than I would have anticipated. I just stare at the far wall. A portrait leans against it, not yet hung up, but I can see where it will go over the mantel. I can also see that the painter didn't accommodate for the changing light while he worked. If I had a brush, a palette knife, and a few hours, I could fix it. That, and the shadow of a very unpleasant-looking mustache he gave Finn. Maybe I will once everyone is done apologizing to me.

"After I woke up next to Kieran—"

"He was dead?"

She flinches. "No. Of course not."

"After you woke up next to Kieran, you realized the Haze could tell you secrets that would otherwise have been kept your whole life." I snort. "That it unlocked potentials you never could have imagined. What potential have I unlocked, other than being pitied for the rest of my life?"

She bites her lower lip and strokes Vespera's head. "Kieran has a plan for how to keep you away from the worst of the gossip."

"Until when?"

"I know you're distraught right now." Raven reaches out tentatively and sets a hand on my knee.

My chest aches. It could be my mark or the fact that I still barely feel like I can breathe. She hasn't reached out to me yet. I've been waiting for this moment, trying to coax her into it. And right now, all I can think about is that I want her to leave me alone.

"I'm not distraught." That's the Goddess-honest truth. I have no idea what the word for this feeling is, but *distraught* seems humiliatingly small and selfish.

Her frown deepens. "I would be devastated if I were you."

"I think I might just be tired," I say. It sounds as true as anything else.

"All right." Raven helps me to my feet. "We will get you back to your room, and you can rest."

Lying down doesn't sound awful, but I don't want to leave this room. "I'm missing something."

"It makes sense that you would miss him, even after—"

"No," I say. "Something here. Something with the Carmine Pox."

Raven stares around the half-decorated room. "The Carmine Pox is here?"

She's not terrified like the other three were. Maybe it's because the plague didn't reach us. Maybe it's another gap in her knowledge, left over from all the tutoring she didn't get. Either way, she doesn't have any answers for me.

And maybe I just think they're here because this is the last place I mattered to this story. Lightning Cape has their answers, and they have Amval's body. They don't need me.

"No." I take a step toward the door, and exhaustion shrieks through me. I didn't even realize I was tired. "It died with him."

"I'm so—" She closes her mouth around the apology before it can escape. "Come on. You and Vespera can nap together."

I stroke my niece's soft, pale curls. Maybe.

Raven shields me from the lingering eyes that chase us through the halls. Just as I expected. If I'd tried to go anywhere without her, I would've been swarmed. Half of these people were already supposed to be gone. They're only still here for the gossip, a look at the princess with a one-day mate.

Not even one day. I didn't get to wake up next to him alive.

Halfway there, Eva joins us. She squeezes my hand once, apologetically, but she has the decency not to say the words.

Instead, she says, "When I heard you were on the move, I thought you could use extra protection. I've cleared the next few halls already."

"Where's Candace?" I ask.

Eva scowls. "King Andri had a meeting set up for this morning, and he insisted Hollis and Candace attend. She sent me."

"At least I'll never have a father-in-law like that," I mutter.

Raven flinches again. Eva's less surprised.

"I spent my whole life engaged to someone who mated with someone else," she says. "And now I still don't have a mate. You can survive, even be happy without what the Carmine Pox took from you."

It's better than apologies, but her words set a bell ringing in my head. No, they make me notice it. The bell has been ringing since Hana appeared.

Why do I know the name Carmine Pox?

We enter the hallway every Solberg in this castle is sleeping on. Eva kisses me on my cheek and promises Candace will come as soon as she can. I nod vaguely. The Carmine Pox. I don't know it from here; I know it from a long time ago.

Raven takes the hand Eva released and ushers me into the room she, Kieran, and their children are sharing. With Moonlight Tower still barely finished, there's not enough space for privacy. Kieran sits on the floor, stacking blocks with Altair, but he jumps up when he sees us.

"I am so sorry," he says as he enfolds me in a hug.

If Eva was still here, I'd look at her. She had the right idea, running away after she caught Candace and Hollis together. I bet she got some of this when she went home, enough to know what my look meant, but not nearly as much.

But Kieran is warm. He's solid. He doesn't let go, even when I can't find my arms to hug him back, and my eyes sting. He smells just a little bit like Father.

Altair and Vespera are lucky. They're getting one hell of a dad.

"I thought, after Finn and Xandra, our bad luck was broken," he says.

"I like to break the mold." I disentangle myself from him. My legs are exhausted, and standing is becoming a chore. I drop onto the couch and look at Altair's wobbling stack of blocks. "Is that Moonlight Tower, Tai?"

He nods with a huge smile. No one told him. "Papa said I make next one."

"Next Moonlight Tower?" I don't glance at Kieran. I don't care how worried he and Raven are. I just want to talk to someone who doesn't know, even if he still pronounces Moonlight *moo-nigh*.

"No!" He giggles. "Next home tower!"

Yet another reason Altair is sometimes my favorite family member —he's got the best dreams. I figure if I encourage enough of them the next Alpha of Dun's Crossing might manage to be interesting.

"Ingrid," Kieran says.

"What?" I offer Altair a block. "What else is there to say?"

"The Goddess gives us the people She does for a reason." He sits next to me. "I wish you'd gotten him for longer, but there's still a reason why all this happened."

My leg twitches. I want to kick over Altair's tower and ask Kieran if there's a reason why that happened. I want to chuck the block in my hands at my brother's skull and ask how he feels about fate now. None of them have any idea what this feels like. At least Altair isn't pretending.

"Carmine Pox," I say.

Kieran blinks, looks at Raven. "What about it?"

"You know it?"

He nods slowly. "I wish I didn't."

"Did you have it?" If he was sick for a while, that could be why I remember the name. It's so fuzzy—I wouldn't be surprised if it were attached to something that happened before I was born.

"Thank the Goddess, no." He stares into the fire. "It never really reached Dun's Crossing."

I finally look at him. Too much emphasis on that *really*; he's leaving something out.

He white-knuckles a block. He's looking at the fire, but his eyes are still, like he's not really seeing it.

The way he always gets when someone brings up yet another crime of Father's that he doesn't want to talk about.

And I know why I know the name.

This is burning clove, Mother says in my memory on one of our many afternoons in her garden.

I grab for it with chubby hands—I was too young to know just how many of her plants would kill me just by touching them.

Careful. It comes from my home kingdom, and it's not very nice. A cure that bites the healthy with what it cures.

Years later, I laughed off the rumors Father had poisoned the king of Lightning Cape with everyone else. He, of course, died of the Carmine Pox.

It was just unlucky that the last burning clove plant in Som Palace, the only thing that would've healed him, disappeared a few months before he needed it.

BLACKMAIL

Amval

THUD...THUD....

Only the spike of pain through my skull tells me that's my head—hitting the bottom of... something. I blink my eyes open, but such total blackness meets them that I try twice before giving up.

Where under the sky am I?

The last thing I remember is....

My mate. Impossibly beautiful in my arms, moaning underneath me. The memory of her scent, ink and violets, clouds my nose as my throat throbs.

That must be my mark. I try to reach for it, to feel its shape, but something scrapes against my raw wrists, and I hiss.

Thick, fibrous rope. Holding me in place.

I have been kidnapped.

Slowly, I breathe in through my nose and then out again. Mother and Father trained me for if this ever happened. The blackness over my eyes must be some kind of blindfold or cover. It reeks of old produce—likely a bag, then. The same rough fabric sandpapers my body, some kind of robe. I test moving one of my legs and find it free. Not a total surprise. The rope around my wrists is thick enough to resist the explosion of a shift for at least a short while, but there is no way to bind human ankles that holds in wolf form. The thudding must be the rhythm of a cart or carriage.

How long has passed? How far away am I?

There is only one way to know.

"Hello?" I call.

The cart slows. "We are miles from anyone. There's no use in yelling."

"I wasn't planning on yelling." There are two ways to deal with a kidnapping—give them no reason to kill you until your ransom is paid or escape before they can kill you. Both require patience and politeness. "I was just curious if you would tell me where we are."

The person—man, I believe—driving the cart snorts. "We just crossed the north border of Lightning Cape."

Rogue territory. It used to be some kingdom or other, but when King Gavin's attempts to overtake it stalled, it fell into chaos. There really is no one to yell for—or at least, no one who isn't just as likely to try to sell me to the highest bidder. I am alone.

My mark throbs.

Oh, Goddess, what happened to my mate? I twist as carefully as I can, feeling out the space. Hay juts into my unbound ankles, but I'm the only body back here.

"Thank you," I say as evenly as I can. "I see no reason why we have to make this unpleasant."

"Of course you don't," the driver grumbles.

That voice…I recognize it. Barely, through the muffling of the bag over my head and my own whirling thoughts.

"Yalim," I say slowly.

The answering silence is deafening.

"You're a member of the palace guard." I can picture him. Narrow face, horrible little mustache. "You had a son this year, didn't you?"

Still no answer, which makes me even more sure I'm right.

I sit up, shoving the implications of one of my own soldiers carting me away in the night to the back of my mind. That's a problem for after I've gotten myself free. "Take the hood off. As you said, we're completely alone, and I already know your face."

Yalim sighs.

A heartbeat later, light floods my vision. I shade my eyes with my bound hands and try not to wince. My whole body groans, my head worst of all. If we're already so far, he's been driving me for nearly a day.

"How did you knock me out?" One of Father's best negotiation tactics—don't ask what you suspect, ask the question after it.

"Some powder," he says. "I don't know. It was at the drop point with instructions."

I smack my lips. My mouth is drier than a sand dune and tastes faintly of copper. Goddess above, I should have paid more attention when Mother worked with us in the apothecary.

"You were hired, then?" I ask.

Yalim scoffs as my eyes finally adjust. Exactly as I expected—thin face, mustache that makes him look like he skinned a squirrel and slapped it on his upper lip. I scratch at my own stubbly cheek and try not to grimace at the sight of him.

Instead, I turn to our surroundings. He doesn't seem to be lying. Scrubby forest lines the narrow path we're traveling on, just as it should at the northern border of the kingdom. A howl issues up from somewhere far away, only to be answered by a pair of others. That sounds like rogues.

Yalim doesn't flinch at the sound. He is more than confident.

Perhaps that's down to the sword on his belt, counterbalanced by the dagger on his opposite thigh. Or the fact that with my wrists bound, I can barely create a stiff breeze.

Still, I try. The wind picks up, tousling Yalim's dark hair.

He flicks his hand, and it dies. "Nice try, but I have my full capabilities."

Under my breath, I curse Father for making powers a requirement of military service. Our army is small, affordable as we rebuild, but extremely powerful.

Including against their own crown prince.

"What do you want?" I ask.

"A little peace of mind," he replies.

I frown. "From me?"

He laughs, long enough and loud enough that I wonder if I could club him with my bound hands and seize control of the horse pulling the cart before we crash.

"If that was all I wanted, I'd ask," he says finally. "I wouldn't have to pay for it in blood."

A chill ices down my spine. That doesn't sound like the words of a kidnapper. That sounds like an assassin.

There are two ways to deal with an assassin: escape before they kill you or die.

"You could ask," I say, hoping he can't hear the new edge to my voice. "I'm sure I'd grant it."

"But then I'd have to tell you." Yalim's laughter this time borders on hysterical. "I'll take my chances with the deal I've got. Stop talking."

I stare at the back of his head, at the swiftly disappearing path past him. He must have a place in mind, or he would've stopped by now. But we've already entered lawless territory, so it can't be far.

My aching thoughts stumble over each other. Whatever he drugged me with was far from restful. I may as well have been awake the whole ride, except then I might have actually learned something.

Slow breath in through my nose then out. Father's voice overlays the old mantra in my thoughts, teaching it to me eons ago. Mother just told me to be brave, but Father understood. He remembered being prince, albeit second in line, before the years he spent hiding from King Gavin's men.

I barely noticed Yalim, other than his mustache. He's a dutiful soldier, not one that tries to be personable with us or climb the ranks. He doesn't ask for special assignments. And he's always worked in the palace, as the presumed son of some minor lord lost when Gavin attacked.

So he has no practice guarding his words. He's already told me everything I need to know, if I can just think hard enough to remember what it was.

What doesn't he want to tell me?

Not the identity of the person who hired him, though I have no doubt someone did. It seemed more personal than that—only his own problems would make him sound hysterical. He has a young son, but killing me doesn't help him at all. There is a reason Yalim is a palace guard, not a noble. He almost couldn't be farther from the line of succession.

"All right." He nudges the horse and leads the cart off to the side of the road. "This is the spot."

"Why this spot?" It looks the same as every other inch of this abandoned road—and any conversation might buy me the extra seconds I need to convince my sluggish brain to work.

Yalim hops off the driver's bench with a sigh. "It's where I met my mate."

"No better place to kill your prince?"

He shakes his head. "That was a joke, Your Highness. It's a random spit of land no one will ever look twice at, deep enough into rogue territory that no one will ever be here to consider looking twice at."

My retort is lost in him grabbing the rope between my wrists and yanking me out of the cart. I stumble so I don't fall on my face.

Two ways to deal with an assassin. I'm not out of options yet.

Yalim leads me to a tree and then forces me to my knees in the dirt, facing the trunk. "If you stay still, this will be nice and clean."

Something hot growls in the pit of my stomach. I test my bonds again. They hold for a little bit after I shift, but I don't need my paws to tear his head off. I'm not just going to sit in the dirt in front of a man known throughout the palace for nothing but his awful little mustache. I am not going to die on my knees.

"Will a clean death clean your conscience?" I snap.

He sighs, surprisingly tired. "I messed that up ages ago. This is just payment."

Wind shifts behind me. I might not be able to wield it right now, but I still feel it like my own skin. That's his sword coming free from its scabbard. That's him hefting it up behind him. A slight pause as he judges the angle.

"I am sorry," Yalim says as he swings.

The wind whispers when to move. At the very last second, I roll out of the way, and his blade bites deeply into the trunk. Wood chips fly, but I barely notice them. I lunge for the dagger sheathed on his thigh, grab it with both bound hands, and shoot to my feet.

Yalim tugs weakly on his sword as I press his own dagger against his throat. When he feels the press of cold metal, his eyes flutter shut.

I snarl, "I'm not interested in apologies."

He clings to his sword, almost leans on it. "I understand, Your Highness."

He's resigned.

And I realized exactly what I was missing.

All his talk about deals, payment, his refusal to tell me what he wants peace for—Yalim is being blackmailed into doing this.

"You have two options," I spit, momentum carrying me forward more than anything else. "Either I can kill you where you intended to kill me, or you can run, and if you ever return to Lightning Cape, I won't bother trekking all the way out to rogue territory."

I hope he chooses to run. He was forced here as much as I was.

Then, I follow the line of his sword in the tree. If I hadn't moved, he would have decapitated me. He might not want to be here, but he is a dutiful soldier.

He exhales shakily against my blade and opens his mouth to answer.

SUPPORT

Ingrid

RAVEN INSISTS I EAT SOMETHING BEFORE I LIE DOWN, SO I STUMBLE
through half of a loaf of bread before leaving for my room next door.
The walls are thick enough that I can't hear Altair playing anymore—
nor can I hear the worried conversation I'm sure Kieran and Raven
are having about me right now, judging by the looks they sent each
other as I left.

I flop onto the covers and stare up at the ceiling. The bread sits
heavy in my stomach. Sleep sounds like a chore now.

Father murdered Amval's grandfather in the exact same way. That
cannot be a coincidence.

My lute calls to me from the corner of the room. I always think
clearer with it in my hands, so I roll out of bed and grab it. My left
hand slides into the slight indentations on the neck, worn from use,
and my right dances over the familiar strings. The sun has warmed it
like I've already been holding it for a while.

Before I think about it, I start playing that air I was working on.
The one my night with Amval inspired a new end to. My mark aches.

Maybe Amval's grandfather had the Carmine Pox in his veins. He must have for the ploy to have worked in the first place. Otherwise, the poison would've sparked a new wave of fear, one that would've made the remains of Lightning Cape's royal family going into hiding together too dangerous to even attempt. But Mother wasn't shy about how pleased she was to "still be living in her homeland." Sometimes, she referred to the annexation of Lightning Cape as her favorite wedding present. And after Kieran took the throne, I heard a pair of soldiers talking about how bizarrely easy that campaign was, implying that they now suspected Father had done something to make it that way.

I set my lute down. In a few days, maybe sooner, everyone here will scatter to their respective corners of the globe, and any chance I have to get to the bottom of this will disappear. When have I let rumors trap me in my room? I can be exhausted when I get home—or when I have answers.

I hurry out of my room and turn down the hall away from Kieran and Raven's door.

Attention follows me. I hold my head high and tell everyone who tries to stop me that I'm too busy to talk right now. Well, everyone but the staff, and I stop them more often than not. Anwen was always so proud that he knew all the secret passages in Solberg Castle, but I would've told him that was a waste of time if he'd ever asked. Sneaking around is far more effort than being one of the only people who treat the staff reasonably. They know secrets that Anwen couldn't even dream of—partially because he only knows about a third of their names.

At the price of a few more *so sorries*, I learn exactly where Joli is staying. If anyone would want to know what I've remembered and dive into this with me, it's her. As I walk, I hum Amval's song. It's a bruise-like ache, and poking bruises makes them more used to the pain when you inevitably smack them against something. Better to get used to it now.

The moment I step into the corridor the Soms are sleeping along, I realize my mistake. The stone walls are garlanded in funereal black and gray. Ribbons of the colors hang on every door. All the usual sounds of a castle die at the threshold, like even noise respects this family's grief. It reminds me of Estrella's family's rooms after King Isai was assassinated. Somber, but overly so. A tactless attempt to support someone going through something so private where privacy is impossible. At least Kieran had the sense not to put up banners indicating the exact spot where all the grieving people were.

And I don't belong here. This is real grief. I want to solve this, whatever it is, out of respect for what might've been. Not what was.

There is no *what was*, other than a scar I'll carry over my heart for the rest of my life.

I turn on my heel and leave, still humming. The more I poke the mark, the faster I'll get used to the pain.

"Are you free yet?" I ask Candace through the mind-link.

"Not yet," she replies. *"I'm so—"*

I cut off the link before she can finish. Even if she's just talking about being busy, I don't want to hear it.

My feet carry me all the way to the twins' nursery. Maybe Hana will be there. She'll have more information, maybe even be willing to listen to me.

Or I just want to stop hearing apologies, and the twins can't talk. Only the Goddess knows.

Lieutenant Sime flanks the door with another soldier, and he nudges the woman to let me in wordlessly. Normally, I'd try to make him break his usually severe expression with some joke, and he'd call me Vivian like he still doesn't know my real name.

Today, I just slide past him into the nursery. Lucian lies in one of the matching bassinets, and Alden squirms in Finn's arms.

"I didn't know you'd be here." I take a step back. "I can go."

"You can be anywhere you want today." He nods to Lucien.

I scoop up the fair-haired twins and wiggle my fingers in his face. He burbles sleepily. "Xandra seemed worried about them."

"We both were, but Hana seems sure it was the inherited version of the disease. Apparently, it strikes faster." He shrugs.

I should've tracked Finn down first. He's the only one who

wouldn't be scared to actually talk to me about this. And this happened in his kingdom—he has the right to make everyone stay, if he wants.

"I don't think it was," I say.

He goes still, curled around his son. "You think it's contagious?"

"Goddess, no. I wouldn't be here if I did." I stroke Lucian's thin, pale hair. "I think it was murder. Poison."

Finn exhales slowly. "That's a relief."

"Right, I'm really glad someone murdered my mate in my arms." It's hard to keep my voice quiet enough not to startle Lucian.

"Not—" He shakes his head, bouncing Alden to keep him happy. "I'm not glad he's dead. I'm glad there's no plague."

"I'm less glad due to the *murdered in my arms* situation."

"I know it was bullshit timing—"

"Oh." I look at Finn, who only has eyes for Alden suddenly. "You don't believe me."

"It's not that I don't believe you," he says.

"Then tell me what kind of murder has good timing," I reply.

He starts pacing, pretending it's for Alden's sake. "I just think this would probably be a lot easier if you had someone to blame—someone you could put your hands on, not the Goddess."

I could put my hands on him, but I'm not going to say that with Lucian in my arms. No one knows what babies remember, and I won't let my nephew grow up hating me just because his father is a bastard. "I understand. You think I'm delusional."

"I think you're fucking heartbroken," he hisses, trying not to wake Alden, who is just starting to fall asleep in his arms. "And I think you should do whatever you need to make that easier, but I'm not going to turn my new kingdom inside out over it. Hana says he was sick. I trust her."

I bite my lip. Hard, harder, until I taste blood. If Finn's not willing to listen, I don't have a chance with Xandra. I stroke Lucian's head one last time, then set him back down in his mountain of blankets and pillows.

"When I'm right, you're going to feel extremely foolish," I say as I leave.

"If you are, I—" The closing door clips the end of his sentence. I hope it was that he'll let me rub his face in it forever. I intend to when I prove I'm right.

After leaving the nursery, though, I have nowhere to go. Xandra will align with Finn on everything, and Estrella isn't even here. There are other people I've had rare pleasant conversations with, but they're few and far between—even if I could be sure they weren't in on whatever plot I'm trying to uncover. Eva is much more Candace's friend than mine, and I can't imagine anything that would make my day worse than getting roped into birdwatching right now.

I find an unfinished window overlooking the sea, not the grass, and plant myself at it. The Windy Ocean lives up to its name—frothy white waves crash one after the next, on the shore and farther out. The swirling gray water makes more sense than anything else right now. I watch the shifting sun change color on its surface.

Finally, Candace says, "*I'm free!*"

I tell her where I am, and she rushes up to me a few moments later. My mark gnaws at my skin. I shoot to my feet and throw myself at her.

All day, ever since I found him, this is what I've been waiting for. I shake in her arms. I don't even know what I'm feeling, what I'm thinking. My best friend is here. That's all that matters.

She rubs my back quietly until I get enough control of myself to pry free and sit back down. Instead of apologizing, thank the Goddess, she waits for me to talk.

"I think Amval was murdered," I blurt out.

Before she replies, I babble every scrap of evidence I have—and it's not much. But I cling to her hand anyway. If anyone will listen to me, it's Candace.

When I'm done, she takes a deep breath. "If you're right... wouldn't that make you the primary suspect?"

"Maybe, but I know I didn't do it." I shake my head. "I need to find the truth."

She rubs her thumb over the back of my hand. "Lightning Cape isn't exactly known for long, thought-out investigations. Having an answer, even a wrong one, might be enough for them."

And I have no evidence. And I've been wandering around, humming to myself, when the rest of the family is in mourning. And my parents committed the original poisoning, which means I would know how to do it.

I stare into Candace's hazel eyes, begging me to let this go. She is right. It would be safer if I did, and I know that's all she wants for me.

But my mark groans in my chest. The Goddess does everything for a reason. Maybe She gave Amval to me because I'm the only one who would get him justice.

Alone, if I have to. Again.

ALONE

Amval

THE CURVED BLADE OF YALIM'S DAGGER GLEAMS IN THE WEAK SUNLIGHT as he swallows and conjures a bead of ruby blood at the tip. I've never killed someone before, much less someone I've known as long as this now former palace guard.

But he's left me very little choice.

"All right," he rasps. "I'll go."

I withdraw the dagger but keep it in my bound hands. "Did you touch my mate?"

"No more than it took to pry her off you," he says. "She didn't even stir."

Relief explodes through the throbbing mark on my throat, but I hold any sign of it tight in my chest. Yalim looks at me. I look at him.

"Do I have to tell you to go again?" I finally ask.

He turns greenish-pale and takes off into the trees. A few feet away, I hear the telltale rip of clothing. He's shifted. Probably smart, with so many rogues in the area.

That's another reason why I need to move quickly. With a single breath of relief, I kneel where he would have decapitated me and use the embedded sword to saw through the ropes around my wrists far more gracefully than I would've been able to with the dagger. I only nick myself once, which feels like a minor miracle.

The skin under the ropes is a nightmare, raw and red. Most of a day of travel, and I look like I've been bound for a month. They sting as I walk to the cart Yalim left behind. I'm glad he did. I've never been this far away from the palace on my own before. I'm not even sure I've been this far into wild territory at all. The path Yalim followed is a sliver on the ground, and I can sort of see the sinking sun through the trees, but it's hard to tell exactly which way it is coming from in here. Hopefully, the horse knows the way back to the palace.

The harnessed horse yawns as I approach, unworried. It—I glance beneath its belly—*he* is a surprisingly handsome gray with a black mane to match his black legs and a white star on his forehead. He's clearly been bred for distance, not speed, but I don't know that speed would help either of us much here.

"Would you like to go for a run?" I ask softly as I drift toward the cart itself.

As I thought, there's nothing in it but a few bales of hay and a cloth strung over the middle, clearly to hide me while Yalim left more populated areas. I grab the cloth and tie it around my neck as a makeshift cloak. Perhaps unsurprisingly, the robe he chose for me to die in isn't particularly comfortable or warm. With the sun setting, I'll need whatever additional protection I can get.

I assume. Nights are often freezing by the shore, especially since it's just barely spring. But out here, with the trees to break the wind? I don't know.

Another howl parts the air. Too much time thinking, not enough riding. I unharness the horse—Cloud, I decide to call him—with only a few mistakes. Father insisted we all know how to saddle our own mounts in an emergency, but a saddle and a cart harness are less similar than I hoped. Still, Cloud is patient while I work. I thank the Goddess he wasn't a hot-blooded breed, chosen to get Yalim here quickly. I'll even take the headache still throbbing at the base of my skull in exchange.

Without Cloud, I have no idea what I would do.

I kick off the cart, swing up onto his back, and urge him forward. He snorts, takes a last mouthful of grass, and then starts off back the way we came. I roll with his swaying gait, catching his rhythm in my body like Mother taught. The triplets were always the best at that, especially bareback, but I am no slouch.

But as I grow comfortable on top of him, thoughts get harder to avoid. Thoughts like whether the rest of my family is well or if they've simply been taken to other locations. Thoughts like the fact that Yalim was a palace guard, so the person who told him to do this is likely waiting for me—or, I suppose, for him—back in Som Palace.

Thoughts like the steady misery of the mark developing on my neck.

Cloud seems confident in his footing, so I let my eyes flutter shut. Memories of last night flash through my mind's eye in vivid color. The moment I saw that gray wolf in the grass, I knew. Her smell may have drawn me to her, but it was that second that I was hers, and she was mine. She was beautiful underneath me, singing like a whole chorus in only one voice. I remember clouds of golden hair, all perfumed like violets and ink, surrounding us even more than the grass and the sharpness of her eyes. Her face is lost to the instinct-lush Haze, but I would know her anywhere. I just need to see her again.

Thoughts of her and Cloud's steady plodding carry me through the rogue-laden forest. The first real breeze on my face feels like my first breath since I woke up. Wind exists in forests like that, but there is a reason Som Palace is perched on the edge of a cliff. Despite the danger, there is no place closer to the element that runs through all our veins. I spin a hurrying gust under Cloud's hooves and look toward the sun, already touching the horizon to my right.

I want to see her, but Lightning Cape comes first. My family and my people need me. Even more, I need to find who did this and bring them to the justice I promised Yalim. Perhaps I'll send his mate and son after him when I get there. If they know where he would go. And if I can prove he was blackmailed.

"That begs the question," I say to Cloud. "Why would he take me away to kill me in the first place?"

He says nothing.

"Not much of a conversationalist, hmm?" I scratch between his ears and wish I had a crisp roseapple to offer him. Not that it would make him talk. In truth, I wish Cirocco, my Beta and brother, was here. I'd be able to figure this all out if I could talk to him about it. I would even take Esen or Hova, the other two of the triplets, just now. Perhaps I would take anyone with Som blood in their veins.

"And yet, you're all I have." I nudge him south at an intersection. Out here, the sun is clear, so I know my directions at least. Knowing the way—or nearly—doesn't ease the strange, hollow pang in my chest.

Loneliness.

I don't know if I've ever been lonely before.

I've certainly never been away from my family for this long. During the years in hiding, we lived side-by-side, trying not to draw any attention to ourselves. We may have a palace now, but I rarely go an hour without talking to one of them.

"You are a fine mount but a poor replacement," I tell Cloud.

His steady breathing sets a reasonable rhythm for my thoughts, at least.

"If I believe Yalim, my mate is a heavy sleeper. He could have killed me then and there with far less effort," I say. "I wouldn't even have been able to fight back. So why drag me a day's journey away?"

The various bruises and aches on my body remind me Yalim didn't take much more care than he would have, killing me where he found me, but the question still seems important. If I can figure out who did this before I reach the palace, things will be much simpler.

"Is there a benefit to everyone believing I disappeared rather than died?"

The question answers itself—perhaps with some princes, but my family knows me far too well to think I ran away. Even during the long years of musty motels and empty stomachs, I trained to be the future Alpha of Lightning Cape. That was one thing we all agreed on —we were down, but we were very far from out. Someday, we would rule our people once again. So I learned diplomatic table manners with crudely whittled forks and knives and traced important family trees in the dirt with sticks. We may have been on the run, but we were raised as the princes and princesses we are.

And no one within Lightning Cape would be foolish enough to think they could convince my family with such a trick.

"Perhaps they were worried about waking people up." I shake my head. "No, they obviously had some kind of sedative. That could have been just as easily given to my mate, even if she did not sleep so deeply."

Cloud bobs his head, and I decide to take that as agreement. Cirocco would certainly be offering his own ideas by now, but even our horses have their limitations.

As soon as I return, my first conversation will be with my brother.

"Why else?" I twist a few strands of Cloud's mane together as I think. He snorts warningly, but I know he would prefer this to me tapping out songs on his neck. My stallion, Seksim, certainly does. "Perhaps it is as simple as not wanting anyone to find my body. I suppose, if I never returned, my family would eventually have to accept that I—"

The words stop halfway up my throat, and I feel like I'm choking on them. There is nothing under the Goddess's sky that I am less likely to do than leave my family. It would destroy them.

I flick the reins, pushing Cloud up to a trot. I've already been gone long enough. Whoever wants to get rid of me must have some plan, and I will not let it happen to my family without me there to protect them.

He leaps into a surprised canter, pounding down the widening road. Soon, we'll reach the border of the kingdom, and news will spread. Whoever thought they could attack the Soms will discover just how wrong they were.

I am still hours of riding away from my family, assuming Mother and Father left Moonlight Tower in the morning like we originally planned. Riding into the kingdom with my head high and a banner flying will only give them a chance to accelerate their plans.

I hunker down on Cloud's back and pull my makeshift cloak into a makeshift hood. Nothing could be more satisfying than riding gloriously up to their side, proving them right for believing I would return —nothing, other than having them all safe and alive when I ride up. I don't have the faintest clue who might have done this to me, other than that it must be someone who had access to Yalim. It seems likeliest that the enemy is within Lightning Cape, but Yalim came with us to the name-blessing. Any noble could have reached him.

Until I am sure who it was, my survival is a secret I'm going to have to keep alone.

My mark throbs. I wish I could release the reins to touch it, read the kingdom of my mate in its growing contours. Her golden, laughing beauty fills my thoughts again.

A pit settles deep in my gut, and within it, a sour question.

The person who was nearest to me when I was kidnapped, who had the best opportunity to summon Yalim and spirit me away, who might not have wished my blood shed right where I was… is her.

Did she order Yalim to abduct and kill me?

If she did, what should my next move be?

LAST CHANCE

Ingrid

The morning after waking up next to my dead mate, I sit in the ballroom, now stuffed with long tables for the vultures who are still here to eat breakfast. Early morning cool wafts in through the unfinished wall. At the name-blessing, that seemed charming. A promise of a kingdom still being built mirroring the twin princes. Now, it just feels exposed, like anyone could reach in through the side and just start snatching people out.

I've been paranoid all morning. It's a miracle I made it down here, with how much time I spent looking over my shoulder. I should've tripped over my own feet and proven the Goddess was right to match us together by dying of plunging through an open window the very next day. My dreams last night were hectic and red. This morning, I'm only more sure that Amval was murdered.

I hunch over my plate of bread, fruit, and porridge, ravenous. Yesterday's distraction meant my rumbling stomach woke me up earlier than most of the castle. Most of the tables lay empty, and only a few benches have any occupants, much less as many as they can fit.

But the few people around me barely glance my way.

Nobles drift in vague clumps, talking lightly among themselves. I looked out the window on the way down here, and I saw the makeshift stable was wild with activity. More than a few families are leaving today, only a day later than planned. King Iraj announced last night that Amval's funeral would take place in Lightning Cape, and it's like that was the last call of the night. The party's over.

I don't want to be the center of attention or the hub of gossip, but it disappearing so quickly raises my hackles. A prince was murdered yesterday—or died, whichever they'd prefer to think. Kaloni is now next in line for the throne, and she's coming of age for the Haze this year. Shouldn't there be… something?

A trio of nobles I don't recognize burst into laughter. I clench my fork in my hand, my mark burning. The lightning-bolt shape is much more obvious now, even through the redness. I picked out a high-necked gown to hide it, and they don't even care.

Someone slides onto the bench next to me. I inhale slowly without looking. There are more than a few people I don't want to talk to this morning. I smell sage and… some summer fruit.

Joli.

"Good morning," I say.

She scoffs slightly. "They certainly think so."

I spear my fork into a thick cut of bread. "It's like they don't even remember that someone died."

Out of the corner of my eye, I watch her sneer. Her hair is piled loosely on top of her head, and she's ashen with exhaustion or crying, but she looks like a force to be reckoned with anyway.

"I told Father that we should ban them all from the funeral. They don't deserve him."

"I would work security at the gate myself if you did." Anger warms my bones, better than the tea I've been choking down.

She laughs bitterly. "He refused."

"Undiplomatic," we say in unison.

There's nothing else to say. I feed the anger in my gut. This is what

I needed. Not confusion, or worry, or the ache in my mark. Someone to take this out on.

Maybe Finn was right. I am looking for someone to blame. But that doesn't mean I'm wrong to look. There's bad luck, and there's this.

"We are leaving today," she says quietly.

My chances of finding the truth are disappearing. I can either slink home to Dun's Crossing and never know or make the safest bet.

I haven't been scared of risk since I fought Mother tooth and nail for a second session with my music tutor.

"I don't think Amval just died," I say.

Joli makes a sound somewhere between a hiccup and a gasp. New tears fill her eyes. Goddess above, she looks so young.

"I shouldn't have said anything." I can get what I need without her. She doesn't need to deal with this.

She grabs my hand and squeezes it so hard it feels like she's trying to pop my bones right out of my skin. "Ingrid, if you walk away from me after saying that, you can consider whatever friendship we had as dead as my brother is."

My mark aches, but I still find the wherewithal to be impressed by her threat. Her dark eyes burn—she'll make good on it, too.

How many times have I been her?

Enough that I know not to underestimate her.

I lean in and lower my voice. "I think he was murdered. Just like Alpha King Notu was before him."

Joli blinks. "Grandfather was sick."

"My mother all but admitted to poisoning him. Burning clove can either help cure the Carmine Pox or replicate its symptoms, and she took the last plant from the castle before she left." I glance around, feeling abruptly paranoid. Anyone in here could have done this, and the hall isn't full enough to cover our conversation. "I am sorry."

"I never met Grandfather," she says slowly, thinking so hard I can almost read her thoughts in her eyes. "All the old stories say Rowena was a gardener, though. And Gavin—"

"He was a monster." I'm used to saying it by now. It helps to think the words long before anyone else mentions them. "That's what I was thinking."

"So you think someone from Dun's Crossing—"

I shake my head. "I considered that, but my siblings didn't do it, and I can't come up with a motive for anyone else who came with us. Soldiers don't care about the crown prince of another kingdom, and neither do personal staff."

She looks up at me, horrified. "You think someone from Lightning Cape did?"

"Honestly, I don't know." Fuck, I wish I had more answers to give Joli. Her hands shake around mine. "I just know that's the next best bet. The kingdom likeliest to hold a grudge against you would be Tansy Beach, but there are only Moonlight Beach loyalists here, and King Iraj was the one who withheld the aid, not Amval."

"But why…." She stares past me—at nothing.

I can only shrug. "That's what I want to find out."

She swallows. Seconds drag as she processes what I said. She could throw my hand back at me, yell at me in front of this whole room, and storm out. But somehow, I don't think she's going to.

"So do I," she says finally. "He deserves that. He was always there for me, even when Mother and Father were too busy."

I taste blood before I realize how hard I'm biting my lip. My mark screams at me to ask more about that, about him. I want to know every single story, every memory she has of her brother.

But those are hers. I'm here to get him justice, not to fall in love with a dead man.

"You should come with us," Joli says. "If you're right, Som Palace is the only place to find answers."

I snort, imagining sitting down in front of Kieran and Raven after the day we had yesterday to request diplomatic permission to visit Lightning Cape. And that's if Finn and Candace haven't already expressed their concerns—vaguely, I hope, in Candace's case.

"I was thinking the same thing, but my family won't let me. Not officially."

Joli's eyes light. "I'm starting to think getting drunk and admitting my little side project to you might have been one of my best business moves."

For her sake, I once again don't tell her I already almost knew. She's too good a smuggler, and Candace helped me solve her client-choice problem for her.

"Ulas!" Joli singsongs as she saunters into the crowded stable. I watch from an empty stall nearby. The reek is lethal, but it's the only place in here that I'm reasonably sure no one needs to be.

A groom in Lightning Cape orange and white looks up from harnessing a pair of horses to a carriage. "Princess Joli."

She skips closer and pets one of the horses. It snorts at her. "I have a small favor to ask of you and Thistle here."

"Thistle is a little irritable today," Ulas says, hurrying forward to separate princess and horse as Thistle almost snaps at Joli. "Can you back up a few paces?"

"Oh, I know her. She just needs to remember me." Joli dodges Ulas and tries to pet Thistle again. The horse lifts one foot off the ground, about to rear. "Come now, girl, relax."

Ulas grits his teeth as he grabs Thistle's reins, trying to drag this situation under control. I barely stifle a laugh. She really is good—I'd be shocked if Ulas remembers they ever talked, with how distracted he is.

"What do you want, Your Highness?" he hisses.

"I've picked up a few souvenirs Mother and Father don't need to know about. Could I stash a trunk in the final carriage's compartment?" She smiles as she reaches for Thistle again, like she doesn't notice the wild look the horse is giving her.

"Yes!" Ulas nearly shouts. "Just put it in and go!"

"Thank you!" she trills before skipping away.

I slip out and meet her behind the building. "You really are brilliant."

She curtsies, but her trademark grin is missing. "Anything for Amval."

Right. My laughter keels over, and I straighten my skirts. "What are we going to do once we get there?"

"The final carriage is always unloaded last—it's all luggage, with one minder. I'll sneak you off before anyone gets around to that. We'll stash you in a garret until a few days have passed and my parents can't send you home." She eyes me. "You're going to have to be as quiet as you were crossing the border into Tansy Beach for the whole ride. Can you do that?"

I barely breathed while she smuggled me past a small army into Moonlight Hollow. "I'll pack a bell in one of the other trunks, just in case."

"Maybe a few." She looks past me, at the chaos in the stable. Counting how many eyes and ears we have to avoid to pull this off, I'd bet. "We're going to find who did this, right?"

Suddenly, I remember sneaking Candace into a diplomatic envoy to Snowcrest a few years ago. My plan was rudimentary compared to Joli's, but the broad strokes feel too similar to ignore. Like history repeating itself.

Except Candace was riding toward her mate. There's no love waiting for me on the other side of this, just a truth everyone else seems content to deny.

Everyone but Joli.

I stick out my hand to shake. "I'll discover who murdered Amval if it kills me."

HOME AGAIN?

Amval

I slow Cloud to a walk at the foot of Som Palace. The sky behind the castle is gray with the rising sun, and every inch of my body moans for a rest. For nearly two days, I've been awake. I look up at the star-shaped outer wall, toward the equally jagged bluestone castle within. One dark window on the southernmost point hides my bed, waiting for my safe return. I would give almost anything to stumble inside and drop into it.

"Anything but the safety of my family," I tell Cloud.

He's gotten used to my talking by now. He's even gotten used to my fiddling with his mane.

I adjust the thick cobalt veil covering my face. The only delay Cloud and I suffered on the journey—a stop in a religious town my family spent a few months in once, home to the largest cloister of the Starlit Oath in Lightning Cape. The makeshift cape I wore there wouldn't have protected me for more than a few minutes inside the palace walls, but the brothers' embroidered face veils, which cover everything but their eyes, is perfect. Starlights, as the brothers prefer to be called, are increasingly common, the longer Father stays in power. We have a few working in the palace already. It's the only path for men who wish to commit their lives to the Goddess.

And I stole from them. I had no choice. Once I unravel everything that happened to bring me here, I'll endow the cloister for the rest of my days. I'll even return the veil.

"The Goddess understands, doesn't She, Cloud?" I murmur as we circle toward the north gate, where staff and all those who hope to become staff enter. "Those starlights were the ones that first taught me to do everything in my power to protect my family and my pack."

He snorts a soft reply. I supposed he's never been inside the temple.

Just before we reach the gate, I hop off Cloud's back, grab a handful of dirt from the side of the road, and smear it over the white spot on his forehead. It doesn't match his coloring exactly, but it should be enough in the predawn gray. He is a palace horse, I'm relatively certain, and the last thing I need is to be accused of thievery.

The wind shifts, throwing the salty scent of the sea at me, and want slams into my chest like a boulder. I'm home—sneaking in through the back door wearing someone else's clothes.

I remount Cloud and hurry the rest of the way to the north gate before the urge to burst in through the front and declare myself overwhelms me. Mother and Father raised me better than that.

The towering gate stands slightly ajar. At its base, Nur, the stable master, stands with a scroll in her hands. It seems she's in need of help today.

I swallow a grimace. I was hoping our cook, Umit, would be here. The nook all the kitchen staff sleeps in, tucked up against the massive clay stove, has always seemed like the second-best place to sleep in the palace.

"You're going to have to help me," I whisper to Cloud. "Only you can vouch for me. Seem well-trained."

He flicks his ears. I pray that's an affirmative. I dismount, and we join the short line of other palace-staff hopefuls.

"New work or old, starlight?" Nur barks when I reach the front.

"New." I deepen my voice and try to copy the blunt accents I heard during my visit to Cirrus Summit. "I was a stable hand out west. I heard the true king had returned."

Nur looks Cloud and I over with her sharp eyes. I noticed her studying my riding posture when she first turned to us. She doesn't need any more testament to my abilities than Cloud—so, hopefully, he is behaving well. I cannot check without seeming distrustful of my horse.

'If you expect us to stable your horse, he'll need to work as well,; she says through the mind-link.

She wants to know if I'm telling the truth about my kingdom. With a smile, I reply, *"He's a carthorse, used to work. And I don't require anything more than food and a place to sleep."*

She scoffs. "We'll pay you. Work will just be a few days. The royals are returning shortly, and they have the remainder of my usual staff with them."

I can come up with a new plan over the course of a few days. "Much appreciated."

She scribbles something down and then steps aside. I plunge forward, headed for the stables before the sun gets high enough that she notices how familiar Cloud looks.

"Wait," she says.

I freeze, suddenly certain my veil is askew, or she recognized my smell.

"Don't you want to know which way to go?"

"Yes." I bow in a starlight's clasped-hand posture. "Thank you."

She gives me directions I don't need and sends me straight into the arms of a pair of senior grooms. One takes Cloud to his own stall. The other, Abir, claps a uniform in my hand and opens a creaking door.

"You can put your things there." He points into the bunkhouse attached to the back of the stable. Inside, beds stack on top of beds, most of them unmade, the reek of body odor and horseshit harmonizing in the worst possible way.

It looks like a place with the Goddess in the stars right now.

"I don't have any things other than Cloud, but I'll rest for a little while." I drift toward the bunkhouse, the threadbare mattresses singing sweet songs to me.

Abir snorts. "You'll get dressed and grab a shovel. We need grooms, but push me, and I'll bust you back down to stable hand."

Someday, I'll get to tell him who he talked to like that. I hold on to that cold kernel of comfort as I stumble into the bunkhouse to change.

MY HANDS SHAKE AS I HARNESS ALMOST A DOZEN HORSES FOR THEIR daily exercise. While I scatter hay in empty stalls, covering the hard-packed dirt and other mess as best I can, my legs threaten to give out. I stumble to the farrier for new horseshoes, my head aching. Somehow, hours pass. I can only blame that on how much time I spend wiping away sweat from under my veil. Perhaps there's a reason starlights are rarely seen doing heavy manual labor. Or perhaps I stole some kind of winter veil—it was in heavy storage.

"Come on, starlight." One of the other grooms, Tek, waves a hay-encrusted shovel at me. "Nur said you had experience."

"I do." The Cirrus Summit accent disappeared almost instantly, but I've been able to hold on to the deeper voice somehow. "But I rode a long way here."

Tek laughs so loudly that I can see every single one of his teeth. "Show me someone in this stable who isn't tired, and I'll show you a liar."

Tired is a pittance of a word compared to the constant, rhythmic shrieking of my limbs. I glance over the tops of a few stalls and make eye contact with Cloud. He understands; he's barely opened his eyes since he finished devouring his breakfast, and lunch has come and gone.

"You'll get used to it." Tek claps me on the shoulder and offers a thin smile.

He's being earnest. Abruptly, I remember one town on the run where we couldn't find a loyalist willing to house us, and Kaloni and I had to work at the local tavern to pay for our stay. More often than not, we stayed away from other people. There was no knowing who would recognize us, who would turn us in. But that time, we had no choice.

Tek's tired smile is the same one Sash, the bartender, would give me after a long night of rowdy patrons. A commiserating smile.

I give him one in return, remember my veil, and nod. "I certainly hope so. I need to impress the stable master enough to convince her to keep me on when the delegation to Moonlight Beach returns."

He hands me a different shovel and nods into an empty stall. We are to muck it out. I close my eyes for a heartbeat and think about my feather bed.

Then, I think about Mother, Father, all my siblings. None of them will have to wake up, frightened and alone, miles away from home.

I open my eyes again and join Tek in mucking.

"Moonlight Beach?" He picks the conversation up as if I never hesitated. "Is that where they went? How'd you hear?"

"On my travels." I am going to have to become a better liar. "The royal twins are being blessed, and it's all anyone can talk about."

"I'll take your word for it, starlight." Tek shrugs. "Do you have a name I should be calling you? All the other starlights work in the palace proper, so I haven't gotten to ask."

A name. Of course. Everyone has a name.

"Sash," I blurt.

"Brother Sash." Tek grins and salutes me with his far grubbier shovel.

I dodge a bit of something that flies off the edge with a grimace. Father made sure I could always control my face in public; the freedom of the veil is strange to get used to.

"I'm pretty sure the Starlit Oath doesn't ban laughing," he says as he returns to work.

"It doesn't… if the joke is funny."

Tek rewards me with another laugh, but my thoughts drift to Princess Ingrid. I've heard all the rumors about her—that she's wild, unconstrained, the most dangerous of the Solberg siblings because one never knows what she'll do next. She surprised me when we met, but not in the way I expected her to.

The mark on my throat throbs. I don't even have the energy to lift my arms high enough to touch the shape any longer. Tonight—or perhaps tomorrow morning.

"Well then, I'll have to come up with some better jokes." Tek nudges me.

I nod in lieu of a smile again.

"A few of us are going into town tonight," he says. "We usually have a few drinks, play a few games, sometimes heckle the awful troubadour off the stage. Do you want to come?"

Behind the shield of my veil, I smile slightly. Bed sounds like all I could possibly want in this life, but a drink and a source of information on what happened while I was gone is a close second. And if the troubadour is so bad, I may have a solution I could offer. As Amval, I wouldn't dare, but Sash follows other rules.

"I—"

"The royal caravan is arriving," Nur snaps. *"All hands on deck!"*

GETTING COMFORTABLE

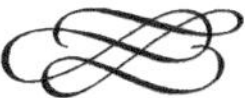

Ingrid

TRUMPETS BLARE OUTSIDE, AND I PRAY THAT MEANS WE'RE FINALLY approaching Som Palace. After almost two days in this Goddess-forsaken trunk, I'm shocked I can still hear them. My lungs hurt. I keep smashing my elbow into the walls—when we go over bumps in the road, so the minder doesn't notice, but that doesn't actually shrink my growing bruises—and I'm ravenous. We barely had enough time to stuff a blanket and some dried fruit into the bottom of the trunk, much less anything more substantial.

I've survived the trip, though. And I survived when my family discovered I was missing. I don't think I've ever received so many mid-links at once. I definitely haven't heard Kieran angrier than when I told him I was safe but not going to say anything else. He made Candace beg me for details.

I reminded her of the time we smuggled her into Snowcrest, and she didn't ask any more questions.

Through the keyhole of the trunk, I've been watching the minder struggle not to get crushed by the overwhelming amount of luggage in here. He's an unarmed man with a very red nose. He huffs and adjusts his position. Candace's voice in my mind reminds me that he's almost certainly not much more comfortable than I am. For almost two fucking days.

I'll have a little more sympathy for him when I can extend my arms fully.

For now, I just curl around my lute—the only thing I wasn't willing to leave behind—and keep praying those are the welcoming trumpets of the castle, not just *another* village thrilled to see the royal caravan.

KNOCK, KNOCK, KNOCK.

I jump, smash my head on the lid of the trunk, and bite my lip so hard it bleeds instead of cursing. The trumpets stopped what feels like a million years ago, so they were obviously a village. What's happening now?

Another pair of knocks, and I remember that's the signal Joli and I set up. Thank the Goddess. I release the interior latch that's supposed to hold the trunk shut, like it's stuck, if anyone else opens it, and the lid thuds back.

Joli stands there, slightly crouched, her head swiveling side to side. Exactly how she looked when she hid me away to cross the border into Tansy Beach.

I suck in my first breath of actually clean air in days and start hauling myself out of the trunk. My muscles groan, and so do I. Joli doesn't bother telling me to shush; she just shoots me a look.

"You stay quiet for two days," I mumble.

"How do you think I figured out I could do this?" she hisses. "We don't have a large window, even with the news."

The news. Amval's death. They didn't tell the palace ahead of time?

A sob punctures the general unpacking noises, and I realize they very much didn't. Low, somber music plays from somewhere.

"People will notice if I'm not part of his procession." She grabs my arm and pulls me the rest of the way out of the trunk. My knees buckle, but I grab the side of the carriage. Nothing in my body will decide whether it hurts or is too tired to hurt—exactly what I'll need to sneak through a crowded palace.

I can complain later. This is my only chance. I grab my lute, and Joli tosses an armful of clothing and a few heavier things into the trunk, then slams the lid shut again.

"You see that door?" She points behind her.

I squint. It's brighter out here than I expected after two days of darkness. But…I nod. There's one darker spot on the deep blue wall.

"In there, first set of stairs on your right, take a left, use this key on the palest door." The music grows louder, and she shoves a metal key into my hand. "I'll visit when I can."

My body groans like it needs to be oiled, but I keep my head down and scuttle across the open courtyard toward the palace that would've belonged to my mate. People are rushing in every direction. More than a few are crying. I hear Amval's name everywhere, which doesn't make my mark feel any better.

I'm doing everything I can, I tell it. *He's dead. There's no being with him. There's just this.*

Somehow, that doesn't improve the situation.

By the time I reach the door, I'm hunched over with pain and exhaustion. I barely notice that it's already open because the word *stairs* finally sinks in. My worthless legs plead with me, but there's no time. King Iraj starts making some kind of speech—whatever additional distraction I'm getting from the news they arrived home with is going to disappear fast. The crowd isn't going in every direction now, just the opposite one.

I clutch my lute for strength. The familiar wood warms under my fingers.

One chance.

I drag myself up the stairs, using my free hand like a third leg. Inside the palace, everything is blue except the vibrant orange mosaics. The bright colors make my headache even worse.

But I reach the top of the stairs, stumble through the rest of Joli's instructions, and throw myself into the room.

It's minuscule, a corner of the weird, pointed shape of the whole palace. The bed is a triangle to fit between sharp-angled walls. A tiny wardrobe sits next to a smaller desk.

And there's a small, cold lunch sitting on the bed.

I kick the door shut and eat without even sitting. Joli is my favorite person in the whole world, a hero among women. My chest aches, and so does my stomach when I'm done, but I couldn't have slowed down if I wanted to.

The triangular bed stares at me. I stare back. I need to take advantage of every second before revealing myself in a week.

I sit next to the door, my ear pressed against it, and wait.

I PASS OUT SITTING UP, MY FIRST ACTUAL SLEEP SINCE LEAVING Moonlight Beach, and the only thing that wakes me up is Joli attempting to shove the door open.

She's pale in the faint moonlight when she finally squeezes herself inside. "I thought you were—"

Dead. Like Amval.

"Just tired." I push hair out of my face and try not to think about what Candace said. People here could think I'm a murderer. And that's if whoever murdered Amval doesn't decide that clearing me out will really simplify their path to getting away with this in the first place.

If I were smarter, that would scare me away.

She gives me a bowl of some kind of rice stew, cold but heavy in my hands. I devour it.

"Curfew is going to be your friend," she says when I'm done. "It's fashionable to be in bed by ten right now, so it borders on a social rule."

I snort. "I can't remember the last time I was asleep before midnight."

Joli smiles. "It was my idea."

"You are good." I rub my eyes, trying to shake off sleep and the ride. Neither of them really wants to go. "Do you have royal death records? I want to start there."

She helps me put on a completely featureless, russet-colored dress —what the maids wear, apparently. Even in the dark, I can tell a little embroidery and a fuller sleeve would work miracles for it, but now isn't really the time to complain.

After, she leads me down to the apothecary. "These books are ledgers. They record every death in the palace, royal and otherwise, as well as anything else important."

"Of course they do." The books cover most of a wall, and each of them is thicker than one of my arms.

"Let me know if you need anything else." Joli leaves.

I light a lantern and pull the first massive ledger onto a small worktable.

About ten pages in is when I remember how much I hate this kind of research. I don't care about plants, despite Mother's efforts. The royal healers aren't afraid of wordiness either. A royal dog gets one page all to himself, and he was attacked outside the walls of the castle. He died of being mauled. I could have told them that immediately.

There has to be someone I can talk to who knew King Notu before he died—and I can't talk to them for almost a week without risking everything. With a groan, I push through another page.

The dog received a detailed examination, but human deaths whisk by with single lines of description. Most of the causes of death seem like guesses—he was found in bed, so he probably died in his sleep; she was found face-down in a pool, so she probably drowned. They're not bad guesses, but I don't know why there isn't more.

And then I remember. The privacy. The whole reason I helped Amval away from that initial swarm. They're not allowed to look any closer than what they can see when the body is first found.

So not only am I bored out of my skull after days of doing nothing in a trunk, there's not even anything for me to find here. I slump back in my chair with a groan and rub my eyes.

My elbow knocks a scroll off the table. It's not nearly as large as one of the massive ledgers, but not small. There's an X-beam rack of them on the wall not covered by ledgers, so I scoop it up to put it back there. Even if I don't find anything, I can at least not get caught looking.

The first few lines catch my eye. *Vernal Flu*, it reads. That, I've heard of—half of every kingdom gets it when the seasons change. Many people get a short but supremely irritating burst of sniffling and coughing every year. Below that, there are a few names, listed alongside ages and symptoms.

They're keeping track of who suffers from vernal flu.

I lurch out of my chair and start opening every single scroll in the stuffed rack. Diseases I've heard of and haven't whistle past. It's hard to remember to put them back before seizing the next one, but finally—

Carmine Pox. I unravel the scroll and study the tight handwriting. There's King Notu, right before the big gap in their records. The twenty-odd years that Lightning Cape spent as part of Dun's Crossing. After that, there are three names listed.

Sozer Kutlu. Soldier. Deceased.

Nabi Emre. Maid. Sent home to convalesce.

And Harun Abdil, who has the Carmine Pox by blood, is a groomsman in the stables right now.

By the time I have everything back in place, the sun is rising. It's late enough to visit the stables, at least. And until I decide to reveal myself, I realize that being nocturnal might be useful. I sneak back into the courtyard. Black and gray have replaced all the white and orange. My mark aches. I don't slow down.

With my head low, I duck inside. If this Harun has it through his blood, he won't show signs, and asking about him will be far too obvious. I need to take a minute, watch, and try to figure it out.

A figure steps out of a stall, and I back into the nearest open door.

"Hello?" a low voice asks behind me.

I wheel, suck in a breath, and almost choke on the reek of manure. The person behind me wears a thick blue veil embroidered with silver constellations—a starlight, Lightning Cape's weird religious order of men. I open my mouth to tell him I'm avoiding someone and let him fill in the gaps, but then I meet his eyes.

Sunlight makes them glow like molten gold, and my heart skips a beat.

FIRST MEETING

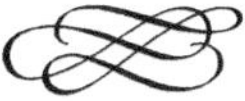

Amval

My mark sings. My body vibrates. The moment the blonde stranger turns around, I recognize her in the depths of my soul.

Princess Ingrid Solberg. My mate.

Memories cascade through my mind, each connecting to the lithe figure in front of me. Her slender body bowed in ecstasy. Her blonde hair, knotted around my fingers. Her pale cheeks pink with exertion.

Her blue eyes, staring at me just like they are now.

My heart stutters, restarts. I need to go. I might not be able to smell her through the stable reek, but I'm not sure how long that will last. Worse, one of the Dun's Crossing royals has a particularly powerful sense of smell, and I can't remember which one right now.

"Apologies." I bow, hiding my eyes as well. "I did not expect to see anyone this early in the morning."

That is true. I rose as early as my body would allow, hoping to review the list of nobles interested in riding today. I don't exactly have a primary suspect yet, but there are certainly a few in the palace

I'd like to spend more time with, and appending my name to theirs is the best way to do that.

Yesterday, while helping my family unload from a safe distance, I learned they don't think I'm missing. They think I'm dead. Staying silent when I saw the coffin containing "my" body was only possible because I was so exhausted. If I could have reliably run, I would have been wiping tears off Mother's face before her feet hit the blue-gray cobbles of the courtyard.

"Sorry," Ingrid says, pulling me back to this moment. "I was… um…."

She's still staring. I can feel her eyes, even if I can't see them. My skin hums, long-buried instincts screaming to go to her, reveal myself, and celebrate.

I inhale long and slow through my nose despite the smell. She may be my mate—but I don't know her from more than a single conversation.

My family comes first.

"I'll leave you to it." Still half-bowed, I hurry out of the stall.

"Wait!" she says.

I close the door between us and turn to see an exhausted Nur.

"Sash!" She looks almost relieved. "Shit, I thought you'd snuck out in the night."

"No, ma'am." I bow to her as well and begin walking toward another stall as if I have somewhere to be. "A starlight always keeps their vows."

She follows, ignoring my religious mumbling. Everyone here seems to. "The royal caravan lost one of their grooms on the road, so a full-time position has opened up. Tek vouched for you. It's yours if you want it."

I grin. The shield of the veil is becoming more familiar, more comfortable. Nur might see my eyes wrinkle, but she won't be able to see how relieved my smile is. "I would love it. Thank you for your kindness, and give my thanks to Tek."

"Give it yourself." She speeds up, already needed elsewhere. "You two are going to be working side-by-side until I'm sure you can pull your weight."

I've certainly heard of worse hells. One of which waits in the stall behind me, if she hasn't already left.

Realization hits me like a gust of concentrated wind to the chest.

What under the Goddess's sky is Ingrid Solberg doing here?

She wasn't part of the royal caravan. I watched, gripping the handle of a trunk and counting heads, as every single member of my family dismounted. She would have been with Joli and the twins in the younger carriage, had she come with them. She would have had a hand on my coffin, like the rest of my family. Even after a single night, my mate has that privilege.

If she wants it.

That sour pit curdles my gut once more, and I remember my worry on the long, dark ride here. Ingrid had access, potentially motive. Her sudden appearance, especially in secret, doesn't exactly seem like a good sign. And she was wearing a maid's dress, one from inside the palace. How she expects no one to notice a blonde beauty like her here, I have no idea, but clearly it worked well enough to get her inside the palace walls. The rumors about Ingrid Solberg mostly paint her as a dangerous wild card, but no one has ever said she isn't smart.

A stall door creaks open behind me, and I hurry for the tack room to make myself busy. She may not have recognized me, but she certainly will if I let her get too close. I just need to find out what she's doing.

I suppose I have my first suspect.

NUR KEEPS ME BUSY ALL DAY. BY THE TIME I FIND MYSELF SITTING across from Tek at the long table that gets dragged into the middle of the bunk room at night for dinner, parts of me I barely knew existed ache.

"Do you feel it in your fingers?" I ask him.

He snorts. "That fades fast. The wrists, though, that's the real trouble."

I roll out my wrists. They don't seem to hurt specifically, but my whole body feels like it has been transformed into a bruise, so it's difficult to say. He laughs at me again, openly and easily.

"I thought you had experience!"

"I do." In riding. "Why does Nur insist we each tend to one horse completely?"

"Not Nur, Abir." Tek shrugs. "And that's just how we do it."

I frown down at my dinner, bland meat over pasta—a pale imitation of what I would be eating inside. After a few days at this job, it seems impossible that it is the most efficient way to tend to the nearly hundred horses stabled here.

"Why?" Tek asks.

I shake my head. My thoughts are far too unfinished to share. Luckily, starlights are known for holding their tongues until ready—just as princes are.

"Do they check our beds to see if we're in them at night?" I ask.

Tek raises an eyebrow. "Not usually. I don't suppose you'll tell me why you want to know that either, will you?"

I smile to myself.

AFTER HOURS SPENT LYING AWAKE, I SIGH IN RELIEF. EVERYONE IS finally in bed. I slide out from under my thin sheet, still dressed, and creep out of the room.

I've been turning the problem over in my mind, and it only makes sense that Ingrid is getting around while everyone is asleep. That is why she was in the stable nearly before the sun rose and why a maid's dress would be enough to disguise her despite her brilliant hair.

There is a side door that's always left unlocked for any staff with tasks outside the palace before or after curfew. Though it is popular to go to bed at the same time as Mother and Father, there is still work to be done. I slip through the door and let my eyes adjust to the darkness. Wind currents are always more muted inside, but I can feel them stir slightly. With any luck, that will be enough to guide me to anyone else sneaking through these halls at night.

For a moment, though, I breathe in the familiar scent. I am home. My limbs ache to slump against the wall and drag me tiredly to my own bed. Or to the kitchen for a proper meal. Or to Cirocco's side, to pour out all the thoughts in my head.

If Mother and Father taught us one thing, it was that luxury and royalty are diametrically opposed opposites. It was our job to live in hiding as long as we did while preparing for the day we'd retake our kingdom, rather than just becoming normal people. It is my job now to hunt down my potential attempted murderer.

I stride deeper into the palace.

The first few currents lead me nowhere useful. I find bakers finishing preparations for tomorrow's bread, a few laundry workers hanging clothes on lines, a soldier or two on rare patrol. Every time, I hug the shadows. Sneaking isn't exactly my strong suit, but I know how to become invisible enough. Duck my head, stay just far enough away. Each of them overlooks me as just another laborer at work too late.

Then, I hear Joli's laugh.

I turn and rush toward it. She and Ingrid are somewhat close. If Ingrid is working her way systematically through my family, Joli would be the next easiest target. She's the youngest, the least well-trained. She spent less time on the run than the rest of us. She doesn't have the same fear in her bones.

"Do you smell that?" It's another voice. Ingrid's.

I freeze just out of sight.

"Smell what?" Joli asks.

"Is someone cooking?" Ingrid replies. "It smells like… something's burning."

My heart crawls into my mouth. She can smell me. I got too close —but if she's going after my baby sister, I'll risk anything.

"Perhaps." Joli sounds unconcerned. "The kitchen works later than almost anyone else."

Why can't my sister smell me? I can pick her out of almost any crowd, peaches and sage on the clean scent of the wind.

"I'm probably imagining it," Ingrid mutters. "Come on. How sure are you that you can do this test?"

"Do it?" Joli laughs. "Not at all. We're sneaking your sample into the pile."

Sample? I risk peering around the corner as their footsteps start to fade and realize they're turning the corner to the healer's office. Once they're out of sight, I wait a few heartbeats and then scurry after.

"If it's that contagious, I should have it, right?" Ingrid's voice floats through the open door.

My mark groans. She has a musical voice, one that always sounds like she's about to laugh. I want to hear it on repeat.

But she may be a killer—my killer.

"I'm not sure," Joli says. "When the Pox is inherited, it's a little strange."

I supposedly died of the Carmine Pox, passed down from Grandfather, and the healers test portions of the palace for that on a rotating basis to avoid another outbreak. But why is Ingrid getting tested? She knows it's all a ruse.

"Well, I know poison isn't contagious," she says.

Poison? My eyebrows shoot up.

"And it's good to know, regardless," Joli says. "This might hurt."

Ingrid sucks in a sharp breath through her teeth, and my mark throbs. I've been tested a dozen times; I remember the slice of a sterile knife across my arm, all to draw a few drops of blood.

"Damn," she mumbles under her breath. "Do you think this will convince your parents?"

Joli sighs, barely audible over clanking glass. She's storing the sample with the others. "I don't know. I doubt they want to be convinced."

"So, I need to find a culprit." Ingrid sighs. "Thank you. I've got it from here."

"Some of us need to make formal breakfast appearances." Joli laughs and then leaves Ingrid alone.

My heart squeezes. She's right there, and I know that, of all my siblings, she's never told me anyone else's secret. I could just reach out and grab her, whisper the truth. Perhaps save her life.

But Ingrid didn't kill her. They seem to be working together. And I need to know how dangerous that is.

I stuff my hands in my pockets and remain still.

When Ingrid leaves, she sniffs the air, and I duck back. She doesn't try to follow the smell, at least.

Instead, I follow her as she visits the head steward's office and studies the book containing the names of all the staff members. Whatever she finds there seems to frustrate her. Afterward, she flips through medical tomes in the library for hours.

Finally, she grumbles, "How the hell am I supposed to prove a murder without a corpse?"

My heart leaps, and when she returns to a tiny room I've never seen before, I can't stop myself from jamming my foot in the door before it closes.

CAUGHT

Ingrid

The door doesn't latch behind me.

Shit.

I whip around and watch... that groom in the veil slide into my room.

Confusion is a luxury. I throw myself across the tiny space and cover the slapdash arrangement of paper scraps I've been organizing my theories with on the desk. "What do you think you're doing?"

"You do not need to be scared." He shuts the door.

"Hell of a thing to say while closing us in." If there were more fabric in this skirt, I could cover more—but maybe the skirt itself is enough to save me. I just wish that cook hadn't burnt whatever they did. The scent of charcoal makes my thoughts fuzzy, even muddled by the stable-reek that hangs around this groom. "I am a respected member of this staff."

"No, you're not." He takes a step closer.

Everything I've learned about defending myself in the last few years rattles through my mind. I reach behind me and unlatch the window. A stiff breeze almost yanks the smell out, which clears my head a little. And now, I have an escape—a dangerous one that will require a very lucky fall.

"Your hair gives you away," he says.

I don't wince. Sure, I haven't seen a blonde here since I arrived, but no one was supposed to see me before I revealed myself. It wasn't supposed to matter.

"What do you want?"

His eyes crinkle in something like a smile. "I want to help."

"I don't need help dusting." I spread myself a little more over my notes and wish I'd thought about the hair. Normally, I'd just scream. Half the palace would come running, and a man in a woman's room wouldn't exactly be treated well. But that would ruin everything.

He laughs, and the sound shimmers through me. It's warm, like his eyes, like nothing I've ever heard before. I get the sense he's laughed a lot.

"I know what you're doing." He holds slim, long-fingered hands out toward me. Beautiful hands. "You think Prince Amval's death was suspicious."

I look the groom up and down. Besides his eyes and his hands, I can't see a single inch of him. The blue veil meets the top of his rough uniform. His posture is straighter than I would expect, but maybe that's a side effect of working so closely with horses.

Goddess above, I wish I knew more about starlights. I'd know how to deal with a holy woman. I don't even know if he's allowed to lie.

And he has those irritatingly captivating eyes that are so common in this kingdom.

"So what if I do?" I ask.

Anwen would laugh at me. At least he got to investigate a very public murder with the full royal support of the palace it happened in.

"I was his personal groom."

I snort. "That's coincidental."

The groom frowns. "I know his horse, Seksim, as well as I know my own. I can prove that to you if you come to the stable with me."

"Of course," I say sarcastically. "I'll just walk alone with you to a secondary location where you know the terrain perfectly. That seems safe."

"I don't mean you any harm, Pr—" He clips the end of his sentence like he knows he just made a mistake.

My stomach flips about a dozen times. This groom knowing I don't belong here is one thing. His knowing my real name is another entirely, and I'm nearly certain he was about to call me princess.

"No, say it." I grow my nails into claws. If I need to go out the window, maybe I can climb. There is no way they screen all their grooms for wind powers as well, though the harsh breeze that keeps blowing in makes me wonder.

He bows slightly, hands clasped over his heart. "Apologies. I know you are hiding for some reason, but I also know you are hunting a truth I would also like very much to find. I will be hunting, with or without you. Wouldn't we cover more ground together?"

He knows who I am. He knows why I'm here. What the hell else does he know? How did he find out so much in only two days? I was being careful.

"I don't even know your name," I say as my nails start to crack into the wood of the tiny desk. Attacking a holy woman is a crime—what about attacking a starlight?

"Sash." He bows again, deeper. "Your Highness, I know things about this palace you won't find in months. I could be a significant boon to you."

I take a deep breath of the clean air pouring so aggressively in from outside that it's flipped my covers back and try to look at this situation without panicking for a moment. There is a strange man in my room. He doesn't seem violent, but I can't really see anything about him. I'm exhausted after days of heinous travel followed by abruptly turning nocturnal.

And someone murdered my mate. Someone who probably knows I'm one of the likeliest people to catch them, someone who definitely does not want to be caught.

If I were them, I'd hire someone in the palace to keep an eye on anyone getting too close to the scent. And, if I were Anwen, I'd have that person I hired ingratiate themselves with anyone they found in order to keep an eye on exactly how close they were getting.

"Well, now I'm sorry." I stride toward Sash with all the confidence I can muster. "You have this all wrong. I'm here to grieve in private, nothing more, so the only thing you can help me with is leaving me alone."

A flicker of dark eyebrow appears in the slit of his veil, furrowed. "But—"

"Like I said, I'm sorry." I grab him by the shoulders, my mark zinging at the fact that I'm touching another man, and spin him around before opening the door. "If I need to pray, I'll find you."

I shove him out, shut the door, and lock it before he can even turn around.

As soon as I'm sure he's gone, I need to find Joli.

The next morning, I stare up at a tall, arched doorway surrounded by orange-red mosaics and sway on my feet in a dress Joli stole from one of her next-older twin sisters. Sibel? Liwar? It doesn't really matter; she said neither of them would recognize it.

She loops her arm through mine, holding me up. "I'll do most of the talking."

"Smart." My mouth tastes like cotton batting, and I yearn for a hot mug of the acrid coffee Magritte is probably making at home right now. Ever since coming back from Moonlight Beach, I've been pushing her to make it stronger and stronger.

I slept for about an hour last night because, when I told Joli about my run-in with the groom, she agreed we needed to steal his ammunition before he had a chance to use it, and she meant revealing me to her parents as soon as possible.

Thus, the dress and the waiting throne room. I take as deep of a breath as I can in the slightly too tight dress. "Let's get this over with."

Joli pats my arm and leads me in.

Banners of gray cover most of the mosaics in here. King Iraj and

Queen Zephira sit on connected blue thrones, holding hands and talking softly to each other. They look about as exhausted as I feel, so maybe this won't be an utter disaster.

"Mother?" Joli says. "Father?"

Slowly, they turn out of their conversation and freeze, looking at me.

That gives Joli the opportunity she needs. "Princess Ingrid arrived late last night, distraught. She regretted not accepting our offer to travel with us. Her grief was too much to bear surrounded by people who didn't love Amval."

Queen Zephira unfreezes first, but only enough to start silently weeping. I grimace. Joli could've picked a slightly less dramatic explanation.

"Apologies." I curtsy.

"She meant to send word, but she just wasn't thinking straight," Joli adds.

"None of us are just now." King Iraj rubs a tired hand over his face, and I realize the usually clean-shaven king is covered in stubble. "We have been preparing for a funeral, but guest quarters are low on the priority list."

"I'll stay—" Joli elbows me, somehow predicting that I was about to mention the tiny, triangular room she gave me. "—in whatever you have available. The only comfort I need is... being surrounded by those who loved him."

The words taste like ash. Like charcoal. I don't belong here. Joli knows that, and so do the king and queen. Claiming it like this, even to solve his murder, is so selfish I think Mother might've balked.

Queen Zephira stands. I brace. If I were her, and my son had just died, I'd slap me right across the face.

Instead, she rushes the few feet between us and throws her arms around me. "I would love nothing more than to get to know his other half, even if he isn't here to be yours."

Over her shoulder, King Iraj nods. When her parents aren't looking, Joli winks at me.

Days pass. I move into a normal-shaped room in a different part of the castle with far more amenities. I'm welcomed into Som family activities, or as much as they seem to be able to welcome me. Clearly, the time on the run gave them a special relationship. The nine of them move like they're dancing together, until one of Amval's parts comes up, and everyone misses a step. Every time it happens, my mark aches, and everyone is silent for a moment.

Still, I try to talk to them about King Notu, their grandfather. King Iraj knows the most—he grew up with the man—but he clearly likes talking about it the least. Cirocco, who was apparently Amval's Beta, is nearly always willing to talk, but doesn't have much useful information. Kaloni turns out to be the most useful, surprisingly. She's awkwardly formal, like Amval was, but she was clearly trained as a potential successor. She knows the family history and is willing to show me places I can find out more. I have to be careful about how often I ask so no one realizes what I'm actually after, but I'm making piecemeal progress.

Before I know it, someone sends for a trunk of my clothes, which arrives with a sternly worded note from Kieran about how he wishes I would have just told him what I was thinking instead of disappearing. When I realize he's not demanding I come home—yet—I breathe a sigh of relief. Maybe Joli's story was a good idea after all.

The results of my test for the Carmine Pox arrive as well. Negative —just like they would be if he were poisoned. I squirrel them away in the desk that locks, which I have now, alongside my growing collection of suspicions. Harun, the groom who was supposed to have the disease, still eludes me. Mostly because I haven't risked a trip to the stables.

Not that my avoidance has convinced Sash I meant what I said. He's always *there*, especially outside and on the lower floors, and I never see him with anyone else. In fact, he tends to disappear when a Som appears, so I try to go everywhere with Joli. If he's avoiding them, he must be involved.

But Joli isn't always around, and I don't want to sit inside, waiting for her to be.

I'm taking a walk on the side of the palace opposite the stables, where he shouldn't even be able to see me, when he appears.

"I'll scream." I have nothing to lose now.

"If you wish," he says. "But I know where you can find everything about King Notu."

MEMORIAL

Amval

I STAND IN FRONT OF INGRID, MY HANDS CLASPED IN FRONT OF ME because I've learned that, combined with the longer sleeves I told Nur I needed for religious reasons, is the best way to hide the occasional gestures I need to stir the wind around us. Only meeting her outside or by the high, arched and nearly always open doors on the lowest floor isn't quite enough. I saw her in the kitchen the day after I broke into her room, asking Umit what had burned last night. Mother always said I smelled like a home fire, but *burned* is another way to put that, I suppose, and I can't risk Ingrid realizing who I am for such a foolish reason.

"Why should I trust you?" She narrows blue eyes at me. "You've been following me around for days, and you just *happen* to have access to the information I've been looking for?"

"It does sound negative," I say slowly, "if you are looking for reasons to distrust me."

"Well, we agree my mate was murdered." She crosses her arms.

I am getting better at swallowing the screaming impulse to tell everyone who says I'm dead the truth. It still flutters in my chest like a trapped bird, one that grows angrier at its captivity every day.

"And who else in this palace would agree with you?"

She studies me, her eyes hard. I squeeze my hands tight enough that my fingertips tingle. This is my last gambit, all I have from the outside. I've taken Lord Faruk, whose loyalties have long been in question, on three rides where he did not speak a word to me. Lady Ceyiz loathes horses, which is only part of what makes her unpopular in court. I am running out of options, and there are only so many excuses for a groom to enter the palace, especially without a royal by his side.

My family would help me if I told them the truth, but no matter who I told—even Joli, who is clearly part of Ingrid's scheme somehow —the information would make it to Mother and Father before long, and then the pressure to come clean would begin. Mother doesn't believe in lying for any reason, and Father won't lie unless it's for the good of the family or the kingdom. This secret is the most I've ever gone against that rule.

Finally, Ingrid sighs. "You tell me what you have, and I'll decide if it's worth working with you."

That seems like the best deal I can expect. "What do you know about memorial chambers?"

THAT NIGHT, AFTER EVERYONE IS IN BED, INGRID AND I CREEP THROUGH the halls together. I keep my hands behind my back to generate an ever-churning breeze. The memorial chambers are high in the east point, where the Goddess can see them as She first rises. The older halls are tight, but I have to risk it.

"Does every dead noble have a memorial room?" Ingrid whispers, looking at the doors stretching the length of the walls on either side.

"Every Alpha and Luna do," I reply, "as well as most royals."

"And this is because of the rules around the bodies?" she asks.

I shake my head. "Memorial rooms are kinder places to grieve than gravesides."

Grandfather's room is near the end of the hall. I've only been in a few times; it was half-finished when Father was run out of the palace, and it reminds him too much of that day.

Somehow, I still don't expect to see a door next to Grandfather's emblazoned with my own name. It sits slightly ajar—it won't be closed until my funeral, so anyone who cared for me can place a memory within. My heart lunges toward it. I have to know what people are leaving, if anything has been left at all.

Ingrid swallows audibly. "We could look there first."

I now know what a horse feels like when abruptly reined in. There is no more foolish place in the castle for me to be. Even with the veil, I won't be able to contain myself.

"Allowing you into King Notu's chamber is sacrilegious enough." I turn to the lock and spin the cogs with a narrow burst of wind I hope she doesn't perceive. It clunks open heavily. "After you."

"Right." Ingrid shoots my door one last look before stepping through Grandfather's. "Oh, shit."

Memorial rooms are always chaotic, but Grandfather's is more so than most. The special locks on these doors, only able to be opened by those of Lightning Cape with sufficient power, mean that these were some of the only rooms in the palace Gavin could not loot. More than a few nobles stored valuables that had nothing to do with Grandfather in here, simply to keep them safe. Some admitted that they had and asked to have them back; others didn't want to announce they'd defiled such a sacred space with material concerns.

The final effect is sort of like a dragon's hoard in a fairytale. Valuables are heaped like sand dunes. Papers slide and crunch underfoot. A portrait of Grandfather, his eyes serious despite the kindly smile pulling at his lips, hangs over everything, and the only clear space is the kneeling cushion before it.

"Anything you wish to know about King Notu, you'll find in here." I bow before his portrait, kissing the tips of my fingers in respect. "But I did not say finding it would be easy."

"It's a good thing we're working together now." Ingrid rolls up her sleeves and ties them out of the way with ribbons I thought were just decoration. "You start on the left side, and I'll start on the right."

I shut the door, and we begin.

She assigned me the side of the room with the most paperwork, so it's painfully slow going. I skim most of the letters to see if they are actually something he ever interacted with or simply written in eulogy after his death. More fall into the latter category than I would hope. The others, I pile beside me to read in more detail later. Ingrid begins with the clothes, mostly sorting through pockets and inner folds. She's looking for something, but I have no idea what.

"What are you hoping to find in here?" I ask.

She sighs. "What do you know about Amval's death?"

My mark hums when she uses my name without the title, but I squash the feeling. "He fell ill and died suddenly."

"Everyone thinks he died of the Carmine Pox—inherited from King Notu." She closes a drawer and opens the next. "I'm not so sure."

I frown. "The Carmine Pox is very visually identifiable. Didn't you see the prince?"

"I did." She pauses for a long moment, just pawing through Grandfather's memorial. "It looked the way people describe it."

"So what confusion is there?" If she suspects I was taken away to be killed elsewhere, I have to be much more careful.

"Let's just say I'm not sure King Notu died of the Carmine Pox either." She shakes her golden head. "You're going to have to earn any more than that."

"Why?" I ask, irritation overcoming diplomacy and caution. "Why do I have to earn everything with you when I have been nothing but helpful?"

"Because I don't know you," she snaps. "And anyone smart enough to kill someone in my arms is smart enough to send a spy to check up on the only potential witness."

"Believe me when I say I would never work alongside Prince Amval's murderer," I say through gritted teeth. "When I discover who it was, I intend to kill them myself."

"You'll have to race me for the privilege," Ingrid says wryly. "And I'm faster than I look."

I glance at her, but her back is still to me. She hasn't said anything about how she feels about me, has only even called me her mate once. Another throb of instinct, like the one that nearly led me into my own memorial chamber, begs me to ask about it.

But that would be beyond cruel. Lying to her like this, allowing her to believe I'm dead—that is a necessity of a difficult situation. Begging secrets about myself is a line I will not cross.

No matter how much I might like to.

"I'm surprised his personal groom cares so much," she says.

I stare blankly at the letter in my hand, trying to find any way to reply without crossing this new line in the sand. Finally, I say, "King Gavin was cruel to those he conquered. We lived in fear of him discovering... any little pleasure we'd gained. When the Soms returned to the palace, everything changed in Lightning Cape."

"I'm sorry." She wanders over to another pile and plants herself on the floor.

"For what?"

She shrugs. "I wish... I don't know, sometimes I wish I'd done something."

"You were Joli's age when your brother took power." I shake my head. "And he was your father."

"That's an excuse," she says bitterly. "I might not have been able to do anything from inside the castle, but I chose not to leave."

"Did you know?" I ask.

She stares at the pile for a long time, sorting through jewelry and mugs he particularly liked and tapestries. "I don't know. Maybe. I could have."

"And I could have stormed the palace myself." I used to have recurring dreams about that, once I was old enough to understand why we moved every few days to months, why we weren't allowed to use our real names in public. I tried to convince Father to attempt it. Every time, he told me that dying for a cause was always a weaker choice than living for one. "But I don't believe anyone holds me responsible for not dying at the hands of King Gavin's brutes."

"Nobody expected you to."

Her words hang bitter in the space where my true identity would go. There are nobles in the palace, Lady Ceyiz included, who resent Father for his inaction. At least. I wouldn't be surprised to learn some have begun resenting me.

Ingrid pulls a laz, a long-necked string instrument, from the pile. Grandfather never played—kings are too busy for pointless pursuits like that—but he loved to listen, so there are more than a few instruments in here. I expect her to move it into the growing stack of useless items beside her, but she twists the pegs, tuning it. Before I can tell her to be careful, that the laz is likely almost a hundred years old to have earned a spot here, her fingers are on the strings.

Notes, light as a summer breeze, drift from strings that should only be able to wheeze. My eyes flutter shut as I let it wash over me. She is an artist, painting pictures in the air. I pick out the refrain of a Dun's Crossing drinking song, but softened like this, the usually bawdy ballad about finding a new woman in every town becomes a wistful plea for one of the women to make the singer stop.

When she finishes, I say, "That was incredible."

She laughs, not quite self-conscious. "I wanted to see how it was different from my lute."

Kings don't have time for useless pursuits—but starlights have almost nothing but time. And I have lied to Ingrid enough. She deserves a little truth.

"You know," I say casually, like this is not the one truth even my family doesn't know, "I've been known to play a few instruments."

ALMOST

Ingrid

I PUT THE LONG LUTE—LAZ—DOWN RELUCTANTLY. I'D LOVE TO SPEND the rest of the night getting to know the slightly off cadences of its new shape. "Which ones? Maybe we could play together sometime."

"The laz, for one." He points at the top of another pile, where a flat string instrument like the inside of a piano sits. "The naqun." He reaches into the pile behind him and unearths a beautifully carved wooden flute. "The vey."

"Impressive." I roll out my shoulders, feeling much less tense after only a few minutes with an instrument that's not even mine. "I play the lute, and anything that's nearly a lute."

"They all produce such different music," he says softly. "You know the laz now, but the naqun has an almost percussive depth in larger bands, and the vey speaks like a voice in the hands of someone talented enough."

I lean back on my hands and turn to Sash with a smile. "You should have told me you were a musician sooner. Even if you were going to turn me over to your evil master, I would've talked to you for a little while."

He ducks his head. "Perhaps."

His heavy veil shifts, and I realize he's curling around the vey almost… protectively. Or secretively. His voice changed when he said that he played, like he was saying something important. I honestly thought he had discovered something at first.

"Have you ever played in front of anyone before?" I ask.

After a moment, he shakes his head.

I hop up and pick my way across the room to him. The firelight of the lantern we brought with us turns his eyes molten again, and my heart skips a beat. My mark reacts immediately, like it always does when I realize how handsome Sash is all over again. It's a betrayal.

But I'm not betraying Amval to sit next to his personal groom, one of two other people in this palace who even think it's strange he's dead, and smile. It's just friendship.

"I'd love to be the first one," I say. "If you're good enough to play three instruments, especially ones that are different, I'm sure I'll be impressed."

"I would enjoy that." He turns the vey over in his hands. "This might sound best with your lute alone, though I would love to hear it alongside the naqun someday."

"Oh, I'll be thinking about a string instrument that sounds like percussion until I do." I grin, my thoughts dancing with possibilities. My mark feels strange, like I just touched a piece of metal in the winter, but not exactly bad. It knows this is just friendship, just music. "But you'll have to be willing to play with more people for that."

"Someday." He inclines his head. "Now that you're here, would you help me with the reading? It's much slower."

"That's probably smart. If you let me back near that laz, I don't know if I'll be able to put it down."

He chuckles. I clear a space on the floor, discover a dusty carpet, and settle in to work.

The paperwork is endless, and so many of them are these long, sprawling passages hiding the fact that they're secretly memorials written after King Notu's death. By the time I hit the third one of those, I'm beginning to regret ever admitting the laz would be a distraction. I could be on the other side of the room, strumming it between other useless objects, actually considering enjoying myself instead of resenting the fact that I now have to be awake all day and all night.

"Oh," Sash says quietly.

I look at him. Silently, he hands what he's holding to me.

As soon as I see the handwriting, my stomach drops. Father, tight and spiky like every word is its own little weapon. The letter is violently effusive, every I dotted and T crossed so aggressively that he struck through the page in a few places. He thanks King Notu for his presence at Father's wedding a few months ago and mentions he didn't know just how beautiful Lightning Cape was until he met Mother.

A shiver runs down my spine. I can hear the words in his voice, heavy with threat. Maybe, this early in his career, King Notu might have read those and thought they were just kind. I know better.

That's when the smell reaches my nose, despite the strangely aggressive breeze that's been whipping through the room all night. Just a hint of cinnamon, something green like a broken branch.

Burning clove. Mother made sure I knew how it smelled. I glance over the letter again, ignoring the words. The blue seal looks like it oozed reddish ink onto the page.

I'm not holding a letter. I'm holding a murder weapon.

"What?" Sash asks. "I just thought you might want to see it."

"Burning clove," I mumble. "It's a contact poison. You have to touch it, the sap, which looks reddish when distilled to full potency."

Sash looks at the stains around the seal, the delicate way I'm holding the letter. "You think—"

"What else?" Father was no military genius. He was just a man willing to take the path that repulsed everyone else.

Sash's eyes dart from the letter to me. "How did you recognize that?"

And there it is. The moment he actually realizes I'm the daughter of these people. That alone is enough of a reason for a girl to seal herself away from society entirely.

"I am not my father's daughter," I say tiredly.

"I never said—"

I wave away the objections. There's no point in pretending, not now that I've seen the look on his face. "Even before I realized what he was doing to the whole world, we never got along. Kieran was his favorite, Anwen his stand-in, and I was a pretty little doll he wanted to polish up and trot out on special occasions. As you may have realized, I wasn't a particularly well-behaved doll. So you can rest easy knowing that I inherited nothing from him other than my looks."

Sash's shoulders rise and fall with a slow, deep breath. "What of your mother?"

I close my eyes. For a few months after Mother was locked up, I practiced a similar speech about her in the mirror. That we never got along, never spent much time together even. And every ridiculous word of it was a lie.

Mother spent all her time with me, or as much of it as she could spare. She wanted me to learn all the important skills Candace did, but when I got bored with them, she let me do what I wanted. Of everyone in my family, she and Candace were the only ones who attended my thousand little presentations of my latest hobbies. One time, Mother let me pin her into an absolutely disastrous dress I was making, and I really think she might have left the room in it, if I could get the two sides to stay together long enough for her to take a step.

She did things that I can't think about. They don't match the woman I knew. Honestly, I have a hard time believing Raven's stories about her sometimes. And I'm not stupid enough to stand by everything she ever did now.

But I can't look into the eyes of this stranger and swear up and down that she means nothing to me. My life would be easier if I could. And it would be much easier if something about his eyes didn't make me kind of want to spill the whole messy thought process into his lap.

"She taught me," I say. "How else do you think I would be able to recognize this?"

"So it was her doing?" He looks back at the letter. "But she is—"

"Dead." That, I've mastered saying without flinching. "So someone else has to be behind the current attack."

He glances at me again. I sigh.

"And if that someone was me, why would I tell you about the poison? You clearly didn't recognize it."

"Of course." He shakes his head. "Apologies. Paranoia is just as contagious as any pox. I… assume that's why you've been keeping your investigation secret as well?"

"That, and that my family thought I was losing my mind," I reply.

His eyebrows raise at my honesty. I want to shake myself. I don't owe him anything. It seems unlikely at this point, but he still *could* be a spy.

"We should seal this room back up," I say. "King Notu was poisoned, and I tested negative for the pox, so it stands to reason Amval was too. We've learned everything we need to know."

"Of course." Sash stands. "And the letter?"

"Can we keep it?" I eye the stains. "I don't think the poison is active, but I'd hate for someone else to find out I'm wrong."

He nods. "King Notu would certainly approve of saving lives."

"And tomorrow maybe we'll… find something Amval touched a week and a half ago with poison on it." I sigh. If I thought this room was like trying to find a needle in a haystack….

"Can you come to me?" Sash asks. "It will be easier to get into the palace that way."

Oh, that's what he needs me for.

Maybe he's not a spy after all.

"At lunch," I say, irritated by how much of a relief that is. "Make sure you can get away."

"I will do what I can." He shuts the door behind us and hurries off into the night, leaving me alone in the hallway.

I almost don't resent the idea of seeing him again tomorrow.

My mark reacts, and I squash the feeling as I head for my bedroom to steal whatever sleep I still can.

MISSING GROOM

Amval

I STEP OUT INTO THE GRIM DARKNESS OF THE COURTYARD AND BREATHE in the wind. Out here, I can finally release my tight control on the air. Grandfather's memorial chamber was so close, I nearly collapsed when Ingrid came to sit next to me.

Or perhaps that was simply because she smelled so painfully sweet, of violets and ink, and I wanted to bury my nose in the curve of her throat. Perhaps because I told her, she played music, and she asked to hear me as well. To play with me someday. I'll have to brush up on the ney; it's not my favorite instrument, just the one that will sound best with hers.

I hum the drinking song she played under my breath.

Instead of turning straight to the stable, as I should because a groom's day starts earlier than a prince's ever did, I circle the long way around. The southernmost point of Som Palace juts out toward the sea, a few windows sparkling like stars. Cirocco is still awake, pacing. He came to the stable for his horse yesterday, and he barely glanced at me. My own brother, perhaps my best friend, didn't recognize me.

It's better he doesn't look at me. I should be pleased, like I should be pleased that Joli didn't recognize my scent or that Mother and Father haven't been to the stables at all. The less of them I see, the safer my position is.

But I still lean against the outer wall and stare up at the room that used to be mine. My back aches for my bed, but that is the least of what I miss. No, I miss seeing Kaloni's light still lit and crossing the hall to talk with her until one of us falls asleep. I miss hearing the twins giggle late into the night, even when it forces me to cram pillows over my ears to keep the noise out. If Cirocco is awake, his triplets, Esen and Hova, will be trying to heckle him to sleep. Joli's light is out, but that means nothing. I've knocked on the door of her lit room and found no one inside. She may well be awake, doing whatever mysterious projects she's always doing under the covers in the hopes no one will see.

It's been a week and a half. That's the longest I have ever gone without my family. If I were given the choice between re-entering the palace by myself or having them back if we all lived on the road again, I would take the second option in a heartbeat.

But those are not the options on the table. My choices are to solve my own attempted murder and save us all or fail and bring us all to our doom. And my funeral is tomorrow.

So I sigh and march to the stable. Somehow, I have to find a way to tell Ingrid everything I know about the day before my murder without revealing who I am. I can't think of a moment when someone would have tried to poison me and failed, resulting in the other body, but I didn't notice those strange stains around the seal, either. Grandfather certainly wouldn't have. His eyesight faded in his later years, and they truly looked like nothing more than an odd wax.

Rage bubbles in my chest. King Gavin has always been the monster in my bedtime stories, the man who destroyed my kingdom, but now I know he killed my blood–he and Queen Rowena, a traitor to her own people. Sly, underhanded monsters. Ones that creep around in the shadows and drag people off to be assassinated elsewhere.

I almost wish they had survived the last few years. Taking the Solbergs' word without seeing their bodies grows harder with every scrap of information I learn about them.

One thing is certain, though: Ingrid did not kill me or attempt to do so. She has been too honest, the opposite of the bastards that raised her. I—we are looking for a liar.

"Come on," Tek wheedles. "You said you would come out next time."

I rub the top of my veil, since I can't run my hand through my hair. Yet another thing to get used to. My legs ache after an energetic, but ultimately useless, lunch with Ingrid where we tried to find anyone who remembered my last day. Really, I should have told her I was there. As Amval's personal groom, I would know enough about his last hours to be useful… but "I" was "here." Another several hours of work have sapped every sliver of energy I have.

"I didn't anticipate how tired I would be," I say.

Tek nods slowly, a dangerous smile growing on his lips. "That's bad luck because tonight is officially mandatory. So, do I have to carry you, or will you walk your tired ass down with me?"

Irritated, far past tired, I mumble, "Carry me."

I realize my mistake when Tek whoops. A heartbeat later, he has my arms, another groom my legs, and they are laughing as they carry me out of the stable. Irritation surges. I am their prince! Then, I catch Tek's eye, sparkling like Esen's when he pulls off a particularly good prank.

This may be where I belong, for now, but I don't have to be alone in it. I go limp in their arms and laugh along with them.

Going out apparently means The Gruesome Pony, a hole-in-the-wall tavern in the town that is slowly regrowing outside the walls of the palace. Almost everything here still bears the burn scars of

Gavin's conquering, but the Pony is worse than most—it doesn't have a roof, just charred walls stretching up into nothingness.

Tek, who set me down as soon as we left the palace walls, nudges me. "Ozkan swears he's never putting a roof back on."

I shake my head. "What does he do when it rains?"

Tek laughs. "Serve stronger ale!"

The whole group, about a dozen men from the stables, guffaws at that. Nur is conspicuously absent—in fact, so is everyone higher ranked than a groom. It seems this is where they go to let off steam without worrying about their superiors. There are even a few of the older stable boys, blending into the crowd like they're the same as the rest.

I smile with them. Drinking has been the trickiest act to master with the veil, so I don't have to worry about whatever watered-down shit Ozkan serves when the sky is as dry as tonight.

A brawny man stops us at the door. "Give me one good reason why I should let you bastards back in."

Tek swaggers forward. "We're the only bastards loud enough to make the rest of the town look twice at your shithole."

The man—presumably Ozkan—scoffs. "You're the only bastards loud enough to get me damn near shut down for noise complaints."

With his wide-set shoulders and heavy beard, Ozkan reminds me of my namesake, Sash the bartender at that inn I worked at. He's not looking for a promise of coin or quiet. This is an old ritual, one I know the next step in still.

"Because we're the only bastards willing to put up with your music," I say, low as I have been but rougher, like my royal diction is an affectation I'm letting slip here.

Everyone stares at me for a moment before bursting into raucous laughter. Ozkan slings an arm around my shoulders.

"Well, if a soldier of the Goddess says it, who am I to disagree?"

We march in through the front door, and the other grooms pull tables together. The one other patron grumbles into his ale but kicks a chair toward Tek when he's looking for one. Clearly, this is their home away from the stables. The place where they belong.

Judging by the shot Ozkan pours me before we even finish sitting down, I belong here now, too. Awkwardly, I slide it under my veil and knock back the burning liquor. I'm not foolish enough to refuse a man like Ozkan.

"I am not playing for them!" the troubadour on the stage shouts.

Ozkan tosses him a coin. "You'll play here or nowhere."

The troubadour scoops it up hungrily and strums a tuneless laz.

I slide into the last empty seat at the table. As I do, the groom who grabbed my legs, Iltas, shakes his head.

"Shit, it's weird seeing someone else there."

"Someone else?" I ask.

"Harun." Iltas raises his mug to the open sky. "How the hell are we going to keep Ozkan in business now?"

Everyone else lifts their cups.

"He could drink like no one else," Tek says. "You've got a lot to make up for, Sash."

I chuckle vaguely, a pit settling in my stomach. "Who is Harun?"

"How do you think you got this job?" Iltas asks.

"When she offered it to me, Nur said… 'He was lost on the road.'"

"On the road?" Tek raises an eyebrow. "Nur told you that?"

"She did." I look from face to face, uncomfortable with the rabid curiosity within.

Iltas whistles. "She only told us Harun was dead, no body to bring home. You think he got ravaged?"

"We'd have heard if the royals were attacked by rogues." Someone smacks Iltas on the back of the head. "Nah, I think he found a tavern and got left behind."

A stableboy winces. "Don't say that. He might stumble back, and Sash would have to give up his job."

"Better than you losing a friend." I raise my glass, thoughts whirling. "To Harun."

"To Harun!" they chorus.

As the drinking begins in earnest, I lean back in my chair and watch the simply awful troubadour pluck his monstrous laz. When Nur offered me the job, I was in a rush. I barely listened to what she said. If I had, perhaps I would have realized the connection sooner.

Someone in the palace, about my age, as all the grooms are, is suspiciously missing just when I am pronounced dead? Harun didn't die on the road, and he certainly wasn't ravaged. I would bet all the money changing hands tonight that he was handed something slathered in a poison meant for me and left in my place.

Tek startles me out of my thoughts by thumping me on the shoulder. "You still with us?"

I nod. "Parties like this are uncommon in the abbey."

He snorts. "I'd bet they are. It's about time to start trying to chase that old bastard off the stage. I don't suppose you sing?"

The troubadour plucks another note so sour it almost makes me wince, and I remember how easily Ingrid held the neck of the laz yesterday. The naqun may be my favorite instrument, but I love the laz nearly as much as she seemed to. I could, at the very least, save the poor beast in this troubadour's hands from its long, slow death.

"Come on," Tek says. "You have to be better than Iltas, at least."

"I'm afraid I don't sing," I say. "I couldn't carry a tune if you put it in a bucket."

Tek rolls his eyes and stumbles away, slung around Iltas instead. I stare into the glass of ale in my hands as they launch into some equally terrible singing. Sash could play here, where others could hear me, for the very first time in my life. But if there is anything this last week has made very clear to me, it's that I am not really living my life—I'm stuck in an afterlife until I unravel the mystery of who banished me here.

And I want to make the first music of my afterlife while breathing in violets and ink, not stale beer.

FUNERAL

Ingrid

I SWAY TO AN UNFAMILIAR SONG AS KING IRAJ, PRINCE CIROCCO, AND Prince Esen carry Amval's coffin into the temple. All of them cry openly, the coffin rocking on their shoulders. Queen Zephira insisted I stand at the front, with the family, and I wish I'd disagreed harder. The whole temple is packed with people who actually knew him, nobles and staff alike, and this is just the procession. After this, there's a meal, all the outsiders will arrive, and *then* it's time for the funeral.

Joli suggested I wear a dress that showed my mark. I told her I didn't have anything appropriate, but honestly, every time I looked at myself in the mirror, it felt like cheating. The throbbing red lightning bolt isn't enough to put me here. I spent one night with him, and I didn't even like him for most of it.

My eyes burn as they set him down at the front. Fuck, I didn't even like him. He was boring, unfunny, one of a hundred stuffed shirts at a dull political event.

Halit, their royal holy woman, raises her arms to the sky. "The Goddess takes to Her side those who most deserve it."

And... that's all I need to hear. I've already sat through enough funerals, and it doesn't seem like this will be much different. She'll give the usual speeches about how he was good enough that the Goddess needed him, and then we'll all leave, wondering what that means for those She doesn't murder. At least here, Halit stands a chance of meaning it, judging by how crowded the temple is. There has to have been more to Amval.

I'll just never get to know it.

And I don't need to. I was happy before. I will be again, once I figure out who did this to him. Sash thinks he has an in with another groom who was at the name-blessing, and I'm meeting with him tomorrow. He, if anyone, might know what happened to my missing groom. After that, I think Sash and I can potentially track him to Amval, or to whoever wanted to murder my mate. I know he's ill, not poisoned, but it's too big of a coincidence to ignore.

My mark nearly jumps off my chest, screaming sharp and jagged. I bend over with a soft curse. Its reactions when I think about Sash are getting worse and worse.

I can't keep dragging Joli into this, I tell it. *She's a kid. He's just a useful ally.*

It doesn't stop screaming. It never does. I just grit my teeth and breathe through it. Queen Zephira rubs my back in small circles, so it probably just looks like I'm upset. It's still hard not to flinch away from her touch. I don't need another family, and I certainly don't need another mother.

No matter how kind she seems or how nice a son she might have raised.

I don't think I take a real breath until we walk outside to eat. Someone looped their arm through mine at some point, and I look to the side to discover it's Kaloni, the now crown princess of Lightning Cape.

"Mother told me why you're here," she whispers. "I wanted to thank you again."

"For what?" I gasp.

"What you did the day we…found him." Kaloni blinks rapidly, prettily. "I don't know what I would have done without you."

The night I met Amval, she was a smear in the background. Another tense, upright Som. Part of the matching set. But she's been helpful, if very formally so, until now.

"What are they going to do with him?" What am I thinking? Their dead get privacy, and I certainly don't have a claim over whatever happens to his body.

She smiles sadly. "He will be burned and dispersed back into the wind. Over the cliff, I would expect. If any of us were going to properly fly, it would be him, I always said."

"What about you?"

Kaloni's eyebrows flicker slightly up. Perfect. If I had any guts, I'd bite my own tongue off. Who asks someone what they want for their own funeral at their brother's? Who asks that question at all? Pain still scrambles my thoughts. I'm irritated I'm still holding onto her in the first place, forget about the rest. I open my mouth to turn it into a joke, but she speaks first.

"There are woods to the north. Deep, dark woods. We lived there when even hiding our faces wasn't enough to get us through towns safely." She stares thoughtfully ahead. "There, I think. Amval's wind was his freedom, but mine is the quiet of safety."

How did they survive on the run for so long if they're all this honest? "That sounds beautiful."

She laughs self-consciously. "You don't have to pretend it makes sense to you. It's just something we all had to think about for a while."

And there it is again. Father's name, what he did. It keeps appearing in conversations with the Soms, and none of them will come right out and say it.

"I'm sorry," I say.

She pats my hand. "There is nothing to be sorry for."

What a perfectly diplomatic response. I clench my jaw to keep from throwing it back in her face. Candace would be disappointed if I screamed at someone at their brother's funeral—even if they deserved it, even if I was just telling them to hit me or hate me or whatever they actually felt instead of smiling.

When Kaloni looks up at me again, a new sheen of tears glosses her eyes. "I don't care what anyone says. You are going to stay here as long as you want, if I have to fight Mother and Father myself."

There's no politics in the roughness of her voice. She reminds me... well, a little of Candace.

"Okay," I say awkwardly. "I don't think they're rushing me out."

"I just want you to know you have someone in your corner." She pulls me closer. "I want to be friends. Close friends. Amval would have liked that."

My mark howls, and I swallow. I can't stay here forever, chasing the ghost of a man I barely met. But I need her help.

Someone taps me on the shoulder, and I turn gratefully. Cirocco, Amval's brother and Beta, stands behind us. His eyes are red and swollen, but he's not crying anymore, at least.

"Can I borrow you?" he asks. Me? Kaloni? I'm not sure.

I disentangle myself from her despite the new spike of pain and nod. Kaloni says something about greeting the newcomers and walks away.

"Why me?" I ask as soon as we're alone. Kaloni used up whatever social graces I had left.

After a long moment, he says, "I was with him until he left for the Haze. I just keep thinking—I should have seen—"

"Hey." I put my hand on his arm. "There was nothing to see, right? That's how the Pox works."

And the poison. But if Cirocco was with him all day, and I remember one of the smears behind Amval being as broad and soft-spoken as Cirocco is, he's the person to talk to about where Amval could have been poisoned. I need him to like me.

My skin crawls. I sound like Mother, ranking who I need to be nice to at a funeral by who I'll need later.

"I suppose." Cirocco sniffles. He's only a year younger than me, even a few inches taller, but he seems strangely young. "I... you were with him last. Did you see anything?"

My brain surges forward with memories of that night, and I shut them back away. I've been over them for clues a million times. Now, they just hurt, and poking that particular bruise hasn't made it hurt any less. It just makes it easier not to poke again.

"I didn't notice anything weird," I say. "Not anything I haven't already mentioned."

His brows furrow. "Who did you mention it to?"

"Sahin, right afterward?" I scan the crowd beginning to gather around the long, outdoor table for the large man. "I was interrogated."

"Oh, before we knew Amval was sick." He relaxes. "I meant signs of the Pox. I keep trying to remember if I missed anything."

"You didn't," I say softly, like Candace does when I keep repeating the same thing over and over again. "But if you want, we can go over what we remember together."

Cirocco gives me a bear hug. "Thank you. I knew the Goddess would pick someone good for Amval."

I rub his back stiffly, wondering what kind of prince chooses Cirocco for a Beta. He's just as big as Sahin, potentially intimidating, but that fades away as soon as Cirocco talks. Maybe it's just a hereditary position, something that always goes to the second son, but somehow, I doubt it.

And here I am, hunting to know a dead man again. I release Cirocco, promise to find time to talk, and keep walking to the table full of food by myself. At home, the funeral ends before the eating starts. My stomach is twisted up in knots, trying to think about eating before we trudge back into an even bigger, longer ceremony for a stranger.

"Innid!" a childish voice shouts.

I wince and smile as I turn. Only one person calls me that—and it's Altair, trying not to stumble over his formal blacks as he pelts across the courtyard toward me. Kieran hurries in his wake.

"Tai!" I scoop him up with a small grunt when he reaches me. Three years old came with a sizable growth spurt, and if I hadn't been training, I wouldn't be able to pick him up anymore. "I didn't know you were going to be here."

Kieran catches up. "I thought we weren't warning people before we came to Lightning Cape anymore."

"Pettiness?" I raise an eyebrow at him. "I thought you were above that."

"I was." He crosses his arms. "Before my little sister disappeared a few days after her mate's death."

"I told Candace," I grumble.

Altair pats my face. "Auntie Innid in twouble?"

I say, "No," at the exact same moment Kieran says, "Yes." Altair looks back and forth between me and his father, confusion building on his little face.

"I did something Papa didn't like," I tell him, "but Papa's not in charge of me, so I can't officially be in trouble."

"Auntie Ingrid scared everybody badly." Kieran pulls Altair out of my arms with a frown. "So Papa's a little unhappy with her."

"Mama says everyone s'posed to be unhappy." Altair nods seriously at me.

I stroke blond hair back from his face. "You didn't know him. You can feel however you like, as long as you're quiet about it."

Kieran pins me with his stare. "Is that right?"

I lift my chin and hold his gaze. I was telling the truth. I'm more than of age. He can't get me in trouble. "I'd say so."

"Then you'll come home with us when this is done," he says, leaning in. "I've already made arrangements, and we brought a carriage with enough space. You're right; the Som family needs quiet to grieve."

I look over his shoulder, past him. The Soms stand in a tight clump of black, one of them peeling off at a time to deal with approaching well-wishers. It's like clockwork, like they made an arrangement. Each Som endures one tense comforting before returning to the group, and then the next one goes out.

As I watch, Cirocco steps away from his family. His chin is higher and his step steadier than when he grabbed me. He looks like a Beta again.

"No," I tell Kieran. "But I think I'll be home soon."

OUTSIDE

Amval

"In this life," Halit intones with her hands raised, "pleasure and pain so often go hand in hand."

My foot slips, and I have to throw my hands out for a gust of wind to catch it before I topple off the side of the temple. No one looks up. Why would they? Most of the palace has been in the temple at least once since the casket ostensibly containing my body was carted in and placed on the altar. Half of the rest of the world seems to have been invited, crowding into a space I never thought was small before.

I remember arriving at the palace for the first time in my life. Prayers of gratitude echoed from the temple's open doors. I followed them, curious, and found the biggest room I'd ever seen up until that time. I've heard that, in other kingdoms, temples are often plain, silver-white spaces so the Goddess's light can be the main decoration. In theory, that sounds beautiful, but then I saw the walls of our temple, covered in mosaics from floor to soaring, arched ceiling. High windows send the Goddess's light into the sparkling stone that tells Her story, making everything the more beautiful from her touch.

Almost everything, I suppose. A section of light is blocked by my body, crammed into a window frame and barely balanced here with the help of the wind.

I couldn't go to the funeral. Tek said the staff was invited to the viewing and first blessing, but I couldn't make my feet move fast enough to carry me there.

"We here have all known the pleasure of Prince Amval's friendship," Halit continues. "His warmth, his kindness."

A chill shudders through me that has nothing to do with the cold. This is macabre. I shouldn't know what people think of me when they don't believe I can hear them any longer. I should have stayed in the bunkhouse. Nur gave us all a half day, and sleep has become too valuable a commodity in my life to waste scaling buildings.

"This is why the pain of his loss strikes so deeply." Halit bows her head. "But as the Goddess hides Her face from us only to show it once more, pleasure will again come where pain now sits. At this moment, the pleasure is Prince Amval's, safe in Her bosom."

A sob cracks the quiet. It's so loud I think I've shattered the glass I'm leaning on for a heartbeat. But it's not me—it is Mother, throwing herself into Father's arms below.

I swallow thickly. Sibel and Liwar close in on either side of her, rubbing her back in alternating circles. Kaloni hugs herself, rocking slightly. Cirocco's mouth hangs open, like he wants to object but can't find the words.

When I realize there is a space between Father and Kaloni, the space where I should be, I lose my grip on the window again. If watching my own funeral is macabre, letting my family sit through it is monstrous.

Instinct sends my hands out, though, and I catch myself before falling. Perhaps this is my just punishment. If I'm going to force them to endure the specter of my death, I should be able to look it in the face.

"I'm here," I whisper against the glass. "I am protecting us all."

If I weren't, there is no force in this world that could keep me from their side. But there is no place I'm more sure my would-be murderer will be than my funeral, which is why I made myself come despite the thousand reasons I shouldn't.

I'm here despite the fact that every broken sob of Mother's is a knife through my heart, a hacking blow like the one Yalim did not finish.

Next to them, Ingrid stands bolt upright. I've never seen her so perfectly poised, so well put together. She looks like she belongs beside my family. Perhaps Liwar helped her dress, or Kaloni coached her in posture.

"The Goddess alone knows when it is time to take those we love from us," Halit declares. "In Her infinite wisdom, She recognized this as the time for Prince Amval."

Ingrid goes perfectly taut, like a hose suddenly filled with liquid, and I realize that her behavior has nothing to do with my family at all.

She is keeping herself from yelling in the middle of my funeral.

My mark throbs. What would she yell, if she could? That it wasn't fair? That she deserved more time with me—or that everybody did?

Halit launches into a hymn, and my family joins her in warbling voices that pluck at something fragile in my chest. Ingrid doesn't sing. She doesn't even part her lips. She is still rigid, ready to explode.

I wish she would yell. It would break the rhythm of Halit's dreary recitations, the percussion of Mother's sobs. Upset the delicate balance within the temple, and reveal what everyone has been hiding underneath.

As I watch the curls of her golden hair quiver, barely trapped in jeweled combs, I think I understand why the Goddess brought her to me for the first time. Ingrid is all passion and movement–a wick about to be lit.

If there is anything—anyone–I can count on to discover the truth of what happened to me, it is her, and she won't stop until she's satisfied.

She deserves the truth.

After curfew that night, I pace the lower edge of the cliff, clutching a ney I borrowed from one of the other grooms. As my funeral ended, I snuck off and left a note on Ingrid's pillow, telling her to bring her lute and meet me here. It feels foolish now. Waves crash, sending up thunderous sprays. The salt air will make the reeds in the ney swell, and I can't imagine it will be kind to her foreign lute.

"Sash?"

I spin. With the noise of the water, I didn't even hear her approach. She steps off the final bluestone stair into a ray of moonlight. Her hair falls loose now, and the soft pinks of her skin turn to pearl. She is wearing a loose dress that a breeze I, for once, did not summon flattens against her body, revealing the slopes of her figure.

My mouth goes dry. She doesn't make any effort to cover herself or even seem embarrassed. If she didn't notice, informing her will be worse—

"Or Sash-statue?" She waves the hand not clasping her lute in front of my eyes.

I blink and return to myself as the breeze dies down. "Sash, I promise."

She laughs, all music already. "I would've been a little surprised if statues could write notes."

"I didn't know if you would come." I lead her to a blanket I've laid out right at the base of the cliff, shielded as much as we can be from the elements. "Today was…."

"The funeral." She sighs. "Honestly, if you hadn't asked me, I would've been playing in my room." She pats the belly of her lute. "This is my closest confidante sometimes."

My mark bellows—she is not my enemy. I could tell her! I close my eyes and inhale slowly through my nose. Every person I tell is a danger. For my family and my kingdom—for Ingrid, since we still don't know who attempted to kill me or why—it is only safe to stay dead.

Which is why I owe her tonight.

"My music is the same to me," I manage.

"Is that why you're so private about it?" She sits and cradles her lute in her lap.

"One of the reasons." I sit facing her, far enough away that I can hear my own notes but close enough to touch. If I were allowed to touch. "Others don't exactly approve. They think I have other responsibilities."

"And grinding yourself to dust by never doing anything you like is obviously the best way to keep up with those." She rolls her eyes as she tunes her lute. "I can't tell you how often I've heard that sort of thing."

"But everyone knows you play the lute." I grimace behind the veil at my mistake. "At least, I've heard about it on the few occasions I've left the palace, so I assume it's well known."

She laughs, but it sounds tired, perhaps forced. "No, you're right; everyone knows. I just decided that being happy sounded better than being what everyone wanted."

My heart lunges up into my throat. She may as well have told me she decided she preferred the sky green. "How?"

She shrugs, no longer a shred forced. "I just did. It's easier than people think—or at least, it is when no one was looking. I don't know if you grew up in a...temple, or wherever starlights stay."

"An abbey," I answer automatically. "I certainly wouldn't say no one was looking, regardless."

"Well, you're out now." Her smile shines like another star. "And I'm the only one watching."

Her blue eyes bore through the late-night dim, inescapable. The veil isn't enough to hide me anymore. My stomach twists around itself, certain that the moment I play a note, she'll recognize me. It doesn't matter that no one has ever heard me play before—she met me, the real me, that night in the grass. That man will appear in my music, and no cleverly wielded breeze will hide him away.

"Well?" She puts her fingers on the frets. "Want to pick the song?"

She deserves the truth. If she sees me... perhaps that is the Goddess's will.

"Let's start with that drinking song you played the other night." I inhale slowly through my nose. "To get a sense of each other."

"Happily." She strums down the strings, I lift the ney to my lips, and the song begins.

I thought, during the Haze, that I would never be closer to another person. That heady blend of instinct and desire was all-consuming, blocking any other thought. Perhaps I was right, physically. But sitting on this beach, playing music with my mate for the very first time, feels more like magic than bending the very wind to my will.

The waves become our percussion, laying down a steadying beat. Ingrid takes the mid-range, transforming the drinking song once again. What was wistful takes on a mourning sadness, undergirded by an anger I can only hear in her strumming. The singer wants to stop, wants to rest, and they are furious that no one will help them.

Her version of the song bleeds into me, catches me, and spins me into it. My ney puts voice to that feeling as a wordless, almost strident melody. The story becomes not a wander, not a quest, but a race against time. How far must the singer go before someone will listen? How long will he have to beg before someone answers?

My mark burns down into my chest like a shot as I watch her play, my own fingers dancing over the keys. I sense her every improvisation the heartbeat before it happens, and she feels mine. We make space for each other, shifting like the tides. She curves around her instrument at first, but as we dance through the song together, she straightens. As the tune starts to reach its climax, she finally looks up at me.

Her eyes are painfully blue, wild and alive to match her unrestrained grin. For once, I feel like that. I struggle not to smile around the mouthpiece; I will not be the one who misses a note in this symphony.

Then, her gaze swoops lower. Her fingers stutter, and they don't catch the rhythm again.

I drop the ney to the blanket. "What?"

"Take off your veil. Now."

LIAR

Ingrid

I CAN'T BREATHE. I CAN'T LOOSEN MY GRIP ON MY LUTE, EVEN THOUGH I can hear the strings groaning. I just....

I can't be right. I can't have seen what I thought I saw in the shadows of Sash's lifted veil.

"What?" He leans back, fixing his veil to cover more. "No, I took a vow—"

"I don't give a fuck about your vow," I spit. "Take it off."

It's dark out here. The veil still covers most of his face. So the mark I thought I saw on his throat, even if it was a mark, could have been shaped like anything.

Even though it looked exactly like a sun. Right where I remember biting Amval.

Where did all the air go? My chest rises and falls, but I feel like I'm choking on nothingness.

"I'm not sure what happened." He starts to stand.

I grab his wrist and yank him back down. "I'm *not sure* why you suddenly think I'm stupid. I saw—I need to see. You. Your face."

"That is forbidden." His voice is all ice, but he won't look at me. He's hiding something.

I open my mouth to keep arguing, but before I can come up with another way to tell him I don't care, my hands suddenly release my lute.

If he won't listen to me, I only have one choice.

I set my lute to the side and launch myself at him. His eyebrows shoot up just before I hit him square in the chest. We both tumble into the sand, and I bracket his hips with my legs. He grabs my shoulders—fuck, he's strong. He'll pull me off if I give him time.

Dodge, then get inside his guard.

Too late to dodge. He has me. But he has both hands on my shoulders, and that means his guard is nonexistent.

I don't bother fighting his hold. I just wriggle an arm between us, grab the bottom of his veil, and rip it up.

High, sharp cheekbones. A thick jaw to balance them. Dark brows. Full lips.

A sun-shaped mark emblazoned on his neck.

I can't breathe.

I fall back off Sash—Amval. Holding myself up is too much effort.

He sits up. "Ingrid—"

"I saw your body," I say. "You were dead."

"They left another body in my place," he says. "I am—"

I slap a hand over his mouth, shock burning away at the warmth of his skin under my hand. His living fucking skin. "If you say you're sorry, I am going to hit you."

He mumbles something I can't understand against my palm. Goddess, maybe I am stupid. With the rest of his face revealed, his eyes are so obviously his. Sash had the same perfect bearing, the same stubborn stiffness that didn't run away when everybody else would have.

Maybe I'll hit him anyway. He deserves it.

"Why did you lie?" I rip my hand back. Touching him makes my skin crawl. How could the Goddess think I belong with someone like this?

"Someone tried to kill me." He scoots back, just out of arm's reach. Smart. I hate him for it. "I don't know who any more than you do."

I laugh, delirious with a cocktail of emotions so thoroughly mixed that I couldn't separate them if I wanted to. I sincerely doubt I do. "And, what, they just missed?"

"I woke up in a cart with an assassin." He shrugs.

"This is not a shrugging situation!" My voice climbs louder and louder, echoing off the cliff behind us.

"Please," he whispers, "can you keep quiet?"

For a single second, I step into the eye of the storm. Total peace, total clarity. His eyes widen. Good. I hope whatever he sees on my face scares him.

Because I am going to kill my mate.

I lunge across the sand again, claws sprouting from my fingertips. The element of surprise has been the cornerstone of my training. If I don't shift, no one sees me coming. Not even my so-called mate. I slash out, shredding his uniform to pieces and drawing blood.

"I understand you are angry." He holds up his hands defensively.

"If this is angry, I've never even been irritated before," I snarl. He lied to me. Over and over again, every time I opened up to him. I ball my other hand into a fist and sock him in the jaw.

His head flies back. When he pulls it forward again, a bruise is already blooming on his chin. "I was protecting my family. Someone thinks I am dead—what do you think they would do if I just waltzed back in, alive?"

"Nothing!" I swipe at his elbow, trying to knock the arm he's holding himself up on out from underneath him. "They targeted you when you were alone with this convoluted fucking plan. Obviously, they couldn't reach you at home."

He catches my wrist with his other hand, crushes it. "And would you risk your family's life on that bet?"

"My family can take care of themselves." His grip is iron, so I twist and sink my teeth into his shoulder.

Blood blooms over my tongue, basil and charcoal. All the burnt food I've been smelling—it's him. I scream against his skin, furious at myself for how much I've missed.

He flips us over while I'm off balance, smashing my back into the sand. "I won't apologize for putting them first."

I tear back from his shoulder and stare up into his face. The perfectly polished diplomat I met is gone. Sash, the formal little monk, is gone. Amval's amber eyes burn as he presses his weight down into me. He's not begging me to understand—he's too confident to even bother asking.

He's alive, the absolute bastard.

I grab a fistful of his hair and yank his mouth down onto mine. He kisses me like the beach is on fire around us, like he can make all his Goddess-damned points with his teeth instead. They clash against mine, but neither of us pull back. Fuck, I've been dreaming about the taste of him. Every morning, I wake up wishing I couldn't remember what happened that night. The char on my tongue burns like embers still too hot to touch; the basil turns into a forest fire.

Clothes disappear with a sound of ripping fabric I barely bother to notice. All that matters is his skin on mine. Muscles I mapped what feels like a lifetime ago come alive under my hands again. I scrape my nails up his bare chest, catching the scrapes I left behind. He hisses into my mouth and grabs my wrist again, pressing into the bruises. I bite his lip as he shoves my hand lower. His cock brushes against my knuckles.

Oh, that's what he thinks he deserves?

I rip my hand away and shove against his shoulders. He doesn't move until I knee him in the hip, just left of where he's made himself all too vulnerable. His flinch alone gives me everything I need to push him over into the sand.

He opens his mouth to say something, and I already know I don't want to hear it. I straddle his face instead, just wanting to shut him up. Amval loops his arms around my thighs, holding me in place, and laves his tongue over my wetness.

I moan. Either the ocean will hide it, or the rest of Lightning Cape will discover their prince is alive while he has his head between my legs. The idea makes me smile, and I grind down onto him. I want to cover him in me, make it so no one can ever doubt who he is again. His breath fans against my thigh. Let him suffocate. This is the best way to kill him I can imagine.

Amval is dedicated, focused. He uses every part of his mouth, his whole face, dancing as deftly as he did over his ney. I see the apex of pleasure only a few seconds before it hits me, hard as a boulder. Shaking, clutching him, I scream my euphoria.

When it's over, I try to climb off, but his grip doesn't loosen. His fingers dent into the flesh of my thighs, holding me in place, and his mouth doesn't slow.

"Amval!" I groan.

His only reply is to fit his tongue inside me. The tingling pleasure threatens to overcome me again, and I rock against him. He more than owes me. The ridge of his nose provides sweet friction despite the increasing slide of wetness between our skin.

But when I tumble over the edge a second time, yanking on his hair and murmuring wordless pleas, he still doesn't release me. I pull harder on his hair, digging my nails into his scalp. Overwhelm threatens like a growing wave.

He pulls back and looks up at me. "What? I thought this was what you wanted."

"I'd rather go back to screaming at you now," I pant.

"I'd rather not have been forced to make the choices I've made." He rolls us over, hefts my knees so high they just about dent the sand next to my head, and presses his face between my legs again.

Pain and pleasure harmonize. I shriek. It's too much, and it's everything I've been missing. All those times my mark reacted to feelings about Sash—it was this feeling. Too intense to look at head on, but good. So, so good it almost feels bad all over again. I wrap my legs around Amval's head.

He releases one of my thighs and sneaks a hand between us. With his tongue still on my sensitive bud, he fits one finger, two, three inside me. I am soaked, a mess, and I part for him like I was always meant to.

One high blends into the next. I shake, writhe, moan. Amval burns himself into me, claims me as his mate. I'm delirious, barely here. For a minute, the waves sound like rippling grass, like we're back at our first night together all over again. Like everything else never happened, and there's nothing to solve on the other side of this.

"Need you." I'm too far gone to be humiliated by the drunken slur in my voice or the words themselves.

Amval smiles against my overstimulated skin like those are the words he's been waiting to hear. He slides up my body smoothly and crushes his mouth onto mine as he aligns his cock. His taste blends with mine on my lips, and I moan. When he slides home, I lose myself completely.

There's no burn, no stretch. I fit him perfectly. He fucks me in slow, deliberate strokes. Still taking his time, wringing everything I have out of me. I kiss him sloppily, struggling to coordinate all the pieces of myself, but he doesn't seem to mind. He just grabs at me, holds me down, makes me his.

"Amval," I moan.

He growls in reply, hips stuttering. I hook one boneless leg around him, pulling him closer, and scrape my teeth over his lips.

With a low, hungry groan, he stiffens on top of me, muscles going taut. His amber eyes still sear into mine, hot and so desperately alive.

When he collapses, I figure out how to control my arm enough to swipe the tears off my face before he can see them.

WHAT COMES AFTER

Amval

I LAY ON MY SIDE, SUCKING IN MOUTHFULS OF BEACH AIR AND TWIRLING my wrist lazily to suction the sand out before it reaches my lungs. Violets and ink fight the salt spray for attention. Someday, I'll figure out how to play the way they smell together. Constraint and wildness, light and dark, the lush purple and the deep green. I've never written my own songs before, but she makes me want to try.

For the first time since I woke up in the cart, my head doesn't hurt, and neither does my mark.

Ingrid had every right to be furious with me, but the ground shifted under our feet when she kissed me. The moment before she did, I looked in her eyes and saw them change. The sparks of rage gave way to something warmer.

Something I might call relief.

That, I understand, even if I don't completely understand what kind of person she turns me into. Blood dries into the sand from the shoulder she bit, and I don't care because doing anything about it would require leaving her side. Her profile stands out against the night sky, pale and lovely. I want to trace it with my tongue.

Perhaps once my tongue has a brief break. The holding her on top of me, pushing her higher and higher—I would risk almost anything to do that again. The feeling of her wrapped around my cock is like coming home, but that was pure power, injected straight into my veins.

Her lips tighten, then relax again, and I realize she doesn't seem quite as thrilled as I am. There is tension in her shoulders, and she picks at the edge of her thumbnail with another finger on the same hand.

But she hasn't moved toward her clothes. I know something ripped in the scuffle, but I believe the only casualties may be my shirt. Her stillness has to mean something. My gaze drifts to her breasts, jutting proudly into the night air. The lightning bolt of my mark stabs across one and into the valley between, making my mouth water. It would be so easy to smooth over this quiet by reaching for it, throwing myself at her again.

I inhale slowly through my nose. We are here because of decisions I made—decisions I was forced to make, ones I don't necessarily regret—but Ingrid deserves better than an animal. I wanted her to know the truth; she knows more than I ever intended, and I still now must be the man she knows I am. I have a duty to ask, even if I would rather go to my grave.

"What does this change?" I ask.

She sighs. Since she hasn't gotten dressed, I let myself watch. She's so slim, but the hidden softness of her chest undulates temptingly.

"Everything," she replies.

A wave crashes, and freezing foam creeps up the beach high enough to brush my spine. I swallow the flinch. I'll have to get used to not hiding behind the veil once more. "I understand. If it means anything to you, I didn't enjoy lying."

"It doesn't." She sits up and stares out over the ocean. "Do you know why?"

I shake my head.

Her eyes narrow, though she doesn't look at me. "Because how am I supposed to trust anything you say now?"

My breath escapes me in a rush. Of course. My family will forgive me because they know I am not a liar. They will understand I had no choice in light of my other behavior.

Ingrid knows me from one conversation, in which I barely understood what she was saying and mocked her sense of humor. I don't know what rumors circulate about the Soms, much less about me in particular. This could simply be what I do, my default solution to any problem.

"I'm not a particularly good liar," I tell her spine, the only part of her really facing me.

She snorts. "You grew up in hiding. How could that be true?"

"Mother and Father lied for us, mostly." It destroyed Mother. I remember waking up in the dead of night to her sobbing more than once, Father always murmuring that this was the only way to keep their family alive. I know what she felt like now.

Just as I know that the clever diplomatic move is to highlight that, show how little I was responsible for my own survival, other than getting very good at obeying orders. But Ingrid won't respond well to clever diplomacy—I think that's why I wanted to give her the little truth I could in the first place.

"A few things are easier, I'll admit. False names are as natural to me as my own."

"Oh, that's a good sign." She draws her knees up to her chest and shakes her head.

"There are a few ways to walk silently with wind powers, and I'm no genius at them, but I'm adept," I continue.

"I appreciate your steadfast commitment to making things worse for yourself," she says.

"I am telling you the truth now." I run a finger softly down the knobs of her spine. She flinches away, and I withdraw my hand. "You have every right to be angry—"

"I'd say so."

"—and my only option is not to lie to you like that again," I finish, sitting up a few inches away. We rolled off the blanket ages ago, so sand crunches beneath me. "I can't take back what I've done. I can only improve."

"What book did you get that out of?" she snaps.

I wince. I didn't even realize I slipped back into old habits already. "I'm not sure, but I can tell you we were in the East when Father read it to me."

She glances at me. "Either you're serious about the 'total honesty' thing, or you have the least ego about your lies of any politician I've ever met."

"The former." I offer her half a smile. This is progress. "We were sleeping in someone's root cellar, and I could read at the time, but the words in the book were too long for me. I tried to read it to him, and he just took it himself."

She snorts then schools her face again. "No. I'm not doing this with you. I can't."

"Why not?" I push forward, twisting to look at her. "I lied, but you can admit I was placed in a difficult position. You may not have known me, but I didn't know you either. You were in position to have the easiest time murdering me."

She scowls, and her grip on her legs tightens. "Absolutely. You shouldn't be talking to me at all. I'm trying to figure out why the hell you decided to cozy up to me instead."

"I was not lying when I said we wanted the same thing." I study her face, looking for that tiny crack in her defenses I saw a moment ago. There is no sign of it now. "When I discovered you were trying to solve my murder, how could I stay away?"

"Because if you're so damn worried about being discovered, that's the smart thing to do!" She throws her arms up. "You wanted to have it both ways, to get me and your fucking secrecy, and you didn't think twice about how that would affect me."

My sleepless nights and endless worrying would say otherwise. "I—"

She holds up a hand to silence me. "Did you try to become your father's new personal groom? Your brother's steward?"

That would have been too dangerous—and hurt them too badly. I drop my gaze to the sand.

"That's what I thought." She turns to face me, arms crossed. "Now, it's my turn to dictate the terms of our relationship all by myself."

I twist my hands together and bite my tongue. The pain is better than telling her I didn't choose the way this happened entirely. I meant to care less, to stay farther away. There is just something about her that pulls me closer.

"We are going to sit here on this beach until you've told me every single thing you remember about the day we met, from the moment you woke up until the moment you fell asleep. When that's done, you're going to give me a list of everyone you think *might* want to kill you." She releases a deep breath. "And then, I'm going to leave and solve this on my own."

My mark screams. Her words hurt more than her teeth or claws, more than the headache I feel creeping back into place again.

"Why not just leave?"

She spears me with a look. "I give up on things for a lot of reasons, but you are not one of them. No matter what you do."

I swallow. She has every right to be angry. Even if that means walking away from the potential of the greatest happiness either of us will ever know. Even if everything I am screams to fight her, to prove why I did what I did, how she can trust me again. Ingrid doesn't want to be handled softly, but I know she'll respond even worse if I try to force her.

If we have any chance in this life, I need to give her time. I need to prove myself with actions, not words.

"All right," I say. "I'll tell you everything."

"Thank you." She runs a hand through her hair, then stands and takes a few steps away.

I close my eyes. Ingrid can't trust me because she doesn't know me, but that is not why she's angry. No, that comes from the fact that I let her believe I was dead in the first place. And I'm not so foolish to believe that she loves me, but she obviously cares or that wouldn't have mattered to her.

Which means my family, who loves me like no one else, is going to be furious. I let them bury me. Ingrid is right—there is no explanation I can give for that. Mother knows that lying is sometimes a necessity. They all know the importance of keeping certain secrets. Perhaps I'm right, that announcing myself to the whole palace is a death knell, but I've lied to the people who care about me for too long.

"When we are done here, I'm going to find my family," I say slowly. "They are going to be furious with me."

Something soft hits the back of my head. I catch it before it hits the sand—my trousers. Ingrid stands behind me, wearing her dress but clutching her undergarments.

"I thought you were trying not to kill them." She stares at me disbelievingly.

"You said, just a minute ago—"

She drops back down on the beach next to me. "You're in danger. Your family is in danger. That comes first, no matter how angry it makes people." She shakes her head. "But I don't envy what comes after."

STARTING AGAIN

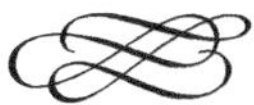

Ingrid

In the morning, I storm around Som Palace. Everyone is still slow and tired after the funeral. I barely slept. But I have—according to my mate, who lied to my face and would have continued to do so if I didn't catch him—an account of Prince Amval's last day, the missing piece I need to solve this mystery and get home.

I don't care that he's alive. There's nothing here for me once this is over. I'm only still bothering because, if he's right and this person is coming for his family next, I owe Joli better than just disappearing.

Cirocco and his other two triplets are in the sunny little room where they always eat breakfast. I shoulder open the door and step inside. Hova, who I think is the youngest, jumps up.

"Princess Ingrid," he asks, "what are you doing here?"

I cut my eyes at Cirocco. "Your brother wanted to talk to me."

Hova and Esen turn in unison. Cirocco swallows whatever he was eating audibly.

"I thought…I mean, we said someday—"

"I thought today would be good." Goddess, my voice sounds like a knife. I stole an hour or two of sleep after Amval finally finished explaining everything, and I woke up feeling more like a hatchet than a person. My skin prickles with needles, and I want to bite the head off everyone who looks at me. Maybe Cirocco doesn't deserve that—I believe Amval is lying to his family as much as he was to me, at least—but I don't seem to have access to whatever lever could turn it down anymore.

"We can talk while you eat with us?" He gestures to the spread on the table, a thousand tiny plates like every meal here in Lightning Cape.

"I've already eaten." It's a lie, but I'm not going to be able to choke anything down now. If I believe Amval is lying to his family, Cirocco is my only chance to validate anything that bastard told me last night.

Every time I think about last night, my legs shake, and my mark burns. It was stupid to have had sex with him again. Even once.

"All right." Cirocco exchanges looks with his brothers then stands up and brushes his hands on his pants. "Try not to eat everything before I get back."

Esen laughs as we leave.

"Is there any reason we have to do this now?" Cirocco asks once we're outside. Bags still hang dark under his eyes, but he doesn't look like the kid I spoke to yesterday. He looks, well, like a Beta. Broad shoulders, stiff posture, head on a swivel. Someone to be reckoned with.

"Yes," I say. "There's a reason to do this now, and I don't want to talk about it."

He eyes me for a long moment.

More flies with honey, Mother trills in my memory.

I shove her voice away. Cirocco isn't a fly; that was always her mistake.

"All right." He opens a door and lets me into a richly decorated bedroom. "On one condition."

"What?" I hesitate in the doorway.

"You'll tell me someday." He sits on a low couch. "He was my brother and my best friend. I deserve to know."

Ah.

"Someday." I step inside, closing the door behind me. "Maybe even someday soon."

"Good." His voice is rough, possibly overwhelmed with relief. My stomach churns. The relief he's looking for is a few hundred yards away, mucking out stalls.

And telling him that is going to kill both of them.

Sometimes I wish I were more my mother's daughter.

"You said you wanted to talk." I drop into a pile of pillows and draw my knees up to my chest. "What are you worried you missed?"

"Any kind of sign?" He shakes his head. "I keep going over and over the day in my mind. We ate in the Tower—arrived the night before."

Just what Amval said, except one detail. "How did you like the food?"

Cirocco laughs. "You sound like him. I devoured everything in sight because I was shocked at how good everything tasted. I thought a kitchen without walls couldn't have pulled it off."

And there is the final detail. Amval repeated it over and over again until I reminded him burning clove was a contact poison, not one you ingested. He was just so sure that, if anyone was poisoned, it would have been Cirocco.

"Why did you arrive early? Delegations from much further away were arriving all morning." And driving Xandra up the wall as they did. The name-blessing had to be pushed back an hour because some important kingdom was stopped on the road.

He shrugs. "Mother says it is more polite not to make your host wonder when you're arriving. We always do."

I didn't ask Amval that last night, but I need to know if anything was different. "And after that? He seemed normal?"

"Completely." Cirocco stares past me, like he's seeing what he thought was his last day with his brother all over again. "We played cards for half the morning, all of us."

"All?"

"My siblings." He offers the wall a ghost of a smile. "We made the game up when we were younger. It only requires half a deck, and you can only play it with exactly eight people."

"I'd like to learn someday." I bite down so hard, trying to catch the words before they escape, that my mouth fills with the taste of blood. Why did I say that? I don't care. I don't want to know, don't want to imagine a group of dirty royals, huddled in some basement around the half-deck of cards they carry from town to town. That puts me at too much risk of feeling bad for Amval, and that's the one thing I'm never allowed to do.

"I suppose we need eight again." Cirocco's smile flickers.

"After that?" I say, too loud. In my lap, I shred the hardened skin around my thumbnail.

"Oh! Um, the girls went off to get ready for the ceremony, and we stayed in the room." Exactly like Amval said. "Esen tried to convince all of us that we should tell Queen Xandra that Lightning Cape has a special blessing from triplets to twins and choreograph something ridiculous. Amval talked him down—he was the only one who could."

My chest aches. I crush the feeling. On the beach, Amval had only said that the four of them lazed around for another few hours. He also skipped the specifics of the card game. I've got no right to be mad that he would want to keep me out of these things. It's not like I want to be included. It's just interesting, watching Cirocco paint a portrait of sibling closeness where Amval sketched the outline of a prince's responsibilities.

"Did anyone visit?"

He shakes his head. "Amval and I went visiting, though. We paid our respects to the remaining lords, as well as Luna Maris, we spoke with people from Birchmint Valley, and shared a drink with the delegation from Lilywind."

"I thought I also saw you with Kash from Starfall Mountain." I didn't, but Amval mentioned him.

Cirocco's eyebrows shoot up. "Is *that* who the dirty guy was?"

I nod grimly. Candace's birth father may be helping to put Starfall Mountain back together, but he certainly hasn't returned to dressing —or bathing—like a prince.

Cirocco groans. "That would be why Amval was so polite. I thought he was just trying to build relationships. It's strange, trying to figure out whether we still have an alliance with a reborn kingdom. Mother and Father have been talking to everyone here, just in case."

Could that be why someone wanted him dead? I shove the thought aside. Information now, conclusions later.

"It sounds like Amval was himself all day," I say. "What about the name-blessing?"

"Normal." Cirocco jumps to his feet and starts pacing. "At no point did I notice anything out of the ordinary. He dressed like usual, talked like usual, laughed like usual. The strangest thing was—"

He stops dead. My heart skips a beat, and not just at the realization that I've heard my mate laugh and didn't even notice.

"What?" I ask breathlessly.

He glances at me, then away. "The strangest thing was Princess Candace introducing you. We aren't the sort of kingdom people usually go around introducing daughters to."

"She was desperate," I mutter before I can stop myself.

"She was right," Cirocco replies.

My mark burns in the silence between us. She was. Maybe she could smell it. And I guess I can't keep wishing she never introduced us so I wouldn't have anything else to remember.

I've spent a week working with Sash. A whole week of memories, where he lied and told the truth seemingly at random, just to mess with me.

No. To protect himself and his family, without any interest in how that might affect me.

"After that?" I ask again with a sandpaper voice that grates on my own ears.

Cirocco keeps his head down as he paces. Maybe he's trying to give me a little privacy. Maybe he's just watching his feet—the room is beautiful, but it's not exactly clean.

Finally, he says, "The Haze fell. I've been with him a few other times when this happened. The change is abrupt, but it's still him underneath. Just less restrained. I remember him laughing when he opened the window." Cirocco stops. "He said he thought that was the night. That he was going to find… you."

My heart thuds a painful rhythm against my ribcage. "He went out through the window?"

Cirocco nods. That's everything Amval told me. He poured his own drink when he met with Lilywind and didn't accept anything from Birchmint Valley. He didn't touch anything someone else didn't touch.

Except me.

"Did you see anything?" Cirocco asks urgently. "When he found you, was he ill? Erratic?"

"How would I know?" I shoot to my feet.

"You met him—"

"He seemed completely different." I have no reason to trust Cirocco, except that he probably doesn't know what his brother is doing. But they could have agreed on this lie ahead of time; they could have been in on it together from the beginning. I know that doesn't make any sense with the Beta's tears, but it's all I can think about right now. "Mostly, he seemed like a person, not a suit somebody blew hot air into."

Cirocco flinches. "You didn't know him."

"That's what I'm saying." My own words echo hollowly in my ears as I storm out of the room again.

That didn't prove anything. Why would it have? I can't trust anyone in this castle, except maybe Joli. There's no reason for them all to lie to me, but I can't count it out. Not when I spent a week working closely with my own mate and didn't notice a Goddess-damned thing.

The haunting melody of his ney echoes in my ears, and I barely resist the urge to smash them shut to avoid it. It was beautiful. Just like Amval himself. But being beautiful isn't enough.

I stalk back down to the apothecary. Maybe they know something else about the missing groom. Anything.

The door swings open as I approach, and I almost run face-first into Kaloni. She jumps out of the way just in time.

"Sorry!" She holds gloved hands up.

I shake my head. "What are you doing down here?"

She laughs self-consciously. "I help out sometimes. Sickness is easier than politics when things get hard."

Realization smacks me like a club to the back of the skull. Sickness is so much simpler than politics.

Why would someone poison a body to pretend to have a sickness and steal Amval away?

They wouldn't. They'd poison him—or they'd leave a sick body in his place–to convince everyone there was no murderer to find.

PACKING UP

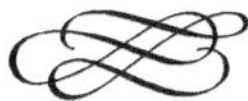

Amval

"ALL RIGHT." NUR CROSSES HER ARMS, STANDING BEFORE THE LINE OF us grooms. "I'm sure you are aware of why we're all here."

"Sadism," Tek hisses in my ear.

I smother a smile. My head pounds, a side effect of another night at the Gruesome Pony, but I'm growing used to the balance of our early mornings and Ozkan's strong, if noxious, ale.

Almost a week has passed since Ingrid discovered the truth. I've seen her in glimpses, here and there, but it seems as if she warned the guards about me. It has been much harder to get into the palace than it even was before.

Which means I have no access to the investigation into my own attempted murder and a head full of quite vivid memories of what my mate looks like on top of me, which I can do nothing about.

Frankly, it may be a miracle I didn't turn to drink sooner.

"The Festival of the First Wind is next week," Nur says. "And—"

"They're still going?" I blurt.

Nur shoots me a look. Tek elbows me. My head pounds in rhythm with my mark. Between that and the veil, I am losing all the skills my parents worked so hard to give me.

But the Festival of the First Wind is an old tradition, from long before King Gavin took over, and one we rediscovered while we were in hiding. In a tiny town called Kubilay, so far to the west some maps put it in Oakspring Dunes, they have a legend that the very first wind in Lightning Cape blew through there, a gift from the Goddess to drop early fruit from their roseapple trees. Ever since, we have made a tradition to return at the high point of the festival and celebrate with them.

I say *we*. In truth, one of the only memories I have of serious misbehavior as a child is, at perhaps six or seven, pitching an all-out tantrum and threatening to scream our names from the treetops unless we returned to Kubilay again. There was never a discussion after that, despite the danger.

"Apologies." I bow, hands clasped. "In the abbey, mourning periods are rather strict, so I was simply surprised to hear of the royal family traveling only three weeks after Prince Amval's death."

"Yes." Nur looks at me strangely. "Well, this is very important to them, and alas, we can't all be as pious as a starlight."

I bow again, clenching my hands tight. Tek rolls his eyes at me. For him, the moment is already forgotten.

I can only hope Nur is also so busy that she forgets before her weekly meeting with Mother and Father.

"They will need two grooms to travel with them. It's a day and a half's travel, so they won't need new horses, but there will be an overnight." She looks us all over. "Who volunteers?"

My hand twitches. I have been every year since I threw that fit. Last year, to celebrate our new ease and control over our kingdom, I went early and celebrated the whole week with the people there. I can smell the breezeloaves baking and see the roseapple blossoms dance in my mind's eye.

But my would-be murderer will likely stay here, as will Ingrid. And containing myself when my family arrives in the stables for a ride is hard enough; not taking their hands when the music starts will be virtually impossible.

Iltas raises his hand, and so does another groom I vaguely remember from last night. Tek shakes his head surreptitiously at them.

"I can't imagine volunteering for extra work," he whispers to me. "You're better off here."

I force myself to nod rather than change my mind and beg Nur to allow me to go on the trip.

THAT AFTERNOON, I AM SADDLING A HORSE WHEN NUR MIND-LINKS us all.

The king and queen are arriving to look over preparations. Whoever sees them first, bring them to me at the carriages.

My heart drops. I need to disappear. This stall is far too close to the entrance.

"Apologies." I bow to Lord Yetir. "I am needed elsewhere, but I'll be returning shortly."

"No." A frown adds another wrinkle to his aging face. "I need my daily ride *now*."

"Shortly, I swear." I hold my hands up as I back out of the stall. He has always been particular, more so since his fall last winter, and he has more than enough power to convince Nur I'm more trouble than I'm worth.

Would Ingrid speak to me if I needed her to save me from being fired? I can't think of another way to protect myself without telling Nur the—

I back directly into someone, and we both grunt. Before I even catch myself on the stable wall, I know who it is.

Father.

"I am so sorry." I spin around and bow as deeply as I dare, my eyes pinned on the ground. "Your Majesties, please forgive me."

"It's all well." Father claps me on the shoulder. "We are all a bit out of sorts these days."

My stomach churns around the half-mention of my death.

"Of course." I can hear Mother's smile in her voice—weaker than usual, but always soft for those who work in the palace.

I steal a glance out of the corner of my veil. Father's trouser-clad legs. Mother's umber skirts. No sign of a groom.

I should have stayed with Lord Yetir.

"May I lead you to Stablemaster Nur?" I ask through gritted teeth.

"I was hoping you would," Father says.

"Allow me to lead." I barely straighten before stepping in front of them both. The manure reek of the horses should hide my smell, and the angle hides my face. This deeper voice I've adopted grows easier to hold on to every day.

The only true threat I face is the throbbing in my chest begging me to reveal everything. Mother would cry. Father would cough to hide the fact that he was crying until we returned to the palace proper. They would have a feast the likes of which Lightning Cape has never seen before ready by tonight, and I would spend all the time in between playing half-cards with my siblings.

I would fall asleep tonight surrounded by my family, rather than strangers. I would have someone to talk to other than Tek who, for all his good qualities, mostly talks about work and ale.

I would stop lying.

"Son?" Father asks.

I jump. They've caught me, and I don't even know what I said. "What?"

"I asked how you came to us. I don't believe I've seen you around," he says.

I exhale slowly through my nose, reminding myself over and over again that Father calls all men younger than him around the palace "son."

"I escaped to Oakspring Dunes while the kingdom was overrun," I say. "And I returned as soon as I heard the true king had. Nur was gracious enough to give me work."

"I am so sorry," Mother says earnestly. "There are too many in the palace who had to abandon everything they loved."

"Far too many," I mutter.

If I told them everything, I would have to return to being a prince while knowing I lacked the spine to actually lead. I have a duty to my family and my people to keep my mouth shut.

Even Ingrid agrees.

"Rest assured we will do everything we can to keep that from ever happening again," Father says severely. "Princess Kaloni is going to be a wonderful queen someday."

The throbbing in my chest becomes something much more like a knife being twisted.

"I am sure she will." I stop in front of the door to the carriage half of the stables. "Stablemaster Nur awaits you."

"Thank you, son." Father nods to me, and both of them disappear inside.

"Could you finish saddling for Lord Yetir?" I ask Tek. *"Last night seems to have caught up with me."*

"Take all the time you need, brother."

THE WHOLE WEEK OF PREPARATIONS IS LIKE THAT OVER AND OVER AGAIN. Iltas and the other groom are mostly responsible for helping them, but they need additional hands often, and my awful habit of hovering nearby to catch glimpses of my family makes me the quickest option more than not.

Kaloni spends half a day organizing trunks due to another tradition—we try to ride all in one carriage, like we did in the backs of hay carts before. Everyone is intended to pack light to make this possible, but with one carriage still being cleaned after transporting "my" body, she can't get everything to fit. When she finally gives up, I want to grab her and pull her back. I don't have another way, but she can't let this lapse, too. Not on the very first trip without me.

My willpower is getting more exercise than it ever has before.

Liwar and Sibel practice their riding every day. There are usually a few small competitions as part of the festival, and the twins are particularly talented at the fancy footwork one requires. I saddle their horses and watch from a window, my hands clasped tightly so I don't cheer them on as if we are at the festival already.

Eser and Hova visit without Cirocco, and that is strange. The First Wind is a spring festival, which usually means pranks, and the three of them plan together more often than not. I help the two of them sneak a bag of supplies into one of Kaloni's perfectly packed carriages —I made sure a space remained after she left—and bite my tongue so I don't ask.

Mother and Father visit sporadically. Sometimes, it seems like they are making a point of seeking me out for a few minutes' conversation. They have so many questions; with each interaction, my lies balloon.

Cirocco stumbles down only once, looking like he hasn't slept since my funeral. He talks briefly with Nur. I am too far away to hear, but later, I learn he was telling her not to include his stallion among the horses brought. He doesn't intend to ride.

I spend the night after that staring at the ceiling, trying to convince myself that Cirocco could keep this secret. Everyone is strange, everyone is grieving, but the others seem to be trying to pull themselves back together more. Cirocco is drowning.

By dawn, I have to face the truth: there can be no exceptions. Whatever leniency I had was destroyed the moment Ingrid ripped off my veil.

The day before the caravan is scheduled to set off, Joli and Ingrid visit. There is no warning, but I know it's Joli by the trail of destruction she leaves in her wake. She loves to stir people up.

I intend to go the other way—but then I smell violets and ink. My mark revolts so violently that I have to follow.

"It's not my favorite, but it is fun," Joli says, running her finger along the edge of a carriage while Iltas loads yet another bag. "You should come if you want to."

"Why isn't it your favorite?" Ingrid asks.

My stomach clenches. Every night I've slept, I've dreamt of her.

Joli sighs. "Because it was Amval's. He loved it too much for anyone else to call it their favorite."

I shift, and something crunches underfoot. Ingrid tenses, turns her head half an inch. I close my eyes. Somehow, I know she knows I'm here.

"Maybe I will come," she says.

Some hot emotion slams through me, violent and soft at once. I can't place it until the two of them leave, until her smell fades from my nose.

I am desperately glad that Ingrid will get to see the Festival of First Wind, even just once.

FESTIVAL OF FIRST WIND

Ingrid

"I still don't understand," Joli says as we disembark in Kubilay.

I follow her gaze to Amval, who is unloading bags from one of the carriages. "I told you, I didn't trust the other groom. There is someone missing from the stables, and we don't know how that's related."

Joli shrugs. I bite my thumbnail. Talking to the stable master, getting him here—it was beyond stupid. I never should have done it. Every time I look at him, my blood boils. He lied to me for two weeks–intentionally.

And I caught him watching the two of us, looking like he'd give just about anything to stand beside us. Joli said this was his favorite festival.

I am a fool.

But at least this way, he can't be murdered while I'm halfway across the kingdom. For better or worse, if anything happens, I'll be right here.

"Do you smell that?" Cirocco asks as he piles out of the carriage.

I take a deep breath, and a fragile sort of sweetness fills my lungs. Sugar and some kind of fruit. It's mouthwatering.

"Breezeloaves." He scans the small town before us. "A cake made with the first roseapples, harvested slightly earlier before the festival. They'll be everywhere tonight."

"They were Amval's favorite." Kaloni blinks furiously.

My mark aches. I look across the lawn at Amval and watch him inhale slowly, deeply.

He meets my gaze. I look away.

"What should I expect from this festival?" I walk toward the little inn. King Iraj and Queen Zephira are already inside.

"It starts at sunset," Joli says.

Esen, one of the triplets, snorts. "It started at the beginning of the week. The party starts at sunset."

Joli shoves him. Kaloni smoothly inserts herself between the two, diffusing any further conflict before it can develop.

"There will be dancing," Kaloni says.

"And horse-riding competitions," Liwar chimes in from where she stands, brushing her mare.

"Pranks." Hova waggles his eyebrows.

"And food." Joli looks ecstatic at the prospect.

Cirocco nods. "More food than we have at the palace most nights."

"If there is dancing," I say slowly, "is there music?"

Kaloni takes my hand. "If you're interested in the music and the breezeloaves, you truly are Amval's perfect mate. He spent most years just eating and listening."

But not playing. I'm standing in the middle of a group of people who know him better than anyone else, who have years of stories and memories, and none of them have heard how he manipulates the ney like a master.

He lied—but in some ways, he trusted me more than he's ever trusted anyone else.

THAT EVENING, I PUT ON ONE OF MY FAVORITE GOWNS. JOLI SAID THE event was muddy, so I might want to be careful about what I wear, but something in the air here is infectious. Every person I've met has grinned at me and chatted like we were old friends. There's no stiff formality. No stuffy politeness. Even King Iraj and Queen Zephira seem more relaxed here.

So I don the elaborate gold gown Candace always says makes me shine. If I stain the hem, I'll have something to talk about at the balls I wear it to afterward. I even convinced Joli to join me in dressing up. She looks wonderful in a sapphire-blue piece I brought on a whim.

When I exit the inn with the rest of the Soms, the first thing I notice is the music. Light, floating, playful. It begs me to come dance, to move quickly and become the wind the whole festival celebrates.

In the shadows of the inn's eaves, I spot Amval. Watching. Wishing.

"Come with us, Sash," I call.

His eyebrows shoot up. "You are too kind. I—"

I loop my arm through his, drunk on the excitement of the night. "I need someone to carry all the prizes I intend to win in these competitions."

King Iraj laughs. "It's a festival for all, son. Please join us."

Amval swallows loudly, audible only to me over the music. "Thank you, Your Majesty."

The reunited Som family—and I—follow the music to the center of the little town.

Apparently, Kubilay pulls out all the stops for this festival. Joli mentioned some crown funds finding their way to help pay for it, and I can see them here and there, but what really catches my eye are the details money couldn't buy. A space that is clearly usually some kind of market has been emptied of everything but tables, a bandstand, and a few booths for competitions. A horse track—standing room only— sits off to one side, and the occasional cheers puncture the music like another instrument. People spin through the center of the space, dancing from one partner to another in complicated patterns I itch to learn.

And everyone is smiling or laughing. After the last three weeks in the castle, that feels like the most dramatic change of all.

"Alpha Iraj!" An older woman grabs the king's hand and bows over it. "We were so devastated to learn of Prince Amval."

The party atmosphere turns maudlin. Amval stares at the ground.

King Iraj sighs. "Tonight, Alev, I intend to celebrate like my son would have."

Alev offers him a watery smile. "We all thought that was what he would have wanted. I would like to show you what we've done."

The parade of us troops after her, through the festival space. Eyes cling to us. Judging by how she grabbed the king, the Soms are treated differently here than anywhere else in their kingdom, but they're still royalty.

Alev leads us to a corner where the music is slightly softer and gestures to a covered form. "He loves the Festival of First Wind so much that we were already at work on this, intending to reveal it for his… his coronation."

She tugs the sheet off, and a statue of Amval, clearly only half-finished, is revealed. Everyone gasps, which seems to cover the choked sound Amval himself makes.

I lean into Joli and whisper, "Why is it full of holes?"

She sniffles. "That's how they know it's time for the First Wind. It's not the same day every year—when the statue sings, they start preparations."

Amval's grasp on my arm tightens, and I realize what kind of honor this is. If I didn't, the heartfelt hug King Iraj and Queen Zephira both offer Alev would clarify. He'll stand forever, a harbinger of this festival he loves.

Making music like he has never been allowed to.

"We'll unveil it to everyone tonight." Alev laughs wetly. "Though it's been an open secret for a while."

"It is lovely." Queen Zephira keeps staring at it, like she's re-memorizing the craggy outline of her son's face. "Thank you."

Fuck, it's hard to know she could see the real thing. Amval has iron self-control.

But I'm still angry. He chose to make it so much harder for me than it had to be.

Still, maybe it's not the worst thing in the world to have brought him here.

After a few more thank-yous, Alev brings us back to the main festival, and the family splits up. Liwar and Sibel hurry off to the horses. I didn't realize the competitive riding they've been practicing also happens at night, but they seem giggly and excited. Esen and Hova disappear with mischievous smiles. King Iraj whisks Queen Zephira into the dancing. Kaloni sees a friend and wanders off to talk.

"What do you usually do?" I ask Joli and Cirocco.

"Get into whatever trouble I can find." Joli grins. "I like to keep people on their toes."

Cirocco looks tiredly around the festival. He's the only one the mood seems not to be touching. "Amval and I usually do all the small competitions first, then ride. But—"

"But nothing." I loop my other arm through Cirocco's and gesture for Joli to do the same. Amval clings to me like a life raft. "I promised I needed a set of hands to carry my prizes—I have to compete!"

Roseapple ale flows freely as we float from one booth to the next. I catapult small sandbags into buckets with a heavy mallet, land metal rings around the mouths of bottles, and attempt to break pottery with a slingshot. Joli is awful at anything that requires a shred of strength, but she kicks my ass in accuracy. Cirocco takes his time, evaluates each game, and inevitably beats both of us. Even if he hadn't said he does this every year, I would know.

At each booth, Amval stands to the side, waiting to accept our various winnings. Baskets of roseapples, small ribbons or lengths of lace, one sandbag sewn in the shape of a frog that Joli technically wins but I find so incredible that she says I can have it. He doesn't say a word, just takes them.

But he should really remember that his veil only hides most of his face—his eyes scream how much he wants to be involved.

We step up to a booth where those with wind powers race tiny ships down lanes of water, and Cirocco pauses.

"What?" I ask.

"This was his favorite," he says quietly.

The person running the booth, a man with a farmer's build, kisses his fingers to the sky in a gesture of respect and grief. He obviously remembers Amval, too.

"You heard Father," Joli says. "We're supposed to be celebrating in his honor."

Cirocco shakes his head. "I can't. Not this one."

Amval crumples, and I grab Cirocco's arm. "Please? I want to play it, if he liked it so much."

"You need wind powers," he says dully.

An idea strikes. "Sash? Do you have control of the wind?"

Stiffly, he nods.

"All right, then," I say. "Sash will compete for me."

"I don't know…." Cirocco turns away from the tiny ships.

"I am half of him, right?" I meet his gaze. "So play with him one last time."

Cirocco stares at me. "I wish I could've seen the two of you together."

Me, too. I push Cirocco forward, then grab Amval. He looks at me with wide eyes, begging to know what I'm thinking.

Well, he'll just have to get used to not having all the information he wants.

The farmer running the booth blows his whistle, and all three Soms pour wind into the tiny sails. Joli clearly isn't quite as strong as the other two, so she quickly starts stealing their wind rather than making her own. They complain, jostle, laugh. The layers of Sash fall away from Amval, and he just looks like a man with his siblings.

My chest aches. I haven't been with all my siblings in a long time—and I don't know if we ever looked like that with each other.

Cirocco and Amval are neck-and-neck at the finish line. Amval starts to edge ahead, then darts a gaze at his brother, and his hands slow.

"Ha!" Cirocco shouts as he crosses the string at the end of the lane first.

Amval bows. "Very good work, Your Highness."

"Uh, yeah. You—you were good, too." Cirocco rubs the back of his neck awkwardly, but he still grins when the farmer hands him a stein and Joli tries to steal it from him.

Several booths later, when Amval has fallen behind with the weight of the prizes the four of us have won, I slow to make sure we don't lose him in the crowd. The later it gets, the more I can smell the ale and see its influence. The last thing either of us needs is some rowdy festival-goer knocking his veil off.

"Thank you," he murmurs.

"Don't mention it," I reply.

SEPARATE CARRIAGES

Amval

THE DAY AFTER THE FESTIVAL OF FIRST WIND, I WAKE WITH A SMILE ON my face for the first time in a long time. I was right. Coming here was painful—until Ingrid intervened. Sailing those ridiculous little boats made me feel the most like myself that I have since waking up in Yalim's cart, and she didn't even stop after that. I bit into the breeze-loaf Esen and Hova managed to switch with an extremely convincing replica made of clay. I cheered Liwar and Sibel to the finish line, even though someone from Kubilay actually won in the end. Joli asked me to help her sneak the clay loaf back onto Esen or Hova's plate, convincing them to fall for their own prank.

And I danced. For hours and hours, my feet lighter than air but still not lighter than the music. Even Ingrid spun through my grasp.

"I usually hate dancing," she confessed, "and parties."

I didn't ask what made this one different. I already know. Kubilay —First Wind—it's special. She fit in just as well as a princess in a mud-spattered gown as we did the first time we wandered into town, a starving family of eight. Alev let us stay at her inn that first year, and she promised she would do it again every time we arrived.

She kept that promise.

After Iltas and I are done readying the carriages, I wander over to the wind statue Alev showed my family last night. Even unfinished, it makes my chest ache.

"I figured I'd find you here," Ingrid says.

"I thought you were too angry to speak to me," I reply. After a whole week of silence, her behavior last night was shocking.

She snorts. "I am. But I'm not too angry to let you get yourself caught for sentimental reasons. Come on."

"Not yet," I say. "I can't visit my memorial chamber, but I could just be admiring the craftsmanship of this."

"Memorial?" She raises an eyebrow.

"What else would this be?" I gesture to it. "A memorial to a life barely lived."

"Goddess above, I know you're dead, but do you have to be so macabre?" She crosses her arms. "They made this because you love this festival, and they love that you do. Not everything is about your legacy."

A statue like this will stand for generations, be its own legacy— but as soon as she says it, I see what she means. Love shines out of every half-chiseled feature and crevice. I didn't have to do anything special, be anything special. In many ways, I wasn't when we first arrived. We didn't tell Alev who we truly were for five years, at least.

I simply loved a tiny festival at the edge of the kingdom.

"Come on." I turn and start walking toward the inn. "I've seen all I need."

We return to the inn, and everyone slowly wakes. After an easy breakfast, we begin loading up to leave.

Despite everyone's best efforts, the family rides home in two separate carriages as well. Mother and Father take the front one, crowded with bags and supplies. Father insists that they need some alone time in a way that makes Joli faux-retch until they leave. I can tell by the way they cling to each other's hands that I am not the only one thinking about the wind statue this morning.

The rest of my siblings and Ingrid pile into the other carriage, the one I will be driving. They barely fit—it takes Kaloni and I working together to squeeze the door shut—but nobody complains. I climb up onto the high front bench and urge the horses to a trot.

The window between the carriage and my bench slides open.

"Sash, Hova doesn't believe that you nearly beat Cirocco at the boats," Joli yells.

"I wouldn't say nearly." I smile at the dirt road ahead, knowing I could have beaten him like usual if I wanted to.

"Can starlights be falsely modest?" Ingrid calls from farther away. "Or is that against the rules?"

"Hey, I won fair and square," Cirocco protests.

"Yes, Your Highness."

"It was close!" Joli insists. "I think his talents might be wasted on groom-hood."

"He should sail tiny boats instead?" Hova laughs.

"Come now," Kaloni says soothingly. "I'm sure he acquitted himself admirably and that Cirocco won. Let's leave him to his work."

"You honor me, Your Highness," I say, my hands tight on the reins. "But I truly don't mind the conversation. The way is easy and the horses obedient."

"And I thought I almost heard him make a joke last night," Ingrid adds. "After this ride, we might just convince one out of him."

"I agreed to take the window seat," Joli decrees, "and I say it stays open."

After a few grumbles of assent, Liwar asks if I can play cards while driving a carriage, and only Kaloni's quick reply laying out exactly how dangerous that would be, keeps me from saying yes.

THE FIRST DAY OF THE RIDE HOME DISAPPEARS IN LONG STRETCHES OF flat road and laughing with my family. I wish I could see any of them, read their responses in their faces, but this is as close as I can get without risking everything.

After a few salvos by Ingrid to draw me in, the others start doing so automatically. Not a topic passes without my opinion being asked. Sash's backstory grows and grows—I spend the hour after everyone else goes to sleep scribbling notes on what I've said so I don't contradict myself. Even still, I have to talk less than I normally would. They may not have recognized my voice yet, but the more I talk, the bigger the threat.

And it still may be the pleasantest drive I've ever taken, despite the hard bench and the jostling of these back roads. On the second day, everyone takes to the same carriages instinctively, the window slides open, and the careful balancing act of how much I miss them and how much I need to protect them begins again. At least there are only a few hours of driving left.

After, I will talk to Ingrid, trying to understand what she is actually thinking. What she's learned. What we are in the aftermath of the truth coming out. I respect her wishes, but they are becoming far less clear, and I miss her almost as much as I miss my family.

"Well, Sash?" Esen says around midmorning. "Do you think the breezeloaves are as good the next day?"

"As good?" I laugh. "Certainly not. But it takes several days of staleness before a breezeloaf isn't still superior to any other cake."

"Oh, you sound like Amval," Liwar complains. "He ate them until they were almost as hard as Esen's clay."

"No, I think he's right," Ingrid says quickly, covering my potential slip. "I don't tend to like sweets, but they really were spectacular."

"Of course, you do," Kaloni says. "You remind me more and more of him, the better I know you."

"Look," I say. "You can see Som Palace on the horizon."

That quiets all discussion of how much Ingrid or I remind my siblings of myself as everyone crowds to the larger windows on the side of the carriage. The first sight of home is another tradition— every time we passed close enough to the palace in our travels, Mother and Father would always point out the shape on the horizon and tell us that was our true home. We weren't homeless—we were just waiting to return.

Which means everyone is watching when the horses attached to the carriage in front of us—Mother and Father's carriage—suddenly rear.

"Hey!" Iltas yells.

One horse bolts left, the other right. He clearly manages to emergency release one of them, as that one charges off toward the woods, but he can't reach the other in time. Wood screeches as the carriage swings into a sharp right turn—too fast. Far too fast. Iltas's yelling turns to wordless alarm as time seems to slow.

A large, jagged rock crouches on the side of the road. The horse dodges it. The carriage lacks the same mobility.

It tips.

Time explodes back into place with the sound of shattering wood. One of my siblings screams. I don't know what spooked the other horses, but I rein in the ones attached to my carriage sharply. They stop, obedient.

Like the horses on Mother and Father's carriage should have been.

"Stay here." I vault off the bench and sprint across the road. The carriage lays in splinters, but that doesn't mean anything. They could be fine or hurt but trapped.

When I reach the wreck, it's silent. My heart pounds in my throat. I drop to my knees and begin tearing through the destroyed wood. Perhaps they're unconscious. Perhaps this is some kind of elaborate prank, even though neither of them have ever played so much as a minor one before. My skin shreds, and I collect splinter after splinter, but I don't slow down.

They need me. There isn't time to slow down.

I find Iltas first, under a trunk of Kaloni's dresses. Any questions I have about him are answered when I shift the trunk and discover he's not lying on his back, but lying on his stomach, with his head twisted all the way around to stare at me with horrified eyes. My stomach lurches, and I shut his eyes.

He was the least protected. They may still be all right.

I cling to that thought until I find Mother with a spoke from one of the wheels stabbed through her gut like a spear. Frantically, I brush the hair away from her face and study her.

There is one last hope—that Mother and Father may also have been swapped for lookalikes and taken away to be murdered elsewhere. I'm not sure how that could have happened while they were in front of us, but someone snuck a corpse into my mate's arms. Anything is possible.

A bruise purples half the woman's face, and her hair is stained with blood. She has dark eyes, like Mother. They could have done a better job finding doubles, knowing that this "murder" would be more closely observed.

So I tug aside the shoulder of her dress, looking for the only sign they couldn't fake.

On the top ridge of her shoulder, as it always has, sits a lightning-shaped mark turned almost maroon by a splotchy birthmark she had there all her life.

Bile scorches my throat. I close her eyes and turn away while my insides scream. Perhaps I've lost her, but Father—

Father lays in a puddle of blood and gray matter, his head half-caved in by the rock that knocked the carriage off course. I check his mark with shaking fingers, but it already feels useless.

My parents are dead.

And I have to tell my siblings—who think I'm a stranger—that we are alone in the world.

CROSSING THE LINE

Ingrid

J OLI CLINGS TO MY HAND SO TIGHTLY, I CAN FEEL MY BONES GRINDING against each other. Like the rest of her siblings, she alternates between craning toward the window and flinching away.

"Do you think we should go?" Cirocco asks no one in particular.

"It is safer in here," Kaloni answers flatly.

Safer from what? Whatever spooked the horses? But it isn't my place to argue. Even with Joli holding onto me, I'm the obvious outsider here.

Me, and as far as they're away, Sash.

Wood crashes outside, and Sibel flinches. How long can he actually tear through this wreckage for? What hasn't he seen?

As soon as I think that, I realize that he's making sure that, if there are bodies, they are truly his parents'.

Ice trickles down my spine. It looked like an accident—but could this be more of the same monster who attempted to murder him?

"He's coming back," Hova whispers.

I glance out the window at Amval. Shoulders slumped, head low, no person leaning heavily on him while they walk away from the wreck together. Joli's grip on my hand tightens. Everyone knows what this means.

Abruptly, I remember finding Candace in the front hall of Kar Castle a few years ago. She was smeared in blood and leaning heavily on Eva. Both of them looked like they'd been crying.

And when I asked if she'd seen Mother, this same silence fell.

Amval stops outside the carriage. He doesn't even reach to open the door. "I'm sorry."

That's all the siblings need. Kaloni bursts into sobs. Joli drops her head onto my shoulder to shed her own silent tears.

"How sure are you?" Cirocco asks.

"Yes." Hova claps his brother on the shoulder. "We want to see for ourselves. I've worked in the apothecary."

"And I have seen enough bodies." Amval's voice rings with certainty. "Trust me when I say that the greatest favor I can do for you right now is keeping you in this carriage."

Kaloni's sobs grow louder, echoing the grief that tore through what should have been the first morning I spent together with Amval. He doesn't look at her. He doesn't look at any of them.

At least when Candace told me what happened to Mother, we both knew what the news meant to each other.

Somehow, Amval hauls himself back onto the front bench, and we limp the rest of the way back to the palace in silence. They've lost three family members—to the best of their knowledge—in the past month. And I thought losing Mother and Father in a single year, even with my relationship to them, was hard. I can't think of anything to say to make this pain easier for any of them.

We arrive in the courtyard of Som Palace, and Kaloni, still tear-soaked, climbs out first. "I want a team of healers sent to a specific location."

Amval climbs down. "Your Highness—"

"Healers." Kaloni swallows. "And a few soldiers. Ones strong enough to carry… bodies."

Whispers flood the courtyard. More than a few people look up at the funeral colors still flying from the deep blue walls.

But Sahin, King Iraj's Beta—former Beta—starts barking orders, putting together a team without hesitation. The rest of the Som siblings climb out of the carriage slowly. Joli drops that frog-shaped sandbag, and picking it up feels like an insult right now. Even a carriage wheel rolls over it, and the whole thing pops.

That seems like a better summary of the trip than anything I could ever come up with.

The siblings move off in a pack, circling around each other like they always seem to. Planets in their own little orbits. I don't think Joli even notices that she's not holding my hand anymore.

Amval, on the other hand, is immediately pulled in by Sahin and the rest of the planning. Questions snap at him from all angles—what happened? Where do they need to go? Did he see the bodies? He answers them with his chin held high and his eyes on the dirt. Something in his shoulders reminds me of the first night I met him. A prince, carrying out his duty.

But no one else is going to see that. At best, they'll see a diligent servant.

Sahin declares Amval will lead the way to the crash site, and I watch Amval choke down some reaction.

At least I didn't have to find Mother's body.

That thought rings in my head as I watch the rescue party leave. As I stumble back into my room and stare blankly at the board covered in my notes. As I listen to the siblings cry down the hall.

So when curfew falls, somehow more strictly despite the king and queen's absence, I get up.

Goddess above, I was so mad at Candace for going after Hollis. He didn't deserve it, and I believe that to this day. But I understand why she gave him that chance now.

My mark throbs like a second heartbeat, murmuring that yes, he lied. Yes, he hurt me. But he had his reasons. He loved his family more

—and, hell, would I have really chosen a mystery mate over any of my siblings if they were in danger? I can see why he did it.

And he's alone right now.

That doesn't make me any less mad at myself, though.

I creep to the window of the stable's bunkhouse and chuck a crumpled piece of paper through. I hear a grumble, and the smell of basil and charcoal intensifies as he rouses from his blankets. I turn and sprint back to the tiny room where I stayed for my first few days in Som Palace, leaving the door open so he can follow.

I can tell he wasn't asleep when he arrives. The whites of his eyes are red, and his skin is puffy.

He was crying.

"Sit." I nod to the bed from the chair I'm perched on.

"Are you intending to yell at me for something?" he asks tiredly. "Because if so, I'd rather stare at a stained mattress."

"No, I—" What? Why the hell did I drag him here? What can I say to make this better? "I didn't want you to be alone tonight."

"Oh." He closes the door behind him, sits on the triangular bed, and pulls off his veil. The stains of exhaustion are even more obvious without it. His lips are chapped from the cliffside wind, and stubble peppers his cheeks.

"How are you feeling?" I can hear Candace laughing at me.

And Amval, much more bitterly. "Splendid, as you might guess."

"That was almost a joke." I offer him a thin smile.

"I am glad this was all it took to unlock my humor." He stares at his hands, not seeing them.

What did he see today?

Even I'm not stupid enough to ask that question.

"I held a private funeral for my mother," I blurt.

Amval raises his eyebrows.

"I know." I chew on my thumbnail, even though that feels doubly insulting while talking about her. "But after the fighting in Snowcrest Canyon, they had a group funeral for 'the fallen,' and the whole thing was about lives given honorably, finding a new future together, that kind of bullshit. She would've hated it."

"But Rowena—"

"Was a monster." I certainly don't need him to tell me that. "Anyone who grew up in my family knows it better than you could dream to know it."

He holds up his hands defensively. "I only know what you said about Gavin."

"I don't know if I loved him." My voice breaks, and I shake my head. "That's off-topic. I held a private funeral for my mother because no one else was going to."

"It's not like my parents won't have a funeral." Amval's voice is acid. "I just won't be invited. I'll have to watch from the outside, just like I watched my own. I'll have to sneak around in the dark to place anything in their memorial chamber, and I won't get to leave the things I want to leave most because those are sealed in a bedroom that is no longer mine."

I lurch up out of my chair and grab one of his hands. "You can't grieve them the way you should be able to. As your parents."

He exhales sharply as he sees the connection I'm making. "It's not the same."

"I'm not saying it is." I run my thumb over his hand and find fresh calluses, ones I don't remember from our night together, what seems like a thousand years ago now. "My sister Candace always says the best way to understand people is to find the place where you relate to them."

He looks past me, amber eyes distant.

"All right. Fine. You are the only person in the world who has ever had this experience, and I was wrong to compare anything." I drop his hand.

He reaches back, hesitates. "I didn't mean—"

"You meant that you want to bury heroes, and that can never be the same as burying monsters." Why am I surprised? I knew this was stupid. Candace got lucky with Hollis. She arrived right when he was willing to change. I arrived right when Amval's parents died. "You know, I don't even think the person who tried to kill you was copying my mother. I think they wanted your death to look like—"

"It was natural." He exhales sharply. "Which means Mother and Father could well be the next victims."

My temper boils beneath my skin. "I said I was going to solve this without you. If you don't want to hear from me, you can just go."

He brushes his fingers over the back of my wrist. The tiny gesture tingles up my arm, all the way to the mark over my heart. I grit my teeth. No one else knows about the funeral I held for Mother, and no one ever should have.

"I'm sorry," he says. "I was just—"

"Lonely," I finish. "So painfully, soul-destroyingly lonely that it seems like you're the only person even grieving."

"Yes. And that is its own form of monstrousness."

I turn slowly to face him. His eyes shine with unshed tears, and his hands are white-knuckled fists at his sides.

"I don't think so," I say.

He laughs bitterly.

"You want to talk about monstrousness? I took a hair comb she gave me out into the woods after we got home," I say. "I buried it in the most beautiful place I could find and said all the right blessings. A woman who abused both my sisters, contributed to the murder of hundreds, if not thousands. That's who I was missing."

"She was your mother. She—loved you."

"She did." The words burn like alcohol, painful and sweet. I haven't said them in a long time. "And you're angry that you can't grieve your parents properly. So, does wanting, feeling the 'wrong' thing make us evil?"

He looks away. "My siblings are in so much pain."

I cup his face, pull his gaze back to mine. "So are you."

It's hard to say who moves first. All I know is that, when his lips meet mine, I don't pull away.

LIFE AND DEATH

Amval

I KNEW I MISSED INGRID. I DIDN'T KNOW HOW MUCH UNTIL OUR mouths meet, and my whole body lights up. I groan softly against her lips, grabbing at her waist. She threads her fingers through my hair.

"Damn," she mumbles.

My chest lights. Everything she was saying echoes in my head. Wanting the wrong things, finding ways to solve this with and without each other—with her hands on me, all the rules I've lived my life by seem so ridiculous. And it's no mistake that she keeps reaching out. When I lick along the seam of her lips and she opens for me, I know what's going to happen next.

We'll solve this together. Hunt down the specter haunting my family and bring them to justice. She won't stop until we do—and neither will I.

Her tongue sweeps into my mouth. The taste of violets and ink, of new growth and beginnings, intensifies. I open, and she presses her tongue deeper. Every breath she takes rings in my ears.

When my breath rasps in my lungs, I pull back. Ingrid's blue eyes light with hungry fire, and she reaches for my head to pull me back in.

With a smile, I dance back a step. "This time, I want to do this right."

We've crashed together and fallen apart enough times. Right now, I don't want the chaos, the craziness of my last month. I want to at least pretend this isn't just another night for me to dream about.

"I think things were going pretty well," she grumbles.

But when I strip off my shirt and lay on the tiny, triangular bed, she looks me up and down like I'm a buffet. Want roars through me.

She licks her lips and climbs on top of me. I stroke her silken hair as she kisses down the side of my face and across my jaw. She drops a soft kiss on my lips, and I twist to press my lips to Ingrid's neck. Her pulse flutters a drumbeat against my lips. I suck on it, graze my teeth over it. She hisses, and my smile only grows.

Today—every day since I woke up in Yalim's cart—has been about death. The Festival of First Wind, though, is about life. About the fact that it persists, no matter how dark things seem, but that it may not always arrive in the form one expects.

Ingrid is the exact same way. Volatile, challenging, never exactly what I anticipate—but so Goddess-damned alive I feel drunk on it sometimes. *Does wanting the wrong thing make us evil?* There are so many things I haven't allowed myself to want, and she wants all of them unflinchingly.

In the wake of all this death, I need a little life, and I love that it comes to me through Ingrid.

I love her.

The thought creeps in on quiet feet, like a cat looking to steal a little affection while it thinks no one will notice. It doesn't scare me. Honestly, it doesn't even surprise me.

I can't imagine how the whole world didn't fall in love with Ingrid Solberg before I got the chance to.

With a hum, I suck a kiss against her throat. She hums back in perfect harmony and then drags her nails down my bare chest. Bright lines of pain meld with the ache in my cock, and I groan.

She smiles softly down at me, a better relief to the pain than any other I could have imagined. I never realized how well she knows me. She repeats the scratching, and I melt like hot butter.

Instinct surges. I seize her moment of distraction and flip us over, knocking my head into the too-close wall as I do. Ingrid giggles like a wind chime as I rub the bump. I bend to drink the song from her lips.

My cock presses into her thigh, harder than before. She threads her hands into my dark hair and pulls me closer. Our mouths crush together, and our tongues dance like the music we made together. I can feel her moves before she makes them. Her fingers twitch, and her lips twist into a shape I half-recognize as a smile.

She's planning something.

Tonight, I strike first.

I pull the neck of her dress down to reveal her breasts. She gasps, but the unmistakable sound of ripping fabric still fills the room.

"You ripped my dress," she says.

"You kept it on." I trace her nipple with one finger.

"If you asked, I would've—"

Once one has made a choice, it can't be unmade. I grab either side of the split fabric and pull, baring her chest completely. She opens her mouth to object, but I press my lips to the newly visible skin, and her complaint turns into a moan. I concur. The taste of Ingrid's bare skin almost overwhelms me after our time apart and the day I've had. Grief burns like poison in the back of my skull, and I trace a promise onto her chest.

Together, we'll fix this problem, and every other that comes our way, for the rest of our lives.

I don't know if she can read the words, but she certainly arches up into me, grabbing at me hungrily. Pleasure jets through my veins, a strong and growing substance.

She moans into a pillow beneath her head.

"No," I pant. "We've been too quiet. I want to hear you."

She picks her head up and meets my gaze, blue eyes burning. I feel pinned in the air, splayed open like a butterfly. Ingrid can read all the dangerous thoughts I'm thinking on my uncovered face; I know it.

And I intend to make the most of the moment before that frightens her. I suck a nipple into my mouth, flick my tongue over it, and drink in her loud, answering moan. The low string of curse words she looses when I drag a hand down to her unruined skirt spears through me. She is impossibly wet, and I have to have her.

With a few fumbling gestures, we work her out of her skirt. It falls somewhere on the floor, and I can't be fucked to wonder where, especially when she starts pulling at my pants. One moan oozes into the next, and we are naked together. Properly. In a bed, safe and comfortable as we can be.

Perhaps I keep hitting my head on the wall, but that just makes the moment real. Death can be perfect, as the memorial chambers so often show. Life, though, is always just off.

Ingrid's wetness slicks my thigh. I breathe in the sweet scent of her. Perfect.

She surges into a kiss and latches her teeth around my lower lip. The pain sizzles as she sucks and nips. I wrap a leg around her waist, and my throbbing cock slides against her center.

"Ingrid," I groan.

Awash in sensation, I just rock with her for a long moment. It would be so easy to fit myself into position, end this moment with climactic pleasure, but just lying here with her underneath me feels miraculous.

She seems to have no such concerns. Ingrid abandons my mouth for a line of teasing bites along my neck. I dig my nails into her shoulders, and she drags her tongue down my body, sweeping over my collarbone and the top of my chest. All I can do is moan and hold on. Every muscle aches like the day after a run, the burn that promises everything I did was worth it. I want to live in this feeling forever.

I need her here with me.

My knuckles knock into hers, and I laugh when I realize we both reached down to line my cock up with her wetness at once. She smiles against my collarbone and threads her fingers through mine. Awkwardly, hand in hand, we position my cock.

I slide into the warmth of her. She moans, loud and long. I bury my neck in her throat, nearly mirroring the position of my mark. Her flavor bursts under my tongue as I fuck her.

Slowly. Very slowly. I want to make this moment last, take as long as it needs to take. Ingrid bites me slightly harder at the end of a particularly slow thrust, a silent bid for speed.

Death is slow. Life is fast and messy.

And I want the mess.

My thrusts race in time with her drumming heart, the bed groaning along with her. I grab every inch of her that I can reach, just needing to touch, to feel. My breath puffs harshly against the sweat-soaked skin of her chest. Our fingers dance messily over her clit, pushing her higher and higher. Every sound she makes drives me a little wilder.

With a sound more like a scream, she explodes first, shaking apart. Watching her face twist with pleasure is all I need. The euphoria is absolute, so all-consuming I can't feel anything but her for long, rippling moments.

I don't want to, even if I could.

CHANGES

Ingrid

By the time we roll off each other and don't just reach for each other again, dawn is reaching hungry fingers through the window. Amval falls right to sleep, snoring slightly. I stare at him.

I can only see Sash, peeking through the eye slit in his star-patterned veil. My stomach churns.

He was lonely, I remind myself. And grieving, and he needed someone, and I was the only one he could have.

And none of that means I had to sleep with him again. I've comforted a number of people in my life with all my clothes on.

I roll out of bed. No matter what he thinks, this doesn't change… much of anything between us. But if he wakes up, and I'm still here, I honestly wouldn't blame him for assuming it did. I have to go.

I gather up my clothes, cursing under my breath when I find my ruined bodice. A few maid uniforms still hang in the closet here, so I slide one on, then pull my not-ruined skirt over it, so at least anyone who sees me might not immediately recognize the shape. With everything else clutched in my hands, I creep out of the room.

Staff members already rush back and forth through the halls. Maybe I should have skipped the skirt and just tried to blend in. As is, navigating the crush is a lot like swimming upstream. Blearily, I wonder why everyone is so panicked.

Of course. The fucking funeral. And, I realize as a cook sprints past with an ancient cake recipe book, the coronation. Lightning Cape is officially leaderless.

I duck my head and hurry as fast as I can to my room. Maybe the Soms will still have the wagons circled, but if they come looking for me, I can't be missing.

As Kaloni's door opens, I scoot inside mine and slam it behind me, then lean against it, panting. She's probably not looking for me. She certainly won't be able to tell where I spent the night—

Three knocks rattle the back of my skull.

"Shit." I wriggle out of my clothes as fast as I can and cover my mouth with one hand. "One moment! I'm just getting up."

Does that make me sound like I'm further away or just drunk? I know Amval said it did one, but I'm not sure which anymore.

"All right," Kaloni says.

It seems like it doesn't matter. I shed clothes like autumn leaves and then seize a robe I left laying over a nearby chair and scramble into it. At least I don't have to worry about mussing my hair.

I yank the door open and meet the exhausted, tear-stained gaze of my mate's sister.

"I am sorry for waking you," she says. "I wouldn't have if I didn't have to."

"What do you need?" I pull the robe tighter and tie it in place. She won't be able to smell him. There's no way.

She glances over her shoulder at the chaos. Even in a hall of nothing but bedrooms, I can still see it. "The palace is a bit hectic this morning. And, as you may expect, the majority of my siblings are in no position to help me."

My head pounds. So does my mark. I want nothing more than to climb into bed and catch up on the sleep I didn't get last night.

"You've been a great help to our family already," she says. "Can I count on you again?"

No. The word tastes so sweet on my tongue, like freedom and peace. I remember Kieran and Raven's coronation; they insisted on a simple ceremony, and it still took all six of us a week straight of running around to pull it all together.

Lighting Cape is not as destroyed as Dun's Crossing was at the time, but this isn't my kingdom. These aren't my people.

"I'm not sure I know enough to be much help," I hedge.

Kaloni breaks into a wide smile, and I know I've fucked up somehow. "Oh, I wouldn't put you in charge of anything as politically tense as the reception seating or complicated as the coronation ceremony. Just simple tasks, the sorts of things I'm sure you were trained to do."

"I really didn't receive all the standard princess training you're imagining," I say. "For that, you want Candace."

"Oh," she says softly.

Shit. She's grieving—she's probably stressed beyond the breaking point, and I've just made her life so much harder. "I—"

"You don't have to explain." She puts her hand on my shoulder. "I should have realized. This is too soon after Amval's death. And, even though you didn't know them that long, I could tell you were growing to love my parents as well."

"Right." I'll take any excuse she'll give me at this point. My bed is singing for me.

"We truly are sisters." She offers me a misty smile. "All the political intricacies aside, that is why I need you."

Well, what the hell am I supposed to say to that? "Just give me a minute, and I'll get dressed."

KALONI IS RIGHT ABOUT ONE THING—SHE DOESN'T NEED ME FOR THE political portion. I spend the day more or less as her assistant. I take notes on two or three dozen different conversations. Everyone from florists to healers to holy women seems to need her attention, and she knows exactly why every single one of them is showing up.

Honestly, it's hard to see the girl I had to save when she found Amval's body in the woman marching through Som Palace now. It's hard to believe she wasn't raised to lead right alongside Amval. Maybe she was. Like I said, I don't know much about Lightning Cape's traditions. But she has almost everything a queen needs already, down to the walk. I just scuttle along in her shadow.

That's not fair. She does need me. It turns out the funeral and the coronation have to be exactly one day apart, to the minute, which means there's a lot to organize. She asks me for the notes I'm taking constantly, and she leaves me to handle a few groups of staff—because she's noticed I'm so good with them—while she takes more private meetings, like those with the holy woman. I even convince the chef, Umit, that she can use the leftovers from the funerary meal to make an incredible soup for the coronation.

But mostly, it's a little like I imagine being close to Estrella in the days after King Isai was murdered. Kaloni needs to look to the world like she has everything under control while her life falls apart around her. She's less self-effacing, more... just more royal than she was before with everyone, even me. It's hard to like her, even though it's impressive.

The other Som siblings straggle in throughout the day. I glimpse the twins standing outside the stable, just staring at it like they can't quite convince themselves to go in. If I didn't have a massive vase in my arms, I'd go stand with them.

In all the chaos, I haven't so much as smelled Amval. I have no idea where he is, what he's thinking. If some maid is going to wander into a room I'm not sure I locked and discover their crown prince, very naked and very much alive.

Instead, I push the thought out of my mind. I have way too many other Soms to worry about right now.

The triplets cause a minor scuffle by trying to eat breakfast after noon, when Chef Umit is already deep in preparations for the funeral. Kaloni asks me if I can handle it while she meets with the dressmaker.

I find Esen and Hova trying to sneak around the burly chef in the door while Cirocco tries to pry them off.

"Hey!" I yell.

Everyone stops.

Oh, I am not used to being the older sibling in situations. I have no idea what to say to get them to stop. Candace usually just asked me, and I did what I wanted—which was more often than not making her happy.

Cirocco sees my hesitation and swoops in. "I know how to cook eggs—and so do you two. Umit, can you spare a pan and a place on the stove?"

She eyes him. "Soft?"

"Wouldn't have them any other way." His smile is exhausted but reliable.

Umit steps back and lets the three of them into her kitchen.

That's why Amval chose Cirocco. Esen is technically the oldest of the triplets. I've learned that he actually could have chosen Kaloni, if he wanted to, but there is some rule about bloodlines. But Cirocco is the one who considers the way his actions affect others, thinks things through, and then decides. Amval needs that—someone who sees the whole picture and doesn't just go with the officially prescribed solution.

As I'm walking back to the dressmaker's room, hoping to catch up with Kaloni before she jets off somewhere new and I have to spend an hour tracking her down, I run into Joli.

She looks like she was in a carriage crash yesterday.

I grab her by the arm and turn her around without a second thought. Her and Kaloni are the only Soms allowed to talk to their siblings that I regularly see alone, and Kaloni always seems to be busy when I see her. I'd bet that Joli has fallen out of everyone else's mind.

I know how that feels. And I know how Candace tried to help. So I'll catch up with Kaloni later.

Back in Joli's room, I sit her down in front of her vanity and run my fingers through her long, dark brown hair, which is somehow thicker than mine.

"What are we doing?" Joli asks.

"Something my sister and I used to do." I grab her brush and start running it softly through the waves. "We called them makeovers, but we only sometimes had something new. The real point is that I'm going to spend the next few hours making you feel beautiful."

Joli frowns. "The day after my parents…."

"It's not shallow." I meet her gaze in the mirror. "Beauty is confidence. And being made beautiful is about letting someone take care of you."

A tear slips down her cheek. "All right. But I'm not spending all day in here."

I grab her chin and offer her the most Candace-like smile I can. "You'll spend as long in here as I say you will."

Joli almost laughs, and that's about all I could hope for.

BROKEN

Amval

WHEN I WAKE AND BREATHE IN A LUNGFUL OF VIOLET-AND-INK scented air, everything seems right with the world for just a moment. There are a thousand pains to face once I open my eyes, funerals, murderers, and my siblings looking past me, but at least I have her.

I reach across the tiny bed, hoping to grab her hand, and find… empty sheets.

My mark sears. I shoot up and search the mattress as though she could be hiding somewhere.

Nothing. But her clothes are gone, the door and window shut. It doesn't look like she's been taken.

It looks like she left.

I drop back down and cover my eyes. All the reaching out, everything she said… I thought she forgave me.

Perhaps she never used those exact words. Perhaps I saw what I wanted to see.

No. Something changed last night, or perhaps at the festival. I get the sense Ingrid can–and has–frozen people out of her life forever. This thaw means something.

It means I have to regain her trust, but the door isn't shut between us.

I roll out of bed, murmur a prayer for my parents, and get dressed.

Down at the stables, no one yells at me for starting my day late. They all know I was part of the team, and the absence of Iltas is surprisingly palpable. Everyone moves slowly today. I join Tek in our usual chores, and all he has for me is a mumbled apology. All I can offer him is the same in return. Two of his friends, gone in a month.

So many lives lost. The grief hanging thick in the air here makes everything feel stifling. My skin crawls with it, and my gut churns. Images of my parents' splayed bodies dance through my thoughts as I struggle through the mundane work.

"I need a few volunteers," Nur says at lunchtime. "We have to see what of the carriage is salvageable."

"I'll go," I reply almost instantly. Traveling there, remembering the path, searching for whole wheels and walls will be far more distracting than shoveling and saddling. And, if I need to regain Ingrid's trust, what better way to do it than to try to glean what I can from the one piece of this mystery that's easier for me to access than her.

Even if the idea of going back there makes me sick.

Nur sends me with a team of two stable boys, a pair of thirteen-year-olds who barely knew Iltas or my parents. They seem more dazed by the change than grieving it, and shortly after we leave the palace, they start playing games to pass the time.

My chest aches as I remember sitting in front of the triplets while they did the same for so many years. How Mother would join in when it was her turn to rest rather than drive.

I am grateful when we reach the site, and they have to stop.

The wreckage is even more scattered than it was yesterday. The team Sahin put together wasn't exactly graceful—their highest priority was retrieving the bodies as quickly as possible in order to prevent any further desecration. That means the scent of blood hangs thick in the air, spread as it is over such a wide area. The stable boys scrunch up their noses as soon as we arrive.

"What is that?" one of them asks.

I point silently at one puddle of dried, crimson gore. Mother's, I think. My stomach lurches, and when the other boy turns to be quietly sick, I can't blame him.

"The stable master wants anything we can save," I say when he's done. "Anything at all. Whole boards, unbroken wheels, even buckles or cushions we can repurpose."

The two boys look decidedly gray as they stare out at the wreckage.

Father's voice echoes in my memory. I put my hands on both of their shoulders. "You can't be brave if you aren't scared."

One of them nods.

"And right now, the kingdom needs you to be brave, so feel free to be as scared as you like."

The other looks up at me. "What if I can't be brave after that?"

"You can." I tousle his dark hair. "Being scared, as big and out loudly as you need to be, makes being brave much easier."

He takes a deep breath, tilts his head back, and screams. The other stableboy joins him, full of pure animalistic fear. My chest aches, and I loose my own howl of both pain and terror at what I might find. It's a primal release of all the hurt of the last month.

When all three of us are done, the wreckage doesn't look quite so terrifying. The stable boys wade into it, and I follow.

They start with the wheels, which at least are easy to recognize breakages in. I head for the front, hoping to find undamaged gear. Iltas's seat is cracked down the middle. It could likely be patched, but —I glance at the horizon—Tek has taught me how to recognize incoming storms, and it doesn't look like there is one rolling in soon. We'll take only the whole pieces and come back for those that could be salvaged in a day or two, when there are more hands to spare. I return the wood to the pile, trying not to replay the argument I had before that we take him back alongside Mother and Father, not in a later trip.

I won. Sahin has always been a pushover, if you know how to talk to him, and Iltas's mother threw herself on me, weeping.

For now, I push that thought away and keep searching. The curtains in the carriage are stained but whole, and one of the benches is still clean. I wrench it out and toss it in a pile of things to take back with us. The boys have found a few things, mostly boards and spindles.

The reins have to be here somewhere. I conjure a small breeze and gesture for the boys to be quiet. They obey immediately, like they refused to on the drive here. I seem to have earned some kind of respect from them.

In the silence, I hear the crash waves, the rise and fall of our own breath, and—there! A small, metallic rattling. I trace the sound to its source and unearth lengths of reins. The boys return to their low chatter as I do.

The reins are in bad shape, nicked and scratched by falling debris in multiple places. I slide the buckles off the ends, pocket those, and toss the leather aside. That'll be yet another piece to salvage later, if we need it. But the reins lead to the harness, and I have higher hopes for that.

Carefully, I run my fingers along it. One of the buckles burst on the right side, where the horse exploded out when the carriage hit the rock, but it's otherwise intact.

The left, however, is a different story entirely. I expected the emergency release to be triggered and it to be fine. I saw the left horse sprint so immediately away from the carriage that it doesn't seem possible for it to have torn through the harness. The material in my hands is good, sturdy leather, with thick stitching and a reinforcing metal core.

But on the left side of the harness, right in the front, there is a huge, deliberate split. Worse than anything on the right side, which the horse actually escaped from.

Almost like someone cut it.

And Iltas couldn't have possibly reached that from the bench.

"Whoa!" one of the stable boys says.

I jump to my feet. He doesn't sound panicked, merely surprised, but the hairs on the back of my neck promise that something is very wrong.

Those hairs seem damn near prophetic. The stableboy holds up a wheel that is almost entirely intact—except the bottom few inches, which are sliced off so cleanly it looks like someone took a saw to them.

"I've never seen a wheel break like that before," the other one says wonderingly.

"Neither have I." There is no awe in my voice. Merely cold, furious certainty.

The crash replays in my memory, as it has every time I stop paying attention for the last day. From a distance, I watch the horses spook at something. I still have no idea what, but with the woods lining the left side of the road, it wouldn't have been hard to secret some accomplice away with a snake or other threat to release at just the right time.

In slow motion, the horses bolt. The left horse tears away immediately—ripping through a harness strap likely sawed partially away before we ever left Kubilay. The carriage veers right, toward the cliff and the rock. The horse dodges the rock. The carriage isn't fast enough—because the bottom few inches of the equally damaged wheel snap before it even hits the rock, slowing it down just enough to ensure that it hits it and flips.

Why bother with the wheel? If not for the rock, the carriage would have simply gone off the cliff.

But there may have been enough time for Iltas to get the remaining horse under control that way.

And my siblings and I wouldn't have had a front-row seat to our parents' accident.

No, not accident. Not bad luck. Not a curse on our family I don't know how to break. Standing on this cliff side, my parents' blood in my nose and the cut harness in my hand, I know a much better word for what happened here.

Murder.

Only Mother and Father weren't lucky enough to escape theirs.

SCREAM

Ingrid

AFTER A LONG AFTERNOON OF TALKING JOLI INTO ONE OF MY MOST ornate dresses, then hiding from Kaloni around the palace with Joli in a ballgown, I sit on my bed, tuning my lute. My pillow sings to me. I'm completely exhausted, but I know I won't sleep.

There's too much in my head. Amval, the carriage crash, the Som siblings and their losses.

As I pluck out the notes of the song I composed the day after the Haze, Amval's song, a tiny voice in the back of my mind asks me why I'm still here. I know the truth about my mate—and I hate him for it. Someone seems to be trying to destroy the Soms, and maybe I can figure out who, but then what? Amval reveals himself, the whole kingdom is furious with him for lying, and whoever is trying to take over gets to do so anyway? Joli deserves better, as do Kaloni, Cirocco, and the rest of his siblings, but am I really helping?

Or am I just setting myself up for Amval to lie to me again?

Something thuds against my window. A branch probably.

But then it happens again. And again. In time with the rhythm of the song. I scramble off my bed and run to the window.

Outside, clinging to the wall like some kind of spider, is Amval, his veil whipping in an aggressive breeze.

"What was that song?" he asks as he reaches for the windowsill.

I put up a hand. "What makes you think you can just come in here?"

"I've learned something important," he says, glancing around the room like he's making sure I'm alone. "I thought you should know."

"Tell me, then." I cross my arms, still blocking the way in.

"I—" He looks at his fingers, then down the three-story fall. "Truly?"

"Truly." The wind can't be a coincidence, no matter how breezy the ocean makes it here. He is holding himself up. "Make it worth my while to let you in, and I will."

He sighs. "I went to the wreck today."

My heart aches. "Again?"

"There was more to find." His amber eyes meet mine. "You would have done it, if you could."

It was on my list for tomorrow. I didn't want to make him go back.

"The accident wasn't an accident." His voice goes hard and dangerous, like I've never heard it before. "Someone murdered my parents, and I can prove it."

My heart skips a beat. I step back from the window. His pockets rattle as he steps inside, looking exhausted. I can't imagine how long he was allowed to sleep before the stable master or one of his friends came looking for him.

Silently, he produces a length of leather from his pocket. No, two lengths. Empty tunnels of leather that once held something thick and stiff—sliced down the middle.

"This is the harness on the horse that broke away first," he says.

"Someone cut it," I say slowly.

"And one of the wheels." A thundercloud gathers on his brow, making him look like a warrior-priest of old under the veil. "It would have been easy to spook the horses intentionally."

"The other groom, you think?" I shake my head as soon as I say it. He was killed with Amval's parents. If he was involved at all, he was a patsy. There's no point in killing the king and queen if one can't even seize power in the aftermath. "No, someone who thinks grooms are particularly disposable, though."

"What do you mean?" He scowls down at the split leather like it personally murdered his family.

"I was telling you the other night." I grab my lute just to feel the weight of it in my hands. "That groom I've been looking for, Harun —"

"You were looking for Harun?" He whips a gaze at me.

I nod. "I told you his name."

"You most certainly did not." Amval starts pacing. "Harun has been missing since the name blessing. You said he was sick?"

"Exactly." I strum a chord, starting to get wrapped up in the quick back-and-forth. "Which would be why someone took you away to kill you somewhere else."

"Three deaths, three so-called accidents," he snarls. "Someone is trying very hard to keep their hands clean."

"And they are clearly not afraid to use people. Harun, your assassin, maybe the groom driving the cart."

"My assassin was blackmailed," he says. "Or at least I believe he was. And Iltas was a lot of fun in the sort of way I suspect wouldn't have made it difficult to get challenging information on him."

"If Harun died, he wouldn't have even needed to be blackmailed." My fingers dance over the strings. "But how could they have pulled off that swap with nobody noticing?"

Amval flicks my question away with a roll of his wrist. "Oh, that would be simple. You sleep like the dead, and I was drugged."

"What about everybody else?" I decide to ignore the comment about how heavily I sleep, what it implies about the hours between when I passed out in his arms and when someone attacked him. Did he watch me? Did he try to wake me for another round? If he'd succeeded, what would that have changed?

Ignoring things is not my specialty.

"They are the much easier part," Amval says. "Close your eyes, and stop playing for a moment."

I do. Nothing happens. After a few seconds, I open them again.

Amval stands almost nose-to-nose with me, veil gone. His eyes burn into mine, and my lips yearn.

I scramble back, knock into the bed, and absolutely do not yelp.

"How did you do that?"

"Anyone with sufficiently strong control of the wind can quiet their steps." He stirs up a breeze and displays the power with my eyes open. Despite his heavy, dusty boots, I don't hear a thing.

"So it has to be someone from Lightning Cape." I fight to regain my breath, clinging to my lute like a shield. "Who is strong enough?"

Stupid question. One walk down the halls makes it crystal clear just how plentiful powers are. Almost every noble has them, even if some are weak. And King Iraj selects—selected–the military based on their magic alone.

The suspects include most of the palace nobles, soldiers, and a large portion of the staff.

That dead end, combined with the suddenness of his presence, knocks me out of the whirl of excitement, and I come crashing back to the ground.

If Candace were telling me about this, I would scream at her to run. Amval proved I can't trust him. If he even decided to tell me the truth, it would be hard to believe. And he was a wholly different person when I met him at the name-blessing, as well. I've met four Amvals, and I have no way of knowing which is the real one.

Worse, every time I give him an inch, he takes a mile. I comfort him when I know he's alone, and he shows up at my room at night. His siblings are only a wall away! He could be caught at any second!

But my screams to kick him out, solve this myself, fall on deaf ears. Something else, something deeper than logic, drowns them out.

"Why didn't you act like this at the name-blessing?" I find myself asking.

He blinks, confused. "At the political gala?"

I shrug. "I'm the same, no matter where you meet me. The only differences are my clothes and how many curse words I'm allowed to use."

"That is a privilege I have not been afforded." He sits on a couch at the end of my bed.

"It mostly gets me into trouble." I sit on the mattress, legs folded underneath me, lute in my lap. Its weight anchors me, promises I'm not stupid for keeping him here instead of throwing him out.

"Yet another privilege." He smiles wryly. "No one expects very much of you."

"You are not the first person to say that to me." Including most of my siblings and my parents. Only Candace and Raven never have.

"I am sorry. I'm sure that hurts." He shakes his head. "But very few people realize just how much freedom that grants."

"I made whatever freedom I have." And I'm damn proud of it.

"It must seem that way to you." His amber gaze goes distant. "My grandfather lost the kingdom. I would like to say it was through no fault of his own, but everyone knows he was a weak Alpha. Gavin always chose his targets well. That we survived the first conquest even as well as we did is a miracle. Now, my father has reclaimed the throne and the family name. If I stumble, if I somehow lose everything the way Grandfather did, Lightning Cape will crumble. I've spent my whole life falling asleep to that like a lullaby in rat-ridden corners of a kingdom we didn't know if we would ever reclaim." He looks at me. "Now, tell me I should make my own freedom."

I open my mouth… and nothing comes out.

Amval smiles tiredly. "I can't imagine you're struck dumb very often."

I shake my head. I knew what kind of pressure Kieran was under —kind of. He had to take the throne, expand Father's empire, fill his shoes. But he didn't have the threat of failure hanging over his head like that. He would have taken over a whole, strong kingdom, loyal to their king.

Clearly, King Iraj had the people's loyalty. But can Amval? Can Kaloni?

"I'm sorry," I say.

"I didn't expect you to understand," he says. "No one does, not even my siblings."

Silence settles between us, an unbreachable gulf. Amval grew up the center of everyone's attention, a prince in hiding or a prince that might be the future of a broken kingdom. I grew up in Mother's lap, trying to get out. No matter what Candace says, there's no common ground here.

Realization crashes over me. "That's why no one had ever heard you play."

He offers me a tired smile. "That's not for kings to do. I had too many other concerns to be wasting my time on it."

I laugh, half in disbelief. "I can't imagine my hobbies being met with anything worse than disinterested disdain—no, sorry, that's the privilege you're talking about."

He shakes his head. "I am sorry no one stopped to listen. They should have."

"I was supposed to be something else, even if I wasn't very good at it." I shrug.

"I like what you are much better." He lays his hand over mine on the neck of my lute.

My mark hums, soft and comfortable. Right.

Maybe there always is a little common ground, even if it's just that neither of us wishes the other one grew up the way they did.

"Are you really that worried about losing the kingdom?" I ask quietly.

He chuckles ruefully. "I was murdered this month, and my parents were murdered two days ago. Wouldn't you be?"

That startles a laugh out of me. "I am beginning to suspect you might be funny."

"Don't tell anyone," he says. "I can't have you ruining my reputation."

"I think it would hurt mine more, if I started going around announcing that a dead man is telling me jokes." I nudge his shoulder playfully, and he leans back into me.

If Candace were telling me about this, I'd scream at her to run. But she's not. All I have to go on is the fuzzy feeling spreading from where my skin brushes his and the bone-deep certainty that he isn't lying to me now. Whatever parts of the Amvals I've met are true, this is one of them.

"If we have too many suspects," I say, "then we have to start whittling them down."

RACING FOR THE THRONE

Amval

"I SWEAR BY EVERY STAR, IT'S NOT USUALLY LIKE THIS," TEK GRUMBLES to me a few days later.

I can only nod in agreement. To actually open my mouth and speak would expend valuable energy that I need to be able to lift the massive Snowcrest Canyon harnesses off their towering, shaggy horses.

For two days, dignitaries have been arriving. More than a few of them, working under the general assumption that staff aren't people in the same way they are, have complained about returning to Lightning Cape so soon after their last visit. In addition to the physical strain, the emotional strain of not hitting them weighs on me.

If they cannot be polite about fucking funerals, the second and third in barely a month, I would rather start the sort of political incident that sends them home than endure their presence.

Someone laughs, and I whirl, searching for Ingrid. Instead, I find another head of blonde hair that takes a moment to place—Candace, her sister, surrounded by her mate and their red-headed best friend.

More than a few Solbergs have arrived, and every one of them has a different trait that sends me looking for her.

Since that night in her room, we've spoken mostly through hidden messages. She is managing the situation inside the palace. It's my responsibility to figure out who spends enough time in the stables to know which of the grooms would be sick. Harun can't have had the infectious form of the Carmine Pox, or Ingrid would have caught it, so those who know the stables well are our primary suspects.

Which means I need to manage my usual duties, handle all the arriving dignitaries, prepare for the Crown Race, which will occur the day before Kaloni's coronation, and pay attention to who else spends time here.

That I managed to nod to Tek is impressive, I feel.

As we work, he keeps up his usual stream of jokes and complaints. I don't know how he does it, with a hangover more often than not, but it does make the work go faster. Once or twice, I even manage to reply.

He is chuckling at a comment I truly did not believe was a joke when Lady Ceyiz walks in on her husband's arm. My ears prick up. She has been in the stables more than I would expect, for someone who purportedly hates horses as much as she does.

"Must we do this?" she asks, and I realize she isn't truly walking. A thin cushion of wind protects her feet and the hem of her gown from the muck that lines the ground here. It also softens her steps to near total silence, though I wouldn't be able to hear them over the chaos here anyway.

Her husband, Lord Mufit, pats her hand. "It's the Crown Race, dear. If I didn't compete, how would that look?"

"Like you are the only one sensible about these beasts." She eyes a stomping red roan suspiciously.

"Like I do not believe our line could ever possibly hold the title," he replies unyieldingly.

He's right, of course. At this point, the Crown Race is nearly a formality—it's not as if losing could actually disqualify Kaloni from taking the throne—but all the nobles of Lightning Cape have sent one representative to compete since the days that it could stop her.

Lady Ceyiz shies away from a pale quarter horse. "Fine. The faster you choose your steed, the better."

I watch the two of them walk deeper into the stable, and she only has eyes for the horses. Not a glance is spared for the staff, and she looks equally at those who live here and those who are only visiting. She doesn't even seem to notice when Nur passes her.

Lady Ceyiz is one of very few nobles who stayed in their ancestral home when Dun's Crossing took over. She claims she had sufficient defenses, but everyone very nearly knows that she made some kind of deal with Gavin. Whenever there is something to be suspected, smart eyes turn toward her.

More nobles from far-flung kingdoms flood in, bringing with them foreign smells of lemon and chocolate, balsam and salt. I lose Lady Ceyiz and her husband in the shuffle. Perhaps she doesn't have any connections here, but her husband certainly seems more comfortable.

LATER THAT EVENING, WHEN THE STABLE IS QUIETER, LORD FARUK Basran comes in to pick his horse for the race. He always skulks around, like he knows those around him are thinking about his bloodline. I certainly am. The last of the line that birthed Rowena Solberg is a figure I want to keep my eye on.

In truth, it's strange that he's here in the first place. Lord Faruk owns his own prized stallion, a buckskin he foolishly named Windrider. However, I know from saddling the thing damn near every day these past few weeks that it's far from fast. Is he spending more time at the stalls of other buckskins? Could he possibly be trying to pass off another horse as his own?

"Can I help you, my lord?" I ask as I sidle up to him.

He barely glances at me. I would be surprised if he knows a

starlight works in the stables. "Must I actually tell you the Crown Race is tomorrow?"

"Won't you be taking Windrider?"

"Perhaps," he says reluctantly.

I grin behind my veil. The Basrans have always been snakes. The only civil war in all of Lightning Cape's history was started by them, and it's frankly childish to call it a war. It was a spat, if anything, put down quickly by my great-grandfather.

But everyone knows they're still smarting from it. And Lord Faruk isn't stupid, though he might be slimy. He could have learned from his ancestors' mistakes—and his cousin Rowena's successes—that the only real way to remove a Som from the throne is to attack us in the dark, like cowards.

"I believe the times for your daily rides have been improving," I offer gladly.

"I don't recall asking for your opinion, boy." He glances at his own horse, then at another buckskin named Tulum, stabled nearby.

My smile burns into a snarl. In addition to everything else, Lord Faruk also has obvious connections to the stable. He rides every day, like a prayer Windrider might bother to live up to his name. And I've watched him attempt to use his powers to speed the horse—he is not weak. He may be dismissive and callous, but he may notice more than he lets on. Iltas wasn't exactly quiet about his own attentiveness, and if Lord Faruk overheard a conversation, he could have very easily tracked down the same information Ingrid did to lead her to Harun.

"Come tomorrow morning, saddle Tulum for me." He turns on his heel, cape flaring. "But I want him announced as Windrider, and if anyone says a word to the contrary, it's your head."

I grit my teeth as I mutter my agreement. Clearly, he is also a liar —and newly at the very top of my suspect list.

NUR WAKES US ALL WITH POTS AND PANS THE FOLLOWING—I CAN'T even say morning. The sun has barely begun turning the sky gray, but there is so much to do for the Crown Race that waking any later would bring the whole event crashing down. My muscles groan—I stayed up an extra hour to pass Ingrid everything I learned yesterday —but I launch myself out of bed. The senior groom assigned to Bayar, Kaloni's chestnut thoroughbred, made the mistake of going out with Tek last night. He lies on his cot now, whimpering slightly.

If, perhaps, I suggested the idea to Tek, I think I can be forgiven. My sister is racing for her throne today. I should be cheering her on from the royal box, but if I can't do that, readying her horse might be the next best thing.

Or at least, it is the best thing I can possibly access. A weight sits on my chest all morning, heavy, dull, and difficult to name. Only when I wander down a familiar aisle of stalls and see a bay-splash thoroughbred dancing to be let out do I realize.

I smooth my hand over Seksim's nose and feed him one of the roseapples I squirreled away in my pocket to ensure Bayar behaves for me. After we retook the palace, buying Seksim was one of my first royal actions. I knew, someday, that I would be making this race, and I'd grown up with stories of how Grandfather won on a mare he'd been riding since childhood instead of the stallion his father picked out for him. I wanted that kind of bond with my horse, even if I had missed so much time already. I wanted to be a proper king–when my time came.

Now, it's Kaloni's time. No matter what happens, as of tomorrow, she will be Luna Queen. When I reveal the truth, she still will be. I won't take it from her.

The ache of loss is far duller than I dreamed it might be. Perhaps I have lost too much else.

Pre-dawn disappears, and the nobles start arriving for their horses. The race is at noon, but that doesn't stop them from arriving in full gear just after breakfast, intending to spend the rest of the waiting time practicing where they might intimidate their competi-tion. I stay with Bayar. Kaloni is never—

Someone raps on the stall door, and I open it to reveal her in crisp riding gear of Lightning Cape orange and white. Mother's, I believe.

It fits her a little awkwardly, but I still have to swallow my reaction when I see it.

Never late. Kaloni is never, ever late.

"I have a request to make." She bobs as if curtsying while wearing trousers. "I only wish I could have made it before you polished Bayar to such fine condition."

She doesn't sound tense, just a little tired. I set the horse brush down and incline my head. "Anything for you, Your Majesty."

"Could you saddle Seksim for me instead?" she asks.

I expect the request to hurt. The horse I handpicked, trained, dreamt of, being ridden by another in a race I'll never run. But it just seems right.

Seksim was chosen for the Crown Race. For a Som to take the throne. Kaloni should ride him—he's faster than Bayar, anyway.

I bow deeply and lead her to the stall. Seksim snuffles my hand excitedly, and I try to hide how happy he is to see me again. I've been trying not to tend to him, so the others wouldn't notice. Luckily, Kaloni just looks out over the edge of the stall, evaluating her competition.

"Seksim is a bit wilder than Bayar," I murmur as I work, "but with a firm hand, you have nothing to fear."

"A firm hand," she repeats, nodding to herself.

Later, when I watch her rein in Seksim at the last heartbeat of the final turn from the grooms' place under the stands, correcting his instinct to always veer wide, I scream louder than anyone else.

Kaloni sails into first place, confirming that she is the rightful queen of Lightning Cape.

And that weight lands heavy on my chest again.

CROWNED

Ingrid

I GRUMBLE MY WAY OUT OF BED ON THE MORNING OF KALONI'S coronation. With everything that's happened, I haven't been getting nearly as much sleep as I should. Hell, I spent half of yesterday with my… uncle, Lord Faruk, trying not to roll my eyes every time he spoke.

Amval might be right about him. At the very least, he's one of the most self-obsessed men I've ever met.

Someone knocks on my door, and I stumble into a robe, expecting Kaloni with a new slate of demands. Instead, I find Candace and Eva, glowing with excitement.

I throw my arms around them. They arrived a couple of days ago, but I haven't had any time to spend with them yet.

"I missed you," I mumble into Candace's shoulder.

She squeezes me tighter. "Then sit down and let me fuss over you."

"Goddess above, that sounds wonderful."

Before long, dresses in every color of the rainbow cover the front of my room, and cosmetics coat the back. Joli wanders in after a while

—I asked one of the maids to wake her so she didn't feel like she missed out on everything—and Candace falls in love with her after only a few sentences. Eva, it turns out, is a wonder with nails. Painting them is a new trend in Snowcrest Canyon, and she insists on doing everyone's.

I say everyone's because more and more people keep arriving. Kaloni has to prepare privately, which is some Lightning Cape tradition, but it seems like everyone else is here. Raven floats through with Vespera on her hip, and everyone helps doll up the little princess. Liwar and Sibel spend more than a few hours with us, cooing over the foreign luxuries and styles. Xandra stops by to ask my opinion of her latest jacket and helps with makeup more than I would have expected. I guess a lifetime of pretending to be someone else makes you spectacular at reshaping a face. Kieran passes through with Altair. Finn has a few teasing jokes—which earn him a puff of powder to the face. I laugh.

It feels... a little like being home again. When I was young, and everyone was home, there wasn't a place you could turn in the castle without company. Then, I was seeking privacy rather than stumbling into it.

No, it's better than that. We're not waiting for Mother to come chide our choices. Raven is here with us, rather than forced to be anywhere else. And all the new women in the family fit into place. Sometimes a little awkwardly—Liwar and Sibel do keep to themselves a little more than most, and Xandra struggles with some of the feminine details—but they fit. It's almost hard to remember the funeral that happened only yesterday and the secrets lining the walls of this palace that I'm supposed to discover. The morning is just about all of these people I love, or am growing to love, coming together in one place.

Eva decides to wear one of my dresses. Joli ends up in a coat that doesn't quite fit Xandra. When Vespera wakes up from her nap, she doesn't even burst into tears.

The door has been open for a while, and a few other noblewomen

I barely know have been in and out. Closing people off right now, when there's been so much loss, seemed wrong.

As lunch approaches, Anwen steps in. "I thought the party was supposed to be after the coronation," he says.

I smirk at him. "Who says we can only have one?"

"I didn't know you were coming!" Candace abandons Liwar's hair to hug our brother.

He chuckles. "I'm just here for the day. Estrella could give birth any minute, but we couldn't miss two funerals and a coronation, and Baz offered to come in my place, so—"

"Smart." His former Beta found a mate, but that doesn't stop him from flirting with every woman in his line of sight. "Want your hair done?"

He shakes his head emphatically. "I actually wanted to talk to you."

I'm probably imagining the room going quiet. A dozen women don't care that this is the first time one of my brothers has asked me for a private conversation possibly ever. But it still feels like it as I set down the earrings I was about to offer Eva and step out into the hall with him.

"We've never done this before," I say as he leads me a little down the hall.

"Really?" He raises an eyebrow. "We should have."

"But then how would you have had all that free time to skulk around the castle?" I watch the stream of staff rushing furiously through the halls.

He rubs the back of his neck. "I wasn't always the best brother. I'd like to make up for that now."

"Estrella really has civilized you," I reply.

"And then some," he says. "But she doesn't know I'm doing this."

My stomach sinks. I already know what he's going to say. "Why not?"

"This is family business. I'm not here on anyone else's behalf."

I squeeze my eyes shut. "You think I should leave."

"Have you thought about how this looks?" he asks. "Three people are dead, Ingrid—"

"I woke up with one and watched the other two die," I snap. "I couldn't exactly forget."

"I'm only saying this because I know how complicated death can be between two kingdoms," he replies. "When King Isai was assassinated—"

"You insisted on leading the investigation yourself, despite your conflict of interest, and followed Estrella home when she left." I open my eyes and glare at him. "You don't exactly get to lecture me on proper political procedure."

His eyes grow sad. "I followed someone. I fought for someone. Your mate isn't here anymore. You don't have a claim to this place."

I open my mouth and very nearly blurt in a crowded hallway just how wrong Anwen is. Maybe he followed Estrella knowing exactly what that meant for his political future, and I have no idea what would theoretically come next for Amval and me, but he's wrong that I have nothing here.

"What?" His brow furrows as he reads the disagreement in my face. Damn him.

"Joli," I lie. I hate lying. It's always harder than the truth in the long run. "She's a close friend of mine, and she's going through a difficult time. I'm here for her, not Amval."

"But to the outside world, it looks like you're here for him," Anwen says quietly.

I fold my arms beneath my chest. "You and Kieran can worry about that. I care about my friend who's hurt. Have a safe trip home, and give Estrella my best."

"To lead is to protect," the holy woman, Halit, declares over Kaloni's head. "To honor, and to take as your own. Kaloni Suat Abda Som, do you accept this responsibility?"

"With honor," she replies. "Lightning Cape is already my own. I've traveled these lands as a commoner and a royal and loved them just as much both ways."

My mark aches. Amval is somewhere outside the temple, I know. He admitted in his last note that he was going to be watching. I just hope he can hear this. On the trip to Kubilay, I realized how much he loves his siblings. It must be killing him to have to watch a ceremony this beautiful from a distance.

Kaloni is an extensive part of the beauty. Her dress, so long it still trails off the altar, is the exact orange-amber of her eyes and Lightning Cape's colors. Her hair is spun up into a towering confection I can already picture a crown around, and she holds herself like a queen.

But even more than that, she's met every simple phrase of Halit's with more. She's talked about how much she loves this place, these people, how much she intends to do for them. She is passionate and focused, her gaze trained upward, past Halit and into the sky, like she's talking to the Goddess Herself.

I'd follow her anywhere. And I hope Amval can see that, for however long it's going to be, his kingdom is in good hands.

"By the will of the Goddess," Halit says, "and the law of this land, I crown you Luna Queen of Lightning Cape."

The holy woman sets a white-gold tiara on Kaloni's head. It stands out brilliantly against her dark hair. Kaloni stands, turns, and lifts her arms to the packed temple.

We all bow.

"I was reading a book on the old traditions," Kaloni says, "and it seems I'm intended to give a speech. To tell you what I intend to do for you in my coming reign. I suppose choosing to make this speech tells you the very first item: I intend to return Lightning Cape to what we were before."

I bite my lip. If she means before the death of Amval as well as her parents, that's going to be a very easy promise to keep, I guess.

"We have suffered enough as a result of being conquered," she continues. "We lost too much of ourselves in the long years of belonging to someone else."

Of course. That makes sense with what Amval was saying about the pressure not only to be as good as his father, but to be better than his grandfather. There are obviously some people in Lightning Cape who blame the old king for letting them be conquered.

"There are so many old traditions to reclaim." A smile leaks into her voice. "So much of our past that we should honor and protect, just like I intend to honor and protect you. That starts with this speech, but I intend to do more. The traditions that truly matter, that made us who we were, will return."

Joli takes my hand. Judging by the quiet tears on her cheeks, she is thinking something very similar. About Amval, and her parents, and all she's lost. Every time I see her cry, it gets a little harder to keep pretending Amval is gone, rather than clinging to the wall of this building somewhere.

"I also intend to reclaim what we've lost in other ways." Kaloni's voice hardens. "The wild lands to the north, currently overrun by rogues, were once fertile farmlands for us. My father built us a strong and capable army; allowing them to sit in the palace like nothing more than lapdogs is a waste of that potential as well as the northern land."

I blink. That's the first time she's actually mentioned her parents, I realize. And not to discuss the loss or her grief over it. I've seen her grief. I watched her cry.

Didn't I?

Yes, of course, she cried on the carriage ride to the palace. She just pulled herself together when we arrived to make the announcement. And obviously, she wept over Amval.

"I intend to lead you fairly and well, like my family has back into antiquity," she says.

There it is. There's the moment she should mention Amval, say something about how he would have led them.

Instead, she says, "And I am truly honored by the trust you've put in me to do so."

Kaloni steps down off the altar and proceeds out of the temple. I straighten, finally, out of my bow with everyone else. That was... strange. It scratches an itch in the back of my mind, one I can't quite place. One that made me wonder if I'd seen her cry over her parents. For some reason, those are tied together.

The Soms leave the temple second, and I with them. As we do, I hear a few murmurs, mostly about the lovely ceremony and how good it will be to have that land reclaimed.

"I thought it was tasteful that she avoided his name," someone says, "with how many Solbergs are here."

"Who, Gavin?" someone replies.

And it hits me. The speech Kaloni just gave—it reminded me of Father.

AFTERLIFE

Amval

I STRETCH MY LEGS IN THE EVENING GLOOM, GRATEFUL AND NERVOUS about the fact that the only windows into the ballroom are on the ground. Climbing the temple—and staying up there—is far from easy, but at least I have to worry much less about getting caught. Especially as the sun sets, I am becoming a shadow against the night, a far more obvious onlooker. I'll have to leave soon.

I don't want to. I can just barely see Kaloni from this angle, laughing at the head table with Sibel and Esen. She suits the crown well, and judging by the endless stream of congratulatory dignitaries, long after etiquette dictates those around her have to pay their thanks, she has done well today. A tired smile stretches my lips, almost enough to dull that ache.

"Hey."

I jump and whirl, but before I even see her, the smell of violets and ink settles my nerves. Ingrid stands before me, resplendent in an indigo gown that bares her powerful shoulders and draping into long capes at the elbows. Her hair is held back from her face with a pair of jeweled combs that almost look dull beside her golden locks, and her face glows with the light of the party.

"I suppose I shouldn't be surprised you spotted me."

She shakes her head. "I just knew you'd be out here. I've been checking every window."

That lifts the weight on my chest like nothing else, even Tek offering to cover for me so I could sneak off. I gave a weak excuse about a girl I loved in Oakspring Dunes arriving with their delegation, and he told me to say no more. But Ingrid alone knows what this really means.

"Also"—she produces a plate from behind her back—"Cirocco said this was your favorite."

A thick slice of gingery cake oozes toffee filling onto the dish. One whiskey-soaked cherry sits beside it, still smeared with frosting that promises she stole it off another slice to ensure I had one.

"I can't believe they made it." I reach for the plate slowly. "He's right, but this is only supposed to be for the turn of the new year."

She shrugs and sits on the opposite side of the windowsill from me. "Kaloni said this was the beginning of a whole new period for Lightning Cape, so it only made sense."

I put a bite in my mouth, and my eyes flutter shut. We've never fed our staff poorly, but flavor has been sorely lacking from my diet. The sharpness of the ginger intertwines with the toffee richness and sweet bite of the cherry in a way that's almost overwhelming after so long.

Kaloni has this cake for me. It doesn't matter what she told everyone else, even our siblings. This is the cake we begged Umit to make when we first returned to the palace, that we stole a slice of off a noble's table when we were only ten and eleven years old. It's no accident. She is thinking about me today as much as I'm thinking about her.

Between this and Seksim, I don't have to worry about that again.

"That good?" Ingrid asks with a smile.

I swallow and nod. "You have to try a bite."

"Candace has more of a sweet tooth." She meets my gaze. "But all right."

I lift a morsel to her lips. More cake, less toffee since she's not much for sweets. She accepts it from my fork with a smirk, but the soft, elated smile that follows is all I need to endure her teasing.

"Now you see," I crow.

She laughs with a full mouth. "Well, you didn't tell me the cake bites back. What is that?"

"Umit's secret ingredient." I smile slyly.

"Maybe I should have been Umit's fated mate instead," she mumbles.

I shake my head as I take another bite. "Some of the old books claim they used to serve this at funerals as well."

She fans her face as she swallows. "It would certainly disguise the tears."

I glance through the window at the golden party whirling by inside. Was Kaloni thinking about those books? I heard her speech about the old traditions. She could be mourning in public, even after her mourning is supposed to be over.

That ache returns to my chest.

"The music isn't even that good," Ingrid says, patting my knee. "I offered to play, but apparently, that wasn't traditional."

My chuckle comes out thick with something other than icing. "Imagine if I had snuck my way into the band."

"We should have done that!" Her eyes light, and she stares into the window. "We still could. Those four have to take a break sometime, and I'm sure one of them wouldn't mind ending the night a little early."

I shake my head. Sitting out here watching all this is hard enough. To be so close and unable to do… I'm not even sure what; I just know it would be impossible.

"Or not," Ingrid says quickly. "Sorry."

"No, it's not—I am happy for my sister," I say. "She deserves this recognition. She is going to be a wonderful queen."

A strange look crosses Ingrid's face, but it's gone so quickly that I'm not completely sure I didn't just imagine it.

"You just wish you could sleep in a comfortable bed again?" she asks.

"I certainly wouldn't mind." I watch Kaloni greet another delegation with the perfect poise we both learned. We all learned. "But I don't particularly hate this new life I've ended up in."

"Shoveling shit?"

"Working," I say, realizing the truth of the word as I say it. "There was such an abrupt change between life on the road and life in the palace. Suddenly, everything was easy—or vastly more complicated. I miss things being hard in a simple way, sometimes."

She nods. "Candace was always so shocked about all my hobbies, like they were the hardest thing I could have possibly done. The lessons she took and obeyed seemed so much harder to me."

"Exactly." My chest warms with understanding. Of course, she understands. Ingrid cuts through the noise like no one I've ever seen, but she's clearly not afraid of effort. "And yet...."

She follows my gaze into the window. "That was supposed to be you in there."

"I died," I say softly, "and the world spun on without me. Who else gets to see so clearly that they are not the hero of the story that they were raised to believe they could be?"

Ingrid takes my hand silently. What could anyone say to something so selfish? My skin burns just hearing the words. What matters is that my people get a leader who will take care of them, and they have. Not that my feelings are hurt because that person couldn't be me.

"I'm glad you died," she says suddenly.

"What?"

She shrugs, gaze trained on the window. "My father thought he was the hero. So did my mother. So did nearly every bastard I've met in my life." Her hand tightens on mine. "I don't like the hero. I don't want him. He's not real."

The weight on my chest disappears. It doesn't just lift, lingering nearby for the chance to drop again. As her words ring through the night, it vanishes entirely.

Heroes are storybook creatures. People out of legends. Father often said that being king was more reading than leading. He and Mother became viciously busy as soon as we returned, busier than they ever were trying to keep eight children a secret. Royalty is a mundane position, not one for heroes.

I died, even if I survived the attempt, and the world kept spinning. I can't destroy the world with a single wrong choice.

When I suck in a breath of toffee, violets, and ink, it tastes like freedom.

"Thank you," I say.

She strokes the back of my hand. "It's an easier lesson to learn from the bottom."

There's an ache in her voice as she says it, and for the first time, I wonder whether Ingrid ever wanted to inherit. But before I can ask, she says, "Would you have had the cake at your coronation?"

I look at the mostly empty plate. "Frankly, I doubt I would have thought of it."

She laughs. "Of course. Perfect Amval would only have the most traditional desserts."

"A nectarine tart." My mouth waters just thinking about it, rich with cinnamon and spices. "And that band you hate so much is traditional as well."

She groans playfully. "So nobody would dance."

I gesture inside at the crowded dance floor. "I disagree, especially after I led the first dance."

She laughs. "You would? Somehow, I can't picture you dancing."

"I danced at the Festival of First Wind!"

"Oh, that's different." She shakes her head. "You weren't Amval there. The prince I met in Moonlight Beach doesn't dance."

"I was quite well trained," I object, but that only makes her laugh more. "I'd also have a buffet, not a banquet."

"Really?" She leans back against the window frame.

"Mother and Father had one for their coronation, mostly because the kingdom was still too destroyed for something more formal." The memory pulls a smile to my lips. "But there was something about everyone serving themselves from the same plates, even the staff, that made the coronation feel truly like a new beginning. A promise that all our suffering under Gavin was over. So, see, I would break one tradition."

"You would continue a newer tradition," she says. "There must be something new you wanted to do, even if it's not with this party. What were your plans when you became Alpha?"

Continue Mother's program of land repatriation after the conquering. Actually put into place Father's idea for a whole new style of farming, taking advantage of the rich soil buried deep in the cliffs with soaring farms.

"I intended to create two units in the army, one for those with powers and one without," I say before I realize that was Cirocco's idea. Well, it was a good one, and it is new.

"More military." She nods slowly. "Not exactly unique."

"I'd make the Festival of First Wind a national holiday," I blurt. It's never occurred to me before, but as soon as I say it, it seems obvious. Everyone should get to enjoy something that special.

"There you go." She grins at me, and it feels better than winning the Crown Race would have. "But somehow, I don't think you would have come up with that before."

"No," I say frankly. "I wouldn't have."

She gestures like that proves her point. Perhaps it does.

"But none of that matters now," I say.

"No?" She looks back inside. "You're going to reveal yourself someday, aren't you?"

"I wouldn't take this from her." Kaloni is already beloved. She will be a wonderful queen.

Ingrid's eyebrows jump in surprise, but she doesn't say anything.

"What?" I ask. "Were you dreaming that I was your chance to inherit?"

She snorts. "Now, that might be your worst joke yet. No, if I became Luna, the whole kingdom would burn down around me."

Her face is set, steady. There's no trace of that expression I might have seen before or the roughness in her voice that suggested she might have missed the opportunity. Ingrid is steadfast—she does not want to lead the way I was raised to.

I squeeze her hand. Perhaps she is right, and it's better that I died.

HAIR ON THE BACK OF MY NECK

Ingrid

AMVAL POLISHES OFF THE LAST OF THE CAKE JUST AS THE BAND INSIDE takes their break. Sweet relief. If I return, at least I won't have to deal with their insipid music or anyone asking me to dance.

"I should go back," I say.

He nods. "Of course. We can't have anyone looking for you out here."

Through the window, I watch Kaloni stand up to make her rounds. I should tell him. That speech… maybe it was old, from some Alpha or Luna eons before, and she just didn't have time to write a new one. Amval could recognize it and end this all here.

But that means he has to listen to me first. And if someone waltzed up to me and implied that Finn may have tried to murder me, I would need a hell of a lot more proof than some speech.

Instead, I just gather my skirts and head back into the party being thrown for my mate's killer.

Maybe.

A juggler has replaced the band, and more than a few of the guests gather around to watch him. People who would swear up and down that this kind of entertainment was "beneath them." I smirk. Maybe I'll start my next boring conversation with that, just to see what they say.

For now, I just take up my usual position along the wall. I squint at the window I just left Amval at—it's too dark to see anything through now. Then, I step out of his view.

Kaloni sails from group to group like an escaped flame in that amber-colored dress. Every person she walks up to seems thrilled to see her. She exchanges smiles, handshakes, and hugs. Just yesterday, she was weeping in black at her parents' funeral. One would never know it today.

I wasn't at King Isai's funeral to see the change in Estrella from one day to the next, but I saw her walking around the halls after his murder. She looked like a queen—but like a fucking miserable one. Perfect posture and beautiful clothes worn like chains, a rain cloud always dragging behind her.

On the days I played assistant to Kaloni, she didn't seem miserable. She seemed busy.

"Did you wander off the wall for once? I could have sworn I already checked here."

I turn to find Candace behind me and smile tiredly. "I need to use my legs every now and again."

She chuckles, then leans against the wall next to me. "How are you?"

A heavy wave of déjà vu crashes over me—this is exactly what happened before she dragged me across Finn and Xandra's unfinished ballroom to meet Amval for the first time. Not Amval. Prince Amval.

My mark burns, and I wish I'd gotten another slice of that cake.

"I've been better," I answer honestly.

She rubs my shoulder comfortingly. "You've been through a lot recently."

"Have I?" My gaze drifts to the table of remaining Soms. Despite the occasion, they look miserable.

Candace takes my hand. "Someone else going through worse doesn't mean it hasn't been hard for you. You also watched two people die."

"After Raven, we all have stronger stomachs than that," I mutter.

She winces. I know she hates it when I bring up the beatings we all watched without saying a word. So does Raven. I think pretending they didn't happen is worse.

"Oh, just ask," I say without any real anger in my voice. She always has to come at these things sideways. I love her more than almost anything, but I am tired.

She tucks her arm through mine and leads me away from the only other person on this stretch of wall. There's never much privacy to be had in a ballroom, but she finds a little by tucking us into an arched window nook that blocks half my view of the party.

The blue stone inside is so much warmer than it was outside.

"Why are you still here?" she asks quietly.

"For Joli," I tell her, like I told Anwen.

She shoots me a look. Dammit. Anwen may have the best eye for false expressions, but Candace knows me leagues better than he does.

"That's not a lie," I mumble. "You saw her today."

"I think she's very sweet," Candace says unyieldingly, "and I also know how much you hate all the formality of a diplomatic visit."

My bones ache with it. I'm tired of trying to remember foreign customs, of people treating me like I do but then don't belong. At home, I'm royalty, and even if that's sometimes the most boring fate I can imagine, everyone knows what to do with me. They don't look at me funny when I ask for charcoal or practice jousting by running up and down the same straightaway for an hour and a half.

I like travel. I like being somewhere new. But staying somewhere new? I've already spent a month here, and I have no idea when I'm going to get to leave.

"Someone murdered them," I remind her through the mind-link.

Candace bites her lower lip. "Ingrid, the king and queen died in a carriage accident."

All the evidence I have to prove that wrong is sitting back in the stables, under the careful custody of the one secret I can't even tell Candace. Maybe it would make her understand if I did. But Kaloni is here somewhere, even if I can't see her right now, and I don't want to give her any reason to go after my family next.

"Let's say that's true," I reply out loud, so nobody wonders what the two of us are talking about so secretly. "It doesn't mean I'm wrong about anything else. Two coincidences aren't any more likely than one."

She shakes her head. "You know who would stand to gain if you're right. You know who they would look at."

"Do I?" I glance around the party, trying to find Kaloni in the crowd. When I can't, the hair on the back of my neck prickles. She wouldn't leave her own coronation.

"Who else?" Candace asks. "He—"

"Isn't the only dead person." I lean close to her, meeting her dark eyes. "Who really stands to benefit at this point?"

Candace's furrowed brow smooths out as she realizes what I'm implying. Her mouth pops open. "If you're right, you should really come home."

"And, what, start a letter-writing campaign?"

"Use our people," she says urgently. "Sleep somewhere safe."

I open my mouth to refuse and almost choke on the smell of orchid and willow as Candace stiffens in front of me.

"Ingrid!" Kaloni says. "I was wondering where you wandered off to."

"You can usually find me here." I gesture at the wall. "Parties aren't where I shine."

"Luna Kaloni." Candace curtsies deeply, trying to cut me off before I make a fool of myself. "Your ceremony was lovely."

"Candace." Kaloni bobs a polite curtsy in return. "Prince Hollis said something very similar. I get the feeling I may be hearing from the two of you—when the time for your coronation *finally* arises."

Did she put extra emphasis on that "finally"? There's no way. She couldn't have planned this many murders this well and then slipped up that stupidly.

"Perhaps." Candace smiles sweetly. "I'll need your dressmaker, at least."

"Oh, this?" Kaloni spins, the orange skirt flaring around her legs like a warning beacon. "Our dressmakers are talented, but it was mostly luck. I was already planning to have a dress made in our colors, so we already had the fabric. Otherwise, there was no way they could have gotten this together in time." She glances at me. "What do you think, Ingrid? You have such exquisite taste, as Joli keeps telling me."

I think that's one hell of a coincidence, and so do the hairs on the back of my neck—but Candace made one good point. I'm on Kaloni's home turf, so there's nowhere I'll actually be safe here if I reveal my suspicions to her too soon.

As much as I loathe biting my tongue and spouting the polite, political lies everyone expects of me, I say, "It's lovely. Especially the train."

"Oh, thank you." She grabs my other hand, then looks at Candace. "We've become almost sisters over this past month, so I feel like you are part of my family as well."

I want to correct her, say Candace is only my half-sister, but only to keep Kaloni further away from the people I actually care about.

"I'll have to come for a visit soon," Candace says, looking at me.

She's scared.

Maybe she's right to be.

"Oh, I was trying to find you because you play some kind of instrument, don't you?" Kaloni asks me.

Anyone with sufficiently strong control of the wind can quiet their steps, Amval said. I know she has wind powers. I just don't know exactly how strong she is.

I nod. "The lute."

"You have to join the band when they return," she says with a smile. "I want everyone to see how talented you are."

Or maybe she just wants me where she can keep an eye on me.

ONE STEP FORWARD

Amval

A FEW DAYS AFTER KALONI'S CORONATION, I WAIT IN THE SIDE ROOM Ingrid let me into. Through a crack in the door, I watch staff rushing past with crisp precision. Ever since Kaloni took the throne, the palace has returned to its old self. Perhaps even more efficient than it was under Mother and Father, though I mouth a prayer to the sky after thinking that. It seems Kaloni is a better leader than any of us dreamed.

I inhale slowly. My people are in good hands—or they will be, just as soon as I root out whoever is hunting my family like a ghost in the night. Kaloni must be their next target, and this time, instead of settling for my siblings and I watching the carnage, they want the eyes of the whole kingdom.

My aching jaw informs me I've clenched so tightly my teeth are complaining. Releasing is an active force of will. The more I watch Kaloni thrive, the more I resent whoever stole so much of her family from her already. She deserves to be queen, and I intend to ensure she gets to keep her crown.

The door I'm watching opens, and Lady Ceyiz steps out. She glances down the hallway, each direction—a sure sign she's hiding something. Then, she locks the door to her bedroom behind her and scurries away.

I breathe slowly until she rounds the corner, then for another few heartbeats, running my fingers over the spare key Ingrid... liberated from one of the maids. When I'm sure the coast is clear, I explode out of my hiding place, unlock the door, and slip inside before anyone can catch me outside the stables.

The luxury of the room barely registers—I only have eyes for the small desk in the corner. Lady Ceyiz rarely ever visits the stables, and even Nur rarely leaves them. She could pull on her husband's connections to convince certain grooms to do her bidding, but mind-linking those of such low status would carry a taboo I'm sure she cares about.

That means there must be a paper trail.

I throw open her desk and begin my hunt, wishing Ingrid could be here with me. She's too busy seeing off the last of her family—and the more we're seen together, the more this murderer has reason to wonder about us. Still, I hum one of her songs for company as I search. Airy, building to a powerful crescendo.

"Goddess above, Lady Ceyiz writes to her sister a lot," I mumble, shuffling through letter after letter. They don't seem to be coded, but I guess I wouldn't know if it were a good enough code. What I do know is that they're marked as if they traveled all the way to the far eastern reaches of Lightning Cape, and that's enough to toss them on the pile of useless items.

Also, there is a small army of stationery and supplies—appropriate for a woman who writes this many letters—and a wicked-looking letter opener that I consider pocketing several times just so that she won't have it. But if she's going to the trouble of these convoluted plans, she's unlikely to just up and stab Kaloni.

And apparently, that's not the only reason she won't be doing that. I ransack the whole desk, even find the false bottom in which Lady Ceyiz has hidden what is obviously some kind of rainy-day fund in a leather pouch, and there's nothing.

No letters to the stables. No scribbled notes. No murderous plans.

For a moment, I sit back in the wreckage I've created. I wasn't sure it was her, but...well, I was sure I would find something. An arrow pointing me to the real culprit, at least.

I glance out the window and realize disappointment is going to have to wait. Clean-up comes first.

"THE WORST THING I FOUND WAS A SLY DIG AT ONE OF MOTHER'S dresses." I groan and drop my head back against a pile of rocks as the sun sets over the distant horizon.

"Damn." Ingrid shakes her head. "You made a compelling case for her."

Passing notes is complicated and dangerous, so when there is too much to relay, we agreed to meet up outside the palace walls, in one of the caves that pock the cliff below. They are sacred caves, only for the dead, but I think that means I'm well within my rights to use them. Even better, we're invisible to the palace above but close enough that we can race back without seeming like we were hiding.

"My uncle was just as charming as always," she grumbles, "and persists in not admitting anything interesting."

I've started to look forward to these meetings more than anything else in my day, even if we're just reciting our failures back to each other.

"Double damn," I say, a phrase she used once and I haven't been able to get out my head since.

She stares at me for a heartbeat and then bursts out laughing. Goddess above, her laugh. I close my eyes to savor the sound.

"Oh, don't make that face." Sand patters against my cheeks, and I open my eyes to see her hiding her hand, like someone else might have thrown the little projectiles.

"Which face is that?" I demand as I swirl up a little tornado of sand.

She makes a moony-eyed expression, and I spin the sand at her because she simply has to be wrong. At the very least, my eyes were closed.

"Not fair!" she complains. "I don't have any magical powers."

"Ah, and that means I should believe you're completely helpless." I reach behind her back and pull out the knife I know she started keeping there since the funeral. It glints in the low light of the cave.

She grabs it. "That's for when my uncle finally irritates me enough, not for you."

"You'd rob me of my murderer's kill?" I feign shock, trying to stay playful. It is more difficult than I hoped.

"Just for that, I hope it's not him," she replies with another handful of sand that I catch in the breeze and send soaring away.

"Who next, then?" My smile fades as I ask the question. We may have chosen Lady Ceyiz and Lord Faruk as our first two targets, but clearly, not all our choices were correct. I know it's just as likely that he has nothing to do with this than that he does. There is a whole castle to investigate, one by one.

"Well... it would be much easier to benefit from these murders if they had some claim to the throne." Ingrid sketches something in the thin sand absently.

I shake my head. "The crown descends along the Som line. Only."

"There have to be some farther-off branches, then." She bends her head, totally focused on her doodle. "A cousin or two who wouldn't mind getting the big seat?"

"Yakup." I swallow. "Father's sister-in-law's son from her first marriage. We don't see him often, but I've never trusted him."

Not since he arrived for the ball celebrating our glorious return and made certain to let me know that he'd sat on the throne while we were in hiding. King Gavin banned anyone from doing that, but he'd made an exception for Yakup for some reason. When I saw the twinkle in my cousin's eye, I knew he wanted that seat again more than almost anything.

"Yakup," she repeats. "Is he here?"

"He has been." Not at the name-blessing, but it wouldn't have been hard to sneak in with all the chaos. And wasn't Yalim from a similar part of the kingdom as Yakup's holdings? "He may still be. I haven't been keeping close track."

"And for him to take the throne—"

"He would have to slaughter my whole family and his parents." My gut churns. Someone with my blood could be the murderer, and I didn't even notice. I didn't think to consider anyone in the family, no matter how distant the connection is. "You are brilliant." I kiss Ingrid on the side of the head and discover she's frowning instead of grinning ear-to-ear like she should be. "What?"

"That just seems like a lot of murder to get away with," she says slowly. "Are you sure there's no one closer…?"

The suggestion sends ice over my skin. "I don't know how your family is, but I assure you, there cannot be anyone closer. Do me the favor of never implying that again."

She holds up her hands. "I know Anwen thought about it. I figured I'd ask."

One of my own siblings? "Not in a thousand lifetimes."

"All right," she says, swiping her hand through her drawing to destroy it. "Forget I said anything. Tomorrow, Yakup."

"Good." I nod, my heartbeat slowly settling. "Apologies. I know our family isn't exactly normal."

She shakes her head, brushing away my apology. There's a look on her face I can't place. "No one's is."

I bite my tongue instead of continuing to explain why it's impossible. She can't understand, not if one of her brothers plotted murder against another.

"This is awful," she says bluntly.

"I'm—"

She silences me with one hand. "No apologies. I mean, we were finally having fun; you were enjoying yourself, and now it's ruined."

I swallow more apologies. "What is there to do?"

"This." She stands, strips, and shifts in a flash. Her wolf stands before me, gray as the early dawn and powerful.

I don't know where she's going with this, but I want to know. My clothes join hers on the ground in the cave, and I transform. Together, we crowd against the stone, too broad to fit. She barks once, high and playful, then takes off.

I lunge after her, blood racing through my veins.

THE CHASE

Ingrid

EVERYONE ALWAYS SAYS ANWEN IS THE FASTEST. MAYBE HE IS—BUT HE'S never been stupid enough to ask me to race, so I can't prove him wrong.

As I tear out of the cliff side cave, onto the narrow strip of stone that winds up toward the palace and down toward the beach, all that matters is that I'm a hell of a lot faster than Amval's muscled form. His feet land heavily behind me, skidding on pebbles as we race away from the tension.

I never should've suggested it was one of his siblings. I knew what he was going to say. It doesn't matter that the palace is a completely different place since Kaloni took over or that she's the one who benefits from these deaths the most. She even did them in the right order to take power. If her parents died first, then Amval, it would have been obvious. This way, it just looks tragic.

But I can't prove it. And without proof, it's just like when I tried to spend time with the whole family, right after Amval's "death"—I'm the outsider, trying to break into a dynamic made of stone.

He's safe. And if I'm right, so are the rest of the Soms. I can bide my time until I can prove what I already know.

And for now, we run.

My paws hit the sand, spraying it in every direction. Dammit. I charge toward the water, for the sturdier wet sand. It still slides underneath me, but at least I don't feel like I'm running in a dream, unable to move forward, no matter how hard I try.

Amval spots my hesitation and cuts me off at a steeper angle. His teeth graze my tail, and I yip as I whip it away. He offers a guttural, wolfish laugh in return.

That's how he wants to play this?

I smile as I race up the beach, saltwater splashing on my fur. He tries to use his ease on the drier sand to corner me, but he just can't keep up. A dock stands up ahead, a single boat knocking rhythmically against its moorings. I'll duck into the shadows there, hide, and surprise him when he comes looking.

Outrunning him is easy. Getting the upper hand is much harder.

We reach the dock. I pour on a little extra speed, dart ahead, and duck under the far side of the worn, salt-stained wood. He huffs, playfully aggrieved. Once out of his line of sight, I sprint to the opposite side, take a deep breath, and duck beneath the water.

Salt stings my eyes when I open them to watch. My lungs burn for air by the time I see his paws stir the ocean floor. Three...two...

I explode out of the water and tackle him. We topple nose-over-tail through the waves. His teeth find my side, mine sinking into his leg. Water very happily makes its way into my lungs, and I splutter.

Amval shifts, and wind clears the ocean away down to the sand a heartbeat later. He stands before me, dripping wet and gloriously naked. All muscle with a smile and glowing amber eyes.

"Can't have you drowning," he says.

I launch myself at him, shifting as I go, and he catches me as our mouths meet. No better way to diffuse tension than this. The water crashes back into place around us, but I barely notice. I'm too busy wrapping my legs around his waist and tasting the smile on his lips between basil and charcoal.

He bites my lower lip like he tried to bite my side. I bite back, and he laughs into my mouth. When he moves beneath me, I pull reluctantly back and look around.

Amval is striding out of the water, arms clasped around me, but he's not headed for the beach.

"I'm not sure a splintery old dock will be much more comfortable," I say, lining his throat with kisses.

"It won't." His voice is almost a groan already. "But the boat has a bed."

I drag my teeth along his neck in answer. There's no point pretending this is a lapse in judgment, something I'm doing just once anymore. Amval lied to me—but I would have lied to him if someone put me in the same position. Maybe I wouldn't have sought him out, but he's just as used to company as I am solitude.

And I don't make a habit of lying to other people. Lying to myself is just childish. He's my mate. I was never going to run away.

So I rock my hips against the taut muscle of his abdomen as he carries me along the dock and then onto the rocking boat. My head swims with the motion, but I just manage to notice between kisses that it's surprisingly modest. Like a normal fishing boat, not a royal vessel.

"Is this your family's?" I ask on a gasp.

"It's how we rode back to the palace, after Lightning Cape was ours again."

The smile on his lips fades just slightly, and I crush my mouth against his to try to coax it back. Once I wind my fingers through his hair and pull, it returns like lighting a fire. Like he's real charcoal, just waiting to be brought to life.

He loves his family. I know that. But I also know the starched prince I met that first night is the Amval they and their expectations built. If he didn't grow up needing to take over a conquered kingdom, he would be this man. The one who chases me when I run, who moves the ocean to keep me from coughing. Who laughs when I laugh and kisses like a man dying of thirst when I kiss him.

This is my mate. Under all that polish, he has the same sort of wants that I do. He just hasn't had the chance to go after those wants.

Maybe I can help him build a world where he can.

He falls with me onto the low-slung bed at the back of the boat, which groans with our weight. When he drags his mouth down onto my chest and over my breasts, I groan in unison. My skin sings with his touch. He seems to be everywhere, surrounding me, consuming me. Hands on my hips, in my hair, in my mouth. Tongue on my chest, dancing lower with a combination of threat and promise. A symphony of touch, threatening to unravel me.

But no symphony is complete without a few harmonies.

I drag a hand down his side, following the lines of his muscles. He speeds his attentions, like I've just set a timer on him. I trace the scratches I left on his back when I discovered his secret, now healing scars, and he shivers. When I drag human nails back up the same paths, his groan vibrates against my skin.

An image floats through my head—the two of us, hand in hand and laughing as we walk back to our clothes. Tonight, I want that.

So I leave my nails blunt as I scratch back down again, all the way onto the curve of his ass. His hardness presses into my hip, and my mouth waters.

When he pulls back to take a breath, I shimmy lower on the bed. My heels knock into the wall almost immediately, and to reach my target, I end up with my legs nearly over Amval's head. But I kiss along the thin skin of his hip, tasting the salt and herb of him hungrily.

He threads a hand into my hair, holding on rather than pushing me forward. I lick my lips, lick him, and his answering groan is all I need to know this is exactly what I want.

I take him into my mouth, run my tongue along his length. His smell surrounds me, overwhelms me until I feel like I'm the one being consumed again. When his grip on my hair tightens, forcing me to slow down, I moan around him.

His hips jerk forward, but his hand doesn't loosen. Slow and slower. He drags his pleasure out, savoring every inch of my mouth.

His amber eyes burn, and so do I, like I caught his fire. I reach down between my legs, desperate for a little bit of relief from the flames.

Amval tracks the motion with his eyes. "Impatient?"

I can only nod, but I'm always impatient. He should already know that.

"If you can't wait." He pulls out of my mouth suddenly, leaving me open and surprised. A string of something wet connects us for a heartbeat, then lands on my bare chest. I make a small, high sound at the absence before he lifts my legs onto his shoulders.

His cock brushes against my hand, against my dripping center. My muscles burn slightly as he bends me almost in half to reach my mouth for another searing kiss. I abandon the warmth between my legs to line him up, and the second I do, he slides home.

The moan that stumbles out of my lips sounds nothing like me, but Amval closes his eyes just like he did when I laughed. Like there's nothing in this world he'd rather hear. So I let my mouth fall open and link my ankles behind his head. I've never been much of a singer, but I have a captive, appreciative audience.

And he shows his appreciation by fitting a hand into the tiny space between us to dance over the bud at the apex of my thighs. My vision goes white with pleasure. I grab his head, his shoulder where I bit him, anything I can hang onto. An anchor in the storm. He puts his hand over mine, locking me in place. His pulse thrums under my fingers as we move toward the apex together.

He meets my gaze, and under the want is something warmer. He opens his mouth like he's going to say something.

"Amval!" I shout as my whole body locks with euphoria. My eyes shut, and I lose myself in the waves.

Everything but our hands, and his pulse. The man he is without anything else around us. The man I've been chasing this whole time.

CHANGE OF PACE

Amval

INGRID AND I WALK HAND-IN-HAND ALONG THE BEACH IN THE
moonlight, our heads down on the long trek back to our clothes. She
hums to herself, a peaceful smile on her face. Perhaps the first actual
peace I've ever seen in her expression, at least while she's awake.

Which is why I will not be saying what I nearly said on the boat. It
is enough for me to know that I love her, at least until we prove who
has been murdering my family.

Then, we'll both have to start answering difficult questions about
what comes next. Her blank disinterest in leading a kingdom rings in
my mind. Lightning Cape is Kaloni's now, but I don't see a future
where I don't at least stay as an advisor. I don't know if Ingrid would
be happy as a politician's wife.

So I won't tell her now. I can't. Not after all she's done for me.

But I can brush a kiss across her cheek and ask if we can meet up
more often. When she grins at me, I know I made the right choice.

A few days later, Tek smacks the back of my head. "You have to come. We all know you've been disappearing at night. If you've got a girl in town, I won't even complain when you sneak off to see her."

"Why haven't you said anything before now?" My face burns under the veil. Have I really been that obvious? Seeing Ingrid every night has made me a bit more distractible. I almost killed one of the horses by absently offering it the saporange I grabbed for my breakfast instead of a roseapple.

Tek stares at me like I have two heads. "You seem happier. No one is going to tattle on whatever's doing that unless you actually poison one of the horses, and even then, Nur will only hear from the hard asses."

"Oh." I glance at Tek—he looks earnest enough. Like he and the other grooms really do care whether the groom who replaced their friend has something in his life.

Ingrid said she would be late and tired tonight. Something with Joli demands her attention. After days of seeing each other, skipping one would perhaps be smart.

"All right."

Tek drags me out of the stable to join the pack of grooms already waiting outside.

"Blessed fucking drinking." Mesut nudges me with a grin. "Invite the girl."

I find myself smiling back. We've worked together occasionally, and he is pleasant enough, but none of the other grooms talk as much as Tek. To me, that is. I just assumed he barely noticed me.

It seems I've been wrong about a lot of things.

We parade through town to the Gruesome Pony. Ozkan meets us at the door with the usual blank refusal to let us in, and I join in on the ribbing.

Inside, the awful troubadour plays his awful music like always, and Tek orders a few rounds. I lose "worst Nur encounter" and have to help him carry them back to the table, but I don't mind. A few more people trickle in as our group starts to get loud, like our noise is what's pulling them in.

Instinct flares, telling me to quiet everyone. We're drawing too much attention.

I tamp it down. We haven't been in hiding for a long while, and it might be time I start acting like that. I drain half my ale—it truly is awful, like Tek warned me—and take what has become my seat, already left open for me.

"And then Lord Yetir looks at me, flat on his back in a horse pie, and asks if I'm quite sure I fastened the saddle correctly." Tek slams his mug down on the table, sloshing ale everywhere, as the rest of us burst into laughter.

"That would explain why he backed away from me while reeking to all the stars," I say.

"I thought starlights couldn't lie!" Mesut gestures accusingly at me.

"No, truly!" I stand and mimic the aging lord's scuttle as best I can. The laughter redoubles, and the troubadour hits such a painfully sour note that I wince before I can smile.

"Oh, give it up!" Tek hollers. "No one wants to hear it."

"I'd like to see one of you do this job!" he replies, awkwardly adjusting the naqun in his lap.

"I certainly could," I mumble into my second ale. I need my wits about me, but I can only avoid so many drinks.

Tek smiles, and I realize the mistake I've made. "My friend Sash here is more than happy to take you up on that offer."

My stomach drops. Ingrid is the only soul alive who's ever heard me play. I shake my head wildly. "It is, um, a sacred practice—"

"Too good for the Pony." Mesut laughs, not entirely unkindly, but he already sounds resigned to my refusal. Just how often have I said no to these people? Why are they so forgiving?

Perhaps because Tek mentioned, before I worked with Mesut, that tightening the buckles hurts his hands, so I made sure to do every single one before he could.

"All right." I stand, heart hammering. "But only for my friends' ears."

They roar a cheer. Two of them try to carry me to the stage, but I manage to squirm out of their grasp just in time. The troubadour shoots me a bitter look, but he hands over the naqun. I tune it as well as I can in the noise before setting my fingers to the strings.

Low, resonant notes roll out of the depths of the instrument. The hardest of my instruments to hide, the naqun is the one I have the least practice with. But my hands remember the strings better than my mind does, and I take up the drinking song Ingrid played for me so long ago. Faster this time, and with more bounce. I wish she were here. A higher string would round out the melody perf—

Tek starts singing, loud but in the neighborhood of the key. Mesut takes up the song quickly, and within a few moments, they're all singing. Not just the grooms, but Ozkan, the other patrons, everyone. Eventually, even the bitter troubadour taps his toe.

Sometimes, I think climbing with the wind holding me up feels a little like flying. This? This may truly be the closest I've gotten.

One song flows into the next, buoyed by the cheers of half the tavern. My heart dips and soars with the movement of the music. My fingers move like they never have before, as if the others' excitement is greasing my every gesture.

Only when a string snaps under my hand—to the boos of my audience—do I realize how much time has passed. Two hours, according to the timepiece over Ozkan's head and the pile of cups in front of my friends.

"I am sorry," I say to the crowd. To the troubadour, I murmur, "I'll replace the string."

He sighs. "You gave the old bastard a better workout than it's ever gotten. You can have the damn thing, as far as I'm concerned. I like other instruments better anyway."

And he walks away, leaving me clutching an admittedly worn, but once-beautiful, naqun. The very first I've ever owned.

Behind me, Tek and the other grooms pound on the table, demanding I come back to them to be properly celebrated. But I need a moment. To recenter, to adjust to the weight of the instrument in my hands. I swallow and wander to the bar.

"The cheapest shot you have." I'll have to replace the string and perhaps pay for it to be serviced.

Ozkan snorts and pours me a finger of something gleaming brown. "After all the business you brought in? My top-shelf is on the house."

I take the shot quickly, under my veil. It's worse than almost anything I've had in the palace, and miles better than anything else I've had in the Pony.

"Another," a familiar voice says.

From a month and a half of control, I do not jump when I hear my brother behind me.

"I'll pay." Cirocco steps up to the bar next to me when Ozkan hesitates. "Clearly, he deserves it."

"Thank you," I say in my lowest, least recognizable voice. "But I've had enough."

"Not if the prince is paying." Ozkan fills my cup again. "Dump it in the gutter if you like."

Cirocco passes him the money then turns to me. "I've heard starlights play before, but never like that."

In my wildest dreams, I never imagined my family would hear me play. I thought I would go to the grave with this secret, as I assume they all have their own.

But tonight, I'm not his brother. I am just the man who played another's instrument for two hours straight, holding the rowdiest tavern in town at attention.

"I didn't learn in the abbey," I reply.

Cirocco laughs. "I don't imagine they teach many drinking songs there. Where did you learn?"

"Privately." I brush the time-softened wood of the naqun. "My family didn't approve."

He nods slowly. "If you played for them, I suspect they might change their minds."

"Perhaps," I mumble. I almost wish he would've responded with a brash insult like Tek. It would be easier to take than the careful consideration of my brother's gaze.

To deflect his attention, I say, "What are you doing here, Your Highness?"

"Cir, please." He shakes his head. "Just while we're here."

"Of course." I bow my head, shocked by the unfamiliar nickname. I thought I knew everything about him.

"I can't claim to like the ale." He lifts his glass to Ozkan, who makes a rude gesture in return. I realize he comes here often. "In truth, I can't give you a reason."

I blink. Cirocco is always sure of himself. He considers every angle, takes his time, and then offers up an answer I wouldn't have dreamt of but fits perfectly.

He glances over his shoulder at the grooms, making an increasing racket to try to lure me back to them.

"Are you lonely?" I ask before I can stop myself.

"In my family?" Cirocco shakes his head. "Impossible."

He's right about that. "Then why are you looking at my friends?"

Terrible negotiation technique. That's the question before the question, not after. But it's easier not to play those games with Ozkan's ale in my veins and the weight of my first naqun in my lap.

"I always see them here," he says, "and that's going to change. Queen Kaloni just signed a conscription order to help with reconquering the north."

"She what?" I say, forgetting who I am to him.

"The public will learn tomorrow. I told her it was fast." Cirocco shrugs, his gaze drifting back to my friends. "Their shouting is part of what makes this place. I spent half my childhood skulking around in corners of taverns even smaller and worse than this one. They never flinch away from the middle table."

I inhale slowly through my nose. Reconquering the north is clever, but our army is already strong. A conscription is unnecessary—

But I wasn't in the meetings that led Kaloni to this decision. I'm not even sure Cirocco was. She has proven herself a good leader thus far, so she's probably right.

"Join us." I stand, holding the drink he bought me. Tek will love drinking the prince's money.

He shakes his head. "The moment someone other than Ozkan recognizes me, I can never return."

I want to insist, to explain that he can trust these people—but he has no reason to trust me.

"But thank you," he says. "And keep playing."

I have to save his life. I want him to know whose music he loved.

YOU AGAIN

Ingrid

"I HEARD THAT STARFALL MOUNTAIN IS BEHIND THE RECENT... DEATHS in the Som family," an officious-looking noblewoman says to her friend as they scurry past me.

I drop my charcoal onto the ledge at the bottom of my easel. After a month and a half of everyone calling the murders accidents, this is the third person today I've heard attribute them to something other than cruel fate. And I may have heard something like that yesterday, but I thought I was losing my mind. The palace is still packed with nobles from all over, lingering after Kaloni's coronation—we've got no shortage of people with no idea what they're talking about.

But this is no longer a coincidence. And this woman is the first with a name, not just "another kingdom."

The pair of noblewomen disappear out of sight, and I wonder if I should chase after them. Then, I consider my soot-stained hands and the filthy apron over my dress. I either need to clean up or seek different sources.

As always, the choice is an easy one.

I pack up my sketch—the Windy Ocean, as seen through a high window—and send all my art supplies back to my room before heading downstairs. At this time of day, I'll be underfoot in the kitchen, but the maids should be between bursts of activity. I find three of them in a makeshift break room inside a linen closet, playing cards.

"Deal me in?" I take the final seat at their table.

"I'm Dilara." The one I don't recognize passes cards my way slowly, like she's too scared to refuse but wishes I wasn't here. "And this is—"

"Karya and Bengu." I smile at them both. "This isn't my first game of cards between the napkins."

Dilara relaxes. "You're that princess, aren't you?"

"Ingrid." I look at my cards. "If that's the one you mean."

Karya nods. "Nothing to worry about with her."

"Well, I'm a decent card player." I grin, and Bengu laughs sheepishly. I beat her badly last time.

"Prove it." Dilara lays down her first set, and the game begins.

My luck is decent, but my bluffing is better. Lying usually isn't worth the time, but I'll say whatever I need to for a card game. In the end, I scrape out a win, two points ahead of Dilara, who has completely lost the hard shell she had when I came in.

"So, what do you want to know?" Karya asks.

Dilara raises an eyebrow.

"I never said I was playing for information." But Karya knows me too well at this point. There's no point in trying to maintain my innocence for long. "All right, but I know I didn't make the bet, so you don't owe me anything."

She grins. "We know that."

Goddess, this is so much easier than trying to worm details out of those noblewomen would have been. "Have you heard the rumor that some other kingdom caused the recent deaths?"

Karya covers her mouth in shock. Dilara shakes her head slowly from side to side, never taking her eyes off my face, like she's trying to read whether I believe it or not. Bengu, though, just turns pale. I look at her.

"I heard it," she whispers.

"Did they say who it was?" Karya asks before I can. "I need to know whether I'm cleaning a murderer's room."

Bengu shrugs. "I've heard a few different answers. Lilywind because they want territory on the mainland—"

"That's ridiculous," Dilara interrupts. "Whaleberry Harbor is much closer to Lilywind. They would start there."

She's right. Moonlight Beach is even closer to the island kingdom than Lightning Cape.

"Starfall Mountain?" Bengu offers. "I have no idea why."

Karya scoffs. "That makes even less sense."

"Anyone else?" I ask.

She shakes her head.

Interesting. Starfall is still rebuilding, and some people are having trouble trusting a former rogue as a leader. Lilywind is almost close enough to suspect, and they've been exclusively peaceful for a long time. Two kingdoms unlikely to actually try anything like this, but whom people could believe would.

So, the perfect kingdoms to start rumors about if you wanted to deflect attention.

"Who did you hear this from?" I ask.

Bengu leans in. "One of the soldiers. Recai."

I SPEND HALF A DAY TRACING THE RUMOR THROUGH THE PALACE. RECAI, it turns out, heard it from one of the visiting Oakspring Dunes soldiers, who are of course leaving today. I just barely manage to catch one of them, guarding the last carriage in the royal caravan. He didn't hear the rumor, but he did see the soldier Recai talking to a chef at a strange time. So I have to fight through the lunch rush to figure out which of Umit's several dozen right hands spoke with

Oakspring Dunes, only to be pointed in the direction of Redwood Nimbus instead.

The contingency from Redwood Nimbus is bizarrely still here with no plans for departure, despite the fact that they have no personal connection to Lightning Cape and not nearly enough political sway to get to do whatever they want. Raven and Kieran left last week; Finn and Xandra a few days after that. My gut tells me there is something to find at Redwood Nimbus, so I do what I've been resisting—stop at my room for a bath and a change of clothes.

An hour later, I knock on Redwood's primary diplomat's door. The Alpha and Luna aren't public people, so Lady Evangeline and her daughter do most of their socializing, according to the book Candace made me that I quickly skimmed through. An older woman with an effusive smile answers the door.

"Princess Ingrid! What a lovely surprise!" She curtsies deeply. "I'm Lady Evangeline. Please, do come in."

And she keeps talking as she sits me on the couch, pours tea, and summons "some after-lunch nibbles" from the kitchen. Somehow, she doesn't actually say anything the whole time. I grit my teeth and try to make it look like a smile. She's the worst kind of diplomat—an expert in worthless noise.

"Oh, I wept for days when I heard what happened to you," she says, laying a hand over her heart. "I lost my mate after two long decades with him, and it is still painful every day. I can't imagine him being taken from me after just one night."

Taken from me doesn't sound like how someone talks about illness. "It was terrible. I just wish I had someone to hold responsible."

Evangeline glances around like someone may have snuck into the tiny sitting room. Goddess above, she's all drama, isn't she?

"I may have someone for you."

And I've never really minded drama. "Who?"

"I heard a rumor, nothing solid...but apparently, Luna Aisha has some designs on Lightning Cape," she whispers loud enough that I wouldn't be surprised if they could hear her in the hallway.

"Luna Aisha?" I say. "Of Lilywind?"

She nods. "It surprised me as well, but what a perfect veil, isn't it? Most people would assume Lilywind would reach for Whaleberry Harbor if they decided to attack another kingdom."

I shake my head like this is new. The name is, I suppose, but it feels distinctly pulled out of a hat. Blaming the Alpha is too standard, the first lie anyone would reach for. Going a step further, calling out the Luna, almost verges on too strange to be fake—but Luna Aisha is coming up on her seventieth birthday, and she has tea with Raven once a month, at which she barely seems like she would kill a fly.

"Can I ask where you heard this from? I don't want to go making accusations if I'm not sure."

Evangeline's eyes widen, like she never dreamed I'd do anything with this information. "Oh, just one of my staff."

Stupid. Another wild goose chase. I sigh. "If you could tell me who—"

A door swings open, and I realize I wasn't wrong at all.

Corwyn Hajni, wearing a steward's uniform in Redwood colors, steps into the room. Thick, gnarled scars cover half his face, and he ducks his head like he's trying to hide the rest of it, but Finn and Xandra made sure I would recognize him no matter what. He even smells like Corwyn, sea salt and balsam.

By all the stars, Astralis is involved in this.

"Lady Evangeline," Corwyn says, disdain grating through his polite demeanor, "you have a tea in half an hour."

"Oh, of course. Apologies." She nods to me. "Kael here makes sure I don't leave my head behind because I'm too busy chatting."

I rip my gaze away from Kael before he can realize who I am. Technically, we never met outside of a brief political introduction. He has no reason to suspect I'd be the one to see through his disguise. "It's no trouble at all."

Lady Evangeline stands, obviously waiting for me to say we should do this again. I curtsy and leave. Diplomats like her are why I'm happy I have no future in politics.

Outside her rooms, I hesitate. I could go right to Amval—but this doesn't prove anything about Kaloni, and I'm still so sure she's involved. Corwyn couldn't orchestrate this on his own, not from Redwood Nimbus, of all places. I'm sure he crawled there because it's the last place anyone would look.

I need more. Amval will believe me, but not about the important parts. For that, I'm going to need to see Corwyn and Kaloni together.

I wait outside Redwood's rooms, tucked away in an alcove, until my feet hurt, and my stomach starts rumbling for dinner. If only I hadn't cleaned up; I'd still have my charcoal and a few scraps of paper in my pocket so at least I could doodle to pass the time. Damn Lady Evangeline and her standards.

Finally, though, Corwyn leaves the rooms. I trail behind him as he hurries away. Frankly, I'm not surprised Finn and Xandra didn't spot him. The few times I saw him, he strutted around with so much confidence, he looked like as much of a prince as Xandra. This version of him has a servant's scuttle down perfectly, dodging auto-matically around ignorant nobility with muttered apologies. If I hadn't noticed his face, I wouldn't have looked twice at him.

And it seems he's counting on that because he doesn't know how to lose someone. Even weaving like he is, I follow him easily through the bluestone halls. He never thinks to check behind him, either. His one remaining scrap of cockiness, I guess.

He leads me straight to a far corner of the palace, not too far away from the room Joli first put me in. The traffic slowly thins, becomes all staff and no nobility. My heartbeat kicks up the tempo. There's a reason Joli put me here—if you need to hide something, it's the best place in Som Palace to do it.

At the top of a tower, under a specific archway, I can just see someone marked with chalk or something else white. Corwyn stops. Alone. I gnaw on my thumbnail. There could be all kinds of magic he's waiting for, secret messages like the ones he was using with Lord Denidor. None of that will be enough proof.

Then, maybe even quieter than Anwen was when he showed me what the wind could do to silence someone, a shape appears at the far end of the hallway. Corwyn straightens. This is who he was waiting for. I squint, begging the person to move a little faster so I can see who it is and confirm my suspicions.

In a dark dress, with her hair piled high to fit her crown once more, Kaloni floats up to Corwyn and murmurs something that sounds like a greeting.

I turn and sprint away as quietly as I can. Amval has to know.

IMPOSSIBLE

Amval

I UNFASTEN A BUCKLE, WORKING QUIETLY ALONGSIDE MESUT. HE doesn't even look at me, but I know now that he notices. I should have realized all along.

"Sash?" Ingrid yells.

I jerk back.

"Your girl?" Mesut asks with a sly smile.

I shake my head, praying he didn't recognize her voice. That no one recognizes her at all. I burst out of the stall and find her standing in the middle of the aisle.

"What are you doing here?" I hiss as I approach.

"We need to talk." This close, I can see her eyes are wide, her chest heaving. "Now."

My stomach drops. The monster struck again. Another one of my siblings is dead, and I let it happen.

"Outside." I drag her into the yard, where at least there's some chance half the stable won't realize I've been sneaking out to see Princess Ingrid at all hours.

She's shaky and slow. Like a bolt of lightning, I realize another possibility, one I didn't even see coming—there was an attempt on Ingrid's life, and she barely escaped. Protective rage surges through me. I've been letting my mate put herself at risk while I take shelter outside.

No matter what she has to tell me, one thing is certain–that ends today. Something massive has changed, and I am tired of hiding and waiting. The slow gathering of evidence is only letting the bodies pile up.

As soon as we're anything approaching out of earshot, I spin up a breeze to disguise our words and nod for her to speak.

"I know who's behind everything," she says.

I sway, almost collapse. "No one else is dead? You are safe?"

She nods, barely seeming to hear me. "Yes, and I don't think anyone else is going to die, as long as we're careful."

Relief hits like a shot of Ozkan's worst liquor, dizzying in its potency. "Thank the Goddess. Who is it? Lord Faruk? Yaqup?"

"No." She swallows. "It's Kaloni."

I laugh, still feeling delirious. "All right, I understand, I don't have a good enough sense of humor. What did you actually find?"

She stares at me as if she was trying to press a thought into my brain. "That's what I found. Kaloni is behind your attempted murder and your parents' 'accident.'"

I want to laugh again, but my mouth feels like it's full of sand. I can't even tell Ingrid how horribly wrong she is. My sister would never do this to me.

"I know how it sounds. That's why I didn't want to tell you until I was sure." She glances over her shoulder. A paranoid gesture for someone who burst into my hiding place and all but called me by my real name.

My anger over someone hurting Ingrid starts to burn into something else, something low and simmering I can't quite name.

Ingrid plunges onward. "There's a new rumor in the palace that the deaths were murders, perpetrated by another kingdom, but the kingdoms people are saying don't make any sense, so I thought that was the perfect cover for someone who thought they might get caught soon. Deflecting blame, you know?"

Somehow, I find myself nodding. This has nothing to do with Kaloni. She wouldn't resort to petty rumormongering to get her way.

"So I followed the rumor all the way back to the source—and that source is Corwyn Hajni!"

"The lord?" I say blankly. "Isn't he dead?"

"Escaped." Ingrid scowls. "And Finn and Xandra decided not to tell anyone this, but Corwyn started the civil war with the help of a group named Astralis. We… don't know exactly what they wanted, just that Corwyn and Lord Denidor were promised positions of power and that Astralis has significant resources."

I am dreaming. That is the only possible explanation for why Ingrid would come to me so recklessly with such an impossible accusation and then explain so little. My head aches, and I wonder if I can just lie down in my cot to end this all.

"Amval!" she snaps, and I realize I was looking away. "Are you even listening to me?"

My mouth is too full of sand to explain my thoughts. She's only a dream, anyway.

Though I did hear whispers that Lords Corwyn and Denidor were implicated in the civil war. Both apparently died in the conflict, so they never amounted to much, but I heard them all the same.

No. If this is not a dream, then Ingrid has somehow lived with my sister for a month and a half and still come to the conclusion she could do this.

"Sorry. I know this is overwhelming." She shakes her head. "Corwyn is going by a fake name, so it's obviously bad that he's here, so I followed him. He went to a secret meeting—with Kaloni!"

"What did they discuss?" I manage.

She looks away. "I didn't stay long enough to find out. But it was clear they knew each other!"

"Lord Corwyn was discussed as a potential marriage alliance for Kaloni, if she didn't mate quickly," I say. "We all met him many times."

Ingrid blinks. "There are other things. The palace runs like an army now. Maids have to hide to take their free time."

"Do they have to hide, or do they prefer their privacy?" My voice returns more and more with every word, powered by that simmering in my gut.

"I—" She scowls. "Have you heard about the conscriptions? I wasn't aware Lightning Cape's army was weak."

"There is strong and there is strong enough to conquer wildlands abandoned to rogues," I reply sharply. Perhaps I wondered something similar, but Ingrid certainly lacks the knowledge to understand why my sister makes her decisions. The very fact that she would accuse her is proof.

Ingrid crosses her arms. "Her coronation speech sounded like something my father would have given, and she's been keeping—"

"Stop." I hold up a hand to silence her. "Kaloni has her flaws. She is overly conciliatory and tends to play peacemaker rather than asking for what she wants. But in a hundred lifetimes, no one would compare her to King Gavin. He was a monster."

"And what do you call someone who murders their parents and brother for the throne?"

"Falsely accused." I take a step back from Ingrid. The simmering infuses my bones, my muscles, and I ache to hit something. To destroy it. There is no other way to vent this feeling.

Her mouth falls open. "I just fucking proved it."

"You have a pile of ideas. Implications. Things anyone who actually knows my sister would dismiss in a heartbeat." I clench and unclench my fists. "I told you it could not be one of my siblings. That is impossible."

"That's why it's such a good plan!" She throws her arms up in frustration.

"For a monster," I reply. "And I am sorry that you were raised in a family of monsters, but haven't I earned enough of your trust that you can believe me when I say my family isn't like that?"

Something sharp flickers across her face, and I know I've crossed some line in the sand. Before, I would have seen that line from a mile away and stayed well clear. Mother and Father taught me to. But they're not here anymore, and I need to find the person responsible, not waste time defending those hurt by them.

"How did you earn it?" she demands. "When you lied to me, or when I caught you lying?"

"When I was perfectly honest and patient with you every second after that," I exclaim. "But I suppose you wouldn't have noticed patience. I doubt you even know what it looks like."

She splutters. "What are you saying?"

"I'm saying you have jumped from plan to theory to plan to theory like each one was burning down around you when we were barely finished with any of them," I reply. "And that's what you're doing now. You saw a shred of something that could imply, in the wrong hands, that Kaloni had some role in what happened to my parents, and you're ready to accuse her."

"I waited!" She throws a glare at me, and I meet it with one of my own. "I've suspected her since her Goddess-damned coronation, and I waited until I thought you would believe me. If we want to talk about who should be trusting who, maybe we should talk about that."

Abruptly, I can see everything clearly. Ingrid, the shape of the weeks we've spent together, even that first meeting—they all come down to one thing.

I take another step back and say quietly, "This is because you don't want the throne."

"What?"

"You told me yourself. You don't want to inherit. If you distance me from my family, I'm far less likely to want to stay here, even if you end up being wrong."

She gestures at my veil and uniform. "Are you honestly accusing me of being the one putting the most distance between you and your family?"

"I'm doing what I had to." The simmering grows cold, intractable. "You could have left at any time. Your family has been begging you to, haven't they?"

She stares at me for a long moment, open-mouthed. "I wanted the truth. I wanted justice."

"And when you discovered my secret?" That was when everything changed. Before then, she had no throne to run away from, scared of all the responsibilities it carried.

"I wanted to fucking work alone!" she yells. "This was your idea, remember? You dragged me into your orbit, kicking and screaming."

Her yelling doesn't impress me anymore. I've seen worse from her.

"If you don't want to hear what I have to say, then I'm very happy to go do exactly what I wanted from the beginning," she snaps.

My mark sears, screaming for me to tell her to stay. Maybe she has a reason that will make this all make sense, and then I can prove to her why she's wrong. If we can just stop yelling, there must be some common ground left between us.

Passion flames in her blue eyes—but I've learned well enough how much and how deeply she cares for all her interests. It's one of the things I loved about her.

Love about her.

Will love about her again, someday, when I can stop feeling like there is a knife wedged in my throat.

"I do not want to hear it," I say, turning back to my work and letting the winds surrounding us die.

A DINNER

Ingrid

After Amval proves that there's no point in talking to him, no
matter what kind of evidence I have, my life in Som Palace barely
changes. No one else even knows he's here.

Joli still hangs out with me when she can, but I realized a while
ago that her smuggling business expands far past wartime needs.
She's often gone from the palace for days at a time—days her siblings
only sometimes notice and always chalk up to "just missing her." The
more time I spend with them, the easier it gets to see why they don't
notice a murderer in their midst. They all still act like they're in
hiding, sharing one tiny room. There's a whole palace to hide secrets
in now, and only Joli and Kaloni seem to have realized that. Even
Cirocco, who seems like he always has his head on a swivel, glances
right over his siblings.

At night, when I can hear them laughing in nearby rooms, I sometimes wonder if Candace and the rest of them are right. I should just
go home, leave them to their stupidity and their ignorance.

Shit, I wish I could.

Too stubborn, Father chides in my memory. Not that I ever really cared what he thought. Mother thought the same, though—she was just smart enough to use it rather than fight it. Now that she's gone, it's much easier to see that. How I got all the training I wanted for my music, endless time with my clothes—and a little bit less on the hobbies she didn't approve of. Did I stop blacksmithing because I didn't enjoy it or because there was always something more interesting to do at home when the smith was available?

I don't know anymore. All I know is that, sure, sometimes I'm a little impulsive. But Amval is going to eat his words when I prove, beyond a shadow of a doubt, that Kaloni is behind all of this. I don't drop things that matter.

So, while Joli is gone, I spend most of my days following Corwyn. Now that I've spotted him, it's so obvious that everybody else within these Goddessdamned walls should be embarrassed they haven't noticed. He's dressed like staff, but the most conversation I see him exchange with a staff member is when someone almost walks into him, and he snaps at her. He never looks over his shoulder. He never has anything in his hands. He's just... always walking.

Usually from one of the remaining visiting nobles to another. A few times, I watch the nobles after he leaves them. Without fail, two of them meet up with each other within the next few hours.

He's a courier. Messages too private to write down get passed through him. Maybe Redwood's in on it. Maybe Lady Evangeline is just another of the many patsies in this scheme. Frankly, I don't care.

Because sometimes, those nobles meet with Kaloni.

Every time, I try to listen, but something in those powers of hers must give her some kind of super-hearing. I can't get close enough to make out more than a few words before her head goes up like a hunting dog, and she ends the meeting.

She hasn't caught me yet, but I know it's just a matter of time. She's not stupid—she couldn't have gotten this far if she were. So every hour I spend skulking around this palace, my mark throbbing, is another hour I'm wasting. I need to do something new—overhear one of Corwyn's meetings, break into Kaloni's rooms—but she always manages to keep me just on the outside.

I could use a second body. But it's not like I'm going to tell Joli now.

So when I return to my room one day to find a formal letter, sealed with Lightning Cape-orange wax, I'm ready for anything.

Almost anything. The formal invitation to dinner with just Kaloni is a surprise—but I'm not going to miss out on any opportunity she gives me.

THAT NIGHT, I KNOCK ON THE DOOR TO HER QUARTERS, WEARING ONE of my more beautiful gowns. Most people would dress down for a private dinner like this. When she opens the door wearing not only a gown but her royal crown, I know I guessed right.

"Ingrid." She smiles warmly. "You look wonderful."

"So do you." I brush a kiss over her cheek and float inside. She wanted me to look like a slob. Her mistake. "The green really brings out your eyes."

"I've been told that." She leads me to a table in her sitting room, already covered with platters of food. Judging by the small plates, though, this is just the first course.

I'm in for a long night.

"I'm a little curious why we're doing this," I say as I sit. My mark throbs as I smell something gingery, like that cake Amval loved.

As usual, I grit my teeth and ignore the feeling. I don't miss him. He's only someone I'm going to prove wrong now.

Kaloni laughs self-consciously. Did it always sound so fake? "Oh, you're going to think it's silly."

"I promise I won't." Full slate of formal silverware on the table. Another trap. I read the books, but I only remember that the rules are different here than at home.

"Well, you were so lovely in the aftermath of the accident." She shakes her head. "I've been too busy to repay that since taking the throne, so I thought you were owed an apology. In my opinion, this meal contains all the best Lightning Cape has to offer."

"You'll have to show me, then." I force a smile. "Where should I start?"

Kaloni's smile tightens slightly as she picks up the fork closest to her plate and spears what looks like a stuffed olive. "For me? Right here."

While I take a bite, she fills my glass with blood-red wine. The food is amazing. Maybe good enough to hide poison. So before I sample every new dish, I wait for her to eat first.

"How has the throne been treating you?" I ask. "A lot seems to have changed pretty quickly."

She blots her mouth with a napkin. "I'm sure it does seem like that. Amval and I—"

I nearly choke when she says his name. Pain rips down from my neck. I haven't heard it since our fight.

"Are you all right?" Her eyebrows knit, worried.

"Spice caught in my throat." I rub my chest, trying not to get sick. He won't be what stops me now. This is all just a physical reaction.

Kaloni offers me a thick cheese on a cracker to calm the burning, then continues, "My brother and I spoke often about his plans for when he became Alpha. I'm just carrying out what he would have."

"Really?" I ask.

She nods. "He hated that we lost that land to the rogues."

Funny that he didn't mention that when I asked him what he would do as Alpha. I take a bite of the cracker and swallow the burning urge to throw that in her face. But I was talking to a dead man.

"I'm sure he's glad," I say sourly.

"I can hope." She kisses her fingers to the sky.

The courses pass like that. Kaloni says something that should be innocuous but doesn't line up with what Amval claimed. I try to push her on it without revealing what I know. She dodges, asks about me. I say as little as I can while answering the questions. We talk about my siblings for a while, including their various kingdoms and relationships. Apparently, it's not common knowledge that Kieran and Raven are going to rule Escuro and Dun's Crossing jointly someday, but Estrella's pregnancy very much is.

It's like a game. Testing each other's defenses, trying to learn what we can. From the outside, I bet this would look like a perfectly polite dinner. During the third course, I use the wrong fork, and she very sweetly corrects me while sliding in a comment about Mother that I frankly deserve some kind of medal for letting slide. I barely stop her before she feeds me a banana, which I'm deathly allergic to, as I told her and every other Som a few weeks ago, in a way that makes her seem like the bad guy.

I hate these fucking games.

Finally, without us ever diving deeper into a subject than the very top layer, the final course arrives. Flaky pastry layered thick with chocolate, cut into neat squares.

Kaloni offers me one. "What about you?"

"What about me?"

"When you realized your mate was a crown prince, you must have thought that meant leadership. What would you do in my position?" Kaloni takes a bite of her pastry, forcing me to answer.

"I didn't realize who he was until he was already dead." I shrug.

"What an awful day." Kaloni shudders and then pats my hand. "I'm sorry. I daydreamed about leading occasionally, even though I hoped I never would, so I thought there might be some scheme or plan you'd like to discuss."

Oh, if Amval could hear her now.

He'd point to the obvious lie that she never hoped to lead and push the rest aside.

"I think there's a difference between being second and being sixth—fifth," I say. "I never thought about it, except to be glad it wasn't going to come to me."

"You don't want to lead?"

I shake my head. "The only part that sounds worthwhile is the traveling."

Kaloni nods slowly. "I take it that's why you've been with us for so long?"

"That and the food." I gesture at the spread. Everything was incredible, even the dessert. It only makes me hate her more.

"I think wanderlust may be a disease common to the last in line. Joli has it."

I force myself not to react. She's noticed Joli's absences. Has she noticed my movements?

"Maybe," I say through a mouthful of pastry.

"Do you think you'll be moving on soon, then?" Kaloni spears me with a gaze over the top of her wine.

There it is. The end of the game. The point of this whole meal. I was right—the rest of the Som siblings aren't in any danger, as long as they stay in line. Kaloni has what she wants. I'm the last loose end to tie up, as far as she's concerned.

"Joli's been having a hard time," I say. "I thought I'd stay until she's doing better."

"She's surrounded by family and friends here," Kaloni says tightly. "I've been talking to her, and while she appreciates your concern, I'm not sure she needs you anymore. You've seen how often she travels, and you just… stay behind."

Kaloni's not stupid—but she's used to dealing with her siblings, not someone raised by Rowena Solberg.

"I should have known I didn't need to lie to you." I look down, like I'm sad. "Your parents offered me hospitality. I've lost the least of you and your siblings, but I am grieving people here." I peek up at her through my lashes. "If it's an imposition—"

"Never." She smiles tightly, chained by the laws of hospitality her far more generous and deserving parents invoked without thinking. To even suggest she doesn't want me here anymore is an insult to the old ways, one she can't risk.

"Thank you," I say.

When I don't get an effusive response or another glass of wine, just a few short words before our goodbye, I know I'm no longer somebody Kaloni thinks she might have to worry about.

I'm officially a danger to her. And I intend to stay that way.

MIRROR

Amval

THE MOMENT INGRID WALKS AWAY, MY MARK SEARS LIKE IT INTENDS TO burn all the way through my skin and kill me, bringing this whole bitter trick to a bitter end.

But I am made of sterner stuff than that. So, I take a heartbeat to catch my breath and then return to the stables. I have a job to do, after all. Mesut needs me.

Thoughts like that power me through the coming days. The rhythm of them is almost familiar. Tek needs me. Nur needs me. Cirocco and Kaloni and every single one of my siblings needs me. The same thoughts that allowed me to trudge through day after week after month in hiding.

This time, at least, there are breaks in the constant throb of being needed. Breaks that come in the form of near-nightly trips to the Gruesome Pony. There are still too many spare nobles hanging around the palace, too much sheer work to do, for even Tek to suggest going every single night. We would drown in horse shit if we did. But we go often enough.

Often enough that, when we arrive, the troubadour just grumbles and steps off the stage. A little bit of my spare pay was enough to get the naqun restrung, and I've quickly developed a repertoire of crowd-favorite songs. I know what will get them to sing and what quiets even my friends' wildest moods. One night, Ozkan approaches me and presses a few coins into my hand.

On instinct, I start to refuse them. I may be living as a groom now, but there is a palace with my name on it, should I ever be able to use my name again.

"Oh, hush," the bartender snaps. "You drag in double the business that worthless lout ever did. If I give you a little coin for your trouble, it's only because I don't intend to owe one of my customers."

I glance at the naqun in my lap, its scratched paint and the remaining, worn strings. "All right."

Soon, the nearest luthier knows me by sight. He even suggests a laz player that I might collaborate with some night.

I almost take him up on the offer—until my mark threatens to burn through me again at the idea of playing with someone other than Ingrid.

"Not yet," I tell him.

Even as I settle into this life, it feels like most of what I say to people is *not yet*. To Ozkan, when he offers me a permanent role. To Nur, when she offers me a promotion—which should rightly go to Tek anyway. And, surprisingly often, to Cirocco when he asks me questions about myself.

He shows up perhaps half the nights we go to the Gruesome Pony. I don't know how he knows we're there. His window is on the opposite side of the palace. But every time he's there, he insists on buying me a drink. And every time, I decide how much I miss my best friend is more important than the potential danger to my cover. He hasn't discovered me yet.

I've spent most of my life talking to Cirocco, but we've never talked like we talk in the Pony. No topic is off-limits. I learn he hates the curfew in the castle and the fact that everyone else still treats it like law. He's worried about Hova—his triplet is covering it well, but his pranks are becoming more reckless. He wishes he had royal amber eyes instead of dark ones. He reads when he can't sleep at night.

In exchange, I tell him anything I think won't give me away. We talk endlessly about my music. Like Grandfather, Cirocco doesn't have a musical bone in his body, but he loves it—and he pays attention. He always asks about slight changes I've made in songs, improvements to my naqun. Explaining this impossible part of myself to him is surprisingly easy. And once I've started doing that, it's equally easy to tell him that I hate being cold more than any other sensation, that Tek drunkenly convinced me into a squiggle of a tattoo on my arm, that I've come to enjoy riding Cloud, the work-horse I rode away from my would-be assassination, better than I ever liked Seksim—albeit with a few details removed.

I grew up right beside him, and somehow, there's still so much we don't know about each other.

"Your friends are waiting for you." Cirocco glances over his shoulder at them one night.

I follow his gaze. The table is a little less full almost every night—those conscriptions he promised, slowly taking effect. Nur is fighting to keep her staff, so everyone knows now that you're less likely to get the letter calling you to the front if you're a good worker. It has made our nights out less frequent.

"Come sit with us," I say, like I do every time he's here.

He sighs. "I can't."

"Why not?" I ask for what feels like the thousandth time. "Why do you have to hide coming here at all?"

"My parents wouldn't have approved." He exhales slowly. "And that means my brother wouldn't have either."

Denial bubbles behind my lips—but it's empty. Mother and Father would have thought that the Pony was a, well, gruesome reminder of what happened to our kingdom. They wouldn't have forbidden Cirocco, just asked in their quiet way why he really felt he *needed* to come here, and that would have been enough. I would have fallen in line, until there was so much pressure that Cirocco couldn't have kept coming.

"They're dead," I say instead.

"The rest of my family isn't." Cirocco pays my tab and leaves me alone with a mirror, showing just how much I let my actions be dictated by those closest to me.

My parents had my best interests at heart—but clearly, they weren't always right.

That night, I split off from the group and take the long way home. I have a slightly later shift, a gift of Tek's new promotion, and I'm not quite ready to go to sleep yet. Instead, I find a chair in the empty market, clearly for a nearby stall. Sticky fruit juice stains the arm, but I sit down in it anyway. A warm evening breeze coasts through, and I look out over the quiet town.

King Gavin put a "governor" of sorts in our palace, one of his soldiers who ruled with an iron fist. This town didn't exactly die, but the campaign to take over almost destroyed it. When we returned to the palace, we took a boat, came up through the back, past nothing but quiet caves.

If we had come this way, is this what we would have seen? A ghost town, packed to bursting with the memories of a once-happy kingdom? Now, I only have to wait until morning to see it come alive again, but the scars remain. To my left, the cobblestones are charred and broken. Who died in that fire? How many people have we lost?

I did everything they even suggested asking because I was supposed to heal those scars. Mother needs me. Father needs me. Lightning Cape needs me.

My mark burns as I remember the night outside Kaloni's coronation, when Ingrid asked me what I would do as Alpha and everyone else's plans danced through my head. My family is brilliant, worthy of emulating—but what am I? Father was right when he said Lightning Cape needs a strong leader to survive this. He was that leader, and so was Mother. I was so lost in being exactly what they wanted of me that I forgot to ever wonder if I was strong, or just a copy of their strength.

I strum the naqun, somber notes drifting off into the quiet night. Nur offered me the promotion I insisted she give Tek because she saw the way the other grooms responded to me. They listen. It's easy to get them to do that—much easier than controlling seven unruly siblings while Dun's Crossing soldiers march by our hiding spot. But Tek is the one who, upon being given the position, started making changes. The later shifts were his idea. There's so much work that it makes more sense to stagger us. The nobles almost never come in all at once.

But now that we're staggered, it's much harder to work in pairs. Working separately would be much more efficient, like I mentioned in my very first week. I've thought that a few times and never said a word to him about it.

When I return to the bunkhouse, I will. Or perhaps in the morning.

What would I do if I were Alpha?

For the first time, with no one but the open air to judge me, ideas flood through my mind. Ideas I always had, tumbling through my mind at night. But ideas I kept quiet because no one else had them first.

I close the door on them, for now. I'm not Alpha, and I never will be. Once I can show my face again, though, I'll advise Kaloni. Then, I'll need them.

For now, I need to focus on making it safe to show my face. All attempts to prove cousin Yakup is behind this have failed. Not proven him innocent, just failed to prove him guilty. Lord Faruk has been going very similarly. He's so dismissive on his visits to the stables that I can barely have half a conversation with him.

Without access to the palace, there is nothing I can do. But the only way I can access the palace is—

Ingrid.

Just thinking her name hurts. I curl painfully around my naqun and breathe through my nose.

It has been nearly two weeks since our fight. Since I told her to leave. Since she ignored everything I said and insisted on a betrayal so deep, it is truly impossible.

And I miss her like someone pulled one of my arms off.

When I'm not thinking about what I should be doing, how I should be acting, that is ridiculously obvious. Even if I should defend my family, I need her.

Which means I need to find a way to get her back.

DRESSED LIKE A PRINCE

Ingrid

After my dinner with Kaloni, I can't sleep. If she were just a grieving queen, she wouldn't need to get rid of me. She wouldn't be sniffing around my loved ones like she was looking for a bruise to punch. No, I'm on the right fucking track, and she's not going to chase me off of it.

I pull my lute into my lap and strum absently. My thoughts unravel into music notes, neat and straight on staves. Mother used the rejuvenation of Escuro to humiliate Candace because everyone was there. She didn't organize it. She just capitalized on the opportunity. Maybe these people aren't all here because some massive evil is happening. Maybe Kaloni is one part of a much bigger plan, and they're just using the excuse to—

Knock. Knock, knock. Knock.

My head shoots up. Everyone should be asleep by now... and that sounds like the call-and-response from that drinking song Amval and I played.

I creep to the door. My stomach churns. My mark aches.

When I open the door, my jaw almost hits the floor.

Amval stands there. Not Sash, Amval. In full princely regalia, like I haven't seen him since that very first night. Coppery embroidery dances over his white doublet, and his white trousers hug the muscle of his legs down to boots so purely white that I can't imagine how long the tanner slaved over the leather. An amber cape dangles from one shoulder, only barely not blowing in a heroic breeze. His dark hair gleams, pushed back off his forehead to reveal even more of his sharp face. Cheekbones slice, nose jabs, brows loom, and mouth—

His mouth is the only thing I don't recognize from that first night, curved up in a faint, sheepish grin I want to kiss away.

My hand snaps out, and the *crack* of my knuckles against his face echoes down the hallway.

"What are you fucking thinking?" I grab his wrist, haul him into my room, and shut the door. "I told you, I hated you when we met."

He rubs his jaw. "Mother had a rule—present yourself at your best when you need to apologize. Then, the person you're apologizing to can see that you're not hiding from what you did."

"And sneaking up here in the dead of night...?" My blood boils. I can barely look at him. He can't be here, not looking this handsome, not after what he said to me. Not after any of this.

"A necessity of the situation." He straightens up, and Goddess, there he is. That fucking prince. The one I honestly couldn't believe Candace was introducing me to. "I owe you an apology."

"And then some." I toss a log on the banked fire just for something to do with my hands. It bursts back to life, crackling and spitting.

It makes *him* an even bigger figure in my room, his shadow crawling all the way up onto the ceiling.

"I am sorry." He bows deeply, and I seriously consider kneeing him in the face just to make him stand up again. "You've more than earned my trust. I should never have accused you of being impulsive or sabotaging me for selfish reasons. You've been tireless in pursuit of whoever is doing this to my family. I should have known you believed what you were saying."

I wait a moment. Another. He has to say that I'm right now, right?

That he's sorry he threw away all the proof I had without looking twice at it?

But nothing comes. He just stands there, bowing.

"By all the stars." I grab his lapels, silk crinkling under my hands, and haul him upright. "Is that it?"

"I...believe so?" He looks genuinely confused. The marks of my knuckles stand out, faintly red, on his cheek. I want to hit him again.

I want to breathe in deeply, charcoal and basil, and bury my face in his chest.

I want to fucking hit him again.

"What's your goal here?" I hiss. "With your fancy little outfit, your hair styled, and your confession? What do you want from me?"

"I missed you," he says frankly.

There it is again—something in the mouth and eyebrows that doesn't match the prince I met that night. Something more like the man I keep dreaming about. He's not lying.

I release his lapels and step back. This would be so much easier if he weren't telling the truth. I just want to be angry, be right, and then leave. He's not allowed to complicate that.

"You expect things to just go back to the way they were?" I ask.

He shakes his head. "I know I have things to make up for—"

"But eventually." The words burn. He expects me to crawl right back to him like a good mate. To cave to the bullshit my body is screaming at me and forget.

I've done that enough.

"No. I told you, I work best alone. Always have." It's how I learned to do damn near everything.

"I don't," he admits.

"Sounds like a problem for you to fix." I march back over to the door and open it. "Take your empty apology and ridiculous clothes somewhere else to solve it."

He crosses his arms but doesn't move. "Find a single word of that apology I didn't mean."

I barely swallow a scream. "I bet you meant it. But you didn't say anything about what we actually fought *about*. You don't even know what you did wrong!"

He grits his teeth. "What exactly do you want me to say?"

"Do you think there's any chance I could be right?" I surprise myself by saying. "Does any single crumb of you think I'm onto something?"

"I—" He swallows and looks at the fire.

I hold the door open wider.

"No," he says. "I don't."

"Then we're done."

"You are closest with Candace, yes?" he asks. "Can you earnestly tell me that, if I came to you with the kind of evidence you had, you would believe Candace arranged your murder?"

I stare out at the empty hallway, at Kaloni's door. And I picture Candace behind it. Someone telling me that Candace had met with Corwyn, or Nessa, or any of the other snakes my family has caught in the grass.

With gritted teeth, I shut the door. "No."

He nods. "My whole family is like that to me. I trust them with everything I am."

"Do you have any idea how much you don't notice about each other, though?" I ask. "Joli goes missing for days at a time, and no one bats an eye."

He scoffs. "No, she doesn't."

"She's a smuggler. A damn good one. She supplied Moonlight Hollow and brought me in on one of her trips." I cross my fingers that she won't be mad I told him, but I need him to listen to me.

Amval blinks slowly. "I would have noticed."

"Are you seriously telling me you don't believe there's any way your siblings have secrets from you?" I can prove him wrong if need be, but I don't want to reveal any more of Joli's than I have to.

"Cirocco drinks with the grooms," he says abruptly. "Or near them, I suppose."

I nod, step closer. "Maybe I wouldn't believe Candace arranged my murder. But if you told me Candace was keeping a secret from me, I'd laugh and ask what was new. Everyone has their secrets."

He shakes his head. "Even you admit there's a world of difference between secrets and what you claimed."

Not after the dinner I just had with her. But conversation isn't going to convince him.

"I have more evidence." I lead him to my wardrobe, throw open the doors, and push aside my dresses.

In the low light of the fire, my web of names and kingdoms Corwyn met with doesn't look like a growing map of a conspiracy. It looks like a craft project. The thread I requested for my "embroidery" certainly doesn't help.

He grabs a sheet of notes from the floor of the wardrobe and reads it silently. This is the part where he tells me I'm just being impulsive again. Or seeing problems where there aren't any. He'll congratulate me on the work I put in, just like everyone does when they hate what you did but don't want to hurt your feelings, and I'll throw him out on his ass like he deserves. I don't need him to understand. I can save him on my own.

"Lord Corwyn was behind the civil war in Tansy Beach—Moonlight Beach?" Amval asks.

"Him and Lord Denidor," I say, feeling stupid. "Finn gave him that new scar when they found out."

"You're sure it's him?"

I cross my arms. "My brother let me stay in a war zone. He wasn't stupid enough to do that without making sure I could recognize the person who started the war."

Amval traces one of the threads with his finger. "He's met with all these people?"

"I followed him to every single one." I point out a few repeats—Birchmint Valley, Whaleberry Harbor, Seedmoss Rapids. "And once he talks to them, they go and meet with someone else on this map. It's that organization, Astralis." My heart pounds, and my words start to run into each other on the way out of my mouth. He's listening. "Who else would have the resources to do all this? Burning clove isn't easy to find; Mother made sure of that. And getting the horses to rear in the exact right spot must have required training or planning. All these people are in on it, but why? To make Kaloni Luna without anyone questioning how she got there."

Amval flinches back, and I realize he was leaning in, even nodding. He was actually listening. I was getting through to him—except for the final part.

"Half of these names are nearly strangers to Lightning Cape," he says. "Why under the Goddess's sky would they conspire to put my sister on the throne?"

"To… steal the world?"

Amval's eyebrows shoot up in disbelief. Fair. That, and something vague about Father, was all Finn and Xandra figured out. I told them immediately that it sounded like Corwyn puffing himself up.

"Right." He looks back at the board, taps the torn paper bearing Corwyn's name in the middle. "I'm certainly convinced Lord Corwyn is a danger and potentially our most promising suspect yet."

I study his face. No laughter hiding behind his eyes—but I guess that's not a shock. He's not turning away from the board, either. He's actually still studying it, like there's some clue he missed.

"Thank the Goddess," I say breathlessly. "If all this couldn't get you there, you'd really be a lost cause."

He almost smiles. "Thank you for your patience."

"Always." My mark hums, like all is right with the world again. I grit my teeth. "But can you see any other motivation in all of this than putting Kaloni on the throne?"

He scans my string-map, the notes I've taken, my rough sketches of the two "accidents." His shoulders slump. "No."

I grin—and stop the second I realize how I would feel if someone proved Candace planned my assassination.

"Blackmail," he says abruptly.

"What?"

"My assassin, he was blackmailed." Amval nods like he's convincing himself. "And we suspected Iltas was. Perhaps Kaloni is being blackmailed, too."

"Maybe." I've only got gut feelings—and her policy changes—to prove him wrong. "Okay. I can... live with that."

Amval throws his arms around me, and if I melt into the embrace, that's only instinct. "Thank you."

He can't hear me through his shoulder anyway. I'm not hiding any thickness in my voice.

"Oh!" He releases me. "There is one more thing, if we've come to a truce."

MAY I HAVE THIS DANCE?

Amval

Ingrid eyes me suspiciously. Of all the risks I've taken coming up here, this may be the riskiest. This is the one that saw me breaking into my memorial chamber to pilfer my own clothes, the one that stands the greatest chance of destroying everything I've earned over the course of this conversation.

"You've mentioned the night we met," I say. "And how you didn't particularly like me."

She nods with a wry smile, her golden hair loose and flowing. Goddess above. I may be dressed in royal colors, but she looks like a work of art in just a simple nightgown.

"I didn't have the same experience," I admit. "I thought you were lovely, if a bit confusing."

She laughs. "I've seen you with your siblings now. You had heard a joke before."

"Not at a royal function," I say honestly. "And not the way you make them. That man you met, he wasn't prepared for that."

"And this one is?"

"I would like to think so." I straighten my doublet—it's funny how uncomfortable it is after only such a short time away—and hold out my hand to her. "I know it was your sister's doing, but we were supposed to dance. For all the time we've spent together over these last weeks, we still have not. The ballroom awaits, Princess."

"Are you being serious?" She looks me up and down. "What am I saying? You're not this funny. Or this reckless."

"You inspired me." I smile, hoping our agreement is strong enough that I can tease her about what happened. I've learned that Ingrid has just as little interest in staying in her own negative emotions as she does anything else she finds boring.

Like I hoped, she laughs. Something in my chest flutters. I love her so much.

"You're making that face again." She shoves my shoulder. "And I have to say no. If you're going to be my partner-in-crime again, I need you not immediately caught and murdered properly this time."

"You are going to have to get used to this face." I catch her hand before she can properly pull it away. "And I suspected you might say something like that, so I'll remind you"—I spin up a breeze around our feet—"that those who want me dead are not the only ones who can use magic to their advantage. Take a step."

She takes one—a heavy one, of course. Always trying to prove me wrong. The golden bubble of her laugh when it lands with the softest *thud* is worth it, though.

"I have to change," she says.

"Aren't I the one who's supposed to be improving my first impression?" I reach for the door.

"Who are you, and what have you done with Amval?" she mumbles as she follows after me. Her grin gives away just how little she resents the change.

"Perhaps this is who I've always been." I lower my voice to a whisper as we step out into the hallway. "Perhaps I'm just through worrying about who else people would rather I be."

She tucks her arm through mine. "Then maybe I can see what the Goddess saw between us."

My mark howls for me to pick her up and spin her around, but we have to move. Quieting our steps will only do so much, if I don't avoid the patrols. Those were Mother's idea. She always suspected that the final assault on Lightning Cape was so successful because one of King Gavin's men snuck in first and let the others through.

I lead Ingrid down a circuitous path, taking side hallways and servants' corridors whenever possible.

"You didn't sneak out before," she says. It's not a question.

I smile. "I didn't stop playing my music after we moved into the palace, and the patrolmen are all vicious gossips."

The shock on her face is so sweet that it makes up for every night I spent making music alone in an empty dungeon because it was the only place the guards didn't check.

"And I needed the occasional midnight snack," I admit. Something about her earnest reaction to everything I say makes me want to be not just honest, but completely honest. Even about the far less romantic of my secrets.

She barely covers a snort. "You cook?"

I shake my head. "I put jam on cold bread."

"Ah, always a good one." She nods sagely. "I know how to make sugar cookies, but mostly I just ate fistfuls of dried currants."

I grin. "My favorite is red currant jam! It's the only good thing to come of the occupation, that some Dun's Crossing soldiers discovered how to grow them here."

"See, I prefer the black." She smiles teasingly as I lead her up to the massive doors to the ballroom.

"Introducing Princess Ingrid Solberg," I say with a formal bow.

"And the undead, no-longer-Crown Prince Amval Som." She bows back at me.

Perhaps there is something to how quickly she moves on from being hurt. Hearing those words in her voice, wrapped around her smile…they are far less painful than I dreamed.

We enter the ballroom, making sure to close the door behind us. Ingrid's nightgown swirls white around her ankles as she skips to the middle of the dance floor. The fabric is so thin, almost fragile. If there were any more light in here, I would be able to see her body silhou-etted inside.

My mouth goes dry as I join her.

"I learned to dance with my sisters," I say, perhaps because I'm determined to ruin this evening.

"I learned with an instructor and the air." She puts one hand on my shoulder, holds the other out to me. "I suppose we'll see which was a better method."

I take her hand and settle the other on the curve of her waist. If I skim my thumb up, I can almost feel the sweep of her rib cage. She is wearing nothing at all underneath the nightgown, her warmth tempting beneath my palms.

But we came here to dance. I start humming the song that was playing when she first approached me at the name blessing, and she steps into a courtly pattern.

I could chart this pattern on the tiles of the ballroom, but I learned it on a hundred worn wood inn floors. Mother usually played our music on a thin, metal flute she always made sure to tuck into her bedroll when we had to run. It was the first music I fell in love with, even though—

"Ouch." Ingrid grins at me, no real pain in her voice as I step on her bare foot with my boot. "It's good you changed into royal cloth-ing. Stable boys' boots are much heavier."

I let the music lapse, though she keeps us spinning to a rhythm I can't hear. "I like to dance, but I'm not especially good at the formal ones."

"How is that possible?" She shakes her head. "I don't like them, but as long as you can hear the music, it's easy."

"We don't have any music."

She rolls her eyes and takes up the humming. Her steps become more exaggerated, and she hits each note on which she moves with particular violence. In, out, steps weaving like embroidery on a tapestry of air.

It's beautiful—and it still makes less sense to me than puzzling out how I would recreate the music on my naqun. She narrowly avoids my foot landing on hers again with a laugh.

"All right, you're hopeless." She doesn't release me, doesn't even slow. "If you're not good at the formal ones, what are you good at?"

"Standing very still." I spin her to a stop, freezing us at a single point on the dance floor, and gather her closer into my arms. Her body presses against mine, soft and pliant. I sway to the beat of the tune she dropped.

She drapes her arms around my neck. "This isn't dancing."

I brush a kiss against her temple. "Oh, I know. I'm also good at improvisational dancing, but I wanted to hold you."

Her chuckle vibrates against my shoulder, so close to my mark that it feels like a lightning strike. "And here I thought we were working on trusting each other again, but you're hiding information."

Letting her go after a week and a half apart goes against every instinct I have, but if there is one person whose opinion I will value until all the stars burn out, it's hers. And despite the humor in her voice, I can hear the very small edge. Our truce is more tentative than I would like.

So I take up the humming, a faster tune, more like something I would play at the Pony, and spin her out. She half-gasps, then spins herself back in. I grab her waist, somewhere between a courtly distance and the closeness we shared a moment ago, and begin swirling across the floor.

She laughs, high and bright. I struggle not to lose the music around my smile as I pull out every trick I know. Dips, spins, crossovers. Ingrid's nightgown furls around her body, around mine, until we're both a flurry of white in a dark blue ballroom. In between her bursts of laughter, she hums with me, a harmony to my melody.

In a thousand years, we would never have danced like this that first night. I would have stumbled through some courtly pattern and made an ass of myself. If we woke up together the next morning, she would have run away instead of waiting to talk.

So perhaps this is better. To have found each other sideways rather than head-on. She already said she likes me better dead, and as much as I found her charming that first night, I don't know if I really could have seen her as anything more than a threat to the stability of the kingdom. Ingrid is many things, but stable isn't one of them. She is a flickering flame, a ray of sunlight casting rainbows through a window. Always changing and more beautiful for it.

"Anyway, I said I wasn't going to do any fucking more of these without a raise," a man says somewhere outside the ballroom.

I freeze, holding Ingrid in a perilously low dip that flattens her nightgown against every swell of her body. She looks at me, then at the door.

Another man snorts. "Good luck with that. You know how she's been about the 'palace purse.'"

"Patrol," I whisper.

"We have to run." Her smile is equal parts worry and excitement, but the excitement is swiftly winning out.

Despite the risk, I bend down and kiss her. She opens easily under my touch, breathing ink and violets that wash over me like the first night in your own bed after a long trip. The kiss isn't easy or gentle, but it still feels like coming home.

I could spend all night here with her.

The large doors crack open, and I pull back, spinning a breeze with sharp flicks of my wrist. Ingrid's work has more than proven that there are larger, more dangerous forces in this palace than I dreamed. Dangerous enough to blackmail a sister I didn't even know had any secrets from me. So, with our steps quiet and the guards hopefully blinded by the pool of their own torchlight, I grab Ingrid's hand and we run through the servants' door.

Once it closes behind us, I realize we're both stifling laughter.

BETTER OFF ALONE?

Ingrid

WHEN I WAKE UP THE NEXT MORNING TO A NOTE FROM AMVAL ALREADY
sitting on my windowsill, my mark hums the song we danced to last
night. I barely feel tired, even though I know we stayed up late. I hum
to myself as I open it.

Has Corwyn been visiting Yakup?

I shake my head and fold the note back up. If he needs to believe
Kaloni was blackmailed, fine. It just means he'll be standing right next
to me when I prove she wasn't. But I haven't heard a peep from his
cousin the whole time he's been here; no matter what Amval wants,
I'm not wasting my time on Yakup.

But even my irritation doesn't have any heat behind it.

I glare up at the morning sun like the Goddess can still see me
somehow. "This is all You, and I'm not going to fall for it."

I shove the feeling aside.

Before going to write Amval a note back.

"You see?"

Amval's veil drifts closer to his face as he sucks in a breath. "*That* is Lord Hajni?"

I nod. "I think that's what he's relying on to keep people from spotting him. That, and the scar."

Amval narrows his eyes, tracing Corwyn through the lower hall we're overlooking, lying on our stomachs. He can only sneak away so often, but I'm trying to make the most of the time we have. He needs to know our target

"He assumes everyone will move out of his way," Amval says softly. "He always did, even when he came with Prince—ah, Luna Xandra."

"He's an asshole." But as I watch, I realize he's right. Corwyn has his head down, but that's still a prince's stride. People move around him.

I completely missed that.

Amval shakes his head. "That always irritated me, but Father thought he was a good match. We hoped—but I suppose I understand why he didn't mate with any of my sisters now. He is an asshole."

"And potentially the head of a conspiracy."

"I'm not sure about that."

I barely bite my tongue before I ask if he's willing to admit it's Kaloni. "Who else, Yakup?"

At least that makes him chuckle. "No, I do think you are right about him."

"Finally." After Amval's note a few days ago, I spent all the time he was able to spare one day proving that, yes, Yakup wants the throne—but he's too dull for an organization like Astralis to even consider using him, much less for him to be leading them. Once I convinced Amval, he asked if I couldn't talk to Joli and get him sent home early. No luck on that front yet.

"Why can't Corwyn be in charge, though?" I ask.

Amval inhales slowly, thinking. I wonder whether he learned that from Cirocco, or Cirocco from him, but they both do it.

I don't know when I noticed that.

"He doesn't inspire loyalty," he says finally. "I would believe that he orchestrated the civil war by himself; everyone on this side of the continent knew King Alden wished Corwyn was his son. But outside of Tansy Beach, he never had many friends, and Tansy Beach doesn't even exist anymore."

"For someone who spent their life on the run, you sure know a lot of court gossip," I say.

He shrugs. "There is a reason people like Lady Evangeline are always welcome in Lightning Cape. Gossip has its value–if you know how to use it."

I grimace. "It might be better to be murdered than spend another afternoon with Lady Evangeline."

"Ah, but then how would you know Corwyn can't be the head of the snake?" His eyes crinkle in a way I know means he's smiling under the veil.

"That's what I have you for."

MY FINGERS ACHE, CLINGING TO THE STONE ON THE OUTSIDE OF ONE OF the spokes of Som Palace in the dead of night. Technically, Amval has conjured some kind of wind behind me that he *claims* means I'm not about to fall to my death. I think, if that's true, I should be able to feel it as more than a gentle breeze.

"Are you afraid of heights?" he asks.

"No," I reply quickly. "I sledded down one of Solberg Castle's roofs once."

"How high was that?"

I close my eyes, listen for a teasing lilt in his voice. Even Candace would tease me a little. Shit, I'm only fifteen feet off the ground—this is just practice for an idea he had about how we could get more information. But the ground seems so much farther away because I can't see it through the night, and maybe because I can barely hear anything over my heart pounding in my ears.

Amval doesn't sound like he's laughing.

"I spent a lot of time in higher towers than this," I mumble defensively.

"Towers have walls." I feel a hand on my elbow. I peel open one eye—he scaled up next to me so fast I didn't even notice. Which doesn't exactly make the fact that my stomach seems to be trying to crawl out of my throat any more impressive. "Ingrid. Come down with me."

Down sounds like a good idea. I'll just climb down. Fifteen feet is a survivable fall if I slip.

But my hands don't move.

Okay, I'll go feet-first. Makes more sense when you're climbing down anyway. I'll just lift up my foot and—

My foot doesn't move either.

"Ingrid?" he says softly.

"Oh, I'm here," I say through gritted teeth. "I just think my body may be teaming up against me."

"Does something hurt?" He sounds urgent, nervous.

I shake my head—oh, shit, that's too much movement. My whole world seems to flip inside out. Am I still holding onto the wall? Is there a wall to hold on to? When did I shut my eyes again?

"Follow my voice." Amval sounds like he's a thousand miles away, at the end of a hallway in one of those dreams where you can run as fast as you want but you never move.

"You can do it," he says.

I swallow. My whole mouth tastes like bile. If I let go of the wall, I would have hit the ground by now, so clearly I'm still holding on, but I don't know for how much longer.

"No." My voice is thin and scratchy. "I can't."

"Then you're going to have to trust me." His voice fades, growing further and further away. "I'm going to catch you. Just let go."

For him, my frozen hands uncurl. My frozen feet slip off the stones. And I'm falling.

With a rush of wind, I land in Amval's arms as softly as if he'd just picked me up.

"There you are," he murmurs.

I blink away tears I don't remember crying, but I can still only see the blurry outline of his face, unveiled because we're the only ones awake at this hour. The breeze really did have me the whole time.

He had me the whole time.

I cup his cheek, lean up, and kiss him until my hand stops shaking.

SOMEHOW, WE WORK TOGETHER FOR A FULL WEEK WITHOUT KILLING each other. Seven days after our dance, I wait inside the tiny staff door Joli pointed me to on my first day here, waiting to see if Amval will be able to sneak away on this break.

I lean against the cool blue stone, trying to figure out how I ended up spending what feels like half my life here, waiting for someone else. With the new schedule Amval suggested to his friend Tek, he has a lot more breaks though they're shorter, but he needs to spend some time in the stables or his friends will get suspicious.

I could be following Corwyn right now. Or Kaloni. Hell, I could be spending time with Joli, who has been asking why I'm so busy lately. But I'm here.

My skin burns where Amval caught me a few days ago. If someone had held a crossbow to my skull, I would've sworn I wasn't afraid of heights. Discovering I was wrong while someone watched? I'd rather take the crossbow to the skull.

But he hasn't said a word about it since he made sure I was safe and put me back on my feet. Not a joke, not even an insinuation. He hasn't mentioned climbing as part of our plans again either.

It's a tiny detail, but I don't know anyone else who would do it. Honestly, I don't know if I would, if I was in his position. Usually, everything is fodder for jokes.

But I don't think I've ever been scared like that before, even when I was watching the people of Dun's Crossing flood into the streets after Kieran and Raven came home.

I rub my arms. It was his idea anyway—or, it was my idea, but I was mostly kidding. Mostly. Except that I'd kind of been planning how I would scale the walls while we were apart.

Which means I would've discovered that I'm a huge coward while completely alone.

The door creaks open, and he leans inside. "Ready?"

I shove off the wall. "Always."

We creep through the halls together. I've gotten used to the wind licking at my ankles. When I complained, Amval turned it warm instead of cool.

But that's the sort of thing that's going to make me think this truce is more than it is.

After all our work, we've mostly managed to connect more of the nobles Corwyn talks to. The string-map in my wardrobe grows every day. None of my siblings' kingdoms are on there, and we haven't seen Corwyn in spitting distance of any of the Som siblings since that one meeting with Kaloni I saw—which does prove she saw me and they're doing something more complicated now. But the relative distance between the people we love most and Astralis is much less comforting when I look at all the kingdoms that are involved. We're up to eight now.

"Here," I murmur when we reach the spot where I left Corwyn to go find Amval, the room of the one remaining diplomat from Whaleberry Harbor, Lord Rik. His Alpha and Luna left almost two weeks ago now, which more people in this palace should frankly find suspicious.

"Here?" he says. "Are you sure?"

"Yes?" I frown at him.

Amval glances around as if confirming something. "He was here at this time yesterday as well."

I blink and then rip the journal I've been keeping my notes in off my hip. Paper hisses as I flip back. After lunch, Lord Rik. After lunch, Lord Rik. After lunch, Lord Rik.

"He's here at this time every single day." How did I miss that? Too much of this palace looks the same.

But Amval noticed immediately. Because every other day this week, he's had to spend this break in the stables.

The door opens, and Corwyn steps out. A long meeting today—no, according to my notes, it's been long every day as well.

"Perhaps watching can only take us so far," Amval says slowly.

"What?"

"We could have a little conversation."

My stomach flips. "If you're looking for a torturer, you've got me mixed up with my father."

Amval grimaces. "Why do you think our dungeons are empty? No, I mean a conversation. We could waylay him."

Together.

The word hangs unspoken between us. I've just been following Corwyn alone because a year or so of self-defense training isn't nearly enough to take on someone Finn couldn't handle with help. But with Amval and his wind powers, I stand a chance.

We stand a chance.

"Tomorrow," I say. "And I think I have an idea."

CATCHING UP

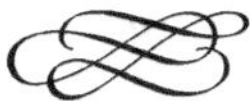

Amval

Ingrid and I lurk above Lord Rik's rooms, waiting. I inhale slowly, exhale slower. According to Ingrid, Corwyn doesn't have any powers, but he has the favor of at least one mage.

We both hope the mage abandoned him. Or, at least, that he is cocky enough not to waste a mage's power on a message-run he completes every single day.

On my next inhale, I slip my hand into Ingrid's. It is time to act. We both know it. But this is the first thing either of us has done that truly risks everything.

The door opens. Ingrid squeezes my hand. As Corwyn steps out— alone, thankfully—I spin a breeze around our feet, and we take off after him.

He doesn't always take the same route from here, but he always uses servants' passages when he can. Ingrid arranged with a few maids she's made friends with to block one of the two most accessible from Lord Rik's room, ensuring Corwyn takes the other.

Like clockwork, he does.

I tap beats on the back of Ingrid's hand. We didn't have time for a cleverer plan than timing our attack to the drinking song that has become so much a part of my life.

We trail after him as the hall slowly empties. Apparently, she's made more than a few friends amongst the palace staff. Somehow, with only a day's notice, she's managed to get this passage all but empty by the time we reach the spot we were hoping for.

The one length of hallway without any windows.

Just as the song reaches the first call-and-response.

Like a summer storm, we both explode from stillness into sudden motion. Ingrid draws a blade as loudly as she can while I spring away from her, wind coasting me along the walls like I barely weigh more than a leaf. I'm just out of his line of sight as he whips to see who's behind him.

"Princess?" he says confusedly, as if he could possibly maintain his ruse now.

"Oh, good." Ingrid smiles. "It would have been awkward if I recognized you and you had forgotten who I was."

Corwyn's posture drops into something menacing, almost feral, but he's too late. I'm behind him, grabbing a heavy fire poker leaning against a nearby wall. The heft of metal in my hands is familiar— when we couldn't train with swords, Father trained us with whatever we could lay hands on. So I know exactly how to rush the wind to send the point of it whistling faster than any human arm could swing.

Thud.

A dull, hollow sound follows—but not a wet one. Corwyn drops to the ground like a sack of potatoes. Ingrid rushes forward and shoves her blade under his nose.

She exhales. "He's breathing."

"I told you I knew what I was doing." I smile and twirl the poker in my hand. For what he's done to my family, I should have brained him. A quiet, worthless death is all he deserves.

But Ingrid is right. We need to know what he knows.

So I help her lift him up, sling an arm over each of our shoulders. She's wearing a maid's dress, like she was the first time I saw her.

Between us, he looks like an overindulgent steward whom we're escorting away before somebody important sees him. Corwyn's head lolls forward limply, and I don't bother picking it up. The fewer people who realize exactly who our...*friend* is, the better. And I don't envy him the headache he'll have when he awakens..

Ingrid grunts. "Come on. This plan is not falling apart because I don't have the arm muscles."

I shift a little more of his weight onto my shoulders, and we take off again. We use only servants' passages, our heads low. I dodge everyone who approaches us, making sure I don't replicate his mistake. He mumbles once, but he doesn't wake up.

Finally, we reach the tiny room Ingrid stayed in when she first arrived at Som Palace and dump him in a chair.

"We should tie him up," she says.

"With what?" I glance around the mostly empty room. "The sheets?"

Ingrid blinks. "You're a groom. Don't you have rope?"

"No!"

She groans. So does Corwyn.

"He's waking up." She rubs her face. "All right. We'll stand between him and the door. What's he going to do, try to rush us?"

I grab the key from her pocket and lock the door, just in case. For a plan that came together in twenty-four hours, a little missing rope is hardly the worst thing we could be dealing with.

As I turn back around, Ingrid slaps Corwyn fully across the face. He shouts quietly and blinks open his eyes.

"Wh—Princess?"

"Glad we didn't knock all the memories out of your head," she says.

Corwyn looks at me, clearly trying to fit the pieces together. I fight every instinct in my body to attack him. If he can tell who I am, we have to kill him, and everything we've done falls apart.

He shakes his head and turns back to Ingrid. I exhale a sharp breath of relief.

"We have a few questions." She prowls back and forth in front of the door like a big cat, graceful and dangerous. "Answer them, and I won't feel compelled to let my brother and his wife know exactly where the traitor they're hunting crawled off to."

Abruptly, I realize Ingrid has never done this before. She may not have even led a negotiation. She is coming on too strong and offering too little stick at the same time.

Corwyn laughs. "Finn and Xandra rule over a broken kingdom miles away. What do I have to worry about from them?"

I step forward. "You have to worry about just how much Lightning Cape relies on our trade agreements with Moonlight Beach. Luna Kaloni would be obliged to hold you if they asked, and it wouldn't be hard for Princess Ingrid to gain control over your accommodations due to her personal connection."

Ingrid glances at me sharply, trying to figure out what I'm thinking. Corwyn looks between us, trying to guess our relationship.

If they don't say no, act like they said yes.

"What is your relationship with Lord Rik?" I cross my arms and lean against the door.

"Friendly." Corwyn sneers at me.

"Friendly enough to visit for hours every day? I'm sure the gossipers would love to hear that," Ingrid says.

She may not have led a negotiation, but Finn and Xandra seem to have given her some insight into him. Corwyn goes just slightly pale, and I nod.

"Luckily for you, we're not interested in gossipers," I say. "We're interested in Astralis."

He narrows his eyes. "I don't know what that is."

I squeeze my hands behind my back so I don't lurch across the room and demand to know if he thinks we're fools. That close, I don't know if I could keep myself from tearing his throat out. I can almost smell the blood on his hands.

Ingrid scoffs. "You're telling me Lord Denidor was leading your little operation in Tansy Beach?"

"That fool couldn't lead himself to the bathroom," Corwyn spits.

Goddess, he's cocky. And Ingrid knows exactly how to use that against him. She is brilliant.

"How did Astralis first get in contact with you, then?" I ask.

"There is no paper trail for you to find, if that's what you're asking," he replies. "As I said, Denidor was the fool, not me."

"So they sent someone." I nod slowly. "Is that what you're doing here?"

Ingrid grins. "Are they making you train your own replacement because you failed?"

High spots of color appear on Corwyn's cheeks. "They understand the risks of what we're doing. Some failure is a guarantee. They know how valuable I am."

Ingrid clicks her tongue. "Sounds like I'm right."

I put a hand on her arm. Corwyn's pride is wounded, but if we hit it too hard—well, he might not try to rush us, but this room is small enough that whoever shifts first wins the fight.

Corwyn tracks the gesture with his eyes, then looks up at me again. "Looks like loyalty is a bit less important in Dun's Crossing than King Kieran keeps pretending it is."

I smile under my veil. If he thinks Ingrid has abandoned her mate, he has no idea who I am. It's good to know that all my effort and hiding has been worth something.

"And what if that's true?" I say. "What if we're just...curious?"

Corwyn's eyes light. Ingrid's arm tenses under my hand, but I smooth my thumb over it. There is more than one way to use his pride against him.

"Why would I believe that?" he asks.

"You're not tied up, are you?" Ingrid replies. "Finn told me what you're doing, and I want to know more."

He eyes us slowly. "He told you about Gavin?"

My heart skips a beat. King Gavin is dead, isn't he?

Ingrid nods. "But I'm not sure I understood."

"Of course, you didn't." Corwyn shakes his head. "I wasn't saying so they'd understand. They can't. It's simple—King Gavin was right. All these kingdoms, these warring interests...it's a waste of time. But people don't like being told what's good for them. And, frankly, his tactics were messy. Wasteful."

Wasteful. Untold thousands of deaths, nothing but waste. My kingdom swallowed whole by the enemy, a simple mess. My blood boils.

Corwyn grins. "Only three people have to die to enact a regime change, you see? And once the right person is in power, they fall in line. Take orders from those who are really in charge."

My knees turn to jelly. Those three deaths—four, really, counting the groom who died in my place and Iltas in my parents' "accident"— those are excusable. Justifiable. Right, so a mysterious group can rule the whole world from the shadows.

"More than three people would have to die to put me in power." Ingrid's voice wobbles slightly, and I pray Corwyn doesn't notice it.

"By my math…five. Kieran, Raven, the kids, and Anwen. Candace can't inherit, and Finn is too needed in Moonlight Beach to extend himself." He shrugs. "We could arrange it in about a month."

"How?" I ask through gritted teeth. "Dun's Crossing is the most secure kingdom in the world."

"In a fight between one wolf and twelve wolves, does it matter how strong the one is?" He smiles, all cocky confidence.

I am going to shred him.

How did I not notice this poison seeping into my very home?

"So?" Corwyn says.

"Let us discuss." I nod to the door.

Ingrid, grimacing, follows me just outside. "Do you believe me now?"

My eyebrows shoot up. "Believe you? He all but admitted they blackmailed Kaloni."

"Where did you get that?" she hisses.

"They only need someone to report to the true power."

She shakes her head. "That doesn't mean blackmail."

"But it could." And the sister I spent so many nights falling asleep hungry beside could not possibly hope to emulate the man who put us in that position. "Regardless, what matters now are names. *If* they are working to get lesser people in positions of power, we just need to get rid of these people first."

Ingrid heaves an irritated sigh. "Okay."

She reopens the door—to show an empty chair and an open window.

Ingrid whips an accusatory look back at me.

NO ONE WILL BELIEVE YOU

Ingrid

When one of the strings on my lute snaps under my fingers that night, I finally have to admit how fucking angry I am.

Angry and fucking tired.

If I wanted to sit around waiting, I could have gone back home. Crossed my fingers and hoped somebody ever bothered to wonder if my mate had been murdered.

If I wanted to be ignored when I talk, I'd go have a conversation at any Goddessdamned ball or gala my family keeps dragging me to. With most of Solberg Castle. Hell, I'd go talk to Lady Evangeline just to hear her prattle on about nothing.

If I wanted to watch someone throw truth out the window to suit their preconceptions—

Well, I'd just go talk to Amval again, wouldn't I?

I suck on the red bubble of blood as I storm to my desk for a spare string. Papers crush as I shove them aside.

Well, most of them crush. One is such thick cardstock that I earn myself a matching paper cut.

I jam another finger into my mouth and glare at the offending missive.

It's the one from Kaloni, a week ago. Inviting me to dinner.

Amval wants to ignore me and then lose our best chance before we get any hard information?

Fine. I'm going to get hard information my way.

I pull out a new paper and scribble down my own invitation to a wonderfully private dinner. Let's see him stop me from the stables.

KALONI KNOCKS ON MY DOOR THE SECOND THE CLOCK STRIKES THE hour. I straighten my clothes—casual, this time—and open it.

I raise my eyebrows at her resplendent gown. "I'm sorry, I thought I mentioned that this would be more informal." I gesture behind me at the low coffee table Dilara helped me set with a beautiful array of snacks and drinks. No courses tonight—we eat like old friends who intend to talk for hours.

Kaloni purses her lips slightly. The stiff train of her gown will make sitting on the couch uncomfortable, and in that corset, reaching the food will be almost impossible. "I must have missed that line."

Still, she strides inside, her chin high. She's not going to give up any ground tonight.

Good. I don't intend to either.

She perches on one of the couches and reaches stiffly for her drink. I drop comfortably into position across from her and grab a bite of a soft herbal cheese on a cracker.

"I'm a little curious why we are doing this," she says with a faint smile, echoing my own words.

"Would you believe me if I said I just wanted to spend time with you?"

She glances at the table, at the crackling fire behind her despite the summer heat, at the smirk on my face. "No."

"Good." I down my drink, refill it, and top off hers.

Her polite patience morphs abruptly into a scowl. "Is that what we were doing? Lying?"

"I think that's a question for you." I stare her down, blood dancing faster and faster through my veins. She's not stupid enough to kill me here. This dinner preparation is local, so she must know Dilara is standing in the other room, waiting to bring out more food as we eat what we have. A built-in witness. But that doesn't mean I can't feel the danger crackling off the woman in front of me like bolts of lightning.

"I didn't have to lie to you," she says acidly. "You could have been one of us. A lost sister, adopted into the fold."

I laugh. "Really? You think I could have fit in here? Your dress is so starched you can't bend over."

She sneers and proves me wrong by grabbing a twist of seeded bread from the far side of the table with barely a wince. "I don't think it's my fault that you lack the breeding of some of our horses."

I affect the perfect posture Mother drilled into me and maneuver a delicate spoonful of a thick, seafood-studded broth into my mouth before slouching back down. "Oh, I have it. I just have more important things to do."

"Breeding makes the world spin," she snaps. "Without it, we would all be rogues."

"Now you really sound like my mother."

"Your mother was a smart woman," Kaloni replies. "Smart enough to see the writing on the wall before anyone else here."

My skin burns. "You know."

Kaloni offers me a smug grin. "Know what, exactly?"

"About the burning clove." I squeeze my hands together so I don't chew on my thumbnail. "About how Gavin took this place over."

"I've known that since I was a little girl, and my mother warned me away from the plant." She stares me down. "You just figured it out now, didn't you?"

"Not right now."

She hums in mild disbelief. My fingers twitch. I could drag her into my bedroom, show her the map I've been working on, knock that little smirk right off her face. She's not some genius I'm strug-gling to keep up with. I'm not some kid she's running circles around.

And I am fucking tired of being treated like I am.

"I don't know if you missed the letter, but my mother died," I spit. "Cold and alone, fighting a losing battle in the snow. So I'm not sure she should really be your role model."

"Murdered by her own bastard." Kaloni tsks. "There are a few mistakes of hers I don't intend to replicate. I certainly won't be letting as much slide."

Mockingly, I cup a hand around my ear. "Can you hear that? It's… yes, I think that's the sound of her spinning in her grave miles and miles away. Mother let nothing slide."

"Except you." Kaloni sips her drink. "Which is why I'm here to tell you I know about your attempted interrogation the other day."

"And here I thought I put together our little shindig." My heart pounds a racing drumbeat in my throat. I didn't see Corwyn all day today, so I hoped he might've run away, too much of a coward to face the fact that he'd been captured by a little trickery and a few lies.

"If you didn't call this, I would have. You and that *groom*"—she sneers the word like it's an insult—"will be dealt with accordingly."

My mark screams. Corwyn didn't recognize Amval, but that doesn't change the fact that Kaloni knows exactly which one wears a starlight's veil. She waited a day—maybe she had to plan something intricate for me, but disposing of a servant wouldn't take more than a snap of her fingers.

I have to warn him.

Even if I'd rather throttle him myself first.

She hums thoughtfully. "Corwyn said you seemed to care for him. Why are you still here, then? Just to profane my brother's memory?"

I bark a laugh as something inside me snaps. "Who under the Goddess's sky are you to talk to me about his memory?"

Kaloni just leans back, still smirking. "Apparently, the one who hasn't yet forgotten him."

"I would think he'd be pretty hard to forget." My voice grows louder and louder. "Considering you fucking murdered him."

She cocks her head to the side. A faraway part of me warns that I'm losing control, giving her all the information she wants. That has to be why she's here—to figure out what I know.

But I've been pushed too Goddessdamned far to keep playing these stupid games with her or anyone else.

"Him and your parents. You made your siblings fucking watch. People you claim to love." I clench my hand, crushing a cracker to dust. "All because you're a member of some fucking group that wants to take over the world? What is Astralis promising you that's worth all this?"

She opens her mouth to respond as the firelight shifts, and for a moment, she looks exactly like Mother. Perfectly poised. In complete control. And about to say one of the cruelest things I can imagine with a smile on her lips.

Kaloni didn't call him Lord Corwyn. She just called him Corwyn.

"They didn't promise you shit," I say as my dinner tries to crawl back out of my mouth. "You're, what, in charge?"

"Oh, none of us are truly in charge." She waves a hand flippantly. "There is a council who decides which kingdoms Astralis will control, and I did find my way onto it, but it's not as if that council has a single leader."

I blink, deflate. "You're just...admitting it?"

She grins. "Your family have been visiting for weeks, trying to give up this mad quest and go home. Everyone knows you're out of your mind with grief. Who, truly, would believe you if you told them?"

Candace. The rest of my siblings, probably.

No one within mind-link distance or who can really do anything but go to war with Lightning Cape.

I deflate slowly. "How? You're younger than I am."

"They need fresh blood, fresh ideas." She sits grandly back in her seat, whisking a bite of food up to her mouth with a gust of wind like any attempt at pretending to be less than she is isn't worth the effort anymore. "A few well-placed inquiries and successful operations can open many doors. My coronation was also my promotion, proof I am fully committed to our work."

"Because you're willing to murder your own family in cold blood." Goddess, I might actually be sick. I knew, but I didn't know. Not like this. "To cry like your heart was breaking while poisoning the knife."

"I planned it all myself," she says proudly. "Did you like the implication that Amval was poisoned? I thought it would add some additional complication to any pesky little investigations that sprung up."

Being right was supposed to feel good. I just feel hollow, exhausted. I don't even want Amval to see this. It's going to destroy him.

I know exactly what kind of damage discovering someone you love is a monster does.

"Well." Kaloni stands with a shallow curtsy. "I am also glad we're not lying to each other anymore. It makes things so much easier. Tomorrow—"

"No."

She raises an eyebrow. "No?"

I've stood by and watched too many monsters get whatever they want. Even when I knew Father was wrong, I didn't do anything.

"You don't just win." I stand to face her.

She smiles apologetically. "I'm afraid I already have."

"You're that confident?"

She nods. I scan the room for any inspiration. There has to be fucking something I can do. If I kill her here, I just lose my life, and who knows who takes over then? I need a way to get rid of her.

My gaze lands on a ticket from a bet I placed on one of the races at the Festival of First Wind.

"How about a little wager, then?" I say. "If I win, you abdicate the throne to Cirocco and leave Lightning Cape forever."

Her smile grows. "And if I win, you marry dear Cirocco. Trying to get rid of you was a mistake. I believe I need you right where I can keep an eye on you."

My stomach churns. The idea of marrying anyone makes me sick at this point. "Deal."

"And the wager?"

Kaloni grew up hiding and scheming. I know Amval wasn't

allowed his music because he was being groomed to rule, but I wouldn't be surprised if she could play something. And draw, and do most of the things I can do.

Except one.

"How about a joust?"

THE JOUST

Amval

MY HEART HAMMERS. THE SUN BEATS DOWN ON ME, DRENCHING MY brow in sweat. People are everywhere, dressed in finery and uniforms alike. I have to find her. I can't be too late.

I spent half of last night awake, trying to figure out how to convince Ingrid I believed her without abandoning my belief in my sister. When Tek woke me early with news of the joust, I barely understood him. All I knew was that we needed to get an early start because there was extra work to do.

By the time it dawned on me exactly what happened, exactly what Ingrid had agreed to, it was too late. I couldn't abandon my friends to do my work for me.

Which is why I am now fighting my way through the frankly enormous crowd, considering how quickly this event came together, trying to reach the track to warn Ingrid.

She told me, one night, about one of her latest interests: jousting. I was excited to be able to relate to her over something. I don't particularly enjoy the sport, but Seksim is well-suited for it, so I've ridden in a few jousts.

Then, she told me that in Dun's Crossing—perhaps in most of the world—they joust as wolves.

Something—likely the sweet curve of her smiling mouth—distracted me before I could tell her just how different things are here.

I try to shoulder through a knot of people to no avail. Perhaps I could say I have some sort of urgent business with the horses, but Lord Corwyn certainly recognized me enough to be able to name the only groom wearing a starlight's veil, and I'm not sure how many members of Astralis dot this crowd. Nothing has happened because of his disappearance yet, but a knife could find me so easily in this crowd. I might not survive the kind of attention that would garner.

I try to dart around the knot instead.

"Sash." Abruptly, Mesut blocks my path.

"What?" I snap.

He eyes me. "A buckle, but…what is wrong?"

The crowd yawns before me, a sea I have to swim through while the current pushes against me. Mother and Father always said crowds were the best places to get spotted. No matter how well you thought you were blending in, trouble still might find you. There are simply too many eyes. So I have no idea how to maneuver this crush of bodies.

I look up at the stocky man I've worked alongside for months now, pray to the Goddess that the friendship I've earned is true, and inhale slowly through my nose.

"My girl?" I say.

He nods.

"She's jousting Luna Kaloni, but she doesn't know that it's on horseback. I have to warn her."

Mesut's eyes widen at the implication. A groom and a princess? One who barely even rides? For a heartbeat, I'm sure I've made a mistake. Loyalty may be strong, but gossip tends to be stronger.

Then, his expression shutters. "We are all here. We will get you to the rail."

I release my breath in a gust and grin at him. "You may well save a life today."

"Are they not using blunted lances?"

"I can only hope they are." Icy fear spiders out from my mark.

Mesut's eyes go distant as mind-links fly in all directions—all avoiding the key piece of information, that I am in love with Ingrid. Grooms answer from what feels like every corner of the crowd, and the sour fear clouding my mind starts to lift.

I have a chance. We have a chance.

"Thank you," I say to all of them.

Most of them don't bother replying because they are too busy coming up with a plan, but Mesut claps me on the arm, just once.

"Shoulders narrow," Mesut says. "Head down. There will be space cleared at the front, perhaps throughout, but for now, you are a rat."

Memories of nights spent trying to patch holes in walls and floors as the vermin tried to squirm through flood my mind. I grimace, but I understand what he's saying.

I maneuver through the smallest gaps my body can fit through, and I can't stop moving until I'm through. I tuck myself smaller and dive into the crowd.

His advice works. I go from slamming into brick walls to worming through the cracks, slicing through the distance between Ingrid and I like a sharp knife. Here and there, one of the other grooms calls out to me through the mind-link, and I find a pocket of empty ground I can dart through while breathing something other than body odor and fear.

My fear. The crowd is all excitement. This is Kaloni's first joust as Luna, and it's against a foreign princess. Vendors hawk snacks and drinks; people chatter and place bets.

And that is what makes my blood run cold. Why I have to reach her, have to warn her.

Kaloni is viciously competitive, always has been, and I know she can't resist a wager.

Just as well as I know how furious Ingrid was with me when she left.

There is no reason for the two of them to be doing this, especially not today, unless there's something on the line.

Kaloni wouldn't normally kill Ingrid. I mostly doubt that Ingrid would kill Kaloni, at least without some more proof than what we have. But they could have bet humiliation, leaving this place, any of a thousand dangerous possibilities.

I don't intend to lose either of them to the other's foolishness.

Which means I need to find Ingrid and convince her to abandon this plan before she discovers that she can't possibly win. As much as I love Kaloni, she is competitive enough not to have warned Ingrid of the differences, especially if Ingrid suggested the joust. My sister will take the advantages people give.

I always thought that made her so clever. Father did, too.

"Sash!" Nur appears out of the crowd and grabs my arm. "Tek said you ran off somewhere. I need to speak with you urgently."

A horn bellows—an announcement. The riders are coming out.

I'm running out of time.

If I don't have Ingrid, this whole masquerade is worthless.

I rip my arm out of her grasp. "Not now."

The stable master gapes after me as I sprint away, diving and weaving through the crowd. Later, I will face the consequences for that. But if it means saving Ingrid, reaching her in time, I'm glad to.

I can see the break in the crowd ahead, hear the rumble of mind-links from the few grooms holding people back from the railing for me. But I can't smell her yet. If I could just smell her, I think I could get my mark to stop bellowing like someone sank a knife into it and keeps pushing deeper. My vision swims slightly with the pain.

"*Come on,*" Tek calls through the mind-link. "*I've got one of the horses, and they're telling me it's time. Where are you?*"

"*I'm coming,*" I reply. "*Buy me a moment.*"

A dizzy thought drifts through my mind—I've already risked so much. If I'm too late, I could just whip off my veil and risk it all.

In my mind's eye, an arrow sinks into my throat before I finish the first word, stopping the duel. Astralis wants Kaloni on the throne—surely, if they thought they could control me, they wouldn't have bothered killing me as well. They must be here to protect her position.

I burst through the final row of the crowd. Ingrid stands there, riding leathers roughly emblazoned with the crest of Dun's Crossing silhouetted in the late-morning sunshine. A few tendrils of golden hair work loose from her braid and fly around her face.

And I can already see the wrinkle of a frown between her eyebrows. She's smart. She must have realized something was off when they gave her the leathers. So why is she still here?

I reach the wooden railing—and the horns blare again. Tek walks out, leading a brown-speckled warmblood beside another senior groom, who has Seksim.

She looks at me and then back at the horse.

"You can still call this off." Splinters dig into my palm when I grab the rail.

Ingrid looks down the lane at Kaloni, who mounts Seksim with effortless grace. Nothing escapes the tight knot of her hair. Backlit as she is, she almost looks like the ghost of Mother, riding again. As Tek reaches us, she looks at the massive crowd I just battled my way through.

And I know what she's going to do. She doesn't have to say a word.

Ingrid claims not to care about the political games I was raised to know like the back of my hand, but she cares deeply about her pride. So deeply she doesn't even realize that is what all the rest of us are playing to protect.

I am too late.

"She is called Beri," I murmur, "and she lists to the right."

Silently, Ingrid fits a foot into the stirrup, and I murmur a prayer that she knows how to ride. No, not just ride. She needs to ride spectacularly to beat Kaloni. They no longer have jousts during the Festival of First Wind because there was no point, with Kaloni there.

And my sister was always there, even when Father asked her to simply rest on her laurels and let others enjoy victory.

When Tek needs to help Ingrid into the saddle, and Beri huffs her irritation, my stomach sinks. Past my toes, through the very ground.

"Thank you all for coming on such short notice," Kaloni calls, her voice amplified on the dancing wind. "Princess Ingrid told me she had never jousted the way we do before, and I was thrilled to offer this exhibition bout to show her. Please, everyone, support her as if she were one of our own." She smiles. "As far as I am concerned, she is."

Kaloni is...lying? A bout against her isn't an exhibition; it's a slaughter. Even she knows that. How much of a hand does Astralis truly have here?

I squint against the sun, trying to see if her lance truly is blunted.

The one Tek hands Ingrid certainly is—but Astralis's modus operandi has been brutal "accidents" where everyone can see.

I clutch the railing until hot blood pools under my palms. Tek leads Ingrid into position. As the horns trumpet the countdown, he comes to stand next to me.

"It's her, isn't it?" he says.

There is no time to answer. The final, mocking, triumphant note sails through the air, and both horses explode off their marks.

I watch Ingrid, hair streaming, charging toward a future I cannot save her from while my mark screams.

RUNNING OUT OF TIME

Ingrid

Beri thunders underneath me, a machine of muscle and sinew I don't know like my own. The lance droops, ridiculously heavy. The crowd roars like a distant ocean. I can barely see Kaloni through the sun behind her, but the basics should be the same. Present a small target, aim for where they're weak, don't fl—

Her lance hammers into my chest, crushing air out of my lungs. My body twists. Vision darkens. Where are the reins? Where are my fucking hands?

I hit the ground like a sack of shit, and any remaining whisper of breath oozes out of me in a pathetic wheeze. Should've taken the helmet they offered me. My ears ring, and the back of my head throbs like my heart is there, trying to patch up whatever damage I did all by itself..

The sun glares down at me with distant disdain. I should've known. The second I saw the armor, I should've known.

Kaloni fucking cheated.

She knew what the fuck I meant. Her little speech made that very clear. *Never jousted the way we do*—if there weren't a few hundred eyes on us, more than a few of whom are her loyal guards, I would've marched down the lane and knocked those words out of her mouth.

Something blocks the mocking sun. Amval? I reach up dizzily, hoping. The fear in his eyes... he knew what happened. He was coming to warn me, like I would have warned him last night if Kaloni didn't oh-so-kindly post a soldier outside my door "to make sure I didn't try to tamper with our arrangement."

A hand grabs mine. Too small to be his. I squint.

It's her. Grinning. Dark hair still in that perfect little bun and barely a sheen of sweat on her forehead.

I try to wrench my hand back, but she holds on. Has she always been stronger than me, or did that fall mess up something important?

"Come now," she says. "It's good sportsmanship for me to help you up."

"I don't give a fuck." I try to pull away again.

"Don't be a sore loser." Kaloni yanks me to my shaking legs with surprising ease. "After all, your engagement party is tonight."

Rage burns through me. I'm about to be much more than a sore loser. I open my mouth—

"Thank you all again!" Kaloni says, the wind amplifying her voice and ripping mine out of my throat. "I have to see the princess to our healers now, but the next bout is coming up!"

Two more riders take their places at the end of the lanes. Kaloni pulls me along with her, away from the noise. I try to speak, to say fucking anything, but the wind jams down my throat like a fist and steals any sound I attempt to make.

Not only can I not tell everyone this was a fucking sham, but I can't even warn Amval. Kaloni might be distracted right now—might have been distracted setting this all up last night, if there's already a party—but she won't be for long.

Amval is running out of time, and I can't do anything.

At least Kaloni actually drops me off at the healer, instead of throwing me in the empty dungeon. To the healer, Tazi, she says,

"Look her over carefully. Recai will be along to retrieve her when she's through."

That's the name of the bastard who stood outside my room all night. I grit my teeth and wait for Kaloni to leave.

"I'm really okay," I tell Tazi.

"Luna's orders," she replies, looking deeply into my eyes, "and, I am sorry, but you're not."

I sigh. "What if I'm trying to get out of here quickly so Recai can have a little free time? My friend Bengu was hoping he could...."

"Your friend?" Tazi pushes me to lie down on her table and begins unfastening my armor.

I nod. "Ask her how much she owes me from the last hand of cards we played, and you'll see."

Tazi's eyes go distant with a mind-link. Bengu only mentioned Recai once, to say that he told her the rumor about another kingdom being behind the accidents, but soldiers and maids don't talk very often. Hopefully, my semi-educated guess is enough.

Tazi smiles faintly, and her eyes clear. "She is terrible at cards. All right, it seems like your head took the worst of it. If you swear you're not in pain anywhere else—"

My mark burns like it's trying to melt through my skin, and I think I might have twisted my ankle, but I nod.

"Bengu should just talk to him." Tazi mutters to herself as she wanders off to concoct something for my head.

Thankfully, her loyalty—or her desire for gossip—makes her hands fast. Within a few heartbeats, I'm out with a sticky, herbal-smelling bandage wrapped around my head. I lurch through the door and promptly slam into the far wall.

Slightly unsteady. I can work with that.

I just need to find someone who can reach Amval. Someone who will believe me and whom he'll believe.

With a grimace, I shed my leathers and hide them in a corner and then begin making my way to the hallway where I've been sleeping for the few last weeks.

My mouth tastes like sick, hidden behind a tapestry, by the time I finally reach Joli's door and knock.

"Ing—whoa!" She catches me as I nearly topple inside. "Kaloni really got you good, didn't she?"

"She fucking rigged it," I mutter.

Joli helps me inside and sits me on her couch. Goddess above, I feel like I've been hit by an avalanche. Or two. I need to lie down.

But I need to make sure at least one of these three Jolis understands me first.

"What do you mean, she rigged it?" The one in the middle offers me a cup of water.

I drink greedily. There, now at least my mouth doesn't taste like something died there. When I look up, she is watching me with worried eyes. The expression doesn't suit her, but neither does all the crying she's been doing.

Fuck, what do I tell her to make her believe?

"I didn't say I'd never jousted like that," I say. "I just challenged her to a joust, and she didn't tell me what that meant here."

"Damn." Joli shakes her head. "I should've warned you. Kaloni is very competitive about her jousting."

I shake my head—*no*, can't do that unless I want to be sick again. "There were stakes. Real ones. I have to marry Cirocco now."

"What? Why?"

"Because otherwise she would have to abdicate." I know I'm not telling this right. I can't find the words in the right order, and Joli is looking at me like I have even more heads than she does.

I pitch to my feet. "My room. Now."

She grabs my arm and helps me down the hall. I'm leaning on her too heavily, I reek of sweat, and she might still be able to smell the vomit on my breath. But I need to explain. She has to listen. She's the only one who will.

In my room, I lead her immediately over to my wardrobe, throw open the doors, and push the dresses aside. "I was right. Amval was murdered, and so were your parents. And they did it."

Joli looks from me to the map with wide eyes. "Ingrid...."

"I'm not crazy, I'm just dizzy." To prove it, I walk all the way to the bed and sit—lie down. "There is someone in danger I need your help to save. Just… just look."

She takes a deep breath but then goes quiet. I've earned her trust. When she came back after her first smuggling trip, she ran to me in a panic, saying she forgot to tell me not to mention what she was doing to anyone. She wouldn't be mad if I did, but had I?

The hug she gave me when I told her she never had to ask made me feel a little like an actual big sister.

So I've earned at least this much. I let my eyes flutter shut as she reads.

SOMEONE IS SHAKING ME. I LURCH UP, AND MY HEAD SCREAMS—BUT slightly quieter than before. Joli pulls her hand back, and I look at her. Only one and a half Jolis. An improvement.

One and a half Jolis looking like they also just got hit by an avalanche or two.

"Astralis," she says.

I start to nod, remember, and just say, "Yes."

"I heard the word once." She sits on the bed next to me, shaking her head. "When I was smuggling supplies to Moonlight Hollow. I drove right by a pair of men, and I heard it. I could tell it was a secret, so I circled back to hear the rest, but by the time I got there, they were gone."

"I challenged Kaloni to a joust because she told me, to my face, that she was part of their leadership. That she'd killed your parents and Amval"—the truth dances on my tongue, but it's not really mine to give—"and that she didn't care if I knew because no one would believe me."

"No," Joli says softly.

Goddess above, I am tired. Where's that anger that got me all the way here when I need it? I'm just cold, scared, and tired.

"I don't lie," I say. "Unless it's to save someone's skin. The truth gets you surprisingly far. And, be honest with yourself—what do I stand to gain if I'm right?"

Joli studies my face, hunting for an answer she's not going to find. I'm too tired to try to use my expression to convince her. If the naked truth isn't enough, then I may as well just run away while I have time. Before Recai finds me. Maybe I could gather some kind of support outside the palace and do…something.

"Nothing," Joli says. "But…Kaloni?"

Through the fog of my all-consuming headache, I can tell she still doesn't believe me. She's leaning away, frowning, staring at the floor. It's textbook, Exactly as Mother taught me.

But her gaze flickers toward me, and there's something there. A kernel of doubt I haven't seen in Amval. She might not believe me, but she doesn't exactly disbelieve me either.

I grab her hand. "Honestly, I don't need you to accept that she's behind this right now. She's no threat to you unless you threaten her, and she finds out."

Joli mouths the word *threat* like it's new. Goddess above, these fucking Soms. If I were her age, and someone told me one of my siblings had murdered another one, I'd barely be surprised. Things might be different now, but I can't imagine them always being this way.

"Okay," she finally says. "Then what do you need? You're obviously out of Tazi's care early for a reason."

"I'm fine." And if the edges of my words are a little slurred, that's nothing another nap won't fix.

"That groom," I say. "The one who drove the other carriage to the festival. I need you to find him and warn him. Kaloni is going to kill him."

Joli opens and closes her mouth. She looks at me, then away. "Kill him? Not just fire him?"

"He's been working with me." That should be safe enough to tell her. "Kaloni knows that, and she said she was going to deal with him appropriately."

No response.

"Do it after she announces the engagement, so you know I'm telling the truth." Fear cracks my voice down the middle. "Please."

Joli bites her lower lip.

A TELLING DINNER

Amval

I STAY AT THE RACETRACK UNTIL EVERY SINGLE JOUST—EACH OF THEM less and less well-attended after Ingrid and Kaloni leave—are done. Mostly, I stare blindly at the dirt, replaying the moment of Ingrid's impact in my mind.

Everyone in the crowd knew that was a hard fall. She clearly didn't know how to land it well, her spine hitting the dirt a heartbeat before her skull. In the moment after, when she just lay there perfectly still, all I could see was Mother and Father's carriage flipping.

Another body I would have to bury. Another life I didn't save.

Finally, though, the last bout ends, and the final dregs of the crowd drift away. Mesut and Tek wander over to me.

"I am sorry," Mesut says.

I shake my head. "No apologies needed. You did everything you could."

We were all just too late.

Tek claps me on the shoulder. "Well, she survived. I heard from a friend in the palace that there's some fancy dinner to celebrate tonight, so I wouldn't be surprised if you don't hear from her."

That, and she stumbled off the track looking like Kaloni hit her in the head, rather than the chest. My mark aches. I should go find her, no matter the cost.

Nur appears at the edge of the track, and I remember what happened when she caught me in the crowd.

"I think someone in the palace knows about Ingrid and me, and Nur wants to fire me because of it," I tell Tek and Mesut as I walk quickly in the opposite direction. *"Don't risk yourselves, but can you buy me a moment to disappear?"*

Both of them agree, closing ranks behind me. I murmur a soft prayer to the Goddess that I ended up in the stables rather than the kitchen. It might be warm there, but Tek and Mesut more than make up for it.

I duck away without a plan, hoping the stables are large enough that I can hide from Nur until I come up with one.

In truth, I doubt she's here to fire me. Or, if she is, I'll receive an escort out of the palace that no one could come back from. I may have escaped death at the hands of an assassin once, but I'm not cocky enough to count on my ability to do it a second time.

Evade an assassin, though? That, I can hopefully manage for at least long enough to learn exactly what Ingrid wagered on that rigged bet.

The rest of my afternoon is more than hectic. I bounce from stall to stall, row to row, avoiding Nur on the hunt.

As the sun sets, I find myself alone in an enclosed stall, listening to footsteps draw closer. They have to be Nur. I've been too lucky for too long. I gather the few things I've managed to pack into my bag—a few pieces of metalwork fine enough to sell but small enough that no one will miss, a change of clothes, some food. If I can pull off this feat a second time, I'm not going with nothing. Tek also gave me the dagger he cuts fruit with, and Mesut swore to watch over my naqun until he can return it to me.

Leaving it behind hurts more than I would expect.

The door opens, and I inhale slowly through my nose.

Peaches? And sage?

Joli darts inside and shuts the door behind her, looking rattled. My stomach lurches like I fell off a cliff. Why is she here? What does she know?

"Sash?" she says.

My stomach jolts out of free fall. Whatever she knows, she doesn't know who I am. Which means I need to get us out of this enclosed room quickly. If I can smell her, I don't have long.

"Yes. I spent the Festival of First Wind with you."

"I know that." She waves my explanation aside frustratedly, and I realize she's not dressed for dinner yet. "Ingrid sent me."

And my stomach drops again, fear and relief commingling in dizzying portions. "Why?"

Joli looks around. "I...I don't know if I believe her, but she says your life is in danger, and I have to get you out of here. You were helping her look into Amval's murder?"

Hearing the way my name catches in her throat is like a punch to the gut. I can only nod.

"Do you also think my sister is behind all this?" she asks, voice wobbling.

I shake my head. "There isn't enough proof."

"Well, Ingrid says she has it." Joli laughs, bordering on hysterical. I itch to crush her in one of the bear hugs she loves. "She says Kaloni admitted she did everything. That's what the joust was about—and since Ingrid lost, she has to marry Cirocco."

"M—Your brother?" Why under the Goddess' sky would she want that?

Joli shakes her head. "They've barely talked."

"Perhaps she wants Ingrid here," I say, mostly to myself. "Where Astralis can watch her."

"Where Kaloni can watch her, Ingrid says." Joli looks torn in a thousand directions. "That's why I'm here. You and I are going to watch the dinner. If Kaloni announces the engagement, then Ingrid is telling the truth, and we have to run. If not, you go back to normal. Perhaps… don't help Ingrid anymore."

She looks like she's choking on the words as she says them. My mark rebels at the idea, but what else can I do? I shoulder my bag, thankful I've already packed to run, and coax a quieting wind around our feet.

Joli shoots me a look. "I knew you let Cirocco win."

I shrug. She can think what she wants. I feel as if I can hear the final strains of this song Ingrid and I have been playing starting up, frantic and terrifying.

We creep out of the stables and in through a side door.

An engagement to Cirocco. I've always suspected my brother's tastes run toward men. This will drive him mad—which Kaloni knows because she and I discussed it.

But apparently Kaloni is having all sorts of discussions.

Why would Ingrid claim Kaloni admitted everything? Just to convince Joli? It seems possible, the kind of desperate move I could see myself making if she were the one who might need to evade an assassin.

But there are a dozen other ways she could have found me. Corwyn's capture proved she has friends in the palace, ones she can count on to go above and beyond for her. She wouldn't have needed to convince a maid of my sister's guilt to get a warning to me.

She wouldn't have risked everything on a wager unless she could hear the same music I am, racing toward a tumultuous crescendo.

Joli leads me to a balcony and then pulls aside a tapestry to reveal a door I didn't know was hidden there.

"Workers' access." She unlocks it with a key on a massive ring and then leads me into a dark, angled space.

Voices echo up through the floor—hundreds of them.

"Sausage again?" a shrill woman complains. "I thought Luna Kaloni promised new prosperity."

"That's coming, darling. We need to conquer the north first."

Joli just crawls over to the one sliver of light. I follow and discover a crack in the floor that stares directly down onto the main dining hall.

I look at her through the gloom. She doesn't look back at me. She's too busy studying what's going on below.

Later, I suppose. I turn my attention downward.

We're just over the head table. Ingrid sits between Kaloni and a stranger, the only golden head amongst the dark. My heart skips a beat when I spot the bandage around it. Something is oozing through the gauze—but that something is green, not red like blood. Every time someone knocks against a cup or scrapes their fork on their plate, she winces. I pray the green is Tazi's headache cure. It works miracles, albeit usually on much smaller headaches.

Kaloni should be letting her rest after a fall like that. Frankly, Tazi shouldn't have let her out.

And yet, she's here, in a sea foam green gown like she's trying to match that green stain. My mark aches in sympathy.

On her left, at the head of the table, Kaloni eats without hesitation. "The conscription means there's more training to be done than I hoped."

"Well, I am sure we're up for the task, Your Highness," the stranger on Ingrid's other side says.

Who is that? I barely recognize the voice, and this angle doesn't show me more than a head of dark hair.

Joli frowns. "Recai? He's a battalion leader, a rising star, but what is he doing at Kaloni's table?"

"More than up for it, I hope," Kaloni replies with half a laugh.

His name sounds familiar, but that's all. Joli is right. He doesn't belong there.

Whatever his response is, it's lost in another clatter of dishes that makes Ingrid wince.

The rest of the dinner carries on like that. We catch snippets of conversation. The rest of our siblings share the head table and talk as if they have no idea something might be happening. Perhaps they don't.

Perhaps nothing is.

Finally, the last of the dessert plates are cleared away, and Kaloni stands. I perk up. Joli straightens from near sleep. Kaloni is either going to announce the engagement, or she is going to dismiss everyone.

My heart patters loud enough that I half expect Ingrid to hear it through the ceiling and look up at us, but she just stares at Kaloni. It's difficult to tell from this distance, but she almost looks... scared.

I've never seen that expression on her face before, and I don't want to see it again.

"Today is an auspicious day," Kaloni says. Her voice carries on the wind, even up to us. "It has been nine weeks to the day since we lost my brother, Prince Amval, and gained a ninth sibling in his mate, Princess Ingrid. She has stayed with us these long weeks, first to grieve, and then because she truly became part of our family." She sets a hand on Ingrid's shoulder.

Nobles coo over the sweetness of the moment, but all I can see is how Ingrid cringes away from her touch—and how that soldier, Recai, moves in response like he's reaching for his magic to push her back.

"Today, we welcomed her into one of our traditions." Soft laughter. "And tonight, we make her entrance into our family official. I am truly, deeply honored to announce that love has touched Som Palace once more. Princess Ingrid and Prince Cirocco are engaged!"

Like the hand of the Goddess Herself is on my chin, I manage to look away from Ingrid in this moment and at my brother. My best friend. After weeks at the Gruesome Pony, I know him better than I ever did.

Shock and dismay flicker across his face, a split-second of discord with the smug pride on Kaloni's lips.

"By the Goddess," I whisper.

Ingrid was right. Kaloni...my sister...arranged my murder. Our parents' murder. Our brother's and my mate's misery.

I should have trusted Ingrid.

Joli grabs my hand. "We have to go."

LAST STRAW

Ingrid

"Thank you," I mutter through gritted teeth to what must be the thousandth dignitary to reach our table.

"Yes, thank you," Cirocco says in a voice so even I can barely hear it. Like it's so dull, it slides right out of my ears.

"It is so wonderful you found love after such a tragedy." The woman curtsies. I have no idea who she is, where she's from. "I'm just honored to be a part of such a historic moment! Thank you, Luna Kaloni, for including us."

"With all I've learned about how families can grow, how could I not, Lady Elyse?" She takes the woman's hand and pats it. "Please, give all my best to Alpha Devan when you return home—though you're of course welcome to stay until the wedding."

Not a member of Astralis, I decide. The only game that's been keeping me awake through this endless slog.

Kaloni, on the other hand, glows like she just got engaged. Like she didn't shackle me to her brother just to keep an eye on me. Cirocco now sits between the two of us, his sweating hand in mine.

On the tabletop, of course. How else will our legions of admirers see the three-banded bracelet that is apparently a betrothal custom in Lightning Cape? The gold, platinum, and copper bands, interlinked like they are, would be beautiful on any other day.

Today, they just look like a manacle.

"Oh, you're too kind," Lady Elyse flutes. "Love and peace to you all." She curtsies again before stepping away—and the next noble takes her place.

My skin crawls. I knock back another glass of the celebratory sparkling wine Kaloni has requested. I would rather dance my way through a hundred balls with any partner of Candace's choosing than keep sitting here. Mouthing a prayer for good luck, I lean over to Cirocco.

"I'm a little tired," I say. "Could you get us out of here before every single person in the palace congratulates us?"

His cheeks pink, and he leans slightly away. Kaloni couldn't have picked a less convincing husband for me if she tried. He hasn't even looked at me since she made the announcement, even though he hasn't objected once. Not when she asked him to stand, to take my hand, to give me this fucking shackle.

"I will try," he whispers back as Kaloni accepts our congratulations happily.

Let her have them, if she wants them. Cirocco leans into his sister.

My thumbnail finds my mouth, and I chew on it. Whatever Tazi put on my head is its own kind of magic; I have a throbbing hangover of a headache, and every sound makes it worse, but I haven't thrown up in a few hours, and all my thoughts are staying in order.

Which gives me enough space to worry about getting out of here and whether Joli warned Amval. She wouldn't give me a straight answer. And even though Kaloni keeps alluding to a wedding soon enough that all these dignitaries should stay until it occurs, I doubt that will keep her distracted enough that she won't have time to deal with one groom. I'm not even sure this dinner was enough trouble. I might already be too late.

No. I'd feel it. This mark has to be good for something. And Joli never showed up tonight, which seems like a sign.

Cirocco leans back with a frown. I don't need him to tell me.

This is Kaloni's show now, and we're going to play our parts until she's done with us.

WHEN THE RIVER OF VISITORS FINALLY DRIES UP, I'VE SHREDDED MY thumb to bleeding twice, and I'm about ready to crawl out of my skin. The wine sets my senses buzzing, but I'm not stupid enough to actually dull them with my guard, Recai, on one side and Kaloni within spitting distance.

Goddess, but I wish I were.

Kaloni stands. "Thank you all for such a beautiful evening. News about the wedding will be forthcoming. All here tonight are invited, and you may spread the news as widely as you wish. Sleep restfully."

The hall fills with conversation and scraping chairs as the roomful of people I've decided I'm going to hate for the rest of my life finally trickle out. The other siblings mutter tired goodbyes—they were the first with their congratulations, mostly filled with confusion, and they don't seem to know what to do now. In another life, they would have been my family, but now, they just look like more bars on my cage.

Kaloni looks at the two of us, flushed with excitement. "I am sorry for the surprise, brother, but when Ingrid admitted what she wanted to me, I simply couldn't wait."

"Of course," Cirocco murmurs.

"And, as Ingrid suggested, you are going to get a start on your life together tonight." She smiles at him and then looks at me with triumphant fire in her eyes. "You'll be sharing quarters from now on. Ingrid, dear, your belongings have already been moved into Cirocco's room." She grabs my hand. "I had them take *special* care with that lute of yours. I wouldn't want you to lose something you've worked so hard on."

A few years ago, I begged one of the trainers in the castle to show me how to fight. Not with weapons or as a wolf, but with my hands. Kaloni's words hit like the punch he landed square on my chin. Blood roars in my ears. Pain reaches spidery fingers through systems I didn't think it could touch.

The very last shred of privacy, of control I had in this Goddess-forsaken palace, stripped away from me when I wasn't even looking. Someone else moved my lute. Hell, if I'm reading her emphasis correctly, they may have broken it. It's the one thing that was truly mine.

"Thank you," Cirocco says dully.

Stop thanking her! I want to scream. I am done with the congratulations, with the apologies for the man I lost who isn't dead yet, with the placid acceptance of everything happening to me.

But as if she can read the change in my eyes, Kaloni's mouth tightens. "Recai will escort you to ensure these crowds don't slow you down enough to steal your first night from you."

I grit my teeth. The message is clear: I lost. I can either marry Cirocco, like I promised, or I can die.

A dark impulse in my chest dares me to push her. The room isn't empty yet. If she kills me here, everyone will know what she is.

But she's not stupid enough to do that.

"Good night." I turn and march out of the room, dragging Cirocco behind me.

That rage carries me all the way upstairs, all the way to his door. I pause and look at him.

He frowns. "What?"

"Don't you have a key?"

"It isn't locked." He shoves open the door easily.

Of course, it's not. "Would you mind if we started locking it? It's an old habit of mine from home."

He grimaces, likely imagining the worst of what growing up with King Gavin could be. "I'll have to find the key, but whatever makes you happy."

I shut the door behind us, and the moment the latch clicks, his hand slips out of mine. I'm probably imagining the whisper of wind, but he certainly seems to dart away faster than otherwise possible. Like he can't wait to escape me.

"My bedroom is through that door." He points at an open archway. "Bathroom there."

Aside from the lush decorations, his quarters look much like mine. The ones that used to be mine. My heart in my throat, I race into the bedroom.

My lute stands beside the massive, canopied bed, as beautiful as if it were always here. I pick it up, strum each string. It's only slightly out of tune. Someone handled it—obviously, they did—but it's intact.

What did Kaloni destroy?

Ice crawls over my skin as I turn to the wardrobe. Cirocco's wardrobe, broader and squatter than the massive one I left behind. Numb legs carry me to it, numb fingers open it, and I don't even know why. Of course, it's not here. There's no point in moving the mix of dresses and pants aside.

There is nothing behind them.

All my research, weeks of work and mapping, every note is gone.

I spend a heartbeat grateful I wasn't stupid enough to write down anything about Amval.

Behind me, Cirocco clears his throat. "Does it all, uh, look all right?"

I let the clothes swing back into place. "I guess I'll get used to it."

"Right." He glances around, his hands in his pockets. "I'm happy to sleep on the couch. I've done it before."

"Why are you going along with this if you can barely look at me?" I ask tiredly.

He blows out a sharp breath. "I am sorry about that. You are...not the sort of person I thought I would spend my life with. I also have some things to get used to."

Irritation bubbles, boils. Where is the Beta who told me that someday, I *would* tell him what I knew about Amval? Soft-spoken, but with a core of iron? Him, at least, I respected.

"Why agree at all?" I advance on him. "You could have said no. I know Kaloni didn't warn you."

He shrugs and stares at the floor. "Amval was my favorite brother. My best friend. I told you once that I knew the Goddess would pick out someone special for him, and I didn't lie."

"So… what? You're marrying me because Kaloni said I wanted you to?" My head feels like it's spinning on my shoulders. If Candace died tomorrow, I wouldn't marry Hollis unless the world depended on it.

Another shrug. "For Amval's memory."

"And because Kaloni said so."

He still won't look at me, and I know I've struck home. Every single one of these siblings is so dependent on the others, I couldn't pry them apart with a bar. They just *trust*. No matter how obvious the signs are.

After hours of politely not screaming and running away, I'm all out of politeness. I'm out of patience, out of composure, and out of fucking time.

"Forget his fucking memory," I snap. "Somewhere else in this palace, Amval is either dying or running for his life because Kaloni is trying to murder him for a *second* time, and I'm tired of pretending that's not true."

Cirocco's mouth falls open.

RUNNING OUT

Amval

With my sister's hand in mine, betrayal ringing in my ears, I scoot away from the crack in the floor. I don't want to keep watching. Seeing Cirocco smooth out his expression into pleasantness and Ingrid struggling to do the same as they went to his room was enough for me.

I want to go back to the moment before Kaloni's announcement, when my whole world made sense.

Joli recovers better than I do, tearing through the dark and dragging me after her. Somehow, she's still dancer-light on her feet. I sound like a stampede.

The wind I've been able to count on all my life leaps to my command almost before I call it. Thank the Goddess. My thoughts alone are heavy enough to drag me through the floor, onto the heads of the revelers downstairs.

Kaloni did this. All of it.

Joli shoots through the door and lets the tapestry swing back into place. "Your bag—what's in it?"

"Essentials," I mumble. "For if I had to run."

"Why didn't you?" she asks.

Because my friends in the stable needed my help. Because I had to know what Ingrid wagered.

I didn't realize she'd wagered everything.

Joli shakes her head. "She's my sister. Pull it together."

Right. Of course. Everything has changed, and nothing has. I reach for all the pieces of Sash, now scattered around my feet.

Armored boots click at the mouth of the hallway.

"Shit." Joli glances toward them, the way we should go to get out the fastest.

But not the only way.

I am not losing another sibling tonight. I whip around and dart in the opposite direction. She stumbles for a moment but then catches up.

"The roof?" she asks through the mind-link.

I nod. She raises a wind at our heels, speeding us up. I'm surprised Esen told her about the connecting stretch of roof he used for a prank he needed my help with, but it seems there are many things I don't know about my siblings. We round a corner into a long gallery of royal portraits, half of which are still missing. We keep finding them in strange nooks of the palace—or in nobles' manors, mysteriously.

"You're back," Joli says, half of an old code from our days on the road.

"You're front," I reply, darting for the massive, locked bay window between paintings.

I don't need to check if she's in the right place. As soon as we could raise an alarm, we were all trained to watch.

The lock glimmers at me. In another life, I would have the keys on hand or simply get a housekeeper to open it for me. In this one, I have to try my hand at a trick Father taught us for emergencies, which I was never particularly good at.

I coax a thin ribbon of air into its teeth and try to feel the shape of the missing key.

"West wind," Joli says. She can hear someone coming from the west but can't see them yet.

I grit my teeth. The air should fly free, not be forced into these tight little curves. My control wanes as the element itself fights me.

And I can hear the boots now, over my hammering heart. They shouldn't even be on patrol yet. Kaloni must be looking for something. My stomach drops. Even if Kaloni hasn't gotten around to taking me out directly, she'll have warned the soldiers.

"My back," Joli snaps, nerves taut in her voice.

I grimace and release my control to swap with her. She was never any better at this than I was, but I'd rather face the soldiers first. If I can shift, I can buy her a few minutes to get away. I pull a spare veil out of my bag and throw it over her head to hide her face before turning to the westernmost door.

The footsteps grow louder. Joli's breathing is even, steady. I flex my hands and prepare to shift.

Click.

She grabs my hand, not wasting time on words, and pulls me out onto the roof. I chase her over the tiles to the next glowing window, my mind spinning. Ingrid said Joli disappeared sometimes, but that was the night she proved Astralis to me, the night we danced. All the other details slip through my fingers.

Joli picks open the next window so quickly there's barely time for me to mount a watch. Still, a soldier steps into the portal of the open window behind us and cocks his head.

"Go!" I push her through the window as she opens it.

She shoots me a look as we barrel forward, but we don't have time to explain.

"Down," I say. *"We can take the northeast servants' door."*

"The window in the map room is faster." She bolts in that direction.

"The map room is two stories off the ground!" I barely manage to dodge a maid exiting one of the many guest rooms. At least her quiet shriek makes Joli tie the veil I tossed around her head properly.

"Trust me."

And I do.

Together, we fly down a zig-zagging staircase and through rooms barely decorated, rooms I forgot we had. We lost so much while we were gone.

At Kaloni's hand, we've lost even more since our return. On the run, we had each other.

Finally, we reach the map room. Wind swirls around our ankles, ready to catch us or throw us forward. Joli unlocks this window, and I see thick, hardy vines curling up over the sill. The sort that disrupt the bricks, that the gardeners are supposed to destroy on sight.

She catches me looking and smiles. *"I've been bribing them to leave these be for about six months now."*

Surprise is a luxury for later. I spin the wind like sugar into a basket to catch us if we fall, and we crawl out the window. New calluses on my fingers come in handy, but the vines make climbing so much easier that I'm irritated I didn't find them, tucked into one spoke of the star, when I first started breaking into my own palace to see Ingrid.

Thinking of her sends a starburst of pain through my mark. I almost lose my grip, and only the wind keeps me in place.

I land on the ground next to Joli.

"No more running until we're out," she says.

I coax the wind back to step-softening silence, and we move. We dodge between pools of light from windows and avoid patrols I didn't even know happened out here. We reach the retaining wall, and she shoves her hand at a curtain of less dangerous ivy.

Instead of shattering her fingers against stone, she reaches deeper, parts the plants, and reveals a faded wooden door. Another key from her ring, and it opens. I stare at my youngest sister as we step out of the palace.

"Follow as closely as you can." She relocks the door and shifts into a dark wolf. *"I have... a few traps."*

Someone shouts behind us. I throw myself into a shift and take off, away from the lights and danger of Som Palace. Following so close I could snatch her tail between my teeth keeps me distracted, at least. The moment I stop, the moment I start thinking…I don't know what comes next.

Joli leads me away from the beach, away from the forest where Mother and Father were murdered, away from the town. After long minutes of running into nothingness, the terrain tilts. A small cluster of low hills sits not far from the palace, toward Moonlight Beach, but they're nearly worthless. Over-mined and over-farmed. I've never even visited them.

She dodges through them like she grew up here. I match her every footfall. Where could we possibly be going?

In a valley between hills, the entrance to an old mine yawns. Joli darts inside, shifts, and shimmies into a set of clothes waiting for her at the mouth. As I shift and throw on some clothes from my bag, she lights a lantern hanging on the wall.

"At this stage, I figure you have more to hide than I do."

The soft firelight illuminates walls lined with bags, boxes, and crates. All of them are labeled. From Oakspring Dunes, to Thunderpeak. From Starfall Mountain, to Seedmoss Rapids.

Smuggling. That's what Ingrid said. Joli disappears for days at a time to be a smuggler.

She shifts a few crates to pull out a burlap sack that moves like grain. "You can sleep here until we come up with a better plan."

"You're a smuggler," I say.

"Yes," she says as if that should have been obvious by now. It is, I suppose. I just still can't imagine how I didn't know. "Do you mind?"

Her posture shifts just slightly toward a pry bar lying on one of the crates. I shake my head.

"Good." She returns to setting up my burlap bed. "You know, I could use a groom. I have horses outside the palace, but we have all the best ones inside."

I laugh helplessly. My littlest sister is offering me a cut of her smuggling business!

"I wouldn't make fun of someone who just saved my life, if I were you." She crosses her arms defensively.

"I'm not." I put a hand on my chest, try to crush the laughter down before the whole storm of emotion behind it explodes out. "I'm just… surprised. How does a princess become a smuggler?"

"She grows up on the run." Joli perches on another box. "And then, when the running's done, she discovers that being a princess is a whole hell of a lot less interesting."

"Have you tried to get involved in the politics?" I already know the answer—no—but Sash wouldn't.

She snorts. "How? Every secondary and tertiary position in the court already has one of my siblings in it."

"I never thought of it like that." I sit on the ground.

"Why would you?" She shakes her head. "I needed something for myself. Something my family wasn't already doing—or trying to do for me."

The realization I had before returning to Ingrid rings through me. "I think I understand. My parents… they had such high expectations of me that they dictated my every move before I made it. They never intended to, I suspect, but that doesn't change much."

"And I can't even complain about my parents anymore." Joli's smile wobbles. "They should have stopped having children before me. Everyone knows it, and I'm not allowed to be angry about that anymore because my sister fucking murdered them."

"You can still be angry," I say immediately.

"To who?" she demands. "My grieving, apparently potentially evil siblings? Ingrid, who barely knew them and is destroying her life to solve their murder? Or all the *friends* I have inside that place?"

"You sound lonely." That shouldn't be a surprise to me either. I should have known, should have made time for her. "I'm so sorry."

"I'm your savior, not your latest penitent." She stands. "You have food in there?"

"Yes, but—"

"But what?" She glares down at me, tears in her eyes, prickling with a fight she doesn't seem to be able to have with anyone. When did we start keeping so many secrets from each other?

"But you're right," I say slowly. "I do have more to hide than you."

"Okay?"

I reach up and pull my veil off. Joli's dark gaze dances around my face.

Then, she bursts out laughing.

PRESS YOUR LUCK

Ingrid

I YAWN AND SCRUB MY HANDS OVER MY FACE. MORNING SUNLIGHT peeks around the edges of the curtains, and Cirocco still hasn't stopped fucking pacing.

"I talked to him," he says for what feels like the thousandth time. "And he didn't say a word."

"He was protecting you." I lean back against a pile of cushions and wonder if I can't sneak in a little nap before breakfast. "From Kaloni, not that he knew it then."

Cirocco shakes his head.

"What do I have to say to make you believe me?" I ask, also for the thousandth time. I've explained everything I know—which was much harder without all my notes, though my best recreation of them litters the table in front of me. I've gone through a detailed timeline, explained to him anything he had questions about. And now, I'm just tired.

Finally, he sighs and drops onto the couch at my feet. "Nothing."

"Glad I wasted this night, then. Enjoy breakfast without me." I roll over, away from him.

"No, I—" His hand brushes my shoulder like he's going to stop me but thinks better of it. Smart. "I don't exactly disbelieve you. It's just… difficult."

"Really?" I peer at him from under my arm, watching that thoughtful face. Cirocco doesn't strike me as a liar, but I have to be sure.

"Really." He takes a deep breath and nods to himself. "I did talk to him. I wasn't thinking about it at the time, but that was my brother." He smiles softly. "Did you know he's a brilliant musician?"

My mark throbs. "I was the first person he played with."

"When this is done," he says, "you'll play for me."

"Does that mean you're in?"

"Someone is attacking my family." He stands, becoming the Beta I've seen in glimpses. "And you have a plan to stop that someone. What else could I be?"

Cirocco and I wander down to breakfast arm-in-arm. It might be part of the plan, but I'm glad to have someone to lean on. The nap I took after my fall yesterday was not enough sleep, and it feels like a particularly angry drummer is nesting in my skull.

"When we enter the hall," I murmur, "laugh like I've just told you the funniest joke."

"Acting is not my strong suit," he replies.

How did they survive on the run? "Imagine Joli's face when she finds out the truth."

I push open the doors as Cirocco laughs and bat my eyes up at him like Candace would. Well, hopefully like Candace would. Judging by the way his laughter intensifies when he looks at me, I might not be pulling it off.

Every eye in the hall turns toward us. I ignore them, draped over his arm like he's the only person in the world.

He bends down to whisper in my ear. "How was that?"

I grin and whisper back, "Perfect."

"You two are so sweet together," someone I'm sure congratulated us last night says as we pass.

"Thank you." I bob a tiny curtsy and try not to want to pull her head off.

Cirocco might not be much of an actor, but he doesn't have a night's worth of sleepless rage to grapple with.

I'm in love, I'm in love, I'm in love.

We flounce up to the head table and take seats next to each other. Liwar, Kaloni, and Sibel are already here.

"Not eating with the triplets?" Kaloni asks lightly.

Cirocco glances at me. "Ingrid prefers the food here, and I didn't want to leave her."

I pat his knee under the table. Good answer.

She nods and returns to her breakfast.

"So," Liwar says slowly, "you seem happy this morning."

"I certainly am." I beam up at Cirocco.

"We talked all night," he replies. "And I realized how much we have in common. Perhaps it's sudden, but I am so glad you arranged this, dear."

"That's lovely," Kaloni says.

I grit my teeth

All right, this isn't my best plan. But Kaloni has been so perfectly controlled, so ahead of me at every step. I just wanted her to be caught off guard once. To think she made a mistake setting me up with Cirocco.

Liwar and Sibel ask more questions as I devour seeded bread, peppery eggs, soft cheese, and a few cups of still too weak coffee. If I can't have a good night's sleep or escape this headache, I at least need this. Cirocco answers gamely, sticking to the script we discussed: this was my idea, but overnight, he fell for me. I sprinkle in enough of my own details that Kaloni could think I fell for him, too, without denying anything in her announcement. The twins seem awkward, but they slowly warm up to the idea.

"I wouldn't mind another sister," Sibel says finally.

My mark aches, and I almost wish Umit had burnt something so I could have a little smell of Amval this morning. He should be the one at my side, murmuring in my ear. Maybe he'd whisper those sly little jokes he's started making when we're alone, a break in his princely persona even where everyone can see him. He'd certainly have his hand on my knee, warm and heavy. Cirocco waits for me to touch him, and every time, he tenses just a little, like he's trying to convince himself not to flinch away.

"And we can share clothes!" Liwar says. "You have some of the most stunning pieces."

"Me?" I shake my head. "I saw that red dress you wore to the coronation, and I nearly wept."

She blushes prettily. "Oh, I was nothing compared to Kaloni."

I wait for Sibel to jump in and encourage her sister, but there's a moment of quiet. Even Cirocco just stares down at his breakfast. Goddess, has everyone always had to come second to Kaloni, or is that new since she took the throne?

"When I wasn't looking at her, I was looking at you," I say to fill the silence, and when I nudge Cirocco, he nods.

Liwar opens her mouth, maybe to disagree with me but definitely to find out exactly how stubborn I can be when someone insults my sister. Before she can say anything, though, the door swings open, and she freezes.

Whispers crash through the room like a wave. The first ones I've heard all morning that aren't about Cirocco and I. From here, I can't make out what they're saying, but they don't have the same giddy tone.

These are shocked.

I turn to see Corwyn. No, not Corwyn—Lord Hajni. The servant's uniform is gone, along with Redwood's colors. In its place, he wears a heavily embroidered cloak in Moonlight Beach indigo over neat trousers and a tunic emblazoned with the symbol of his house.

"What is he doing here?" I hiss.

Kaloni doesn't look up from her breakfast, but I can see her tiny smile. She knew he was going to do this. She gave him permission.

She doesn't think he has to hide anymore.

Where the fuck is Joli? Where is Amval?

Cirocco grabs my hand and squeezes it almost tight enough that it hurts. The small burst of pain gives me enough space that I can breathe. Barely.

Corwyn marches toward us so confidently I expect him to pull out the empty chair that should be Joli's, but Kaloni still isn't that cocky. He sits a table away, with his precious Lord Rik and a few other nobles I know he's been visiting. This close, I can see bandaged scrapes on his hands, likely from whatever happened to him after he crawled out the window, and a bandage on the back of his head from where Amval hit him. It oozes green, just like mine did yesterday— Kaloni sent him to the fucking royal healer to be patched up.

My blood boils. I squeeze Cirocco's hand back as hard as I can. It's the only Goddess-damned thing keeping me here instead of bolting across the room to finish what Amval started.

He was right. We should have brained Corwyn and been done with it. The spiraling web of Astralis looks more and more like a distraction when Corwyn and Kaloni sit within arm's reach.

"Well, I am glad to hear you two have hit it off so well," Kaloni says, suddenly looking up from her clean plate.

My pulse jumps like a deer smelling a wolf. I've stumbled into another trap. How does she keep laying them out when I'm not looking?

"We have," Cirocco says warmly, not seeing the jaws about to swallow us.

"In that case, why wait?" She smiles graciously. "Without a mate bond, you must be missing some intimacy."

"Uh...." Cirocco looks at me.

Kaloni's smile brightens a shade, and I know we've lost. She saw right through us.

Dammit, where is Joli?

"Given how many pieces are already in place or leftover from the other… events we've had recently, I think I could plan a lovely wedding for you in, say, a week?" She looks around the room. "So many dignitaries are already here, so we wouldn't need to worry much about invitations."

"What about my family?" I blurt. "They are farther flung."

"Oh, are you speaking to them again?" She blinks innocently. "Well, we'll send our fastest messengers. I'm sure they can get here in time for the reception if they really try."

Candace is in Snowcrest, at least three weeks away. Estrella just gave birth. Excuses crowd my mouth, but there's no point.

The trap is sprung, and I'm right smack in the middle of it again.

"Thank you," I mumble.

Cirocco echoes me. Listening to Liwar and Sibel chattering about wedding preparations makes the rest of my breakfast taste like ash.

When we can finally escape, I shuffle out into the hallway like a zombie. Kaloni has already assigned me a strict schedule of dress fittings and tastings. What little time I had melts away.

She is winning.

"Ingrid!" someone hisses.

I turn to see—Joli! She has dark bags under her eyes, is covered in dust, and leans around the corner, waving at us.

Fuck whoever can see us. I dart toward her. She has the news I've been waiting for.

Cirocco charges after me.

Joli starts to pull me away but then pauses and looks at her brother. "Is he…?"

"As up to date as you are," I reply before shooting a warning glance at Cirocco. He can't mention Amval. Not yet.

A smile I don't understand flickers over Joli's lips. "If you say so."

She leads us into a tiny nook hidden by a painting. Close, breathless air clouds the space. My heart hammers in my mark, in my skull.

"Well?"

She takes a deep breath. "Amval is safe. Now, what are we going to do about our traitorous fucking sister?"

REUNION

Amval

I PUNCH THE BURLAP SACK, TRYING TO MANEUVER IT INTO SOMETHING comfortable. Grain crunches under my fist, but when I lay my head back down, it feels exactly the same. Morning reached the cave hours ago, but I barely slept last night. Every time I managed to pass out, I had the same dream—Kaloni, standing over me with Yalim's sword. Every time, I woke up just before I either escaped or her blow landed true.

And this burlap bed isn't exactly helping me to rest.

Frustrated, I sit up and abandon sleep altogether in favor of pulling out a roseapple for breakfast. Joli said she would be back when she could. When she knew more. But if one of these crates has some method of keeping time, I haven't found it yet, and I don't know what I would be counting down to anyway. At least I don't have to bother with my veil anymore. The air in here is stale enough after she dragged a false cave-in, just stones attached to a thick wooden board, into the entrance without muffling it further.

Something rustles outside. I jump to my feet and grab that pry bar

Joli almost used against me last night. It could be—should be—her, but I don't intend to take that risk. The cave-in shifts aside. I inhale deeply through my nose.

And smell violets and ink.

Before Ingrid even fully enters the cave, I throw myself at her, pry bar forgotten. She grunts softly as I wrap her in a desperate embrace, gulping lungful after lungful of her scent. A heartbeat later, she folds herself around me, shaking slightly.

"Joli and Cirocco are coming behind me," she mumbles into the crook of my shoulder, her voice washing over the tender skin of my mark like warm water. "I asked them to wait. I needed...."

She doesn't have to finish the sentence. I needed her, too. There are so many things I have to say, but first, I press my mouth to hers.

Everything in the world realigns in the clash of lips and teeth. It's messy, hungry, as desperate as my arms around her. She grabs at my hair, my tunic. I touch every inch of her I can reach.

I only let her go when I can't resist my lungs' screaming any longer, but neither of us backs more than an inch away. My gaze roves over her face like I'm memorizing it all over again. Her pointed chin, the sweet bow of her lips, the pink in her cheeks. Goddess above, I missed her like a limb.

"I am so sorry," I say. "Kaloni is... out of control. I don't recognize her anymore. The sister I knew never would have done this."

"People change." She drags a thumb over my stubbly cheek. A shaving razor did not make the list of emergency items to pack. "And your siblings have far more secrets from each other than you expected, clearly."

We both look around at the crates and boxes proving I barely knew Joli. Ingrid knew before I did.

"I've missed so much," I say. "I've been too busy trying to be the hero. Be my father."

"I'm just glad you listened before it was too late. I saw soldiers headed to the stable on my way out," she says.

My heart skips a beat. "Nur was looking for me, but I hid from her. Could you make sure she isn't punished?"

Ingrid stares at me and then smiles helplessly. "And your friends, too?"

"If you can." Tek and Mesut shouldn't be in too much trouble, but I'd rather be sure.

"That," she says.

"What?"

"That's the kind of king you should be, if you ever get to." She cups my face. "Someone who thinks about his boss when he's on the run for his life."

King. What an impossible thought, after all this time. But there is a glow in Ingrid's sky-blue eyes that almost makes me believe it could happen.

"I...don't know what I would've done if you actually died," she whispers.

"Avenged me," I say with a smile.

Her only answer is another kiss. Hungry, all teeth, and I need more. I grab her and crush her closer. Her moan pours into my mouth. It lights me on fire, barely starting to fill that pit of need. We've made too many mistakes, almost lost each other too many times. I love her too much to ever let her go again.

With my hands, my lips, I swear to her that she'll never have to avenge me.

"We don't have much time," she mumbles against my lips.

"Then let's make the most of what we have." I kiss away from her mouth, down her throat. She tightens one hand in my hair, and with the other, starts untying the front of her dress.

I've never seen her wear a dress that ties before. I slant a crooked smile up at her, wondering if this was what she planned, why she asked the others to wait all along. Ingrid just smiles back at me as she strips out of her undergarments and lets them fall to the ground.

I graze my hands up the backs of her legs as I kiss down to her breasts. She rolls into my touch. Goddess above, if we had the time to spend.

But we don't. And though I know all I need is the sweet heat of her, I don't intend to leave her without the kind of apology she deserves.

My mouth trails down her chest, down to the thin web of skin over her hipbone. Her groan echoes through the mine, and I shush her teasingly.

Her hand tightens in my hair, driving me toward the apex of her thighs. Exactly where I want to be. Her legs fall open as I lick between them and find her already drenched, already wanting. I lap up how much she has missed me. She is so warm, the taste of violets and ink on my tongue like the sweetest liquor I can imagine. A life spent drunk on this might be the best one I could live. She rocks into me in desperate rhythm, crushing my nose and smothering all breath from my lungs.

I move with her. For the first time in my life, the air can wait.

Her legs start trembling, and I hook them over my shoulders in one smooth motion, taking all her weight. She muffles a cry against the back of her hand, just barely. My cock throbs when I look up at the whole length of her, golden, shining, and splayed. All mine.

A new flood of wetness soaks my face as she yelps my name. I hold her and kiss the faint burns my stubble left on the inside of her thighs until she stops shaking.

Finally, I set her back on her feet. "How far behind are—"

She pushes me to sit on the burlap-sack bed, then straddles me, open dress flaring behind her in a riot of color. Any answer disappears in another claiming kiss. I lick her taste back into her own mouth, and she rolls her hips against my lap. She kisses me harder, deeper, pushing me back until I'm reclining on the sack. My hardening cock lines up with the wetness of her entrance, and I moan as she grinds down onto it.

Abruptly, she pulls back, glancing at the doorway. "Not far, but I don't want to wait. Can you be fast enough?"

I smirk. "Can you?"

She nips my lower lip, and I hiss. In revenge, I thrust my aching cock against her through my pants.

"Point taken," she murmurs.

I lean up to capture one of her nipples in my mouth. She gasps and clutches the back of my head. We've only been separated for a few days, but every day I woke up expecting the worst. My timing isn't what I'm worried about. I swirl my tongue over the skin, coaxing every nerve to life. Ingrid rocks against me, the fabric of my pants clinging stickily to my legs.

Hunger and need rumble through me like the first strains of a growing storm.

Ingrid and I both reach for my pants in unison. Our fingers tangle, holding hands more than racing forward for a moment. The wanting ache of my mark makes me press my mouth, my teeth to hers. She moans low in her throat.

My cock springs free, and Ingrid positions herself above me. I bite down on her vulnerable skin to stifle my groan, and she lowers herself down, stretching to fit me perfectly. I could spend forever here, with Ingrid staring down at me and my cock inside her. Every morning I woke up without her wound my nerves a little tighter; all of that melts out of me now.

Never again. We will never be truly separated again.

I sit up suddenly, crushing her to my chest and changing the angle. We don't have time for me to sit here and marvel at her beauty, how she glows in the lantern-light and must be memorialized. I swallow the moan she almost chokes on from her lips, and together, we set a bruising pace. She kisses back as hard as I do, leaving behind the sting I know means marks in the morning. Pleasure rips through me in tidal waves, threatening to pull me under.

Not without her.

I thread a hand between us to find the bud at her center, and she jerks as if struck with lightning. I strum her in rhythm, another instrument I intend to learn to play to perfection. Luckily, I've always been a quick learner. A few cycles, and she shakes apart on top of me again.

This, I can watch. Her head thrown back, hair stuck to her face in sweaty swirls, her mouth open in euphoria. Seeing her undone throws me over the edge, muffling her name in the crook of her neck.

Even after pleasure returns my limbs to me, I just hold her there, tight against my chest. Feeling every single inch of her.

Alive. Warm. Willing to give me another chance. Willing to fight what seems like the whole world at my side. She kisses the side of my head weakly, boneless and spent.

Someone raps on the false cave-in.

"Really hoping I didn't just hear what I thought I did," Joli calls. "This is my cave, and I'm happy to kick you out of it!"

Ingrid laughs helplessly against my shoulder.

"Just give us a minute," I reply.

Joli groans.

LIKE A HAWK

Ingrid

"So then we'll—Cirocco?" Amval says, looking at his brother.

I glance at my fake fiancé to find him staring through the sweltering cave. Amval hasn't bothered with his veil in this little mine, and Joli has been slightly more careful about the looks she's been stealing at Amval—maybe because she had all of last night to look at him—but Cirocco doesn't have that tact. Still, he hasn't been outright staring until now.

He clears his throat. "Apologies, I just—"

"You thought I was dead." Amval pats his brother's shoulder. "I wanted to tell you."

"But you couldn't," Cirocco says slowly. "For our safety."

"Clearly, Kaloni is suspicious of those she thinks know anything." I jingle the metal manacle around my wrist. "She wouldn't have put me with you if she didn't still trust you completely."

"Right." Cirocco sighs. "I know all that."

Amval looks at me, his amber eyes shining with hurt and want. It's

345

a plea for me to have the right words to fix all of this. The Goddess put us together for a lot of reasons, but my way with words wasn't one of them.

"You'll get used to it," I say.

That just earns me another forlorn nod.

Joli leans forward. "What if we kick his ass? This whole plan we're coming up with... we don't need him for it for another week, right?"

That startles a laugh out of Cirocco, and I grin.

Amval holds up his hands protectively. "Hey, I've had my ass kicked enough recently."

Cirocco and Joli both look at me, wide-eyed.

I chuckle. "Let's just say you're taking the news much better than I am, all right?"

As Joli laughs and Cirocco looks back and forth between the two of us disbelievingly, I only have eyes for Amval.

Amval, who's alive. Who kissed me and touched me right here. Who let me kick his ass on that beach to deal with what felt like such an all-consuming betrayal.

Who apologized to me the moment I walked in the door.

Quietly, trying not to think about everything that has happened and everything that could and what any of this means, I take his hand. The steady warmth of his palm on mine makes it easier to take every breath.

"To refocus," he says over his siblings' chatter. "I think the end of this plan is good, but it would be much better if we had some additional manpower."

"The twins and the rest of the triplets," Cirocco says immediately.

Joli scoffs. "You said you only believed Ingrid because of all the nights you spent with *Sash*. No one else is going to believe us without seeing his face."

Cirocco grimaces. "And we cannot bring them out here without potentially leading eyes to this exact location."

"Eyes we really can't risk right now." I glance around at the walls of smuggled supplies and wonder how many secrets Joli is hiding in here other than her own. "Are there any soldiers or palace staff you trust?"

Joli opens her mouth, but Amval speaks over her. "No. It's not a matter of trust. I trust many of them with my life, especially those in the stable. But if a royal arrives with a question, they will have no way of saying no, regardless of what they want. I won't risk their safety."

Something throbs in my chest. There he is again, the man I think would make an incredible Alpha. Was he always lurking under the stiff prince I met so long ago, or is he an undead invention?

"What about your family?" Joli asks. "The strength of a half-dozen kingdoms wouldn't be a bad thing to have."

"And they would show up in a heartbeat," I say, "except the ones who are actually close enough to do so in a week. Moonlight Beach can't handle another fight right now."

"Dun's Crossing?" Amval asks. "I'm not sure if Joli could speed the travel time—"

"Not with two children," she says.

"And they won't leave them behind." I rub my eyes. "I think extra bodies would be useful, but Kaloni made that impossible. We're just going to have to make do with what we've got."

"So… just us," Joli says.

Amval looks around the tiny group, exhaustion weighing heavily on his face. I can feel it on mine, too. It was one thing to ask what we've been asking of ourselves. Cirocco's just a year younger than I am, but Joli…I know why Candace made me stay out of the battle in Snowcrest now. She's too young to be dealing with all of this.

"Royalty hold some innate power over their staff," Amval says, "and I hold that over you as your older brother. So, for now, pretend I am Sash again. Are you both certain about this? You can turn back now. Keep this secret and stay away from the upcoming battle."

For once, Cirocco answers first. "How long has it been? I didn't think you'd forget me that quickly."

A slow smile grows on Amval's face. His brother shines with determination, with offense at ever having been questioned that reminds me just a little bit of Finn.

"Our family is under attack," Cirocco says. "If I ever choose to sit back and watch when that happens, kill me immediately. They've put some kind of imposter in my place."

Joli nods. "Astralis isn't getting one of their tentacles in here. We've been through enough."

"And if we were doing this whole scheme just for a laugh, you'd be in anyway?" I smirk at her.

She shrugs impishly. Amval and Cirocco laugh. Goddess above, is that what I seem like to other people? She's one of the most charming people I've ever met and probably the scariest.

I glance at the mouth of the cave. Orange sunset oozes in around the fake rockslide covering the entrance, a ticking clock I resent. Kaloni has plans for dinner tonight—apparently, Cirocco and I have to figure out our seating charts *while* sitting in the dining room, or they'll never truly work.

Which means she wants to see us. Escaping Corwyn's unsubtle but persistent tailing to get here was hard enough—Kaloni's schedule is a transparent ploy to make sure she knows where I am as often as possible. Just like engaging me to Cirocco. As soon as the wedding's over, I'm sure he'll be her next source of information.

Or at least, that's what she thinks.

When I look back, Amval has already followed my line of sight. "I suppose you have to go, then?"

"We will be back," Cirocco says.

"As often as we can," Joli corrects. "Which… might not be all that often."

Amval grimaces, just for a second, and just with his mouth. It's a habit he formed while wearing the veil; I can tell. He doesn't want us to go.

I don't really want to go.

Quietly, we all shuffle the supply crates and bags we've been sitting on to stand, partially hunched. Amval and Cirocco exchange an intense goodbye. Joli looks at me.

"One more week," she says.

"What?"

She nudges me. "You weren't my first human passenger. I know how people desperate to get back to someone look."

I swallow. Charming and scary. "Why don't you worry about your part of the plan, and I'll worry about me?"

She shakes her head, unintimidated. Fuck. When Amval turns to me, a knot settles in my gut. We got him out safe—but how long will he be safe for? I have to go plan a wedding to someone else and just hope.

That same fear echoes in his eyes. He'll be alone, but I'll be sleeping down the hall from Kaloni. Neither of us are safe.

And there's really nothing to say about that, so he just kisses me.

AT DINNER THAT NIGHT, I DRAPE MYSELF OVER CIROCCO IN A beautiful, cool hall and try not to let my resentment leak onto my face. Kaloni is watching us like a hawk. Recai has expressed concern three times over what a long *nap* I took this afternoon. When I decided I was done being followed, turned on my heel, and ran directly into Corwyn, he asked if I was sure I didn't need to visit the healer for my head again because I'd been behaving so erratically. Everywhere I turn, there are eyes.

How does a sweltering smuggler's cave with only dried meats and uncooked grain to eat sound more comfortable than the dining hall of a palace? I stab my knife into a hunk of meat and try to choke down some of Umit's finest work—apparently, tonight is also the first of several tastings.

"You don't seem to like that one particularly," Kaloni says.

"I love it," I lie through a full mouth. The hair on the back of my neck has been on end since we stepped through the door, and I doubt it will settle until the wedding is over.

"What about you, honey?" I ask Cirocco, saccharine-sweet.

He swallows audibly and gives some answer I don't hear while I stare lovingly up into his face and picture his brother. My hand on his tenses, and I watch his knuckles turn white.

Release. Relax. The hawks may be watching, but we need them to roost for this plan to work out.

And I will not be the reason I don't get to spend the rest of my life with Amval. Not now.

BELIEF

Amval

THEY'RE GONE AGAIN. IT'S JUST ME AND THE CRATES. THE ECHOES OF my siblings' laughter and Ingrid's smile all fade too fast. I end up lying on the burlap sack, staring at the rocky ceiling, not quite sleeping.

Just thinking.

When I let my mind wander free, it wanders to Kaloni. Her coronation gown, so lovely and ready so quickly. Somebody should have noticed that. The speech Cirocco and Joli both confirmed that she gave. The proud, victorious look on her face when she announced the engagement.

It's all just a few shades off from the look she gave me when she invented half-cards. Just the two of us, awake late, watching while the younger ones slept. It had been a long day of traveling, and Mother and Father were out trying to learn if an old ally still lived in the area. I think she even found the deck under a loose board. I told her it was worthless, and we might as well leave it here.

Nothing is worthless, she told me, *if you know how to use it.*

Which means I was the one who found the cards because I handed them over to her and dared her to prove it. Make something out of them. Her eyes sparkled like they always do when she gets competitive, and she made up a game we all still play to this day, with half a hundred decks of cards in that palace.

I scrub my fingers through my hair. She betrayed us. She orchestrated my murder, Mother and Father's murder.

Night falls, I'm restless for hours, and then, like always, the sun rises again. Despite how hot I know it's going to be in a few hours, I light a fire in the small, covered metal bucket Joli gave me for that purpose, to keep anything old in the mine from catching. It spits a pitiful amount of warmth, but it's enough. I don't have to go rifling through these boxes to find spare blankets and more proof my siblings aren't who I thought they were.

As I warm my hands, another memory tumbles to the surface. One I haven't thought about in years. Kaloni and I were older. It was only a few years before King Gavin was felled, and we regained our kingdom. I had fallen head over heels for this girl in a village we were passing through. The idea of that makes me smile; the girl was sweet enough, but I had no idea what love actually was then. Still, at the time, I was sure, and Mother and Father didn't want to hear it. We weren't allowed relationships. Knowing someone outside the family that well was too risky and left too many loose ends behind when we inevitably had to run. So I was dutifully hunting when Kaloni found me in the woods.

She's waiting for you, just like she promised, Kaloni said. *I made sure you were hunting tonight for a reason. What are you doing?*

I'd never broken a rule before, really. Not for anything other than the Festival of First Wind. But Kaloni pushed me out of the woods, took over the hunt herself, and never breathed a word to anyone. We ended up leaving the next day, but I had that one lovely night because she created it for me.

The quiet must be getting to me. I pull my hands away from the fire and… lie back down on my burlap sack. There isn't much else to do in here, and I didn't exactly pack games for my escape to save my life. Hiding out with my siblings is much more interesting.

So when another silent day rolls by and my mind turns to Corwyn's smirk as he bragged about Astralis's size, I find myself thinking the one thing I should not be.

Nothing in that engagement *proves* Kaloni isn't being blackmailed.

I try to push the thought away, but it gnaws at me like a dog on a bone. I trust Ingrid. Cirocco and Joli obviously do. There must be a piece that I'm missing.

But as the proof of Joli's years-long smuggling ring stares down at me, it's hard to resist wondering if the thing I'm missing isn't simply the sort of secret Kaloni could be blackmailed into doing the worst things possible over.

I roll off the burlap sack, free a stick from the front of the fake rockslide, and start sketching in the dirt. Things I know. Things I dismissed. Anything that could lead me closer to the truth.

Kaloni had a romance while we were traveling with an innkeeper's son.

Once, Kaloni was forced to kill a woman who was about to scream the truth about us to the sky. She's not alone in that—I think Joli may be the only one who didn't have to do something drastic—but I know it eats her alive. I caught her crying herself to sleep for weeks after that.

She is extremely competitive and can be lured into bets with odds strongly against her.

Kaloni is horrifically afraid of spiders, and she's even more frightened of anyone finding out.

Anything.

I sketch them out, draw lines between them, rank them by what I think she would do to keep them hidden, and step back.

Goddess above, they look like the scribblings of a madman. Worse than Ingrid's string map before she explained it to me. My sketches look like smudges. Every word looks like it's written with a different foreign alphabet. And not a single line makes a shred of sense.

I need air. Three days in this cave alone is too much. I shove aside the false rockslide and shift at almost the same moment, so even someone watching could barely see me in the moonlight.

Sucking in lungful after lungful of clear air, I run. Past the memories. Past the doubts. Past anything but the rhythm of my paws on the hills beneath me. Miner's madness is real, and it was reaching for me. There is nothing more to it than that.

Right?

Every time I hesitate, every time I have to ask again, I run a little harder. My unused muscles ache. My lungs wheeze. I should have been running every night. It is cool and safe now, especially for a single, dark brown wolf a few miles from the palace, which stands barely darker blue than the night sky itself.

The Goddess shines soothing light down on me. I repeat a prayer for clarity in my head. *Make my way bright, make my path right.* Simple, a child's prayer. One I learned with Kaloni next to me.

I run a little bit faster.

When I hit a stream so far north of the palace that I can't even see it anymore, my legs shaking like they're going to give out, I finally give up. There is no outrunning my mind.

It's not miner's madness. It's the sinking doubt that we are going to kill my sister for nothing.

I bend and lap cold water from the stream. Somehow, I have to get back. A run is one thing; staying out all night is another entirely. Perhaps Cirocco will come visit me, and we can talk. He was the most reluctant, I thought. Perhaps if I can just understand what he believes is true, I can stop thinking this might be a mistake. Wind rustles through a patch of reeds beside me.

There is one other way to quiet my mind.

I slice one reed from the bunch with a claw. It tumbles to the ground. The shape is not quite right, far less even, but it's all I have. And this is the one precise, fiddly task I know how to do all too well with the wind. I shift and then I feed the air through the reed, carefully boring seven holes into it.

A shoddy ney sits in my lap, familiar and comforting already. I put it to my lips and test the sound. The pitch is thin, far from anything I could produce with a real instrument, but it's mine. An echo of a hundred nights I spent on the run, though I had to find tiny pockets of lonesomeness rather than running from it.

With my eyes closed, I play that silly little drinking song Ingrid and I have played so many times now. The one I played constantly for my friends in the Gruesome Pony, which never failed to get the whole bar singing. I sway with the rhythm, trying to find the old hidden comfort of my music.

And I just keep thinking that the song is missing lower notes. Something to anchor the "voice" of the ney, to bring it back to the dirt where it belongs.

It's missing Ingrid and her lute.

I throw the shitty reed into the stream and watch it sink. A growl, maybe a yell, catches behind my teeth. My mark throbs painfully.

The song was missing Ingrid, and so am I. All these concerns about Kaloni, they're nothing but the product of a restless mind. I want to believe Ingrid, so I do. It is as simple as knowing that I need her, and she needs this.

No. It is as simple as knowing that she is right. Ingrid has lost a lot, but she's never been forced to kill like my siblings or me. She wouldn't charge into that without thinking. As Joli said, Ingrid believes Kaloni confessed to her.

We've come down to belief again.

I throw myself into a shift and start the long run back to the cave. If it's a matter of belief, I believe Ingrid. I swear it on every star in the sky. She never needs to know I hesitated, and nothing has to change.

And if I'm right, the truth will come out in the end anyway..

UNSHAKEABLE

Ingrid

Two days before my wedding, I sit in the temple in front of Halit, the holy woman, and struggle not to fall asleep. She has that cadence to her voice, more lullaby than stirring religious rhetoric, and the temple is muggy-warm with late summer heat.

And, of course, Kaloni has been running us fucking ragged.

Cirocco sits beside me for the first time in—shit, has it really been two days?—fighting his own losing battle. There have been a thousand and one things to do for the wedding, enough to keep both of us more than busy. While I get my dress fitted, he engages in ancient rituals Kaloni *just thought* needed to be brought back for this particular wedding. While I review seating charts, he organizes rooms for all the visiting dignitaries in a palace already crammed to the gills. I've spent what feels like most of a week running past him, and when we finally stumble into the room together at night, both of us are too exhausted to do more than exchange a few mumbled pleasantries. I know he doesn't think Kaloni or Corwyn suspect him. He knows Recai is still following me around. Nothing else.

If Cirocco has been an afterthought, Joli has been a ghost. I see her for a few minutes at a time, just often enough that Kaloni hasn't commented on it. She looks exhausted every time I do, and she always manages to pull me aside to report some other piece of our plan has been moved into place. Even without Kaloni's eye on her, she is falling apart.

"Princess?" Halit asks.

"Yeah?" I jerk and discover my eyes were shut. A little bit of drool crusts the corner of my mouth.

"This is where you agree to love the prince for the rest of your days." Judgment edges her voice.

"Absolutely." I scrub the evidence off my face and elbow Cirocco. He shoots me a tiny smile. He definitely let me fall asleep on purpose. "For all my days and every star."

Halit nods. "Right. Then—"

"We're pulling up!" Raven calls through the mind-link.

I shoot up. We couldn't get them here in time for any sort of plan, but Kieran and Raven are too important not to invite to the wedding itself. "My family is here. I have to go."

As I start almost running out of the temple, more to get away from its soporific effects than anything else, I hear Cirocco apologizing for my behavior. I'm just an excited bride.

That excuse has been getting a lot of wear lately. I've gotten used to the strange shape of Cirocco's hand in mine, his thyme and orange smell. We share the bed, albeit with a wall of pillows between us to make both of us happier. And I know that this plan is going to work. That we're closing in on the final strains of a symphony we've spent all summer playing out.

But anybody who expects me to be *patient* on top of all of that can go fuck themselves.

I bolt out into the main courtyard as the gates open, and the familiar carriage trundles in. It's a piece of home, even if Candace is the piece I truly want. I gnaw on my thumbnail, and Cirocco steps up next to me.

Altair is the first one out the door. "Auntie Innid!"

I scoop him up in a massive hug, showering his face with kisses. He wriggles, laughs like he doesn't have a care in the world, and I turn to introduce him to—

Cirocco. Goddess above, I actually forgot for a second. My mark scorches as I force a smile. Altair has a better eye for people's emotions than anyone thinks. Of all of them, he'll catch me first.

"This is a new friend of mine," I manage. "Cirocco."

"Seer-ukko." Altair sticks out a serious hand to shake.

Cirocco takes it with a small smile as the others catch up.

"I would like to meet the man marrying Ingrid as well," Kieran says. He stands tall and proud in Dun's Crossing colors, looking like a true Alpha.

I grit my teeth. He has all the subtlety of a brick to the back of the head. Obviously, he is trying to intimidate Cirocco.

Bravely, my betrothed bows. "King Kieran, Queen Raven. I am pleased to meet you properly."

Kieran looks him up and down witheringly. Raven curtsies, a sleepy Vespera balanced on one hip. The two of them exchange a glance, and I realize there's a scheme playing out.

"I've always been fascinated by Som Palace," Raven says lightly. "Cirocco, could you give me a tour?"

For the thousandth time today, I wish I could mind-link anyone in this place. I just look at Cirocco, trying to will him to refuse with my eyes alone.

"Right now, I am needed elsewhere," he says.

Yes!

"Well then, walk me there with a short tour on the way." Raven cuts between us and takes his arm, starting to pull him away. "We can do the rest later."

No!

"And you can show Altair and me to our room," Kieran says inexorably.

"He's gone," I mutter. "You don't have to pretend that wasn't a set-up anymore."

Kieran sighs. "Does it improve your opinion if it was for your benefit, not his?"

"Mine?" I set Altair on the ground, my grip tight on his hand, and walk them inside. "I saw right through you."

"I was hoping you would." He looks around at the chaos inside the palace. Staff and nobles run in every direction. Quietly, as I re-enter, Recai detaches from the wall he was holding up while I was in the temple and falls into step behind us. "But perhaps we can talk more in the room."

I glance at him. He isn't even twenty-five yet, but the first few gray hairs dull his blonde, and he looks haggard. But then, he's been haggard since Vespera was born. Maybe since he took over the kingdom. I watch him spot Recai once, on a quieter upper floor, and his shoulders go tight.

He's worried about something. How much does he know?

Finally, we reach the room assigned to them. Recai stops outside, a few feet back. Kieran takes Altair and settles him for a nap. There's a little bit of crying, but it ends quickly with a promise that Altair can see me later. A promise my schedule can't keep.

I just sit on the couch. After Cirocco finished assigning bedrooms, Kaloni went through and made "a few tweaks." Tweaks that coincidentally placed my only family on nearly the opposite side of the palace from me. The room is lovely, at least as nice as mine, but the smell of fresh lacquer in the air promises Kaloni might have spent a few days justifying moving them with a little decoration.

My brother steps back into the main room and sits across from me. "Are you safe?"

My stomach swoops. He knows. And if he knows, anyone else could—

"This boy, this Cirocco, is he making you do this?" he asks intently.

I laugh, a bubble of pure relief. The plan is safe. "Absolutely not."

With a frown, he leans back. "I can get rid of that soldier outside if that makes the truth easier to tell."

"I promise, I've chosen to be exactly where I am." True enough—it was my idea to play up how happy we were.

"Why?" he asks disbelievingly. "I last saw you at your mate's funeral, when you refused to come home until you finished grieving."

My bones ache as I settle deeper into the couch and exhaustion threatens again. Weeks and weeks of lying weigh on me. I miss Amval, and I am tired.

Two more days.

"You saw Cirocco and I talking at the funeral, didn't you?" I say. "We spent a lot of time together after that, and something just… changed between us."

"That, I can understand." He shakes his head anyway. "But a wedding? So quickly Candace can't even be here?"

"Kaloni suggested it," I say tiredly, "and it seemed right."

Maybe, if everything goes wrong, he'll remember that I said that. Maybe he'll wonder if I wasn't right all along. Maybe Kaloni can be brought to justice another way.

"Is that all?" I stand.

"No." He stands to face me. "I know grief is hard—"

I tut. "You already gave me this lecture. The morning after my mate was murdered."

He huffs. "Ingrid, you're leaping headfirst into something you don't understand."

"I'm not a child anymore!" I throw my hands up. "I haven't been for a long time, and I don't know what it's going to take to get you to see that."

"I am treating you like a child because you are throwing a tantrum like you are one," Kieran replies. "Running off? Refusing everyone who is worried about you? Ingrid, you are about to marry a man you don't even know."

"Almost everyone does!" My hands shake, and I don't even know why anymore. "That's what a mate is. I just picked this stranger out for myself, so you don't like him."

"A wedding is forever." He takes a step closer, lowers his voice— one of Mother's tricks for defusing a situation.

I vault over the back of the couch to get away from him. "Don't. Don't act like you're my parent."

He clenches his hands tight and then releases them with a long breath. "I know how far your impulses have carried you before."

His voice echoes with Amval's accusation. Everyone thinks I'm impulsive, incapable of thinking things through. As he said, a child throwing a tantrum.

"This time, I know what I'm doing." I storm to the door. "And you arrived too late. I don't have time to see Tai tonight. Enjoy telling him that."

With my head held high, I storm out. Kieran doesn't chase after me, potentially aware of how fighting in front of my shadow would look. As I head for the all-night pampering party I'm expected at next, Recai clings to my every step, as usual. Kaloni doesn't even need to threaten me herself; she just attaches this armed dog to me, and the rattle of his armor does the rest. In every clink of his sword against his thigh, I hear the message. *Marry Cirocco or die.*

I gnaw on my thumbnail, wandering in circles.

If all goes to plan, I'll do neither, and Kaloni's reign of terror will end tomorrow.

Is the plan good enough?

What am I thinking? Of course it is. I helped come up with it.

But the brassy confidence that usually keeps me going when I hesitate rings hollow. Kieran is right. Everyone in my life has told me to stop, even Amval. And the stakes of tomorrow are a thousand times higher than usual. This isn't jumping off the roof or testing out a new hobby. The future of Lightning Cape—potentially of the world —rests on tomorrow going exactly right.

My mark throbs, and I know what I need.

Finding Cirocco is so much easier than remembering where I need to be. My feet carry me to the armory, where he is choosing his royal blade. Recai, as always, pauses at the door. I pull Cirocco away from the armorer with a breathless half-smile I hope makes me look like I'm in love.

With my arms around his neck, I whisper in his ear, "I need you to get a message to Amval. I don't have the time to get all the way there."

Cirocco nods.

"Tell him I have a few minutes tomorrow night, and I need to see him." With so little time, he needs to be ready.

Just like I need to hear from my mate that we're not making a mistake, the night before I'm supposed to marry his brother.

NAKED TRUTH

Amval

After days and days of loneliness, pacing the confines of this mine and trying to convince myself the chart I scratched on the ground is nonsense again, someone finally speaks to me.

"Amval?" Cirocco says through the mind-link.

I leap to my feet. *"Where are you?"*

"At the edge of the range," he replies. *"I don't have long—"*

"Then, I'll meet you." I know that he's just here to tell me something, or he wouldn't have called from the edge of the range, but I am clawing at the walls. I need to see someone else, not just hear their voice from a distance. So I shed my clothes, slip out of the rockslide, and shift while ignoring Cirocco's objections. Two more days remain until the wedding. One conversation is all I need to remain sane until then.

I hope

At my insistence, Cirocco tells me where he is. I dart through the hills, following the pattern of Joli's footsteps I remember to avoid setting off her traps. He occupies the nearest zig-zagging path down

365

the cliff face, almost equidistant from the mine and the palace. His wolf has always been a little bit lighter than mine, chestnut brown rather than walnut but just as broad. I barrel toward him, a grin splitting my lupine mouth, and bark in greeting.

Despite everything, he crouches playfully. Excitement surges through me.

"Do you have a minute for a run?" I ask.

"Just a minute." He turns and bolts down the cliff path toward the beach below. I surge behind him. If the path was a little wider, I could pass him. I've always been just a little bit faster. But, just like at the Festival of First Wind, I don't mind letting him win this time. He's lost enough.

We tumble onto the sand, kicking up sprays. The length of the beach stretches before us, and I watch him look down it, likely imagining a true race.

"Message first," he says, reluctantly straightening. *"Ingrid made me promise."*

Anything Ingrid has to say, I need to know. I squash the rush of excitement at seeing anyone and nod for him to continue.

"She's getting a bit worn down," he says. *"So, tomorrow night, she wants—"*

A scarred, coppery-tan wolf lunges out of a cave in the cliff and slams into Cirocco. I whip around as two more wolves barrel out of the same cave toward me.

He was followed.

I run at the two attacking wolves, forcing them to dodge or take the full weight of my shoulder. They both scatter. To my left, I see Cirocco struggling to his feet against the lead wolf, teeth flashing in the moonlight. I whirl on one of the two I separated, my claws out. One paw scrapes over his chest, but he tucks his head before I can reach his throat. Cirocco's enemy yelps as he lands a bite.

Teeth sink into my flank—the third wolf, forgotten in my focus. I snarl and try to turn, but he remains attached. With my screaming, injured leg, I kick at him until my foot finds home and then turn back to the one in front of me.

Cirocco scorches out of nowhere, tackling the wolf about to try to rip out my throat. His attacker scrambles to find his footing in the sand. He rolls away with the one who would have killed me, leaving me with the remaining two again. My back leg weeps blood, moving slower every time I give it a direction, but I ignore Cirocco's former target to deal with the wolf behind me. Bloody saliva drips from his lips. I rake out with my claws, not at his throat but at his front legs. He topples, and I pounce, slicing neatly through the important muscles that would let him regain his feet.

Behind me, Cirocco whines. My stomach drops. That's not all pain —there is a note of submission that makes me sick. I turn to see him pinned beneath the wolf he saved me from, teeth at his throat. Yield or die.

I try to charge the distance and save him, but the coppery-tan wolf shoulders me out of the way and digs his claws into the wound on my back leg. I scream and fall.

That wolf shifts into Corwyn, who smirks down at me with such cocky disdain I can almost forget the pain barreling through my leg and the threat leveled against Cirocco just to knock the look off his face.

"I told them," he says. "Damon, knock this bastard out."

The world goes black around me.

I WAKE UP TO THE SYMPHONY OF AGONY IN MY HEAD AND LEG. THEY shriek in mocking harmony as I struggle to sit up and figure out where I am.

Human hands push me upright. The silver manacle rattling around my wrist would explain that—Corwyn forced me to shift back. I pull on the thin, brown robe they left me achingly and look around.

Thick, craggy bluestone. Even thicker bars. I should have recognized it by the salt and mildew smell alone.

I'm in the dungeon.

My stomach drops. I stumble for the door, but the chain attached to my manacle yanks me back. My fingers just barely brush the bars, nowhere near the heavy padlock holding them shut. The wedding is in two days, and our plan doesn't work without both Ingrid and me.

"Cirocco?" I call through the mind-link. I can't see him, but these cells are bored into the rock, bars only at the front. He could be next to me, and I'd have no idea.

"Here," he groans. *"Alive, but hurting. I thought you—"*

He doesn't have to finish the sentence. He's already been to my funeral once.

"Alive, but hurting," I repeat. *"Cor—"*

"All right," a woman says, her voice echoing off the stone so I can't identify it. "I'm impressed."

Kaloni strides past the bars of my cell, and my heart skips a beat. A pair of soldiers, Yasa and Pak, follow in her footsteps.

"Release him," she says.

And there it is. The moment I've been waiting for. The proof Kaloni isn't behind this so much as forced into it, the line she will not cross, no matter what they hold over her head.

But Yasa and Pak march past me, and a different cell door creaks open. I suppose they're freeing Cirocco first. That's not an issue. I struggle closer to the door. I should be ready when they come for me.

Kaloni tsks. "Two days isn't much time for that bruising to go down."

"Then you shouldn't have sent people to attack me," Cirocco replies stiffly. "Ingrid is going to know."

"You're not going to see her until the wedding has already started." She snaps her fingers. "Get him upstairs. Quietly."

Yasa leads a heavily bruised Cirocco past my cell. I press as close to the door as the manacle allows.

"Why are you still going through with the wedding?" I ask.

Kaloni steps back into view of my cell and looks at me. "What do you mean?"

"Corwyn is going to know you're not obeying his blackmail

anymore when he discovers we're not here," I say. "So why bother with the wedding?"

She smiles very slowly. Hungrily. "Goddess above, you think *Corwyn* is in charge here?"

This time, my heart doesn't just skip a beat. It stops beating altogether. "Who is?"

"Me." She grins. "I told the council I could gain control over Lightning Cape by myself, and I very nearly have. Corwyn is a loan, a spare body for the jobs that weren't worth my time."

I sink to the floor. Ingrid was right. Kaloni betrayed us. No blackmail. No excuses. Just simple abandonment of every principle I thought she believed in.

"You had me assassinated," I say numbly.

"Well, I tried." She frowns. "How did you escape?"

"Yalim is dutiful, but he's not—no." I shake my head. It seems I saved that man's life, and I am not going to give that up now. "I'm not answering your questions. You should answer mine."

She cocks her head thoughtfully. "Your impression of Mother was always better. You don't have Father's… intimidating tone."

I grit my teeth. "That was not an impression. That was your older brother telling you how wrong you are. How did this happen? When did I lose you?"

"My older brother?" She laughs. "I led this family more than you did, more often than not."

"You kept the peace, but—"

"I managed everyone while Mother and Father trained you to lead." She sneers at me. "And you couldn't even learn to do that."

I stare up into her face and realize, with icy clarity, how my sister really feels about me.

"How long?" I ask.

"Astralis contacted me—"

I shake my head. "How long have you hated me?"

She leans against the bars, her face cast in half-light that makes her look like a stranger. "Since the day we retook the palace. Father gave that speech, standing on the throne, and I realized that in a few decades, you would be saying the exact same words unless I wrote something else for you."

The day we retook the palace. The happiest day of my life, before I met Ingrid.

I wish I could argue with Kaloni, but I remember making sure a scribe took down every word of Father's speech. I knew I was going to need it someday.

"So you decided to kill me?" I ask. "Kill them? Ruin the lives of our siblings? All because I was too much like Mother and Father for your liking?"

"No." She crouches, her eye-level with me. "That would be cruel. I did it because Lightning Cape deserves better. We deserve to be the heart of a new world, not another stumbling kingdom, ripe for whoever next decides to conquer us. You would have made us weak. Susceptible. With me—and Astralis—we can be strong."

I stare into her eyes, an amber mirror of my own. Part of me wants to see a bonfire of power-hunger and greed so obvious I should feel like a fool for having missed it. I want to see a stranger.

Instead, my sister looks back at me. The one who kept the peace between our siblings at any cost. The one who always needed to prove herself, winning every bet and competition. The one who stood beside and behind me while my parents trained me for the throne.

I couldn't find something Kaloni was hiding from me for Astralis to blackmail her with because she hasn't been hiding anything but how truly far she will go.

"I'll make certain my next assassination attempt takes," she says as she stands. "After the wedding, of course. I want to see your face when your mate marries someone else first."

STOOD UP

Ingrid

Somehow, Kaloni manages to squeeze even more activities into my schedule after I pass that message to Cirocco.

The night of pampering is an absolute frenzy, noblewomen attempting to slip off to bed before Kaloni or one of the other women she has clearly deputized lassoes them back in for another round of primping. Lady Evangeline is there, of course, though she's notably not one of Kaloni's posse. I almost wish she was. Then, maybe every other woman in a fifteen-foot radius wouldn't be compelled to talk about the exact same nothing as she does. Tucking myself in a corner with Sibel or Liwar or—during her brief appearance—Joli doesn't even save me. People seek me out to drag me into new and worse inanities.

When I finally stumble out of that powder-choked room, the sun is rising, and Kaloni catches my arm. With a voice like she's just had the best sleep of her life, she informs me that she's cleared her schedule to ensure the last day of wedding preparations goes exactly as planned.

I seriously consider just screaming in her face. Full volume, as long as my voice will hold out. Just to see what she'll do.

But instead, I let her whisk me off to breakfast—another parade of dignitaries, all the lucky men who actually got to sleep last night—and then a florist, the kitchen to give final approval for the menu, and my final fitting. Every Goddess-damned time I turn around, there she is. Always smiling. When people can see us, she glows like a proper sister. When they can't, she smirks. The stars will disappear from the sky before I stop wanting to tear that smirk off her face with my claws.

And I don't. It almost seems to frustrate her. We have lunch, at least partially, with Kieran and Raven, and I catch them both shooting me confused looks, like I've been replaced by an exact copy of myself who somehow has all the manners and patience Mother tried to teach me.

That doesn't bother me either. Because I know I'm just counting down the second until tonight. Until I can escape these walls, escape Kaloni's ever-watchful eye, and kiss my mate again. Every petty jab is just another minute passed before I get there.

Goddess, I deserve some kind of medal.

But finally, finally, night falls. Kaloni squeezes in a last few activities, which are complete nonsense. A blessing that hasn't been done in so long that Halit struggles to read the faded handwriting. I have to approve the *chairs* for the banquet hall. And then I'm free. I flip Recai a salute as I enter my room, wishing I had the key to lock the door. According to yet another "ancient rule" Kaloni dredged up, Cirocco is the only one allowed to carry it.

Cirocco isn't here yet. I was counting on him to help me with this next part—but it's for Amval. It's to stop the constant throb of worry in the back of my skull that I am risking my mate and his whole kingdom on another stupid bet. I take a deep breath, open the window, and stare down at the trellis Joli arranged to have put in.

Fuck me, the ground is far away.

I climb out the window. My stomach pitches. Hands, feet—where are those? I can't move. I am going to fall.

Follow my voice, Amval says in my memory.

He's not here to catch me when I jump this time. Instead, he's waiting for me in that tiny hole of a cave. Counting on me.

You can do it.

For him, I can.

Slowly, painfully, I scale down the trellis. Every twitch of the wind makes me sick. My vision spins like it's trying to knock me off on purpose. But I reach the ground.

Not just reach it. I drop to my knees and kiss it just for being flat. Getting back in when the only thing waiting for me is a surly soldier and a fake wedding is going to be harder, but that's a problem for later.

For now… Amval!

I take Joli's hidden door out of the retaining wall, strip, shove my clothes into a bag, and shift. The night wind tears through my fur as I run. The throb of my worries, my mark, my sleepless headache all die down as I draw closer. The hills feel like old friends. I pelt up to the mine, through the pattern of traps Joli taught me, and push the false rockslide aside.

And no one is there.

I shift. This can't be happening. I scaled a fucking tower. He has to be here.

"Amval?" I try to say, but there's a breath caught in my throat, so it comes out as a pitiful whisper.

Shockingly, he doesn't emerge from a nonexistent corner with apologies on his lips.

No.

I tear into the cave like there's somewhere he could hide. Things scatter in every direction. My voice comes back to me at some point, which I only know because I just start muttering his name like a spell. Like if I say it enough, he'll return. He'll never have been taken.

But slowly, I realize there's no sign of a struggle. Everything is neat and folded. Even the fucking rockslide was in place.

And then I find the diagram. A twisted mirror of the one I had, the one Kaloni destroyed. Except, instead of showing all the obvious connections between her, Corwyn, and Astralis, it attempts to exonerate her. It shows every way the *real* enemy could have gotten her, everything they could have held against her.

He doesn't believe me. He lied.

And now, he's gone. Not kidnapped. Not missing. He fucking left.

My blood boils.

I destroy the ridiculous drawing in the dirt, grab every scrap of evidence that he was ever here, and throw it out of the cave. A net trap captures his worthless bag of supplies. The metal jaws of a foot trap scythe out of the dirt and shred his veil. If he wants to risk his life with Kaloni, so be it, but he's not dragging his siblings down with him. I slam the rockslide back into place, shift, and run back to the palace.

The trellis seems like a complete waste of time now. He wanted me to trust him? He should have stopped fucking lying. Goddess, all the time and effort we put into keeping this ridiculous secret was all for nothing. I put on my underdress, slip through the servants' door, and find a maid's uniform in that tiny, awful room I started my stay at Som Palace in.

How much have I endured for him? I should have stayed at home. I would have been better off never knowing what his laugh sounded like or how his fingers move over the strings of a naqun like they do over my skin.

I have to warn the other two.

Disguised, I storm through the palace, not to Joli's bedroom, but to the tiny, abandoned workshop on a low floor of the palace she admitted to me after she smuggled Amval out. What feels like half of our plan waits there. I shouldn't be going there myself—she's the only one who can actually navigate this nightmare without being seen—but fuck it! Amval already saw fit to abandon our plan. It doesn't work without him.

I shoulder open the door, and Joli jumps, throwing her hands defensively across the sprawl of paper in front of her.

"Ingrid?" she says.

"He's gone," I spit. "Your fucking brother lied, and he's gone."

"Gone?" She closes the door behind me. "As in… missing?"

"As in, he still thinks he can trust Kaloni, and he ran away to test his luck." Rage boils under my skin. "He *lied*. To my face. Again."

"How sure are you?" Joli frowns, worried. "No one knows about the cave. The only way they could have found it—"

"They didn't find it!" I shout. "Everything was perfect. Just the way he always leaves things. If he could have folded the burlap sack, he would have."

"That sounds like Amval." She gets off her stool but doesn't approach me, like I'm some kind of wild animal.

Maybe I am. My hands itch for something to shred.

"How do you know he lied?"

"I found his so-called proof," I sneer. "He was trying to explain how Kaloni was blackmailed. Still. After telling me he believed she did this."

"Maybe—"

"Maybe nothing!" The way Joli almost flinches, then stands her ground makes me sick, but I will worry about that later. I'll apologize later. For now, I can only burn. "I've watched him do this before. Time and again, he gives into the mate bond, only to choose her over me. Well, this time I'm not waiting for him to realize the truth."

"What does that mean?" Joli asks.

"Warning Cirocco," I say, "and then going ahead with the plan as much as we can."

Her eyebrows shoot up. "But we need—"

"Not anymore, we don't," I snarl. "I'm sorry your two oldest siblings are worthless."

I storm out of the workshop, swirling with the same rage I carried in with me. It scorches me all the way upstairs, to the bedroom I should be asleep in. Recai is standing gua—Recai is *fucking sleeping*, leaning against the wall outside my room. The sword on his belt gleams, and I consider for a long, long moment that I could just grab the damned thing and run him through with it. Kaloni has so many pets. She won't miss just one, especially with her absolute sucker of a brother dropping himself right into her lap.

The sound the sword would make unsheathing is the only reason I instead creep past him and try the knob. Unlocked. I fucking told Cirocco we should lock the door. No matter how safe he's used to feeling here—

I bluster inside and discover the real reason the door isn't locked. My precious would-be husband still isn't here. I saw his schedule when I got dressed this morning. He was done with all his Kaloni-assigned activities at least an hour ago now.

I snatch one of his silky pillows off the couch and shriek into it as loudly as I can.

The only reason Cirocco wouldn't be here is if he's fucking helping Amval. I knew he wasn't fully convinced either, but at least he didn't lie to me about it. At least he said he was going along with things until he was convinced one way or the other.

I just thought he was smart enough to realize the truth staring him in the face.

Pieces of the maid uniform fly as I shed them. No point in hiding them now. Kaloni is probably sleeping blissfully right now, certain that she's already won. And I'm glad she is. Let her rest on her laurels.

Because I don't need Amval or Cirocco to save their Goddess-damned kingdom for them.

WEAKNESS

Amval

I CROUCH ON THE FLOOR OF MY CELL, WATCHING THROUGH THE BARS and ignoring the persistent ache of my wounded leg. Heels click along the stone floor—yes, there is the third round, again. There are three soldiers down here with me now, I'm sure of it.

And none of them are Yasa or Pak. Those two, Kaloni made sure to take with her.

Just thinking her name twists a knife in my gut. She truly did this. Arranged it all. She looked at Mother and Father and thought they were weak. That she had a better path, one she could only pave with their blood.

Theirs–and mine.

The soldier making the first round returns again, sharp and precise. If I snapped a breeze out fast enough, I could trip him and snatch the jingling keys off his belt. But there is a stalagmite jutting out of the ground right where he would fall. Visions of blood and viscera, brains splattered on grass still my hand. Kaloni wants to paint the world with blood. I need to find another way. Without Yasa and Pak here, I can't even be sure these men know who they're guarding. My hair has grown long in the long weeks under the veil, and I did not shave my beard while in the cave. Wearing a filthy prisoner's robe, I could be any cutpurse or liar. Trying to convince them of my identity is a waste of breath. It doesn't matter that I know every one of their names.

Except in that it makes the idea of splattering them over the stone that much more sickening.

But my mark throbs with an urgent need to escape. There's no light down here, no way of telling time. All I know is that Ingrid's wedding is coming, and if I am not there, she has no plan.

Goddess above, does she even know that I've been captured? Did she visit me and find an empty cave? I reach through the nothingness between us, trying to force the knowledge that I am alive, that I am coming for her, through impassible air.

Joli joked that she ought to sneak a holy woman out to wed us in the cave so we could all communicate. I have never more resented failing to listen to my youngest sister.

I roll back to sit, my leg still screaming from the deep bite, and survey what I have. A silver manacle, trapping me in this form. A reeking bucket in the corner that I don't much want to investigate. A wooden board of a bed, chained to the wall. As many pebbles as I could want. Nothing that I can use without hurting a trio of soldiers who have done nothing but obey their Luna, as they should.

The second round does not pass by. I twist, my heart leaping. A mistake? A rescue attempt?

"Oh, this is worth being late," Corwyn says as he steps into view at the front of my cell.

"With a smirk that large," I reply, "I'm surprised the weight of your swollen head doesn't topple you right over."

His smirk sours. "Some people just never know when they've been humbled."

I chuckle in his face, hearing the harmony of laughter I know Ingrid would share if she were here. "The mirror might show you another."

"Those fools would never have been able to pull it off without that ridiculous mate bond you all cling to." He sneers at me. "She ruined you, you know? You used to know respect, at least."

I straighten to my full height, all princely bearing as my father taught me. "Ingrid taught me respect is only worth the trouble with those who deserve it. A bastard like you does not."

"Silence." His hand flashes to the ruby-encrusted dagger at his belt, and I realize that, for the first time since he reappeared within the walls of Som Palace, Corwyn is wearing noble finery. The crest of house Hajni covers him in intricate embroidery.

And, I realize as my gut drops, he's wearing Som colors. His very outfit is a declaration of loyalty. Moonlight Beach won't have him, not after everything he did to them, but my fucking sister will.

"I will scream from the stars themselves if I can." I stride up to the bars, unafraid. "Corwyn Hajni is an asshole!. He couldn't earn a kingdom, so he tried to steal one, and he couldn't even—"

Corwyn seizes me by the throat, choking the words to death on my last gasp of air. My pounding headache returns, dancing from temple to temple.

"You stumbled into a throne you could never dream to deserve," he hisses. "From the day I met you, I knew you were going to be a weak king. Conciliatory, unable to stand on your own two feet without asking someone if those were really the two they thought you ought to use. Perhaps I failed—but I fucking tried something. What have you done?"

Answers pound the drums for my dancing headache, too busy to reach my gasping tongue. I claw at his hand, but the silver holds me back from any real shredding, keeps me weak.

With a sneer, Corwyn drops me. "Kaloni is right. It's better for Lightning Cape that you die here, forgotten."

I gasp in a lungful of mildew-stained air as he strides away. My chest burns, my head worse. He beat me on the beach. He beat me here, without even drawing that blade I know he can't use, or at least couldn't until recently. He snuck into my palace under my very nose

—every carriage passed through the stables, and I didn't so much as spot him. And Kaloni....

Kaloni played me for a fool. More than three years ago, we retook the palace. She has hated me for more than three years, my own sister, and I never noticed. I just plunged forward, business as usual. If she was around less, well, so was everyone. We had a whole palace to spread out in. If she never appeared with exactly the idea I needed, I had other advisors. If she never gave me the permission I didn't realize I was waiting to choose for myself, I didn't need it.

I roll onto my back and stare up at the stone ceiling. These weeks since my death have proven over and over again what a worthless king I would've been. Ingrid proved that I have no policies I want to enact on my own. I refused leadership in the stables and forced Nur to give it to Tek instead. I refused to see the wisdom my own mate was handing to me because I didn't like what it implied.

With a sour stab of pain, I realize Corwyn and Kaloni are correct. Lightning Cape is better off without me. They need a king with new ideas. Brave ones. Father was a good king, but he wanted too much to stay the same or return to how it was. My kingdom deserves to grow, to truly be reborn in our freedom. And I don't have those ideas. Not now. Perhaps not ever.

Much too late, the second patrol comes by. Aydolun walks with a slight limp, his left knee damaged in a fight early on in King Gavin's rule. I couldn't mistake him for the third patrol if I wanted to.

That's the kind of king you should be, Ingrid says in my memory. Someone who looks out for their friends, she meant.

I think she was wrong about that. When I thought about my policies, I could only think about the Festival of First Wind. Something small and personal. A king needs to see the whole map, think about everyone without personal feelings getting in the way. And no matter what Mother and Father tried, they never taught me how to do that.

Late. Corwyn said he was going to be late—but for what? Those clothes outstrip anything he would need for all but the most formal occasions.

Like a royal wedding.

Achingly, I sit up. I am not the kind of king Lightning Cape needs —but my people are not the only reason I need to escape this cell. Somewhere else in this palace, my mate is about to marry someone else.

Lightning Cape doesn't need me to stop that.

I do.

The wind struggles to my call with the silver still clamped around my wrist, but I clench my teeth and channel every iota of power I have ever possessed.

The third patrol, Ekca, is approaching.

For the first time in my life, I unleash the full storm roaring inside me. In a single blast of wind, the stone my manacle is embedded into explodes into nothing but gravel.

"What the–" Ekca's boot lands in front of my cell.

I launch myself forward, a whip of wind exploding out of my palm. It bands his ankle rather than tripping him and yanks him up.

"Hey—!"

I rip his voice out of his throat.

Ekca hangs, silent and bug-eyed, from the ceiling. I reach up and snatch the keys dangling off his belt. A few tries find the right one for my cell. I unlock it, drag him inside by a snare of wind, and dart out. He mouths furious words as I lock him inside.

I turn down the hallway with the ring of keys on my hip. I cage up two more soldiers before I so much as escape the dungeon.

Tomorrow, I'll give them a rest, time with the healer, whatever they need.

Today, Ingrid needs me.

CEREMONIAL

Ingrid

"I STILL CAN'T FIND HIM," JOLI WHISPERS AS SHE HANDS ME A CLUMP OF
nauseatingly sweet wildflowers I'm apparently supposed to hold
during this shitshow.

"Of course you can't." The stems groan, threatening to snap in my
hands. "He's gone."

The doors to the temple swing open, and I step inside to a swell of
music that's supposed to sound triumphant. I know because Kaloni
made sure to tell me that with the same little smile she's wearing right
now, standing at the altar beside Halit. Apparently, that's the traditional place for the Alpha and Luna during a royal wedding.

What I wouldn't fucking give to make her show me where she's
finding all these convenient old traditions.

Every eye in the temple turns toward me—every single one, that
is, except Cirocco's. He stands on Halit's other side in a suit of
wedding white to "complement" the garish orange Kaloni stuffed me
into, his head piously bent. I seethe. A few stems do break, the flower
heads falling away behind me. The fucking coward never returned to

383

the room last night, and now he's avoiding my very eyes. What a surprise. I made the mistake of trusting these siblings, and even Joli is sticking with Amval to the end.

I hold on to the scorching anger because it almost drowns out the shrieking of my mark, hidden beneath layer after layer of orange satin. Apparently, Lightning Cape wedding dresses are heavy and hot, too. Perfect for a sweltering summer evening. Rivulets of sweat slide down the back of my neck, into the low knot of my hair Kaloni insisted on.

Amval wouldn't like it, a tiny voice in the back of my head says. *He liked your hair long and loose. A waterfall.*

Well, then it's a good thing I don't give a single fuck what he thinks.

As I march through the temple, I count allies and enemies. Representatives of every single kingdom I caught Corwyn calling on are here. Lord Rik, the Whaleberry diplomat he kept visiting, smirks at me as I pass. Finn and Xandra are here, Kieran's worries infecting Finn's white-knuckled grip on his mate, but I'm a little surprised not to see Hana. Raven waves with Vespera's tiny hand as I pass, and Altair grins, but Kieran seems distracted, staring at Taner like they're having a conversation through the mind-link. Maybe he's unable to face me, too.

Fine. I'm just as happy to prove him wrong while everyone watches.

I reach the front of the temple and kneel on the massive pile of rustling orange skirts. My knees don't even feel the rough stone of the altar. Kaloni drops a smug kiss on my brow, just like Halit said she would. A few more stems snap in my grasp. The flowers shed like dead skin off my dress as I stand to face Cirocco.

Still staring at his fucking feet.

Halit raises her arms, her iridescent sleeves sliding up toward her shoulders. "The Goddess works in mysterious ways."

Out of the corner of my eye, I spot Joli slipping into position in the shadows of a high ledge. She holds a pull-rope in one hand, ready for my signal. But what signal am I supposed to give her? Amval was supposed to be our key piece of evidence. She holds nothing but supporting documents. The shit that couldn't even convince my mate to believe me, much less a temple crammed to the gills with strangers.

"She gives us our mates," Halit says, "those with whom we are most suited to face the world. But She declares that we do not share one lifespan. That we may, at any point, lose that other half with which She gifted us."

My mark screams even louder, praying to an unhearing Goddess that the only gap between Amval and I was life and death. But no. The gap is his fucking sister, the tyrant, looming over me in the gold-soaked sunset. She looks like a bird of prey, decked in glistening feathers. After everything, he still chose her. He lied to my face and either got himself killed for it or will soon. Kaloni is too smart to leave a weapon like him alive.

Whether he wants me to or not, I would find a way to use him.

At Halit's instruction, Cirocco takes my hands. He's clammy and limp like a dead fish—terrified. And he's fucking right to be. I squeeze his hands until he winces. Wasn't he supposed to be the Beta who thought things through and stood by his convictions? Who is this wilting fucking flower in front of me now? Marriage holds about as little appeal as ever kneeling before Kaloni again, but I would never choose a man like the one Cirocco turned out to be. I wish I could recant introducing him to Altair.

I suck in a breath through my gritted teeth as Halit intones about the complexities of fate, how perhaps Amval dying was all part of Her cosmic plan for Cirocco and I to end up together. Maybe it was part of Her cosmic plan for me to punch a holy woman in the mouth.

No. Joli is counting on me. Lightning Cape, even though they don't know it, is counting on me. I don't have much time, but I have to come up with something.

My mind spins as Halit marches through the endless ceremony— another idea of Kaloni's, and a stupid one. It gives me enough time to come up with a new plan before the line we were already waiting for, the line that was supposed to let me reintroduce Amval. Almost every inch of space in the temple is taken up with dignitaries. The rest bristles with soldiers. Proper, powered ones, not Kaloni's reedy new conscripts. Two flank each of the four doors, and more line the walls in between those doors. Kaloni is prepared for me to try something. And, though she appears unarmed, her skirt is almost as bulky as my own. She could be hiding anything under there. An out-and-out attack is going to get me thrown in the dungeons if I'm lucky, murdered in front of my favorite nephew if I'm not.

I could just declare that Amval is alive—but without him here, who would believe me? Nothing Joli has even supports the idea. We didn't think we'd need to. I grit my teeth. At least that option is likelier to secure me a trip to the dungeon rather than immediate death.

Refusing the marriage gets me killed, whether fast or slow.

Calling on Cirocco to support me, given his continual refusal to look anywhere but his boots, gets me humiliated by a second would-be husband.

I could try to run for the mines or the stables, see if Amval left behind some proof of his true identity. I've never met someone fast enough to catch me before I get there. But that requires a whole lot of luck, and clearly, that has not been in my favor of late.

I can't count on my family to save me. Raven using her powers could start a war Kieran would never want to draw Dunn's Crossing into, even if it meant sparing me.

Kaloni smiles serenely at me, her teeth wolf-sharp. Backlit as she is by the window, no one else *should* be able to see her. But it's over-the-top, bordering on cocky. The more she wins, the more ambitious she gets. I first noticed it when she announced our engagement—she changed a story I could have told people without flinching. It was even worse than the smug, unshakeable confidence that telling me about her involvement with Astralis wouldn't change a thing.

That night, I thought I'd lost everything. Amval could have been dead, Joli might not have believed me, all my notes were gone...but I talked to Cirocco. I convinced him, just like I had convinced Joli earlier. Okay, maybe she didn't believe me right away, but Kaloni's actions showed the truth. Just like they showed me.

Maybe that's all I need.

Maybe, if I accuse her this publicly, when she's so sure she's already won, she'll lose the increasingly fragile grip on her control.

"As the Goddess takes the sky once more," Halit says, "She shines Her blessing on this union. One that She did not create, but one which found itself in Her image."

This is it. In a few seconds, Halit is going to ask me if I am ready to be united to one man for the rest of my days.

"Princess Ingrid Mayra Solberg," Halit says. "Under the eyes of the Goddess, are you—"

Cirocco finally lifts his head and looks straight at me. One side of his face—the side facing away from the onlookers—is absolutely covered in mottled purple and green. His eye is swollen and reddish with burst blood vessels. For a heartbeat, I think of the body I woke up next to so long ago. Cirocco has the Carmine Pox!

But then I realize the purple and green is a brutal bruise, maybe a day or two old. Like he got it the last day I saw him. His dark eyes, suddenly unafraid, burn into mine like he is trying to force a thought through the air between us.

The hair on the back of my neck prickles. I missed something.

"For the rest of your days?" Halit finishes.

But I'm out of time. I open my mouth, my mind whirling, with no idea what's going to come out.

The largest door explodes open.

THE RING OF TRUTH

Amval

"SHE WILL NEVER BE READY TO MARRY MY BROTHER!" I SHOUT AS I storm into the packed temple, a sword lifted high above my head and a trail of allies collected from every corner of the palace behind me.

Gasps ripple through the crowd, buoying my name forward. Ingrid turns, her jaw falling slack. The last rays of sunset bathe her in gold…but Goddess above, Kaloni dressed her like a fucking pumpkin.

"Imposter!" Kaloni replies. "A lookalike. We stumbled across him while in exile, and I told Mother and Father he would be trouble someday."

"I am Prince Amval Temir Akintan Som, heir to the crown my sister wears." I storm toward her. "Victim of an attempted assassination at her hand, and her prisoner until an hour ago."

Something dark and sour in Ingrid's eyes dies, replaced by a glow even brighter than the sun. "And I am more than ready to be *re*united with one man." She grins and releases Cirocco. "For all my days and —"

"Seize them!" Kaloni shrieks.

The temple explodes in movement, and I realize why it was relatively easy to sneak through the palace after I escaped from the dungeon. Half the soldiers are here, lunging off the walls with perfect coordination. I launch myself forward, land on all fours as a wolf, and charge toward the altar. Kaloni can have whatever fight she wants, but she's not keeping me from Ingrid any longer.

A gale whips into my path, attempting to tie up my legs. I leap over it. Father trained our soldiers well—but he trained me better.

"She murdered our parents!" Joli releases the pull-rope overhead, and a banner strung with a recreation of that chart Ingrid showed me, connecting all the kingdoms to Corwyn and Kaloni, falls into place across the center of the temple. "As part of a scheme with Astralis, a group trying to take over the world."

"Astralis? They attempted to conquer Moonlight Beach a few months ago," Luna Xandra declares. "They used Lord Corwyn and Lord Denidor to do it."

More murmurs. Perfect.

"Amval!" Tek calls behind me.

Every instinct screams to keep running toward Ingrid, scrabbling for something in her massive, orange skirt as Kaloni grabs one of her wrists. But I want to be the man she loves—so I turn to see the friend I dragged into this mess, locked in a grapple with a soldier whose teeth are snapping ever closer to his throat.

My claws skid on the stone as I whip back. The wolf on top of him doesn't expect my shoulder ramming into his exposed ribs. His breath bursts from his lungs, and he tumbles off Tek. General Hana, the Moonlight Beach woman I ran into and managed to sway with only the word *Astralis*, claws out the soldier's throat before he can even try to stand. She nods, a silent promise that she will protect the small army of grooms that rallied behind me the moment I stepped into the stables.

A wolf flies out of nowhere, attempting to tackle General Hana. I leap into his path and ram him out of the air. Father would trust the people he brought here to fend for themselves, would likely charge the altar and shift to give some kind of speech. But my speeches have always come off stiff and unapproachable. And, despite the endless shout of my mark, I trust Ingrid.

She chose to be here. Every moment of these last weeks, she has fought. For me. For my people. She knows what she's doing.

Those I led here need me right now.

The wolf underneath me snarls and gnashes at my forelegs. Pain spiders up into my shoulder as he makes contact. I scrape my claws across his ribs, and he whimpers.

King Kieran stands, only a few inches away. "I believe my sister. I have heard of Astralis, and I know she doesn't lie." He looks around the room. "And I think we all know how much Prince Amval loves his family. For him to level this accusation...."

He doesn't bother finishing the sentence before shifting into a massive, silver wolf and slamming a paw into the skull of the soldier underneath me, who instantly goes limp. I leap off the body and charge deeper into the fray. The tide may be turning, but I don't intend to lose a single person I brought here.

We've lost enough.

My world dissolves into a flurry of fur, claws, and blood. I spin this way and that as mind-links fly. A few of Ingrid's friends amongst the maids whisper different soldiers' weaknesses from hidden corners of the temple. Nur saves Mesut's life. A trio of stable boys manage to drop a smaller soldier together. Other dignitaries join the fight on various sides.

The reek of balsam and sea salt reaches my nose, and I turn.

Corwyn.

The back of his coppery-tan wolf appears out of the battle. I don't hesitate. My teeth find the joint of his hip, and metallic blood spills over my tongue. He yelps and twists, trying to reach me with his claws. I spin out of his way without releasing. Perhaps I would have been a weak king, but I am not weak here. I spent my whole childhood waiting, training for the day someone would appear and try to kill me. Some trumped-up former lord certainly will not be the one to do it.

My teeth split muscle and sinew, scrape against bone. He bends at an impossible angle, one that must hurt him, but the hate alive in his face makes it worth the pain. His claws rasp across my muzzle, up into my eye, and I release with a scream as half my vision goes dark. Pain blurs my thoughts, makes me stumble. Corwyn looms over me, a vicious sneer on his lupine lips.

And that is his mistake. The heartbeat he wastes on gloating gives me just enough time to slash at his unprotected throat, tearing through fur and old scar tissue.

Blood waterfalls onto me, hot and fast. I wriggle out of the way before he crumples. Dead.

Or at least it seems so. My halved vision makes movement difficult to track. Wolves seem to jerk and almost teleport across the battlefield. My head pounds.

Someone fits their shoulder under mine, holding me up.

"Come on," Tek says.

"The Pony?" I reply weakly. *"Now?"*

He laughs in my mind and leads me toward the altar. *"Your girl is waiting."*

Even though I know it's just a nicer way of saying I'm too hurt to keep fighting, it warms me like a shot of whiskey. The idea of going to Ingrid is like a fire. It scorches through me, hot and desperate. A small squadron, a ring of protection forms around us. King Kieran. Hana. More than a few Lightning Cape nobles, including, to my surprise, a bloody Lady Ceyiz. Yet another apology I owe, when the fighting stops.

"No one will believe you," Kaloni spits.

"Tell that to everyone who fucking does," Ingrid replies.

The battle parts, and I see the two of them, alone at the altar now. Kaloni holds one of Ingrid's wrists, one silver manacle clamped around it and the other swinging free while she fights to capture the other arm. Ingrid leans so far away from my sister that she looks like a diagonal line, straining to escape.

My heart pounds. I surge away from Tek, clumsy with injury and blood loss. The three stairs up to them might as well be a mountain. I miss one, smash my chin, and keep running.

"Brother." Kaloni spits the word like it's poison, like she's actually saying *traitor*. "It seems Mother and Father didn't teach you how to die."

Ingrid meets my gaze, her blue eyes burning with hope and trust. My thoughts spin. I can't fight Kaloni—she received all the same training I did, in this arena at least. But perhaps Ingrid can.

I circle half-blindly away from her. The hate that focused Corwyn is even more intense in Kaloni. I saw it in the dungeon. She spins without a second thought, her glare boring into me.

"Everyone knows now," I say. *"If you yield, you don't have to die."*

She laughs in disbelief. "Of course, you offer mercy. That's going to kill you someday, you know?"

"It hasn't yet." I gather the shreds of my shattered thoughts as much as I can and tamp down the storm raging inside me to a single thread of finesse.

"Luck," she sneers. "Yours has always been better than mine. That's why I know how to fight."

"I am sorry," I say honestly. *"I wish you'd told me earlier."*

While my sister's eyes bug out of her head, I feed a sliver of wind into the lock on the manacle around Ingrid's wrist. Control has never come easily to me, and it's harder now. But my mate needs me.

"You aren't even angry?" Kaloni shrieks.

Joli's quiet, even breathing as she picked the window lock rings in my ears. I match her rhythm just like I matched her steps at the mine.

"I'm furious," I say. *"But, Goddess help me, I still don't hate you."*

"Oh, and that makes you so much bet—"

Click.

Ingrid's silver manacle snaps open. With a sound of tearing fabric and an explosion of orange satin confetti, she shifts into a sleek, dangerous gray wolf. Kaloni starts to turn, her features morphing into horror.

And Ingrid slashes out her throat before Kaloni can so much as shout.

My sister falls dead between us with a hollow *thud* that echoes up my spine. Despite everything, I can't look at her. I truly don't hate her. I just miss the sister I once had.

Ingrid rushes to my side, shifts, and cups the bloody, blind side of my face. I lean into the warmth of her touch. Tears sheet down her face. I shift and curl around her, emotions too complicated for the air caught in my throat.

Quiet slowly falls over the temple. Without Kaloni giving the orders, there's no reason for the soldiers to keep fighting. Someone drapes a blanket over us. Others are removing bodies. I don't look over when someone comes for Kaloni. I can't yet. Tazi, the healer, tends to my eye, stopping the worst of the bleeding and giving me something for the pain. No one speaks. No one has to.

We are all wondering whether Astralis is dead or if we have just cut off a single head.

Finally, Ingrid sniffles and looks at me. "Can you do that voice-amplifying thing?"

I nod and spin up a breeze to carry her voice to every corner of the temple.

"I meant what I said," she declares. "I'm ready to be reunited. And we've got a wedding all set up."

Goddess, I love her.

FOR EVERY STAR

Ingrid

"THE GODDESS' WILL IS OFTEN FAR MORE COMPLICATED THAN ANY OF US can guess," Halit says, blood streaked on her cheek from the arrow she took to the shoulder before fleeing the altar.

Laughter ripples through the temple. I know, from my second march up here, that the healthy hold up the wounded from every side of the battle that just occurred. The battle that shines on the pale white of the bandage covering half of Amval's face in the moonlight.

Tazi says she's not sure if his sight will ever come back in that eye, but she's sure he'll survive. And, fuck, that's all that really matters. That's why I needed to marry him now. Even though he's wearing a bloody blanket tied around his waist, and I'm wearing a cloak Raven made Altair and Vespera hide under before she shifted to join the fight. Even though my head throbs with the one attack Recai got in before Cirocco tackled him away, before Kaloni grabbed me and declared to all the other approaching soldiers that I was "hers." Whatever she had planned for me died with her, and I don't particularly mind that.

Amval squeezes my hands, warm, steady, and simply…him. Just like the fact that none of the people he brought with him into this temple are dead. Some are injured, even severely, but every casualty was on Kaloni's side. I watched him turn away from me, and I knew. He trusted me enough to save myself while he saved everyone else.

Halit continues, "She is mysterious in Her many—"

"I'm sorry," I say, "but my wedding has been going on long enough. Can we skip to the good part?"

More laughter.

Amval grins. "As you wish."

Halit sighs, but I can see a little bit of a smile playing around her lips. "Under the eyes of the Goddess, are you prepared to be united to this man for the rest of your days?"

"For all my days and every star," I vow, staring into Amval's one orange-golden eye. "I love you. I don't want to spend another second apart."

He laughs, a throaty rumble I can almost feel through our joined hands. "I love you. I have for a long time now."

"Prince Amval," Halit says with mock-sternness. "Under the eyes of the Goddess, are you prepared to be united to this woman for the rest of your days?"

"Yes," he says impatiently. "Can I kiss her while you do the rest of the blessings?"

The laughter and Halit's semi-grudging agreement fade away as he grabs me and crushes his lips to mine. I kiss him back hungrily, like I could devour him and keep him inside me forever. While we were getting all this ready, I asked about the diagram I found, and he explained everything. Loneliness drove him to draw it.

I am happy to make sure he's never lonely again.

We only break apart when Amval sways, still unsteady on his feet from all the blood he's lost.

"You are one," Halit says simply.

"I love you," Amval says in my mind almost before she's finished her sentence.

"Ha!" I spin giddily, like a kid, too excited to stand still like a princess ought to. *"I love you, too."*

He watches me with a glowing smile.

"Yuck," Joli says.

I stick my tongue out at her.

"All right," Cirocco says. "There is a reception awaiting. Tazi has called enough healers so that we might actually all be able to enjoy it."

Somehow, he manages to usher all of us out of the temple, into the ballroom. At the door, Liwar and Sibel catch my hands, their faces tearstained but alight.

"We're so sorry," Liwar says.

"I should have known." Sibel shakes her head. "You and Cirocco don't make any sense together."

Liwar smacks her arm. "We should have known something was going on with Kaloni. That's why we're sorry. And we'd like to apologize by loaning you something nice to wear for the reception."

"Oh." I glance at Amval. Cirocco waits by his shoulder, clearly about to demand something similar. All the pressures of life suddenly descend back into place. With Kaloni dead, Amval has no rival for the crown. There's going to be a coronation and then months of cleaning up what happened here. I'm going to have to be Luna.

That thought maybe isn't as terrifying as it once was, but it's too big for tonight, when Amval is still wrapped in bandages, and I can't let go of him for fear he'll disappear again.

"Go with them," he says through the mind-link.

"No," I reply. *"I won't leave you."*

Amval grins. *"Go with them. They'll leave you alone to bathe. Slip out onto the balcony, and I'll meet you there."*

"What about the reception?" I glance into the glowing room. Music is playing, and a few of the healthiest guests are spinning across the dance floor.

He raises an eyebrow. *"You want to go to a ball with a bunch of diplomats?"*

My chest feels like it's about to burst. "Thanks, Sibel, Liwar. I'd love to clean up and get dressed."

They lead me away. Conversation wends like a river between them, colors and fabrics and dresses I haven't even seen yet. No one mentions Kaloni again. I understand. They can't solve her right now, but they can solve my wedding dress.

Or so they think.

When they usher me into the bathroom, just like Amval suggested they would, I take a moment to write a quick note in lipstick on the mirror thanking them again and promising I haven't been kidnapped. It'll have to be good enough because I've been away from him for too long. I leave it and sneak out onto the balcony.

Cool night air kisses my skin. Then, a warm, familiar mouth does the same. Amval appears from a pool of shadow and wraps his arms around my waist. I twist in his grasp and claim his lips. It's taken too long, but he's here. He's safe.

"They'll check eventually," he murmurs against my mouth. "Do you trust me?"

"Completely."

He pulls back and points past the balcony, at a low roof that leads to a glowing window. "I'll keep us from falling."

Tonight, not even climbing down the palace walls could scare me. I clamber over the railing and onto the tile of the roof. Wind tears at the cloak wrapped around me.

"Is that you?" I ask with a smirk.

He shrugs playfully. My head swims, delirious with victory, drunk with him. I unfasten the clasp of the cloak and let it spiral away into the night, leaving me completely bare. Amval's eyes darken with want.

I laugh and start across the roof. He chases after me with a low growl. The wind presses in on either side, keeping me balanced like his hands on my waist. I jump, skip, dance across the roof without ever looking down.

When I tumble in through the open window, I find a tiny music room. Dust-covered instruments lean off shelves, and a blanket lies on the floor in the middle.

"Joli told me about it," he says as he climbs in after me, all his clothes lost to the wind as well. "I wanted to see if—"

I crash into his mouth. Tomorrow, we'll open this place up and see what we can save. Tomorrow, we'll fill these halls with music. Tonight, he's the only instrument I want to play.

Amval's hands trace the lines of my body like he's starving, and I am his meal. He plucks, crushes, devours. I laugh into his mouth. Being swallowed whole by my mate, my husband, seems like the sweetest possible reward.

He grabs my thighs and lifts me off the ground and then lowers me to the blanket on the floor. I knot my fingers in his hair and lock my legs so he can't dream of going any further away. He seems happy to comply, pressing his warm weight down onto me as he licks into my mouth. His cock hardens against my stomach. I groan and roll my hips, wishing for friction a little lower, unwilling to release him to get it. He laughs, teasing and delighted. It feels a little like when we snuck down to the ballroom, like we're getting away with something. Sneaking around because we can, not because we have to.

On a whim, I try to roll him over, not expecting the iron cage of his arms to so much as shift. But he flips easily with a soft noise of surprise. I pull back, worried.

"Apologies." He smiles ruefully and taps the bandage on his face—on the side I rolled him to. "I think this will take some getting used to."

I kiss along the edges of it, far from the heart of the gore. "At least the scar will make you look like the men I've always dreamed about. A dashing adventurer." I wiggle my eyebrows.

His gaze turns thoughtful, and I frown. He is thinking about tomorrow, and I need him right here. I reach between us, position his cock, and sink down onto it.

Euphoria blots out all contemplation on his face. He grabs my hips and drags me deeper. I gasp at the fullness, straining to contain all of him so quickly. But the ache is sweet, perfect for a night like tonight. I roll my hips, not that he needed the invitation. He is already lifting me up to pull me back down again, fucking me on his cock with the sheer strength of his arms alone.

There is nothing but his hands, his mouth, his dick, the hum of laughter and victory on my skin. I lose myself in him happily. And when he starts to fall apart underneath me, it is the look on his face that sends me careening over the edge with my name on his lips.

I crumple onto his chest. Climbing off him right now seems impossible. He is so warm, so alive underneath me. He wraps a lazy arm around me and kisses the side of my head.

"Those adventurers you dreamed about…" he says.

I shake my head. "It was a joke. I know you're not so good at those."

"I don't think it was." He traces undulating lines up my side. "Lightning Cape is going to need a new leader."

Tomorrow's thoughts. They found us, even in here. I want to push them out again, but the easy rhythm of his hands on my skin makes them easier to swallow. He makes them easier to swallow.

"I… might be able to get on board with that," I say. "Being Luna doesn't seem quite as horrible with you at my side."

"I'm glad." He chuckles. "But that's not what I want."

I crane my neck to look up at him in profile. Despite the injuries he's taken, he looks almost completely relaxed. Something changed while I wasn't looking. "What do you want?"

"To figure out what I want." He squeezes me. "Other than you."

"And your music."

"Our music."

The words burn through me, hot and bright. "I started playing the lute because I loved the troubadour's puffy pants."

"What?" he asks with another laugh.

"I wouldn't mind wearing them for a few years," I say. "Until we're ready."

His smile grows like the best kind of crescendos. So slow you almost don't notice it at first, reaching an explosive apex. He looks like my own personal sun. "I wouldn't either. A few years of traveling. Making *our* music. And then, we can lead the way they deserve."

"We should leave Cirocco in charge," I say. "He kept me from doing anything stupid in the temple before you arrived."

"Brilliant." He kisses me again. "I love you."

"I love you too." I pillow my head on his chest and listen to the percussive thrum of his heartbeat. "For all my days and every star."

Thank you for reading! If you're interested in me continuing this series with the next generation, please leave me a review on your favorite retailer and let me know!

Driven by the Secret Billionaire by ID Johnson

Wolf Shifter Alpha Kings series

Ravens and Ruins (free!)

Sundrops and Shadows

Snowflakes and Sabotage

Waves and Wickedness

Breezes and Bodies

The Vampire King's Feeder series

Claiming the Alpha's Daughter (free!)

Loving the Alpha's Daughter

Finding the Alpha's Daughter

Bewitching by the Alpha's Son

Writing as B. Moon

The Boy Who Died

Sign up for Bella's newsletter here.

Or get a free novella from The Alpha King's Breeder series when you sign up here:
The Beta and the Maid

Follow Bella on Facebook here.

Follow Bella on Bookbub here.